DREAMS FROM THE HEART

–Tales of Hope & Love –

by C. R. STURGILL

ISBN: 0988565307
ISBN 13: 9780988565302
Library of Congress Control Number: 2012918438
DreamHeart Books
Marion, Virginia

"Sturgill offers a poignant, punchy debut four-part collection of short stories.

This sweet, honest collection is divided into four sections about love, family, hope and loss. Many of the stories here describe male writers who receive encouragement from women who act as their editors and inspirations. In "A Little Mystery," for example, a downtrodden writer, Carl, meets a beautiful postal worker while mailing his love stories for publication. In "First Love," quarterback and country boy Max falls in love with New York University–bound Julie; they part ways when Max refuses to leave his blue-collar life but are reunited years later when Max, now an author, goes to New York City to meet his new editor. A similar theme is carried over into a story in the "Family" section; "Open Field" is about a father, grappling with his son's high school football injury, who remembers all the times he persuaded his son not to pursue his other love: writing. The book closes with a story about a son who teaches his mother to skydive at the end of her battle with pancreatic cancer. Sturgill's collection largely centers on romances with playful details, and tales of happy accidents and passionate moments. The author's prose is frank, honest and not overly sentimental...When Sturgill excerpts his characters' writing, it often expresses their unsaid desires—such as wanting to be with an unattainable woman—which give the stories added dimension...Overall, this first outing provides a...substantial read for short story lovers.

A fine short story collection, bound together by resonant themes".

— *Kirkus Reviews*

Other Books by C.R. Sturgill:

Fantasy World

Blood Tides

Sea of Hearts

For More Information & Updates:

Follow on Facebook
https://www.facebook.com/crsturgillauthor/

https://www.facebook.com/dreamsfromtheheart/

Visit my Website
http://www.crsturgill.com/

In loving memory of my mother, Janet Wilcox Sturgill, who succumbed to pancreatic cancer on January 12, 2012. She was the sweetest, kindest, most caring, most supportive, most selfless, and most loving woman I've ever had the pleasure to know. This book could not have happened without her loving support and encouragement over the years. I regret that she didn't get to see the final product, but fortunately, she was able to read about half the stories. I hope this book can reflect at least a small part of the dreams, love, and hope that she embodied and that her memory can live on through my words. I love you, Mom.

Table of Contents

Dreams of Love & Romance

The Gift

"OK. You can remove the blindfold," Tom said.

Finally, the pickup truck stopped. The past ten minutes had been a rough ride, up and down hills, rocking side to side, and jostling Helen back and forth in her seat. The blindfold made it even more disorienting. She was a little agitated as her husband grabbed her hands and helped her out of the truck. "This better be good!"

She quickly removed the blindfold and looked around. Tom had parked the truck on a flat area near the top of a large hill, or small mountain. In front of them, the hill fell away to a view that extended for miles until the next mountain range. Below, the hill sloped less steeply through open fields and into a pine forest. Behind lay another unobstructed view of the blue mountains to the east. Above the truck, on the other side of the cleared flat area, trees covered the slope to the top of the mountain.

She was speechless as she stared at the most beautiful scenery she'd ever seen. The cloudless deep blue sky, joining the grass and trees just turning green with spring, made it that much better. She gazed at Tom's face, with his grin and the twinkle in his eyes. After the shock finally wore off, she smiled too.

"Happy anniversary!" Tom exclaimed.

"What is this place?"

"Heaven."

"Seriously, what are we doing up here? Whose land is it?" Helen asked a little more forcefully.

"It's ours," Tom replied, laughing at Helen's expression.

"You're joking!"

"I made an offer last week, and they accepted today."

"You're serious?" she asked with a mixture of amazement and concern.

"Yep. It's our dream land, honey."

"Can we afford this? And what are we going to do with it?"

"We'll be paying for it for a while. But it's ours, baby. One day, when the kids are grown, I'm going to build us a cabin, right in this spot, and we're going to live here in total privacy—just me and you, enjoying all this," he said, spreading his arms wide. "We'll get to see all the seasons change right from the rocking chairs on our front porch."

With tears moistening her eyes, Helen reached out and hugged her husband. "Oh, Tom, this is wonderful! Are the kids grown yet?"

Tom laughed, especially since they didn't even have children yet, and squeezed her back. Then he leaned back and kissed her softly on the lips. "You're the only thing more beautiful than all this."

"You are the sweetest, kindest, smartest, handsomest man ever!" She kissed him back, this time longer and with more passion.

Tom was the first to break away. "OK. We'll have to save that for a moment. I have another surprise for you." Helen could only grin like a schoolgirl in love for the first time as she watched him retrieve an armful of items from the backseat of the pickup and then drop everything on the tailgate. He then vaulted up into the bed and began setting up his surprise. He spread out a thick bedspread, opened a picnic basket, and scattered its contents across it.

"First, we have a bowl of strawberries and grapes for an appetizer. Second, we have two sandwiches, made with my own hands. I hate to get too romantic on you, but I went with bologna and cheese. Next, a bag of chips to accompany my romantic sandwiches. And, to wash it down, a bottle of the finest wine." He finished spreading out the food and added plates and napkins. Then he hopped out of the bed, went back into the truck cab, and returned with two pillows, placing them against the cab.

"Now, my dear, would you like to join me for a picnic while we watch the sun set over the mountains?"

"You're amazing! Do you know that?" She still couldn't stop grinning as he assisted her into the truck's bed. They sat down side by side against the pillows.

14

Tom poured them each some wine into two plastic cups. "Nope. You're the amazing one. I'm just the one lucky enough to have landed you."

They sat and ate, talking and laughing as the sun dropped in the sky. It was such a special moment. They had only been married for a year, but it had been a great one. Tom always did things to surprise Helen and make her happy. She tried her best to do the same for him, but he made it hard to keep up. They were a story of high school sweethearts and first-time lovers that was turning out perfect. They had been each other's first serious relationship, but they got it right. She couldn't imagine anyone better than Tom.

After they ate, Tom quickly packed everything back into the picnic basket. Then they lay down on their backs, their heads on the pillows and Tom's arm behind Helen's head. Helen turned to look at him as he stared up at the darkening sky. He wasn't what she considered gorgeous. She hadn't really noticed him in high school until Tom sat behind her in chemistry class. Once he broke the silence and turned on his charm and wit, she was hooked. Average-looking and average body became handsome and sexy. Now, he was everything she needed and wanted. No other man could catch her eyes—they were only for him.

He finally turned his head and returned her gaze. "What are you staring at with those big ol' eyes?" he asked, smiling.

"Just you, stud muffin," she replied, smiling back.

"Ewww, yuck!"

"Shut up!"

They turned so their bodies faced each other, and Tom wrapped his free arm around her and pulled her close. They stared into each other's eyes, grinning stupidly as the last rays of the sun caressed their bodies.

"Do you have any idea how much I love you?" Helen asked.

"Hmmm…no. Can you show me?" Tom laughed.

"Why, yes, I think I can." She kissed him softly. Their kisses quickly turned passionate, and soon their hands caressed and explored each other's body as they quickly removed their clothes. Within minutes, they entered into another part of their relationship that was always incredible. They made love as the sun set over the mountains and well into the darkness, their bodies hot despite the coolness of the air.

***

That first summer, they went back to explore their land a few times and even camped there once. They returned in the fall, when the leaves had changed, and Tom did some hunting, killing a four-point buck in

15

November. During the cold, harsh winter, they gave little thought to the land. Their first child, Ethan, was born in March, and most of their free time was gone after that.

Tom was as good a father as he was a husband, helping Helen with bottles, diapers, baths, chores—everything. They didn't have as much alone time, but they were always together as a family. They drove Ethan up to the land that summer, but that was the only trip they made that year. That fall, work and Ethan left no time for hunting.

Laura was born the following May, and any thought, dream, or hope of alone time vanished. They stayed busy from before daylight until well after dark, but they were happy. They shared all the work, stress, and joy. What free time they had came late at night when they were both exhausted. But they took advantage of that time the best they could.

Their lives as busy parents didn't leave much time for picnics and wine, but Tom still worked in little surprises here and there. Occasionally, Helen came home to a candlelit supper waiting on the table. Of course, the children were there in their high chairs, but it was still a sweet surprise. He also made breakfast in bed a recurring treat, among other occasional surprises.

***

One night, after struggling to get Ethan and Laura to sleep for two hours following a very stressful and aggravating day at work, Helen finally got Laura to join Ethan in slumber. Helen was so tired and stressed she could scream and wanted nothing more than sleep at that point. She gently eased out of Laura's bed and tiptoed to the door. She slowly turned the handle and began gently pulling the door open. A squeak made her freeze in place. She didn't even turn to look at the beds. Her heart pounded in her chest, and she dared not breathe or flinch. After a tense moment, she heard nothing but deep breathing behind her. She quickly slipped through the narrow crack and pulled the door shut behind her.

As she wearily shuffled up the hall, she noticed some small red scraps on the floor. She shook her head, sighed, and bent down to pick up the first piece. To her surprise, it wasn't paper or plastic. It was a rose petal. Still crouching, she looked up the hall and realized it was a trail of rose petals. Her fatigue and stress suddenly melted away as she stood and followed the red trail to their bedroom.

She spotted the candlelight flickering even before she entered the room. Once she passed through the doorway, she saw the candles on the dresser and nightstand. The rose petals continued past the bed and into the bathroom. In the bathroom, candles surrounded their Jacuzzi tub.

16

Bubbles filled the tub, hiding the water below. Only Tom's head and shoulders were visible as he sipped a glass of wine. The bottle sat on the back edge of the tub next to an empty glass. He turned his head as she entered.

"What's all this?" she asked with a big smile.

"I knew you were having a rough day, and it's been a tough week. You need some relaxation."

"But all this, on a weeknight?"

"Why not?" Tom asked. "Now get naked and get in here!"

She shook her head and complied, quickly disrobing and climbing into the opposite side of the tub. He poured her a glass of wine, which she eagerly grabbed and drank a large sip.

"Honey, I'm not sure if I'm up for anything tonight," Helen said. "I'm exhausted."

"Well then, we'll sit here for a while, sip some wine, and, after we get out, I'll give you a massage on the bed until you fall asleep."

"Have I ever told you that you're the best husband ever?"

"Probably, but you can say it again if you'd like."

***

The years quickly passed as the children grew. It was their tenth wedding anniversary when Tom again had her don the blindfold, climb into their pickup truck—a newer version of the original—and go driving. Once the truck left the road and began its tortuous climb up the side of the mountain, Helen knew where they were going. Despite the lack of surprise, she would be happy with the results.

"OK. You can take off your blindfold," Tom said as he helped her out of the vehicle. She complied and once again marveled at the same view she'd first gazed upon ten years before. Everything was just as beautiful. Once again, the sun was beginning its downward journey through the blue sky and toward the mountains, and once again, Tom retrieved the picnic basket and set up the same picnic they had experienced years ago. Soon, they were both in the truck's bed, eating their sandwiches and sipping their wine.

"How's the cabin coming?" Helen asked with a grin.

"Great! In my mind anyway."

"So, no chance of building it ahead of schedule?"

"Now, did I say that? Actually, we have twenty thousand dollars saved up. I figure it will cost around forty thousand to build it. So maybe, just maybe, we can get it done in the next ten years."

Helen leaned over and hugged him hard. "Oh, that would be great! Can you imagine living up here?"

"Yeah, it would be pretty great: see the sun rising over the mountains each morning and setting over the other range in the evenings; listen to the sounds of the animals and insects at night; watch the deer in the yard. Maybe not too long."

They completed their routine of years before and made love in the setting sun's light and then cuddled late into the darkness.

***

Problems filled the next ten years. Helen had her gallbladder removed the following year, and Ethan and Laura both required braces a few years later. They also moved into a larger house so each child would have their own room and a bigger yard to play in—just months before Helen's job was eliminated. They steadily depleted their nest egg until it was pretty much gone.

They performed their tenth-anniversary ritual on their twentieth anniversary, Tom still insisting on the blindfold. The only difference that year was the cold rain. Tom parked the truck in the opposite direction, so they could sit inside and enjoy their picnic while experiencing the same view. This anniversary felt much different than the ones before. The weather definitely didn't help.

"I guess we ran out of luck this year, huh?" Tom said as he stared straight ahead, sipping his wine.

"I guess it kind of fits in with the past few years," Helen answered, also staring straight ahead at the rain spattering against the windshield.

"Yeah, we've had a bump or two. Maybe the real world finally caught up with us." Tom turned to stare at Helen and grabbed her left hand in his. "But it's still a fairy tale." He kissed her.

Helen smiled. She couldn't blink fast enough to stop a tear from running to the corner of her eye. He always said and did the right things. No matter how tough it got, he was a rock. "You're my Prince Charming."

"And you're my little damsel in distress." Tom leaned forward and kissed her. Suddenly, the dreary, melancholy moment changed. His soft, warm lips instantly swept her away to a different place. Even after twenty years of marriage, she still loved his kiss, especially when he made it passionate. She melted as their kisses intensified, and his hands explored her body. Soon, hers were doing the same to him. In moments, their clothes were off. He slid his seat back, and she climbed onto his lap, facing him. They made love in the truck as the rain poured around them.

"Wow! We still have it, don't we, babe?" Tom said when they'd finished.

She turned on his lap so her back rested against the door and her legs lay across the passenger's seat. She laid her head on his chest. "You're still amazing," she said, smiling a very satisfied smile, her cheeks glowing.

"Only because of you."

They sat in silence for a moment. "How's the cabin coming?"

"Pretty good…in my head. Well, you know all the money we've spent over the past ten years. Unfortunately, we're not in as good of shape as we were back then. But now that you're working again, we should be able to get back on track."

"But Ethan will be going to college next year and Laura the year after."

A moment of silence passed before Tom replied, "Yeah, I hoped they might get scholarships. I guess we're running out of time for that."

"We'll eventually get there. It'll work out in the end."

Tom smiled at her and kissed her again. "I promise you, honey, that we'll have that cabin. And we'll get to watch every season come and go on top of this mountain."

"I know we will. I know we will."

***

The next five years brought more financial strain, with both children attending college. Although they encouraged state schools, Ethan went out of state, and Laura went to a private college in-state. Both children worked during college to help pay expenses, but Tom and Helen still footed most of the bills.

But it was also a good time for them. They had plenty of time for each other now that the house was empty. Their physical relationship was not what it had been in their younger years, but their cuddling, kissing, and acts of romance were better than ever.

They went away to a resort and spa in Palm Springs for Helen's birthday one year. Arthritis in Tom's hands didn't allow him to give massages up to his standards, so he let a professional do it for her. Another year, they went on a cruise for Thanksgiving since Ethan and Laura didn't come home from college that week. These trips were expensive, but Tom assured Helen they could afford them. He still prepared his share of candlelit dinners, baths, and breakfasts in bed, and they went dancing, traveled, and lived life to the fullest.

They really began to save money after the kids graduated college and managed to pay their house off early, in their twenty-sixth year of marriage. Without a house payment, they were able to pay off their vehicles. Other than their trips, food, and entertainment, they were able to save for their ultimate dream.

***

One cold, snowy December evening, during their twenty-ninth year of marriage, Tom sat down heavily in the recliner. Helen looked up from watching television to stare at him. He rubbed high on his stomach absently. He had complained about stomach pain for a couple of weeks, a bad pain in his upper abdomen that went straight through to his back. He didn't look well, and he hadn't eaten much over those past weeks. He said he just wasn't hungry. He wouldn't say how much weight he had lost, but she knew it was a lot. But he was too stubborn to go to the doctor.

"Honey, you need to get checked out," she pleaded.

He looked at her with a weak grin. "Just a little acid reflux or something. I'll keep eating the antacids."

"You're an old fool!"

"But you still love me," he said, chuckling.

"Occasionally. But you'd better get to the doctor or at least start eating! You're wasting away to nothing."

"Yes, dear. Oh, speaking of changing the subject, guess what?"

She shook her head. She couldn't help but admire his spirit, no matter how bad he felt. "What?"

"We have forty thousand dollars in the bank!"

"Really?" she exclaimed.

"It's taken long enough. But yep, we've got it. I'm going to start pricing out a cabin next week."

"Wow, that's great!" Helen said. "Do you think forty thousand dollars is enough?"

"I'm not sure. I'm thinking about looking at the cabin kits. My brother Mike said he could help me build it in the spring. If it's not enough, I might be able to borrow some from my 401(k). One way or the other, baby, we will have that cabin next year!"

She stood up and walked over to him, leaned over, and gave him a kiss and a big hug. "I love you," she said.

***

Two days later, Helen awoke to find Tom still in bed. He was always up before her. His skin appeared yellowish and pale, and his breathing was heavy. She gently shook him until he awoke. He opened his eyes weakly, revealing that the whites were also yellow. Suddenly, he doubled up in pain, grasping at his stomach.

20

"We're going to the hospital, *now!*" she said firmly. She quickly dressed them both and helped Tom to the truck. He didn't protest this time. A half-hour later, they sat in the emergency room. She quickly explained his symptoms at the registration desk, and within minutes, he was on a stretcher in the examining room.

The doctors did a battery of tests, including ultrasound and an MRI. Tom and Helen had some time alone in the examining room between tests. Tom acted like he felt a little better, but he was still very weak and obviously in pain. She stood beside the bed and held his hand. "Sorry I'm so much trouble," he whispered weakly, squeezing her hand.

"You're not any trouble, silly!" She leaned over and kissed his forehead.

"I'll be back to myself soon. I'm sure it's nothing serious. Probably that acid reflux or, worst case, an ulcer."

"I'm sure it's nothing too, dear."

A few days later, they returned to the hospital to review the results of his tests. Dr. Jacobs, an oncologist, informed them that Tom was suffering from pancreatic cancer. It was also classified as stage IV, which was very advanced. He explained that pancreatic cancer had one of the highest mortality rates of any cancer. In Tom's case, it had metastasized out of the pancreas and into the liver, causing his yellow color. Surgery was not an option at this point.

Tom and Helen could only stare at the doctor in silence as he rendered Tom's death sentence. Chemotherapy and radiation could slow the growth and extend his life. Still, even then, his life expectancy was only six months. If he did nothing, he would not last longer than three months. The doctor gave him some strong pain pills and scheduled him for an evaluation at the cancer research center at the college two hours away. They would give Tom a second opinion and, if it were the same, would set up the chemo and radiation treatments.

The news from the cancer research center was just as grim. They confirmed Dr. Jacobs's prognosis and set Tom up to begin chemotherapy and radiation treatments the next day. They also referred them to a local hospice for when, or if, he became too weak to travel back and forth. Tom was mostly silent as Helen drove them back home.

"This kind of throws a wrench in the cabin plan, huh?" He chuckled weakly.

"That's the last thing you need to worry about!" Helen couldn't keep the tears from rolling down her cheeks. "You can beat this. You're strong.

They said that chemo could work well in some patients. All they have to do is keep it in check until a cure is found."

"You know this will take all our savings, even if I don't need the hospice."

"I don't care about our savings! I want you to get over this, Tom! You have to beat it."

They were silent for a while. "Helen, I have to ask you something."

"What?" she asked with some hesitation.

"I want you to keep working. I can drive by myself to get my treatments."

"No! I want to take care of you, Tom."

"You need to keep some normalcy to your life. You need your work and your friends. If I get so bad that I can't drive, I'll let you know. But until then, keep working. You can take care of me every night. Please, Helen."

She couldn't respond. It was all she could do to drive with tear-filled eyes.

***

The following two months were tough. Helen did as she was asked, as much as she hated it. She went to work while Tom drove himself to the cancer center. It was a four-hour round-trip drive, but he assured her he was OK. By the time she came home from work, he was worn out. She usually found him on the couch or in bed. He tried his best to perk up when she arrived, but she knew he was steadily getting weaker. It was so hard to see him like that. He had always been the rock in their relationship, steady and strong no matter what kind of storms they encountered. Now, she had to try to be the rock for him.

Tom deteriorated into a shell of his former self. Thin and frail, he had lost at least thirty pounds and still had the yellowish tint to his skin and eyes. The pain medicine eased his pain some, but Helen knew Tom still hurt. He also looked a lot older than his years. She guessed that losing the weight had made his face appear more gaunt and wrinkled. He hadn't lost any hair yet, which was surprising with the chemo treatments. But to her, he was still handsome and sexy, just in a slightly different way.

She spent most of her time caring for him and trying to make him comfortable. They climbed into the Jacuzzi tub nearly every night, where she would rub and massage him and sometimes just sit behind him with her arms wrapped around tight. Every night, they ended up on the couch together. He would usually lie down with his head on her lap, and she'd rub his head until he dozed off. Sometimes, they would lie together side by side. If he slept well, they would stay there for the night. If he woke up, they went to bed.

"I'm sorry you have to spend so much time taking care of me," he said one night on the couch, his head in her lap. He rolled over onto his back so he could look up at her.

"I wouldn't be anywhere else in the world right now! You've taken care of me for the past thirty years, more so than I ever deserved." She wiped the corners of her eyes. "It's my turn to take care of you now."

He smiled at her and then wiped his own eyes. "Can the patient have a big, wet, sloppy kiss?"

"As many as he wants." She laughed and leaned down to kiss his lips.

***

Tom insisted on Helen donning the blindfold once again on their thirtieth anniversary. The past few days had been hard on Tom, and she knew the pain pills were doing little to help, but he had insisted on keeping up their tradition. Once again, they took the ride in the pickup truck, the third version of the original. At least she thought they were doing the same ride, but something was different. The ride up the mountain wasn't nearly as rough, and she could swear she heard gravel crunching beneath the tires. Maybe he had taken her to a new destination this year.

After he parked the truck, he once again came around and opened her door. "You can remove the blindfold now," he said, grabbing her hands to help her out of the vehicle.

She took off the blindfold and looked around, screamed, and burst into tears. She grabbed Tom and hugged him tightly, squeezing so hard that she was a little scared she might've hurt him. She couldn't speak. She just buried her head into his shoulder and cried. She felt Tom's tears dripping onto her head.

Finally, she raised her head and peered around again. It was a beautiful March day with a sky as blue as the first day they'd come to the mountain. The sun shone bright and warm, and the grass and trees were just starting to green. They had parked on a gravel driveway, and on the other side of the truck stood a brand-new log cabin. It was stunning: with red cedar logs, a shiny green metal roof, and lots of windows. A large porch on the front wrapped around its sides, and wooden columns joined the roof to the railing.

They climbed up the stairs arm in arm. As they neared the top, Helen saw the rocking chairs on the porch. They walked up to the chairs and sat down. She still couldn't speak. She rocked in the chair and absorbed the view all around her. Tom held her hand as he rocked beside her. "How?" was all she could finally utter.

"Helen, I have to tell you something, and I hope you'll forgive me. I've lied to you for the past couple of months. It's the only time in our marriage that I've ever lied to you. I haven't been going to my treatments. I didn't go at all."

"Tom! Why?"

"First of all, they already said I'm incurable. I didn't want to spend my last months getting even sicker and weaker from the chemo. Second, I've promised you this cabin all of our marriage. Those treatments would have taken what money we've saved. Plus, if I tried to wait until after the treatments were over, I know I would've been too weak to help build this and enjoy what time I could with you in it. Working on this cabin has taken my mind off my illness. It's given me a much greater purpose than being fried in a hospital."

"How did you build this, feeling like you do?"

"Mike took FMLA from work. He did most of it. And Ethan and Laura actually helped some on weekends and after work."

"They knew?"

"I had to recruit all the help I could. But they were more than happy to give their mother a gift."

"I can't believe you!"

"No matter what you say about me, you know I keep my promises. Can you forgive me for lying?"

"Of course! How could I hold that against you? I think you should have been getting treatments, though, but you are still the sweetest man ever."

Tom leaned over and kissed her. "Good. I can go out on a high note."

Tom stood, took Helen by the hand, and escorted her inside the cabin. It was small but beautiful, with two bedrooms, one bath, a small kitchen, and a small living room. The living room and bedroom both had fireplaces. They made their way back out onto the porch and into the rocking chairs just as the sun began to set over the blue mountains.

"Is this as good as you dreamed?" Tom asked, grinning weakly. She saw he was getting tired.

"Oh, Tom, it's so much better than I dreamed! *You're* so much better than I could ever have dreamed."

"Happy anniversary." Tom smiled.

"This is the best one yet, honey," Helen replied and leaned over to kiss him.

"But I'm afraid we might have to skip the wild lovemaking. I don't think I can handle that right now."

"All I want is to be with you," Helen said and kissed him again.

Tom was silent for a moment as they both watched the sun disappear.

"What's wrong, dear?" she asked as she grabbed his hand.

"I think I've told you another lie."

"What?" She turned from looking at the mountains to stare at him.

"I promised you I would build this cabin…."

"And you did!"

"I also promised I would watch each season pass with you. I might be able to watch winter end and spring begin. I don't know about summer and fall."

Helen burst into tears and pulled her hand away from his to cover her face. Finally, she composed herself. When she looked back at him, she saw tears streaming down his cheeks. "You will, honey. I know you will see them all."

***

Ethan, Laura, and Mike moved enough of Tom's and Helen's belongings into the cabin the following week so that they could move in. Tom took a turn for the worse, and Helen asked for a leave of absence from work to be with him. They spent most of their days rocking in their chairs on the porch. They saw deer each morning and evening, and hawks cried out overhead as they glided on mountain currents. They saw a lot of other wildlife too: turkeys, squirrels, rabbits, possums—even a skunk. They just sat and talked the hours and days away. At night, they would cuddle on the couch in front of the fireplace. Everything was perfect, except the obvious.

Tom died in his sleep on April 21. The doctors said he had lived much longer than he should have and commented on his strength. Watching his passing unfold over the past few months didn't make it easier for Helen. She had him cremated and set the urn on the mantle in the living room, where it glowed in the light of the rising and setting sun. Laura and Ethan stayed with her for a week before they went back to work. She assured them she was OK.

She returned to work the following week. In the evenings, she came home, took the urn, and went out onto the porch. She set it in the chair beside her and rocked. She talked to the urn, to Tom. She knew she wasn't crazy. Somehow, it helped to fill the enormous void in her heart. She knew his spirit was on that mountain with her. Together, they watched summer and fall come and go and winter begin.

At first, her children thought she was losing her mind. Over time, they realized just how deep a love their parents had—it transcended death. It was sad to watch, her rocking beside the urn, but they knew it made their mother feel better. She did well living on her own, as well as could be expected.

***

The following March, Helen passed away. Mike found her body on the living room floor after she hadn't answered the phone for two days. The doctors said it was probably a heart attack or a ruptured aneurysm, and no autopsy was performed. The family knew better. She had just let go of living. She had left to be with Tom. Laura and Ethan placed her urn beside Tom's on the mantle and worked together to keep the cabin and land up. They even brought their families up to stay a few times that spring and summer, and they sensed their parents' presence all over the mountain.

At one such get-together that Fourth of July, Laura and Ethan stood in the living room as their families played outside. "You know, this cabin was the ultimate gift," Ethan said to his sister.

She was silent for a moment and then turned to turn at the urns. "No. That wasn't the gift."

Ethan looked at her puzzled and then followed her gaze to the mantle. Slowly, he smiled and nodded.

Red-Pen

She felt his hot breath just before his lips brushed the exposed skin. He softly kissed her shoulder, the same gentle way he used to kiss her lips, and slowly worked up toward her neck. She felt his tongue gently lick as his lips kissed and sucked. This was too much! It was time to end things before they went too far. She turned her head toward his. "I don't think this is a good idea…."

Leah laid the stapled papers down on her chest, needing a moment to cool off. The story definitely had an effect on her. She sighed and briefly glanced over at her sleeping, snoring husband. He lay facing the other direction. For a moment, she thought about waking him up and taking her building desire out on him. It was only for a brief moment. She knew he would be angry when wakened and definitely not in the mood to give up his precious sleep.

She sighed again and turned back to stare at the ceiling. She couldn't believe how talented a writer Robert was. She had been glad when he finally got back into it a few months earlier. Her mind drifted back to their high school days together, some twenty years prior.

They became almost instant friends from their first day of tenth-grade English together. He was nerdy, goofy, gangly, and not at all in her friend class. He was also funny, intelligent, spontaneous, sweet, and cute.

She had tried to ignore him when he sat in the chair behind her the first day, but he wouldn't allow it. For some reason, he chose her to throw all his attention at, and he eventually wore down her defenses. Once she gave in and laughed at the tenth corny joke, it was over.

They were never more than friends. At first, she thought he was interested in more, but he never openly gave any indication if he was. She dated whom she wanted to date, and he occasionally dated as well, although not much and with little success.

Their friendship quickly evolved into a strong one. They reached the point where they confided everything in each other—they didn't have to keep their guards up with no thoughts of a romantic relationship. They didn't put up barriers or act like people they weren't. They bared all—the good, the bad, and the ugly. She shared her guy problems, and he told her his girl problems, or lack of girl problems. They went shopping together, hung out at each other's house, went out to eat, went bowling, went to movies, and did pretty much anything two friends could do together. If she didn't have a date, she picked up the phone and called her best friend.

As she reminisced about their beginnings, she couldn't remember exactly how they became so close. Robert was just so different from most other boys, with no hint of pretentiousness about him. He didn't care what people thought. Many considered him a nerd, and others started rumors that Robert was gay, but he was neither. He was just Robert. He dressed how he wanted to dress, said what he wanted to say, and did what he wanted to do. Very few people in high school were like that. Everyone else strove to fit in and be a part of their chosen clique. Individuality was rare. Despite being a cheerleader and a preppy girl, Leah really admired, and was drawn to, him.

Early into the class, she saw his talent at writing. Since he sat behind her, the teacher paired them up. They had to read and red-pen each other's paper for every writing assignment—marking errors and recommending changes with a red pen. Their teacher apparently loved writing, at least her students' writing, so they got lots of practice. Writing came easy for Robert. If their assignment were to write two pages, he wrote six. While most of the students moaned, groaned, and struggled to write about the next topic, Robert didn't hesitate. His creative mind translated well to paper.

Near the end of school, one of Robert's stories, red-penned by Leah, won a local contest the teacher had made them all enter. He was the only one from their county to place. She told him that he should pursue writing, that he had a gift and needed to take advantage of it. He did go on to write several good short stories and even started a few novels. However, by their senior year, they didn't share any classes together, and he seemed to lose interest. When she asked him about it, he merely said he'd lost his editor. His one weakness was the technical part of writing, which was her strength. But with their different class schedules, there wasn't time for him to write or for her to red-pen. They drifted apart somewhat during those years.

She picked up the papers and continued reading.

> He stopped kissing and moved his lips up to her exposed ear. "Are you telling me to stop?" he asked in a heavy whisper, ensuring his hot breath caressed her ear. Before she could answer, he began kissing her earlobe. He drew it into his mouth, sucking and flicking it with his tongue. As he pulled his mouth away, he let his teeth rake against it, sending shivers down her entire body. He continued kissing her ear, from the lobe to the top, and even flicked his tongue inside a few times. *Please, stop*!

***

"Good morning, buttercup," Robert chirped as he poured his mug full of coffee and sat down on the couch in the teachers' lounge.

Leah glanced up from the newspaper and smiled at her friend. "Good morning to you, lover boy!"

"Lover boy? Who have you been talking to?" he asked with mock surprise.

"Just reading your story. And may I say, you should be ashamed!"

"Hey, I just write the stuff! Don't hate the player; hate the game."

Leah laughed. "You're the player, huh?"

"You know me. I just don't know what game I'm playing or how it's played. So, what did you think of my little story? Did it, uh…have any effects on you?"

Leah looked around the small lounge, ensuring the other teachers milling about weren't paying too much attention to their conversation. She felt her cheeks growing hot. "It was…it was a little stirring in parts."

"Hmmm…stirring, huh? Did you wake up the old man?"

"Robert!" she said a little too loud and punched his arm.

"Sorry! I was just asking a question," Robert replied innocently.

"You need to worry about your passive and active voices. You never did know the difference. Not to mention your run-on sentences…."

"OK. OK. Blah, blah, and blah. I'm going to pretend you liked it anyway."

"Yes, Robert, it was very good. But I did red-pen quite a bit." She reached into her large shoulder bag, withdrew the story, and handed it to Robert.

He glanced through it briefly and then looked back at her. "Uh, I think you messed up. There's one sentence without a red mark on it."

She hit his arm again.

***

After her last student fled the room, Leah walked up to the door separating her and Robert's classrooms and gently opened it a few inches. Robert sat at his desk, turned to the side, engaged in conversation with a female student. She started to close the door but, for some reason, stopped. Robert had certainly changed since their high school days. Other than still wearing glasses, he bore little resemblance to the young, gangly, somewhat nerdy boy of twenty years ago. His body had filled out nicely, aided by his continued weight lifting. His once acne-covered face was now smooth, tanned, and adorned with a goatee. Although she had never really noticed, he was rather handsome.

"May I help you, Mrs. Peters?"

Leah was startled to realize she had been caught daydreaming at Robert's door. His student now gone, he stared straight at her with his steely blue eyes. "Uh, I was just making sure you were behaving yourself. I'm not sure if you need to be left alone with young females." She walked into the room and up to his desk.

"Yeah. You know me, a real horn dog."

"So, what wild plans do you have for this weekend, stud muffin?" Leah laughed.

"As if you don't remember!"

"Huh? Oh, yeah. Your date with Miss Watkins!" Leah exclaimed.

"My date with Miss Watkins," Robert echoed mockingly. "Like you forgot! Yet another evil scheme of yours to torture me."

"Torture you? You'll have a great time! She's so sweet and cute."

"Sweet and cute? So are baby wolverines, until they're gnawing the flesh from your bones!"

"Oh, Robert! She's a librarian. How crazy could she be?"

"They're the craziest! Have you never watched a movie with a female librarian in it? They're all quiet and nice, until they take their glasses off, let their hair down, and get freaky."

30

"That's just in the movies. But even if it came true, what's wrong with a little freakiness? She might rock your world. Then you could write a story about it!" Leah couldn't keep a straight face for more than a few seconds.

"Yeah, and do you remember the last time you set me up with a freaky girl?" Robert asked, not finding the humor in the conversation. "She was a sweet, quiet bank teller."

Leah tried her best to contain her laughter. "Can you refresh my memory?"

"You remember the story, when she invited me back to her apartment for a nightcap."

"Still fuzzy; go on, please." Leah covered her mouth with the back of her hand.

"And we went into her bedroom."

"Hmmm…sounds good so far."

"And her naked male roommate was in her bed!"

"A threesome? Pretty wild!"

"And he was more excited about me than her!"

Leah lost it. She cackled out loud, even bending over and pounding the desk with her hand. She finally stood and wiped tears from her eyes. When she saw the expression on Robert's face, she lost it again.

Finally, he gave in and laughed a little too. "You do love torturing me, don't you? I'm like your little circus monkey," Robert said dryly.

"I'm just trying to find you a good woman to use all your romantic, erotic story ideas on." She still struggled to regain her composure.

"Let's just remember that my romantic fantasies don't include me and another man or making an adult Internet film."

Leah burst into another fit of laughter. Eventually, it died down to just a chuckle. "Oh, yeah. Pam, the wannabe porn star! Hey, but I can't claim credit for her."

"But who signed me up for Find-A-Date-Tonight?"

"You really should give that another chance. I bet there are a lot of normal, sexy, romantic women just waiting for the right man to come along."

Robert growled, flashing a glare that only evoked additional laughter. "Let's see if I survive tonight first."

"So, do you have some more reading material for me?" Leah asked, wiping her eyes one last time.

"Yeah. 'Final Exit, Part Two.'"

"Come on, silly. Give it up!"

Robert reached into the open briefcase beside his desk and handed her another story. She quickly grabbed it and read the title out loud. "'True Love.' Hmmm…very creative."

"Don't judge a story by its title. It was kind of a rush job, so you might want to have an extra red pen ready."

"I'm sure it's great. I'll be reading it while you're off on your big date, little monkey."

"Shut up!"

***

> We stood on the end of the pier, overlooking the dark, moon-streaked water. The waves lapped at the poles below and crashed steadily on the beach behind us. A strong, salty breeze blew into our faces, wafting Amy's long hair against me and her sweet perfume to my nose. I shifted slightly, my body softly grazing hers. I thought she might move away, but instead, she moved back against me. I felt her warm, toned body pressed against mine through her thin dress. I slowly wrapped my arms around her, joining my hands over her stomach, a flood of memories rushing through my mind. It all seemed so familiar, just as it had so many years ago. I felt alive again.
>
> She slowly turned around so we faced each other. My hands were now on her lower back, and she placed hers on my shoulders. The look in her eyes was one I recognized from long ago, as if we were suddenly transported back in time. She slid her hands behind my head and pulled me toward her. Then her luscious lips touched mine. I thought my knees would buckle with the flood of sensations that surged through my body. I had forgotten exactly what it was like to kiss her lips, but it was as if we had never stopped. Our mouths, lips, and tongues moved perfectly together, struggling to get more. Our bodies and minds melded into one. My heart raced, my head swam, my stomach fluttered, and my body tingled from head to toe.

Suddenly, the phone rang, dragging Leah out of the engrossing story. She quickly tossed the papers onto the couch and ran into the kitchen to answer it. She glanced at her watch as she reached for the phone—eleven o'clock. She looked at the caller ID and saw it was Robert's cell phone. She smiled and quickly answered.

"I know your date can't be over already," she said in mock surprise.

"Other than jail time, name one reason I shouldn't drive to your house, wrap my fingers around your neck, and slowly choke the last breath from your body?" Robert nearly shouted into the phone.

"You sound tense."

"I'll give you tense!" he stammered.

"OK. What have you done with sweet, innocent Miss Watkins?"

"You knew, didn't you?"

"Knew what, dear?"

"Don't play coy with me!"

"Coy? Me?" She heard only silence on the other end. "OK. I heard that she might be a little on the adventurous side, but I thought you might need a little excitement. So, did you have a good time?" She did her best not to laugh.

"Adventurous? *Adventurous?* I don't think that word describes my date tonight!"

"Do share."

She heard him sigh into the phone. When he finally started to speak, the edge in his voice had softened a little. "Dinner went OK. We ate at the Steer Shack…."

"Steer Shack? Wow. You pulled out all the stops."

"Shut up, please! Anyway, we chatted politely and ate a decent meal. I suggested we go to a movie, but she said we could watch a DVD at her place instead."

"Oooohhhh. You didn't waste any time, did you?" She couldn't silence a snicker.

"Once again, shut up. Anyway, for some ungodly reason, I agreed. So we went to her house. We got comfy on the couch, and she put in a movie. The lighting was really dim, and she snuggled close to me. Well, when the movie started, guess what it was?"

"*Gone with the Wind?*" Leah cackled.

"Ha, ha, and ha. No. It was an *adult* movie."

"No way!"

"Oh, yes way. But not just any adult movie. Very soon, I realized just what type it was."

"Kinky?" Leah managed to spit out through her laughter.

"Just a bit. It involved the women having their way with the men."

"Having their way with?"

"Yes. As in the women used certain tools and attachments and played the role of the men, and the men played the role of the women."

Leah bent over the counter, dropping the phone in the process, and laughed hysterically with her head buried in her arms. Tears ran down her cheeks and onto her sleeves. After a moment, she managed to pick up the phone again. "You're making this up!"

"Are you enjoying yourself, Leah? Are you really enjoying yourself?"

"I'm sorry. I'll do better," she said, trying to catch her breath.

"I couldn't move or speak. She put her arm around me and bored a hole into the side of my head with her eyes. Finally, she placed her hand on my inner thigh and asked what I thought of the movie. She followed that up by asking if I was open-minded about that sort of thing."

"And were you?"

He growled in response. "I leaped up and ran from her house. It was like a horror movie. I kept looking over my shoulder as I struggled to open my car door. It finally opened, and I hopped in, locked the doors, and prayed that it would start. Thankfully, unlike in the movies, it did, and here I am talking to you. Although, for all I know, she might just appear in front of me in the middle of the road, toys in hand!"

Leah could do nothing but laugh. "So that's your story, and you're sticking to it?" she finally asked.

"Well, gee, I'm home and look at the time. Have I thanked you yet for setting me up on yet another therapy-inducing date?"

"Why, no, you haven't."

"How about I do it with a click?"

Leah was still chuckling to herself as she hung up the phone and went into her bedroom.

"Sounds like you've been having a good time," her husband grumbled from the bed. "Who were you laughing it up with?"

"Robert. He just got back from his date with the librarian," she answered as she climbed into her side of the bed.

"I don't know why he continues to date women. I think he's going after the wrong sex."

"Richard! Why do you insist on believing he's gay?"

"Let's see: he writes girly love stories, teaches English, and never has a second date with a woman. I rest my case."

"So a man can't write or be sensitive or single without being gay?"

"Pretty much sums it up."

34

"It wouldn't hurt if you were a little more sensitive and romantic, you know. Every woman likes to be romanced once in a while," Leah said, her good mood quickly wearing off.

"Well, you knew how I was when you married me. If you wanted all that, you should have married Tooty Fruity. Now that you've stopped your cackling, I'm going back to sleep."

***

Robert opened the door after the second knock. He issued a glare as her welcome.

"Are you still sore at me?" she asked, her head slightly cocked to the side and her bottom lip pushed out.

"Always. Now get in here."

She followed him into his apartment. She had been in it a few times before. It was small, fashionably decorated, and always immaculate. Her eyes followed Robert, who was dressed more casually than usual. He wore black sweatpants and an old Washington Redskins jersey. Although unshaven, he had combed his hair, and she caught a whiff of nice cologne. He led her into the kitchen and merely pointed at a chair on the near side of the table. Two stacks of papers lay on the table, one in front of the chair she sat down in.

"Coffee?" he asked gruffly, pouring himself a cup.

"Why, yes. Thank you very much," Leah replied with a grin at his morning demeanor.

"Two sugars and an ounce of milk?" Robert rumbled.

"Why, yes. I'm impressed!" She marveled that he knew how she liked her coffee.

He prepared her mug, set it down in front of her, and then walked to the other side of the table and sat down. "I'm just freakin' nice like that."

"Wait a second. You didn't poison it, did you?" Leah asked, staring into her mug.

"Of course not. I don't have time to dispose of a body today."

"I'm thinking you're not a morning person, are you?"

"Just depends on what happened the night before. OK. Here's my last story, which you so generously red-penned last week. I have to get a final draft together to mail it off to the contest on Monday," Robert said, all business.

"How do we do it? Are you going to read it?" Leah asked, trying to be a little more serious.

Robert looked at her a moment as if gauging whether she was joking. When he saw she wasn't smiling, he said, "I guess we could do that. It is a

35

little easier to catch mistakes when you read it out loud. In addition to the obvious mistakes, I'm also open to suggestions for changes."

"Yes, sir, boss!"

Robert growled and then began reading out loud. The further Robert got into the story, the harder she found it to concentrate. He had a soft, strong voice, and something about the way he read pulled her into the story, as if they were characters in it. She always wondered when she read his stories if he was actually a romantic person in real life or just had a good imagination. Now, the honesty and sincerity in his voice made her believe the former. Suddenly, she could picture him being the romantic man in the story. She usually just saw his humorous, best-friend side. Even though he was merely reading a story, she was picking up on a lot more.

The dialogue in much of the story was similar to theirs—a relaxed humor mixed in with the more serious, romantic conversation. When Robert came to some of those parts, he looked her in the eye and flashed a grin. He knew the story so well that he had most of it memorized. She returned the grin and then quickly stared back down at the words, trying again to focus. She did manage to throw in some suggestions: different ways to phrase specific sentences, along with several additions and subtractions. Some he would agree to; some they would debate.

The toughest part came during the love scene she'd read just a couple of nights before. As he read the very descriptive and detailed pages, neither made eye contact. She knew her cheeks were red and hoped he didn't notice. Actually hearing him read the words intensified the effects she'd experienced while reading. She tried to think about anything else, anything other than the words he spoke. She thought about her husband and wondered if he was catching fish on his trip. She thought about what she needed from the grocery store later that afternoon. But her mind kept coming back to that table, that story, and the intense love scene he painted with every soft, sensuous word.

At last, finishing the scene, Robert looked up at Leah, his cheeks also slightly red. "That was weird enough." He chuckled.

"Just a tad," she answered with a nervous laugh.

"Other than that part, did you like it? I mean, was it believable?"

"Uh, yeah. I thought it was pretty good."

"Kind of like every night with you and Richard?"

"Please! It took you longer to read the scene than it would take us, and about once a month at that." As soon as she spoke, she realized she shouldn't have. That was way too personal to share with Robert. She changed the subject quickly, saving them both an embarrassing moment. "So, are all your stories from real-life conquests?"

Robert laughed. "Considering you set up most of my real-life dates and know the ugly outcomes, that would be a no. Somehow, I don't think people want to read about my experiences—at least not in a romance novel. Maybe they could be *Tales from the Dark Side* or *Twilight Zone* episodes."

"Hey, now there's an idea! I'll need to set you up on some more dates, so you could have, like, a whole series."

"I think I'm done with your dates. I like my life of solitude just fine. I'll just write my stories, and hopefully novels, and live through them," he said in a moment of seriousness.

"Awe, that's sad! Don't give up on me yet." Robert raised his eyebrows slightly, so she hurriedly continued, "I might find someone good for you. Or you might find someone on your own. You're a good catch for any woman," Leah said, laying her hand on top of his on the table.

"Aren't you just sweet all the sudden?" Robert replied with a slight grin.

"All the sudden? All the time!" She laughed. She noticed her hand had rested on his a little too long and discreetly pulled it back. "OK. On to the mushy stuff!"

They worked together for the next few hours, hammering out a polished version. They ordered a pizza for lunch and took a break from their project long enough to eat and talk about subjects other than the story. They never had any problem finding something to talk about, from the mundane to the off-the-wall crazy. They had no moments of silence. Finally, at four, Leah had to head home. Richard was supposed to be back by six, and she had to buy groceries and have supper ready by then.

***

Over the next few weeks, Leah and Richard's relationship deteriorated. He started going out more and more with friends, leaving her home alone. He came home late at night, hardly spoke to her, and went to bed. Jake, their sixteen-year-old son, was rarely home since getting his driver's license. This gave her a lot of alone time, and she began spending more time on the phone with Robert, calling him nearly every night. She also went to his apartment for a few more red-pen sessions as he entered more contests. They discussed his stories, both current and future ideas, Robert's love life—or lack thereof—and her marriage. She tried not to talk about her personal life at first, but they spent so much time talking that it became unavoidable.

"Why did you marry him?" Robert asked one night on the phone when Leah was in a particularly bad mood.

She thought for a moment before answering. "We were young and thought we were in love. He was cool and spontaneous, and we had fun together."

"And he was a jock."

"What's with you and jocks? I'm sure not all of them turn out bad," she said defensively.

"OK. Name one who hasn't."

She was quiet again, running through a mental list of every boy they went to high school with who was still around town. As badly as she wanted to, she couldn't dispute Robert's theory. "I'm sure there are some out there somewhere. Hey, wait a minute! What about some of the professional football players? Let's see, Payton Manning seems sweet, and Brett Favre...."

"Pros don't count, just washed-up high school jocks. But you know what your real problem is?"

"Oh, this will be good coming from a professional bachelor!" Although she valued his opinion on most things, she didn't always like it when he offered her advice on family-related subjects.

"That hurts! I read a lot, and I watch a lot of chick flicks. That makes me qualified. How old were you when you got married?"

"Nineteen, Dr. Phil."

"Your problem, like so many others, is that you married too young," Robert said, a hint of smugness in his voice.

"What if we were madly in love?" she argued.

"What do two nineteen-year-olds know about love? What do nineteen-year-olds know about themselves? Think about how many changes you've gone through since you were nineteen. You really don't fully mature and know who you are until your thirties. How can you know what you want in a partner without knowing who you really are? What are the chances that a person meets someone in their teens, and they both grow and evolve into mature adults and end up still being one hundred percent compatible and in love? I mean, I'm sure it happens, but how often?"

"Wow, so deep!" Leah said with heavy sarcasm.

Robert growled. "Let me go one step further. What are the chances, considering you really only dated one person in your life, that in a town the size of this one, the person ends up being the love of your life and your soul mate? Again, it might happen, but how often?"

"Hmmm…So, Oprah, what are your solutions for these two problems?"

"I'm glad you asked, grasshopper. It's simple. First, you travel the world and date lots of people. Second, you don't get married until your thirties."

"That's your personal plan?"

"Kind of, but I don't travel, and I date nothing but freaks and will probably never get married. Now, back to you…."

"But I'd say most people get married by their early to mid-twenties, and many of them stay together and live happily ever after," Leah shot back.

"Well, half end in divorce. Out of the other half, how many are happy? I mean truly happy. Think about all the couples you know well and your parents and my parents. Sure, they're together, but are they happy and totally compatible? Or are they just comfortable or too scared to start over again?"

Leah silently debated whether to continue the argument. She decided she didn't have the energy. "You have too much free time on your hands."

***

Two weeks later, on a Saturday night, Leah pounded on Robert's door. It was nearly midnight and pouring rain. She knocked for several minutes until the outside light came on and the door opened. Robert stood there in a pair of gray shorts and a black tank top, his hair a mess. "What's going on?"

"Richard is gone!" she sobbed.

"Huh? Gone?"

"Can I come in? It's freezing out here!"

"Sure, come in." He shut the door behind her and led her to the couch, where they sat down beside each other. He grabbed the blanket from the back of the couch and spread it over her. She smiled faintly. "OK. What's going on?"

She told him about her fighting with Richard all day about the amount of time he'd been spending away from home. He informed her that he was going camping with the guys that night and that she could just deal with it. She told him that if he went camping, he'd better pack a lot of clothes because he wouldn't be welcome back in that house. He said, "Fine," packed a suitcase, made several trips to his vehicle, and left.

"Wow. I'm sorry to hear that," Robert said, shaking his head.

"He makes me so mad!" Her anger began to replace the tears.

"Where's Jake?"

"Luckily, he's spending the night with a friend."

"That's good." Robert put his hand on her knee, on top of the blanket. "I'm sure he'll come back tomorrow, and you two will make up—and have all kinds of freaky makeup sex."

Leah elbowed him in his left arm but couldn't hide a brief smile. "You know, I really don't think I want him to come back."

"Really?"

"You know how our relationship is. We're not in love. Maybe it's time to move on. I mean, he's made the first move. Why not just go with it?"

Robert fell silent for a moment. "Well, believe it or not, I'm really not comfortable counseling you on this."

"What? You're missing a chance to throw out a theory or some free love advice?"

Robert squeezed her knee hard. She groaned and hit the back of his hand with her fist.

"I don't know," he said. "I mean, you're a married woman in a single man's apartment at midnight. I'm here for you, but I don't think I need to give marriage advice right now."

"OK. Fine then. But can I ask something of you? And please don't take this the wrong way."

"Not liking the sound of this, but go ahead," Robert replied apprehensively.

"I don't want to be alone tonight."

"Oh, well, you can sleep in my bed, and I'll sleep here on the couch."

"No. I'll sleep on the couch, but I want you to stay here with me."

"Huh? Do I need to go brush my teeth really quick?" Robert asked with a nervous grin.

"No, stupid! Just stay here with me until I fall asleep. I'm tired, upset, and right now, I just want to lie down on your couch. You lie down there, and I'll lie in front of you, and no funny business!"

She stood so Robert could get up, cut off the living room lights, and lie down on his side, his head on the armrest. She then lay down in front of him, her head on his right arm and her back pressed against his chest. They spread the blanket over them, and he placed his left arm around her.

"OK. This is going down as one of the strangest nights ever," Robert said with a nervous chuckle.

She replied with an elbow in his stomach. "Shut up and go to sleep. And no messing around back there!"

Leah didn't fall asleep for quite a while. It was such a surreal situation. Her marriage was falling, or had fallen, apart. It really hadn't fully hit her that Richard was gone, and she didn't know whether he would come back or she wanted him to come back. Then she thought about what all it would mean if he didn't return. What would Jake do? Would she be able to keep the house? How could she get by on her own? Her mind was reeling.

Then there was her spooning with her best friend. She couldn't help but think about his last story. The couple in the story had started out in the same position, leading into the erotic scene. She knew nothing would happen that night, but the thoughts still crept into her mind. She went from worrying about her future to imagining Robert whispering into, and then kissing, her ear. She wondered if he, the story's author, had any of the same thoughts. She almost got up and went home several times, but she really didn't want to be alone in that house. It was a long night.

***

The phone rang five times before a gruff voice finally whispered, "Hello?"

"I'm sorry to call so late, but I really need to talk to you," Leah blurted out, her voice tinged with fatigue and tears.

After a moment of silence, Robert, barely awake, said, "You just have something against me and sleep, don't you?"

Leah ignored his ill-timed attempt at humor. "It's Richard!"

"Did he come back?"

"No, and he's not coming back!" Leah spoke in choppy sentences, trying to keep from crying again.

"What? Why?"

"Turns out he's staying with his girlfriend!"

"Huh?"

"Apparently, all his nights out and this weekend's getaway were with another woman! Oh, and get this: she's nineteen years old!"

"Oh, my God! I knew he was a useless excuse of a man, but I had no idea," Robert said.

"I was shocked too. First of all, cheating when he never even wants sex with me. And second, a nineteen-year-old!" Her anger overrode any thought of crying.

"Wow. I'm floored. How's Jake doing? Does he know?"

"Yeah. We've talked about it most of the day. Richard came back this morning to get more of his stuff, and Jake overheard most of our fight. I guess he's doing OK. His first instinct, like mine, is to hate him. He just went to bed a little bit ago. That's why I'm just now calling you."

"Can I do anything for you?"

"Just stay up and talk to me."

"Sure. Sleep is overrated anyway."

"A nineteen-year-old! What would a nineteen-year-old see in him?"

"Probably the same thing you did years ago. He's probably turned on the charm—or faked it. He's mature, has a job, and is probably exciting for her."

"I don't know how! And what about the…the sex? Why would she want that five minutes of *nothing*?"

"What do nineteen-year-olds know about sex? That goes back to my argument against getting married young. I mean, what did you know about romance, foreplay, and good sex back then? Sex was exciting because it was new and naughty. She probably looks at him as more experienced than guys her age and a better lover. But you—people our age—need more than five minutes of just sex. It's no longer new or naughty. You want the romance: the wine and candles, the foreplay, and the cuddling afterward. It's about the entire experience now, not just the orgasm."

Leah was silent for a moment. She hated to admit it, but sometimes Robert said all the right things and was very perceptive concerning relationships. "Why doesn't *he* want all that stuff?"

"He's a former jock." They both laughed. "He's a rude, crude, self-centered man. He's just worried about his own gratification. He knows with a nineteen-year-old, he doesn't have to worry about all the other stuff you want. He's back to being a stud again."

"Why are you so sensitive and romantic?"

"Oh, I'm just making this crap up as I go. Five minutes sounds good enough to me."

They talked until five in the morning. Although nothing in Leah's life changed in those hours, she felt better about everything by the time they hung up.

***

The following week was tough, though being back at work helped some. Leah spent her evenings with Jake—they needed each other to cope with Richard's absence. They went out and ate, shopped, and did things to take their minds off the obvious. She spoke to Richard a couple

42

of times, as he gathered the rest of his belongings. He had moved into an apartment with his girlfriend. She knew there would be no reconciliation. Their marriage had been on a downhill slide for years, and she had nothing to fight for. It was still tough, though. The fact that he'd cheated on her hurt badly, and being single again was a difficult concept to grasp. She had been married pretty much all her adult life.

But she would survive, and having a friend like Robert really helped. Even though he had never been married, he was a rock for her, and his sense of humor could make her laugh no matter how hard she had been crying. She talked to him on the phone every night after Jake went to bed. She didn't go over to his apartment that week. Although the thought of spooning was very tempting, Jake needed everything to be as normal as possible. That Friday, Robert gave her a new story to red-pen. She couldn't wait. She had been rereading his old ones almost every night. That night, she read the new one, entitled "Old Friends."

> Her legs shook as she stood face-to-face with the man who had been her best friend for years. Now, suddenly, everything was different. When his hands grabbed hers, electricity shot up her arms and into her body, leaving a trail of chill bumps in its wake. She had been nervous the entire date, which was strange considering they had been friends for so many years. They knew everything about each other, and, for most of the date, they had laughed and had fun like every other time they were together.
>
> Now they stood on her porch at the end of the date—the moment of truth. *How do I kiss someone I love like a brother? What if there are no feelings at all?* It was like her first date in high school. They gazed deeply into each other's eyes, and she noticed the subtle change in his eyes and face. She knew he was thinking of her as more than just a friend. He wrapped his arms around her waist, and she placed hers around his neck. She was afraid he could feel her trembling against his strong body. She felt more than just friendship toward him too.
>
> She realized at that moment just how attracted she was to him, how much she always had been. As they stood in the moonlight, their bodies pressed tightly together, lust and

desire replaced any thoughts of friendship. He slowly leaned toward her. She closed her eyes and waited for the touch and taste of his lips. Her heart pounded in her chest, and her stomach fluttered wildly.

At last, their lips met. He was so tender with the first kiss. He kissed her top lip, then the bottom. The sensation was indescribable. Her body tingled from her hair to her toes, and she felt the flush on her cheeks. His hands moved up and down her back, and hers ran through the hair on the back of his head. Their heads moved back and forth as their wet lips glided effortlessly together. He slowly sucked her top lip between his, then the bottom. Soon, their mouths opened, allowing their tongues to explore each other.

She had no more worry or concern about his being like a brother. They had quickly transitioned into much more than that. Their first kiss was better than any she'd ever imagined. It seemed so natural, so right. She couldn't get enough of his lips. The more they kissed, the more she wanted. They kissed for twenty minutes, standing on her front porch. Finally, they stopped long enough to catch their breaths. Then she opened the door, and they stumbled into her apartment.

Leah put down the story. It was the best one she had read yet. Then she realized she'd forgotten to red-pen it. It was a little strange that the storyline dealt with old friends becoming lovers. She wondered if it was based loosely on them. In many of his stories, she knew he took bits and pieces of real-life and then developed them into a fictional tale. That must have been what he'd done here. She needed a quick break before finishing. She didn't know exactly what was coming next, but she had a pretty good idea that, whatever it was, it was going to be graphic and intense. She doubted it was the best idea to be reading that kind of story, especially considering she was sleeping alone—and would be for a long, long time—but it definitely beat watching television.

***

"You have to!" Robert pleaded.

"I really don't think so. I mean, Richard has only been gone for three months. It's too soon."

"It doesn't have to be anything serious. Just go out, meet this person, and have a nice dinner. You know full well what Richard has been up to. It's time for you to start the next phase of your life. You can at least go out on an innocent date."

"This isn't supposed to work this way! I'm the one who sets you up on dates. We can't both be matchmakers," Leah replied, trying to come up with as many excuses as she could not to go.

"That's exactly why I owe you one. You've tortured me numerous times. Now, it's my turn. Well, not to torture you, but to set you up," Robert argued desperately.

She sighed and shook her head. "What's his name?"

"Uh, I can't tell you. It's going to be a truly blind date," Robert said evasively.

"Oh, God, this can't be good. OK. What does he look like?"

"Tall, dark, and handsome. And he has a great personality and a good sense of humor. You'll love him!"

"I don't know. I really don't need another useless man," Leah whined.

"Oh, come on! If it doesn't work out, I'll never try to fix you up again. It's a one-time deal," Robert offered.

"Really? Never?"

"Yep. Promise plus."

"Can I get it in writing?" Leah asked, resigning herself to the fact she was going out with a man who was not her husband.

"Great! He said he'll meet you at the Little Italy restaurant on Main Street at eight in the corner booth."

"I think I'm going to be sick."

***

Leah stopped halfway across the restaurant and stared at the man sitting in the corner booth, her mouth hanging open. He wore a long-sleeved black shirt and khaki pants, a simple yet effective outfit, and he looked very handsome. She quickly surveyed the entire restaurant and then slowly walked toward him. He smiled the entire time she approached.

"What are you doing here?" she asked, not hiding her puzzlement. "My date is supposed to be here. Did he stand me up?"

"Nope. He's here. Even arrived early," Robert said, still grinning.

"Where's he at?" she asked, looking around the restaurant again.

"Sit down, stupid! It's me."

Leah dropped onto the bench on the other side of the table and stared at him, her face expressionless.

"Are you that disappointed?"

"Uh, no. I'm too shocked to speak," she stammered.

"Something can actually make you speechless? I should have done this years ago." He laughed.

"Is this whole thing a joke, or are you serious?"

"I'm pretty serious."

"This is like a date, date? Not just hanging out as friends?" Leah asked, her face still ashen.

"I'm not liking your reaction too much. Is this a terrible idea?"

"No. I don't guess so. I'm just stunned."

"I need to tell you something." He grabbed both of her hands and stared into her eyes. "When I'm done, you can decide what comes next."

"Um…OK. Shoot," Leah said, beginning to regain her composure.

"Leah, I've loved you since we were sixteen years old. Well, at that time, it was probably more lust. But over the years, it has developed into much more."

"Really?" she asked, not hiding her surprise.

"It's been hard all these years to settle for just being your friend when I wanted to be so much more. It's killed me to watch how badly Richard treated you. Do you know how many nights I lay awake, thinking about how that jerk was lying beside you, totally ignoring you when he should have had you wrapped up in his arms, cherishing every second he was allowed to spend with you? I kept asking myself, how could someone be with you and not do everything within his power to make you happy in every way possible? Do you know how close I was to finding him and hurting him badly when I found out he cheated on you?"

Leah sat in stunned silence. The more Robert spoke, the more he let down his guard and allowed his true feelings to come spilling forth. He spoke like he wrote in his stories. He had never shared feelings like this in all the years they'd been friends. She felt happy, flattered, and overwhelmed. "Wow. I don't know what to say!"

"And you know all my stories? We *are* the main characters. Every one of them is about us."

A tear ran from Leah's right eye. She removed a hand from his and quickly wiped it away. "Why didn't you ever say anything, at least before I got married?" She placed her hand back on top of his.

46

"Would you have gone out with me then? Honestly?" She stared down at the table. "I didn't think so," he continued. "And I didn't want to say anything over the past several years while you were married. I didn't want to interfere with that, even though I hated Richard for neglecting you."

"What would have you done if Richard hadn't left?"

"I guess I would have kept writing love stories about a woman I could never be with."

Leah took both hands and wiped her eyes. "I'm available now," she whispered in a shaky voice.

"So, do you have any feelings for me?"

She stared back at him, looking deep into his blue eyes. Now that they were expressing their true feelings, she fully saw him as so much more than a friend. "I've developed very strong feelings for you over the past year. I think it was red-penning your stories that allowed me to see the real you. I saw more than my goofy, funny friend. I used to feel so guilty reading your stories, with my husband in the bed beside me, and imagining it was us in the scene. I found myself jealous of the women I set you up with. Although I felt bad for it, I was glad they didn't work out for you and took away our time together.

"Any doubt about my feelings for you disappeared when Richard left, and we started spending so much time together. Then I knew that you weren't just making up the words—you really felt and meant what you wrote. You have been so kind and sweet and supportive of me. You were always there when I had no one else. You've been there for me for twenty years now, and you've never asked for anything in return."

"Good answer!" Robert said with a nervous laugh. "Now, what the heck do we do?"

She rubbed his hands gently and smiled. "Whatever we do, we have to make sure we don't mess up our friendship. I hope it will develop into more than that and be story-worthy, but I can't afford to lose my best friend in the process. I can't get through this without you. Can you promise me that?"

"If you couldn't get rid of pesky nerd-boy in the tenth grade, do you think you'll get rid of him now?" They both laughed. "We will always be best friends. All we're saying now is that we're free to think of each other as more than friends. I don't want to rush into a situation we're not ready for or force something that's not there."

They were both silent for a moment. Finally, Leah spoke. "So, Mr. Romance Writer, what happens now? What would you write next?"

"I'm thinking a make-out scene."

"You pig! Besides, if that happens, it has to be on my doorstep at the end of the date, like in your last story," she said slyly.

"Oh, yeah. I guess that will be the big test, huh? We have to hope it doesn't feel like kissing a sibling."

"I'm thinking it won't. But yeah, I guess it will be a test. And if we pass, I have another test."

"Hmmm…another one?" Robert asked.

"Yep. I have some toys in my bedroom I've been dying to try on you. Rumor has it you're kind of kinky like that."

They burst into laughter, disturbing everyone around them.

Happy Birthday

"Did it ever occur to you for one minute to do something romantic today?" Valerie asked, dropping the lame "funny" card about turning forty onto the table.

"I guess we can, but it has to be quick. I'm running late," Rex replied, barely glancing her way as he walked into the kitchen.

"Not sex, you idiot!" she yelled. For some stupid reason, she thought today might be different. Maybe a milestone birthday would cause him to give some thought to a gift or a gesture of love. *She* was the idiot. Rex was Rex, and that was all she should expect.

"We ate out Saturday. I thought that was your birthday supper," Rex said defensively as he reentered the room, lunchbox in hand.

"The buffet was wonderful, *dear*, but for some reason, I thought…." She stopped. It was no use going there.

"Thought what?"

She responded, against her better judgment. "I don't know, maybe breakfast in bed, flowers, a thoughtful gift…a card with something special written in it…."

"You've been watching Lifetime too much," Rex said as he kissed her cheek and headed toward the door. "Oh, happy birthday," he called out as he shut the door behind him.

She screamed.

***

Valerie walked quickly through the office door, her eyes still red despite reapplying makeup. She was late and obviously not in a good mood. She actually looked forward to working and taking her mind off the worst birthday ever. When she reached her desk, she froze. On the middle of it sat a beautiful bouquet of flowers. The vase held several types of flowers, but her eyes were drawn to her favorite—the orange tulips in the middle of the arrangement. A small basket in front of the flowers contained Hershey's Kisses and dark-chocolate bars—her two favorite indulgences.

She stumbled forward in disbelief and amazement. *Did Rex come through after all? How did he get the flowers and candy here so early?* She threw her purse down, grabbed the card, and opened it with shaking hands. "Like a fine wine, you only keep getting better each year. Happy Birthday to the best secretary and friend I could want. Your best boss ever, Kevin."

She fell into her chair. *Kevin?* Kevin had been her boss for the past three years. They worked alone in a small, three-room office suite. Close friends, they shared much of their personal lives with each other. Their friendship was based on more than just working alone together all day, though. They had similar personalities and senses of humor. He was funny, intelligent, and, though she tried not to notice, good-looking. He made her laugh on days she wanted to cry. He was also a good listener and very intuitive. Although he was a man, and she hated that entire half of the species much of the time, he understood her perspective, or at least pretended to.

He was also very thoughtful, as demonstrated by the flowers and candy. She couldn't remember mentioning her favorite flower to him. Still, she knew it wasn't a coincidence that they were the bouquet's centerpiece. If only her husband were that thoughtful! Kevin always had a knack for doing and saying the right things at the right times. She couldn't understand how he was single or why his wife had left him the year before for another woman. When she would ask him if he had started dating again, he would answer that he wasn't interested in finding another ex-wife and didn't want to drive any more women to lesbianism. He still joked about it, despite the pain.

"Good morning, birthday girl!" a deep voice said from behind her. She was so caught up in the moment that she hadn't heard Kevin come out of his office.

"You didn't have to do all this," she said, turning to face her boss.

"OK then. You owe me forty-five dollars." He laughed as he playfully squeezed her shoulder. His touches were innocent, but she experienced a chill each time. She hated herself for it, but it was beyond her control. "So, am I the bestest boss ever?"

"Uh, let me think…I'd say top ten easy." She laughed. Kevin swung his hand in a pretend slap to her face. "No. You *are* number one. Thank you very much, Kevin." Their eyes met in a gaze that lasted a little too long.

Once again, Kevin knew when to speak and broke the awkward silence at the perfect moment. "I've noticed you've been a little down lately. I figured you could use a pick-me-up. If flowers and chocolate don't do it…."

"It's been a rough morning. I'm very impressed: tulips and kisses!"

"I just hope you have enough room left on your desk for the roses your husband will send shortly."

"Yeah, right! There'll be room in my seat because I'll be passed out on the floor!"

"Got to keep the faith. People can change and surprise you," he said with a smile and turned to walk back into his office.

Valerie watched him walk away. She knew he was good-looking, but lately, she'd been feeling an attraction to him. The physical attraction was only a small part, though. He was so sweet and caring, and she had no doubt that he could be very romantic if given the opportunity. He was everything Rex wasn't. She loved her husband very much but was getting to the point in her life where she needed more than just comfort and security. The children were out of the house, and it was time for her and her husband to find the spark again. Now they had time for the romance they didn't have time for when she became pregnant just out of high school.

She needed to have a long talk with Rex, and what better time for a life-changing conversation than her fortieth birthday? If they couldn't find the spark, or make one, it might be time for something drastic. *Life is too short to be miserable. If he's not the one…*She didn't want to fill in the blank.

***

"Rex, we need to talk." Valerie was sitting up in bed reading when her husband entered the room.

He took off his dirty work clothes and sat down on his side of the bed. "Oh, God. What now?"

"That's an excellent way to start off, *honey*," she replied with a glare.

He lay down on the bed and stared at the ceiling. "I'm sorry I didn't get you a present."

"It's not a present I want!"

51

"Then what do you want?"

She took a deep breath. She wanted them to have a civil discussion without it ending in one of them storming off to sleep on the couch. "Do you know what Kevin gave me for my birthday?"

"A pony?" Rex used humor to deal with conflict. Valerie had found it endearing twenty years earlier. Now, it was infuriating.

"He got me orange tulips, Hershey's Kisses, and mini-dark chocolate bars."

"Man, what a good boss! Mine didn't get me anything."

She gritted her teeth and paused before continuing. "Do you know what really made it a good gift?"

"It was free?"

"That is my favorite flower and favorite candy! I don't even remember mentioning it to him. He pays attention to what I say, remembers the things I like, and gets them for me when I'm not expecting anything. It's not the gift; it's the thought behind it. How much thought went into your stupid card?"

"Hey, someone at Hallmark had to think about it!"

She snapped. "Is this all just a big joke to you? Is our marriage a joke? Is me being miserable funny? Is me walking out the door and leaving your sorry butt going to be funny too?"

Rex turned to look at her red, angry face. She hardly ever yelled and had never said anything like that before. "You're going to leave me over a bad gift?"

"You need to listen to me! I don't care about a gift! I want you to love me and care enough about me to put some thought into things. I want you to be sweet, thoughtful, and romantic occasionally. I want to be surprised for once and not always disappointed. How about wine or roses or breakfast in bed? Maybe a trip somewhere…." The blood slowly drained from her face as the anger turned to frustration.

Rex was silent for a moment and then turned back to stare at the ceiling. "You never used to care about that stuff," he said quietly with no humor or sarcasm.

"Rex, we were eighteen when we had to get married. I had to worry about raising a child when I was still one myself. I didn't have time to think about romance. But now we're adults, and we're by ourselves. Now, I do have time to think about it. I need more than pecks on the cheek and funny cards."

They fell silent again for several minutes. "Valerie, I love you with all my heart. I know I don't always show it, but I do. I just don't know how to be romantic like that. My mind doesn't work that way. I don't know anything about wine and roses, and I can't cook anything but toast." He turned to look at her again.

Valerie wasn't sure, but his eyes appeared a little moist. She reached out and grabbed his hand. "It doesn't have to be wine or roses, and it'd be the best piece of toast I ever ate if you surprised me with it and a glass of orange juice when I woke up. If you love me, then you should want to make me happy. That means just paying attention to me and my likes and dislikes, thinking about ways to surprise me. You don't have to be something you're not."

"Do you listen to me and do things to make me happy?" Rex asked, suddenly defensive.

"What did I get you for your birthday?"

He thought for a moment. "Oh. My metric toolset."

"How did I know that's what you wanted when you never asked for it?"

"I guess I must have mentioned it at some point."

"And for Christmas?"

"Uh, a Remington 760."

"Did you ask for it? So how did I know what to get you when I know nothing about guns?"

Rex didn't respond.

"What about fixing your favorite meals on your special days? And don't forget about the other special things I do for you on special days and sometimes just out of the blue." She knew he knew what she was referring to. "If you liked wine and roses, I would get you that, but I listen to you and know what you want and what makes you happy. I just want the same from you."

Rex was rarely ever at a loss for words. He started to speak a time or two but stopped. His face revealed the struggle within.

"Rex, I love you too and want to spend the rest of my life with you, but I need more right now. I need you to show me you love me and not just say it back to me. I need you to spend less time in your workshop and hunting and more time doing things with me. I probably *have* changed. But this is still me, the person you married. If we can't change and evolve together, then we're going to have to look at the other option."

It was the only time Valerie had ever seen tears run down her husband's cheeks. She felt bad for him at that moment, but there was nothing else she could say. She couldn't take back the words because she had finally spoken the truth and exposed what had been weighing her down for a long time. She reached out and placed her arm around his head and gently pulled it over to rest on her chest. As his warm tears soaked into her nightgown, she cried softly too.

***

No radical changes took place over the remainder of the week. If anything, Rex spent more time in his workshop in the evenings. Valerie wanted to discuss things again but decided against it. She had clearly expressed her feelings. It was up to her husband to do something with the information.

Kevin didn't do anything to ease her troubled thoughts. He actually added fuel to the fire. She didn't know whether it was her imagination or he sensed her weakness, but he seemed more charming, good-looking, and sexier than ever. He made her laugh more than usual, he was sweeter than normal, and his cologne smelled better. He was more handsome; his body appeared tighter—and on and on. She knew it had to be just her frame of mind, but that thought did little to comfort her when she spent her evenings at home with her "missing" husband. Friday wrapped up the worst birthday week ever, and she found herself dreading the weekend. She'd rather be at work, where she at least received some attention and could laugh.

***

"What are we doing this weekend?" she asked when Rex finally came to bed.

"I'm going hunting in the morning. Then we're going together tomorrow afternoon," Rex said, seeming more cheerful than usual.

"We? When did I start caring about hunting?" *Why do his few surprises always have to irritate me so much?*

"Well, tomorrow, you're going. It'll be fun. I promise," Rex said, flashing a grin she hadn't seen in a long time.

She sighed. She was at a loss for words. *Hunting?* "What season is even open? It's just October."

"Deer season for bows."

"Do I have to shoot a bow?" *Bowhunting? Really?*

"Nope. You can just watch," Rex said as he turned off the light.

"So we'll just sit there in silence and wait for a deer to walk past close enough for you to shoot it?" She didn't try to hide her irritation. *From my wonderful birthday card at the beginning of the week to hunting at the end.*

"More or less."

"Why do you need to go twice in one day?"

54

"You'd be too grouchy at five in the morning, and it's pretty chilly. Tomorrow afternoon will be nice. Now, I need some sleep. I have to get up early." He kissed her on the lips and rolled over, facing away from her.

She angrily turned in the opposite direction.

***

Valerie completed her usual weekend chores Saturday morning and occasionally thought about having to go hunting that evening. She desperately hoped he would get a deer that morning and not want to go again. She'd rather just stay at home than do that. It was probably his way of trying to be sweet, but sitting in the woods in silence just didn't sound too exciting. At noon, she went to the grocery store and ran a couple of errands.

Rex's truck sat in the driveway when she arrived home. He opened the front door of the house just as she reached it.

"Did you kill a deer and cancel our trip?" she asked, walking in and setting the first two handfuls of bags down on the counter.

"Nope and nope," he said with a smile. Once again, he was in an unusually good mood. Then he walked out to the car and retrieved the next load of groceries, shocking Valerie a little. Helping out around the house was not his strong suit. "We need to leave by four," he said as he passed her on her way back to the car.

"Great."

***

Precisely at four, Rex told her it was time to go. He said everything was already packed, and she didn't need to bring anything. She felt stupid wearing one of his old, faded camouflage shirts and a pair of jeans. He wanted her to wear the complete camo outfit, but she finally convinced him that she would be really still so the deer wouldn't see her. One piece of camo was one too many for her. He wore his usual camo overalls.

They drove for nearly an hour on gravel and dirt roads before Rex finally parked on the side of one particularly narrow one. Although her mood was not the best, she couldn't ignore the beautiful fall day. The sky was a deep, clear blue, and the leaves on the trees were a brilliant display of yellow, orange, and red. The ride brought back long-buried memories of the hikes and picnics they had gone on twenty years earlier. She really loved the outdoors, but somehow children, housework, and a job had made it one of the last things on her mind. Maybe, just maybe, this wouldn't suck as much as she'd feared.

"OK. We've got a short hike to get to my spot," Rex said as he placed his large backpack on his back.

55

"Lead on, Rambo."

The air was warm but definitely had the crisp fall feel to it. The trail started off in thicker growth but eventually led into a mature patch of woods. A few squirrels chattered and played around them. Something larger crashed in the distance. "Probably a deer," Rex whispered to her. She breathed in deeply, appreciating the earthy forest air. Surprisingly, she was more relaxed than she had been in a while.

But her tension returned when they stopped at a giant oak tree at the far edge of the forest. Wooden boards nailed up its side led to a large wooden platform twenty or thirty feet above. "Oh no, we're not!" she exclaimed as Rex grinned at her.

"That's where we have to hunt from. Come on, honey. It'll be fun."

"Fun for you. I'll be in the truck."

"Please go up there with me. I'll come up behind you and make sure you don't slip. Just keep three points of contact, like climbing a ladder."

She glared at him for a moment and then finally surveyed the wooden steps and platform above. The stairs appeared solid and ended at a square hole in the bottom of the platform. That part worried her some, but she really didn't want to walk back to the truck alone. Her anger had also kicked in, overriding her fear or concern for the ascent. Wordlessly, she grabbed a board and started to climb.

"Wow! Nice view," Rex called up as he started after her.

"Shut up!"

After a few shaky minutes, she finally pulled herself onto the platform. The structure actually impressed her. A double railing ran all the way around it, and two stools sat in front of her. The floor was soft, and she quickly realized that it was a sleeping bag, unzipped and folded open. Rex pulled himself up behind her and placed a wooden cover over the hole in the floor.

She walked over to the railing and took in the view. The forest thinned out, and the land fell away in front of them. The hill led down to a beautiful blue lake. She realized it was probably a remote part of Claytor Lake, absent of any development. On the far side of the lake stood a forest; a chain of mountains rose beyond. The sun hovered a little bit above the peaks. She flinched slightly when she felt Rex's arm wrap around her waist.

"So, how do you like hunting?"

"This place is unbelievable." She continued surveying the scenery on all sides. "Do you actually hunt here?"

"Not with a bow. I rifle hunt here some. A buddy owns this property, and we built this stand many years ago. I just like coming here sometimes."

"So why are we here now?"

"Next to you, this is the most beautiful place on earth. I thought it was time to introduce you to each other. Beautiful wife, meet beautiful place." Rex laughed.

Valerie turned and looked at him with newfound respect. She placed both arms around him and hugged him tightly. "Thank you," she said and kissed him on the lips.

After a moment, he broke off the kiss. "Slow down, honey; there's more. Come over here and sit down."

She followed Rex, and they sat down at the back of the platform with their backs against the tree. He grabbed his pack and rifled through it, extracting several plastic bags and spreading them out between them. "I packed us a romantic supper to eat as we watch the sun set." He handed her one bag containing a sandwich and a bag of chips. "I believe chicken salad is your favorite, with sour-cream-and-onion chips, of course." She watched in amazement, her mouth open, as her husband prepared their meal.

He handed her a third bag. "Dessert. Since someone already gave you kisses, it's a piece of your favorite cake: German chocolate. And no, it's not homemade." He retrieved a couple of more handfuls of items with another reach into his pack. "I wasn't sure what kind of wine goes with sandwiches and chips, but I went with white. I think it's pretty good because it cost a lot more than the others." He handed her the bottle and two plastic cups, causing her grin to turn into a huge smile. "And a little lighting if we need it," he said, setting down a battery-powered fluorescent lantern. "I thought about candles, but something about being on a platform made of wood, in a tree made of wood, in the woods, made me a little hesitant…."

She quickly set the feast to the side and placed her hands behind his neck, pulling him close and kissing him like they hadn't kissed in recent memory. Suddenly, the feelings of love, and lust, came rushing back through her body. A surge of heat raced from her lips to her toes. She wasn't sure if she had ever felt like that kissing him. Suddenly, he was a great kisser, and their lips and tongues moved in perfect harmony. After a few moments, they finally paused for a gasp of air.

"Wow! I never knew you liked chicken salad *that* much."

"You're an idiot," she said, playfully for a change.

"Before we get too carried away, I do have a birthday gift for you."
He reached into his bag again, withdrawing a long gift-wrapped box, and
gingerly handed it to her.

She looked at him, shook her head, and slowly unwrapped the box.
She then carefully lifted the top off—and gasped. Tears instantly filled her
eyes. Inside lay an orange tulip, made entirely out of metal. The stems and
leaves were painted green and the flower beautiful shades of orange. The
leaves were made of some kind of paper-thin pieces of metal. The flower
part was thicker but intricately shaped and painted to resemble an actual
tulip. She couldn't speak for a moment. "Did you make this?" she finally
whispered.

"Believe it or not. I had planned on making a dozen, but it'd be, like,
May when I finished," he said, chuckling softly.

"It's so beautiful!" Tears flowed freely down her cheeks now.

"I never could see spending a bunch of money on flowers that only
last a few days. I wanted something that would last forever, or at least as
long as we last." Rex's face was serious for a moment as he gazed into her
eyes. "Are we going to last forever?"

She laid the flower carefully back in its box and placed her hands on
the sides of his face. "If you can just occasionally be the sweet, thoughtful,
and charming person you are today, we will last forever. See, you don't
have to do anything special or fancy. Just be you, and just be thoughtful."
She pulled him close and kissed him passionately.

They finally paused after a minute or so. "Do you have any special
requests for me, or do you want me to use my imagination?" Valerie asked
with a devilish grin.

"What do you think the sleeping bag is here for? As soon as the sun
sets, baby…."

Rex opened the wine and poured them each a cup. He reached into
his bag a final time and brought out a blanket. He covered them up, and
they sat sipping wine with their arms around each other as they watched
the sun set over the mountains. At that moment, Valerie was exactly
where she'd always wanted to be. All other thoughts melted away. She was
with the sweetest, funniest, sexiest, most romantic man in the world. And
she was enjoying the happiest birthday ever.

A Little Mystery

Carl's life sucked. He wasn't afraid to admit it, and he didn't try to spin it. It was his life. He sat down at the kitchen table with the bag of Chinese food and two bottles of beer. Takeout was a rare treat, but he occasionally needed a break from macaroni and cheese, Ramen noodles, canned soup, and frozen dinners. The beer, of course, was a staple either way.

He stared blankly at the fuzzy television sitting on the stack of milk crates. He couldn't afford cable, so he made do with the three channels he could somewhat see. He wasn't into television too much, though. He read a lot and occasionally rented movies, VHS of course, and watched them on the VCR a friend had given him a few years back. The rest of the time, he wrote.

His small laptop computer sat on the kitchen table. He'd purchased it used from the same friend who'd given him the VCR. It was old and ill-suited for much more than a word processor, and it had dial-up Internet access. It was all he needed; it beat the typewriter he'd used before. An old laser-jet printer also sat on the table, completing his home office.

Carl threw away the empty Chinese boxes and turned on the laptop. He had to put the final touches on his latest short story so he could mail it in for the contest tomorrow. He'd been writing and submitting for contests over the past few months. It was his only viable hope and dream for escaping his current existence. The contests paid over $1,000 to the winner and offered publication. The money would be great short term, but publication was the bigger prize. Getting published could open doors to developing stories into novels and getting those published too. It was a long shot, but his other options were limited at the time—and he had plenty of free time to write.

He'd been laid off from his white-collar, middle-management office job six months prior. Now he worked a very blue-collar factory job. His daily existence consisted of bolting pieces of metal together eight hours a day, five days a week. It was excruciatingly mind-numbing. He'd started writing shortly after losing his office job. He liked writing in high school and college and had some early success, but he left the writing behind as his career took off. Now, not only was it his dream, but it also kept his mind somewhat sharp—and staved off, or at least delayed, insanity.

He opened Word, clicked on his latest potential life-changer, "Just Friends," and started reading it, spot-checking for any remaining errors.

> They were only halfway through their run and nowhere near the car when the downpour hit. They were dripping wet by the time they sprinted into the semi-shelter of the trees. They stopped at a large oak, laughing and breathing hard. Sarah leaned back against the tree and shook her head, slinging water out of her long hair. Dustin faced her and stretched his right arm out, so his hand rested against the tree beside her head.

> They looked at each other, smiling as they caught their breath. Then she noticed something different in Dustin's gaze, a hunger in his eyes she'd never seen before. Instantly, she experienced a stirring deep inside. Dustin reached his left arm out, placing it on the tree on the other side of her head. He was squarely in front of her now. Suddenly, she felt an overpowering attraction to her best friend. She reached out, grabbed the front of his soaking-wet shirt, and pulled him toward her.

It was ironic that he found himself writing romance stories. He wasn't really sure how or why. Single, Carl had never been married and wasn't currently in a relationship. Conventional wisdom said to write what you knew, and he was doing the opposite. He had never really been in love. He dated occasionally and had been in a serious relationship or two, but he'd never felt that spark. He'd never experienced what he wrote about in his stories. He was very aware of what he wanted out of a relationship, though, and he had a perfect woman—at least the template of one—in his mind. He just had to find her. When he did, he could be the romantic leading man of his stories. Until then, he just had to keep writing.

> Sarah closed her eyes and hoped he knew what to do. After a brief moment, his wet lips touched hers. They were cold from the rain, but only for a second. As their lips moved together, they quickly heated up. He pressed his body against hers, pinning her against the tree. She felt the heat of his body through their wet clothes.
>
> The kiss was incredible and the scene surreal. The rain still poured and splashed around them, but they were oblivious inside their warm cocoon of passion. Despite the cool rain, their bodies were hot now, and their lips slid effortlessly across each other. Sarah grabbed the back of his head and tried to pull him even closer. He moved his hands behind her and caressed her lower back. Slowly, his hands moved lower as his lips left hers to assault her wet neck.

***

Carl walked up to the post office counter when it was finally his turn. He was surprised and pleased to see that the attractive blond lady would be the one to wait on him. He'd seen her working there often but always ended up in the wrong line. It was never a bad thing to have an encounter with an attractive woman, however brief.

"May I help you?" she asked in a sweet, friendly voice, with a warm smile. Her name badge read "Nora."

It was funny, and maybe a little sad, that his heart raced with merely a smile from a good-looking woman. "I just need to mail this, first-class, please."

She took the large envelope and placed it on the scale. "So, Carl Rogers, a writer, huh?"

"Huh? Oh. How did you know?" He realized he was an idiot as soon as the words left his mouth.

"Might be the address label," she said with a playful laugh.

"Yeah. I guess that might be a clue. I'm sorry. It's been a long day."

"What type of story is it?" She printed the postage label and affixed it to the envelope.

He hoped his cheeks weren't turning red. "Uh, a romance."

"Really? A manly guy writing romances? Wow. That's really cool! I love reading romance novels. What's it—"

A man cleared his throat from behind the "Wait Here Until Called" sign. Nora rolled her eyes so only Carl could see. He smiled. "That will be a dollar eighty-one."

He quickly handed her two dollars and received his change and receipt.

"Good luck, Carl Rogers."

"Thanks, uh, Nora…."

"Jenkins. Nora Jenkins."

***

Carl sat down at the kitchen table again that evening with an opened can of pork and beans and a beer. The TV was on and turned to the somewhat clear nightly news. He couldn't believe how far he had fallen from the downtown condo he'd owned just months before. He'd actually had cable and furniture and could afford to go out to eat and drink after work. He'd sold it, at a substantial loss, soon after losing his job and traded his Lexus for a considerably older Corolla. He sighed and turned up the beer. Oh well. It could be worse, he guessed.

His thoughts turned to Nora as he choked down his cold meal. "Nora Jenkins," her sweet voice had said. He replayed their brief encounter in his mind. Despite his stupid question, he thought it had gone well. *She's attractive, seems to have a good personality, and likes romances! Is she married? I didn't even think to look at her finger! How can I talk to her again?* He didn't have another contest until the next month, which was the only reason he had to go to the post office. He couldn't just go in to talk to her. He wasn't, and never had been, that kind of confident guy—which probably explained why he was eating pork and beans alone in his dump of a studio apartment.

He turned on his laptop and opened his folder of short stories. Suddenly, he had an idea. The submission deadline for the contest he'd just entered wasn't until tomorrow. He could enter another story and possibly get to see Nora again! There was no rule against multiple submissions. It would just cost him another twenty dollars. He smiled as he printed off "Perfect Strangers," one of his favorite stories. He quickly assembled the packet and prepared it for mailing.

***

The next day, work could not pass fast enough. Several times, he swore the hands on his watch had stopped. Finally, mercifully, the buzzer rang, and he quickly clocked out and headed across town to the post office. He grabbed the envelope and nearly ran inside. One person stood ahead of him, waiting for the next clerk. He took his place in line and surveyed the scene. Two clerks were working, each helping someone. A man stood behind the counter in front of him. In the other line was Nora. She smiled as she talked to the elderly lady in front of her. Carl's heart skipped a beat or two just watching her. Her shoulder-length blond hair appeared to radiate light, and her green eyes glowed. Even a drab postal uniform couldn't hide her shapely figure.

Carl's heart sank a little when the lady Nora was helping finished first. Nora called "Next" with her sweet voice, and the man in front of him strode to the counter. Carl glanced over his shoulder and was relieved to see a man walk through the door and toward him to get in line.

As the man arrived, the other clerk called, "Next."

"Uh, you can go ahead. I need to double-check something," Carl said quickly, stepping aside to let the man go to the counter. He opened his envelope and leafed through the papers.

In a moment, the sweet voice again called, "Next." Carl looked up to meet those beautiful green eyes and that deadly smile. He smiled too as he took the short walk.

"Hello, Nora," Carl said, smiling and trying not to sound too nervous. He handed her the envelope as he spoke. "I need to mail this, please."

"Hello again, Carl," she replied as she placed the envelope on the scale.

"Did you really remember my name, or did you cheat and read the envelope?"

"Don't know, do you?" She looked up and smiled and then printed off the postage label. "Another entry for the same contest?"

"Yeah. I figure it couldn't hurt. And it's a while before the next one."

"Another love story?"

"Uh, yeah." Carl was always a little uncomfortable admitting to writing romances.

"A dollar fifty-one. Great! What's this one about?"

Carl glanced over his shoulder and was relieved to see no one in line. "It's called 'Perfect Strangers.' It's about two strangers meeting on the subway. They slowly become friends during the morning commute. Over time, while complaining about their personal lives and situations, they slowly start falling in love—only they don't realize it until the end."

"Hmmm…Not bad. But is there any mystery, or surprises, or twists and turns? Or do they just meet and fall in love?"

"Uh, no, not really, I guess. Most of the contest stories have to be fairly short. There's not a lot of time for twists and turns."

"But you have to have a little mystery to make a good love story! Try to throw something in there so the characters, and readers, don't know exactly what's going to happen."

Carl was silent for a moment. *Beautiful and intelligent too!* "I will definitely think about it. I'll have to start a new story and see what I can do."

"And can I read it?" She smiled and winked.

The question took Carl totally off guard. "Uh, yeah…I guess. If you really want to."

"Sweet! Now, I'm afraid I have to 'next' you."

Carl just remembered to glance down at her left hand before leaving: no wedding ring. "Thank you, Miss Jenkins."

"Thank you, Mr. Rogers. Despite your lack of mystery, I hope you win your contest," she said with an impish grin and a wink. "Now get to work on the next one!"

***

Carl couldn't even remember walking out of the post office, getting in his car, or driving home. That night, after finishing his macaroni and cheese, he turned on his laptop. He was anxious to start a story Nora could read. However, he was out of romance ideas. After writing half a dozen stories over the past two months, his well was dry.

He logged into his online writing group to see if he had any emails. He'd just joined the site a couple of weeks prior. It allowed him to create his own home page with his picture and bio, upload his stories for others to read and critique, and read and critique other people's material. He hadn't used the site much other than to upload his stories, and he used that email address on his cover page for writing competitions. He hoped that an interested editor or judge might view his site and read all his material.

He was surprised to see an actual message in his inbox from someone with the user name Romance Lover. He excitedly clicked on it. "Hi. Really liked your stories but have some suggestions. If you're interested, email me back."

Carl raised his eyebrows and grinned. He clicked on Romance Lover's name and pulled up the profile. The attached picture was of a red pen. A short bio explained that Romance Lover was a thirty-year-old single female who enjoyed reading good romance stories. She wasn't a writer but liked to read and would help critique and edit if allowed.

Cool. He was always open to advice, especially from single females. He started to reply to her email when he noticed she was online. He chose "chat" instead.

"Hi, Romance Lover. Thanks for your email." He waited patiently for a response.

"Hello, Carl. Thank you for IM'ing. You're a very good writer, although you do have a little work to do."

"Well, I'm open to suggestions. But do you have a name? Romance Lover is a little long."

"Don't you like a little intrigue? Just call me RL for short."

"OK, RL. Which story do you want to start with?"

"Let's do 'Perfect Strangers.' Open the file, and we'll go through it."

Carl smiled. This was a strange situation, but it definitely beat his usual evenings. He clicked on the link to his story and assumed she did the same. He moved the chat window to the side, so he could view the story and instant message simultaneously. "OK," he typed. "Lead on."

It was a little time-consuming, but they went through his storyline by line as she pointed out grammatical errors and made suggestions on how to rephrase certain parts. He tended to use a few extra words in his writing and was fond of using commas and dashes. She apparently liked fewer words and simpler sentences. Her editing skills impressed him. Despite his having reread the story at least a dozen times, she spotted several obvious errors. Finally, over an hour later, they made it to the end of the story.

"Is that it?" he typed.

"For the technical part."

"Uh-oh. What's left?"

"I think you need to add something to the story."

"Really? What's that?" Maybe this wasn't going to be as fun as he thought.

"You need some kind of surprise or twist to it. I knew where it was leading the entire time."

Carl chuckled out loud. "A little mystery?"

"Yeah, that's it!"

"It's funny you say that. I received the same suggestion from a woman who hasn't even read the story just earlier today."

"A woman? You didn't mention a girlfriend in your bio."

"Oh, she's not a girlfriend. I just met her this week."

"Hmmm…So, do you like this woman?"

Carl hesitated before responding. He wasn't sure how much to say about Nora when he had just met this online person he was hitting it off with, even though it was only over the computer. Of course, he had no idea what this woman looked like, if it was indeed a woman, and where in the country or world she lived. He decided to be honest and let the chips fall where they may. "Yeah. I really like her. It's actually funny that I met her at the post office, mailing 'Just Friends.'"

"So she works at the post office?"

"Yeah. She's the clerk who waited on me, and we just struck up a conversation. She asked what kind of story I had written and commented that she loved romances."

"Just like me, huh?"

"Yeah, I guess so. Two in one week!"

"So, continue. Tell me about this post-office woman."

"Well, her name is Nora, and she is very attractive, with blond hair and green eyes."

"What is it with men and blond hair?"

Carl smiled and continued, "She's outgoing and funny, and, I don't know. We just really hit it off."

"Ask her out."

"I can't do that! I hardly know her."

"What better way to get to know her? She's not married, is she?"

"No. At least there's no ring. But she could have a boyfriend. I can't imagine a woman like her being single."

"Why not? Are only unattractive people single?"

"Well, no. But…I don't know. I just figure someone like that has a boyfriend." It was amazing how quickly she'd put him on the defensive.

"You're single."

"I don't consider myself attractive."

"I've seen your picture—you're rather handsome."

"Thank you! But I guess I'm a little shy too." He could feel his cheeks turning red, despite being alone.

"Maybe she's shy."

"I don't think so. She seemed very outgoing and bubbly."

"It sounds like you did your share of talking too."

Carl paused for a moment. "Oh, yeah. Good point."

"Ask her out. What happens if she says no?"

"I don't know. Embarrassment and disappointment for me, I guess."

"There's nothing wrong with getting turned down, and it's no reflection on you. There are many reasons people do or don't find other people attractive or their type. But doing nothing is the worse crime. Without risk, there is no reward."

Carl went to the refrigerator and retrieved another beer. He shook his head. It was strange taking advice from a computer monitor. It seemed somehow very impersonal but also like having a close friend to talk to, only without the talking part. "I'll think about it. Now, tell me about you. It's not fair that you've seen my picture, but I haven't seen yours."

"Whose fault is that? You shouldn't have posted yours if you didn't want people to see it."

"No. You should have posted yours if you're going to be chatting with people!"

"Maybe…but like I said, nothing wrong with a little mystery."

"You're not a dude, are you?" he typed, not entirely joking.

"LOL! No. I assure you, I'm all woman."

"OK. I guess we'll go with the mystery then. But you know, that might be someone else's picture instead of mine."

"Surely you would have chosen better than that!"

"That wasn't very nice!" Carl responded, smiling at her quick wit.

"LOL! OK. Now, back to your story. Why don't you rewrite and add a little mystery to it? Then I can critique."

"I'll work on it."

"That's your homework assignment. Email me when you've finished and reposted, and I'll critique. Good night."

Carl wasn't sure what had just taken place for the past two hours, but he liked it. Only now, he had to rewrite his story. He had to maintain a reason to talk to RL. He closed his browser, opened the story file, and sipped on his beer as he rubbed his head and stared at the computer screen. Finally, an idea came to him. He jotted down a few notes on the pad of paper he kept by his computer and then began typing feverishly. He finished at midnight, saved it, and uploaded it to his webpage. Then he sent RL an email asking her to read the story and saying that he would be online the following evening to discuss it.

***

Once again, he slogged through another slow day at work. His mind was torn between two sets of thoughts. One was about Nora. He thought about what RL had said. Should he just go in and ask her out? He might be able to ask her out for some coffee and to discuss his stories. If she said yes, a whole new chapter might open in his life. If she said no, then that fantasy was over. Then there was the true fantasy woman, whom he knew nothing about but had spent two hours typing back and forth with. He couldn't wait to see what she thought about his revisions and to learn more about her. He was confused, and slightly overwhelmed, but guessed it wasn't too bad of a situation to be in. Maybe he was a player now. He laughed out loud at that.

Back home, he quickly devoured two chicken potpies, downed a beer, and turned on his computer. In a minute, he was on his writer's group webpage and saw a new e-mail from RL. He smiled as he opened it.

"I'm impressed! Not a bad revision, especially in that length of time. I think we can work with that. IM me when you're ready."

He grinned. In his revision, he'd backed off a little on the two characters falling for each other and played up the friendship part. Then he had the leading lady talk the leading man into going out on a blind date with one of her friends. He finally agreed. When he arrived at the restaurant, he discovered it was really her. It ended with them admitting their feelings for each other. He quickly sent an instant message to Romance Lover.

"OK. Let's get to work."

"Good evening, Carl. Good job again on your story! Do you see what Nora and I were talking about?"

He was impressed she remembered Nora's name. "Yeah, I guess it was better. Any typos?"

They went through the story again, and she made fewer corrections this time. After they finished, they "chatted" about Carl's personal life. He was a little nervous to answer all her questions, but for some reason, he felt at ease with her, whoever "her" was. He pretty much gave an overview of his entire life and current situation. He thought about trying to make it sound a little more interesting, and a little less pathetic, but surprisingly he kept going with honesty. Then they came to his interest in writing romance stories, his thoughts on love and relationships, and what he personally wanted out of a relationship.

"What's your definition of love?"

Carl hesitated for a moment. That was a deep question. "Well, my definition has nothing to do with feelings or emotions."

"Hmmm…Do go on."

68

"I think love means doing anything you can to make the other person happy, satisfying their every need in every way, whatever those needs are, and the other person doing the same for you. If two people can do that, and it's from the heart, everything else will take care of itself."

It was a moment before RL responded. "I've never thought about it that way. Not bad. But what about physical attraction?"

"Well, you have to have some form of physical attraction. My answer assumed you had already met a person you were attracted to. But if you don't want to be with that person all the time, miss them when they're away, and want to make and keep them happy, then you don't have love."

"Interesting…"

After answering all her questions, Carl turned the tables and questioned her. She remained a little mysterious, but he managed to glean some information. They shared similar views on love and romance. She wanted a man who could appreciate her for her, who would be her best friend, and to whom she would never tire of talking. She wanted to laugh and have fun, enjoy life, be spontaneous, and avoid the drama that seemed to dog her previous relationships. They also seemed to be in a similar place in life: single, lonely, and close to broke.

"OK. Now that we know each other, let's talk about your current love life."

"You mean lack of?" Carl typed, the nervousness returning somewhat.

"We're going to fix that."

"We are? How are we going to do that?"

"I bet Nora would like to hear that you updated your story."

"Hey, I could go by the post office and tell her!" Carl's heart sped up at the prospect of another trip to the post office.

"No, idiot! You go into the post office and ask her to join you for coffee at some quaint café after she gets off work. Tell her she can read your story there and let you know if she likes it."

Carl paused and stroked his chin. "Maybe…."

"Carl, for once in your life, make a move. How many girls have you missed out on? If she says no, what do you lose? If she's not interested now, she probably won't be in the future. I mean, how well are you going to get to know someone only seeing them for five minutes once or twice a month?"

"You know, I might just try that."

"Tomorrow is Friday. Go to the post office and ask her to meet you for coffee. Email me when you get back, or if she shoots you down, and let me know what happened. Now, go to bed. Good night."

"Good night," he typed back.

He barely slept that night.

***

Once again, he sped across town to the post office after work. He got in line and was relieved to see Nora working again. He carried an envelope, although he wasn't actually going to mail it. He had to let two people go in front of him this time before being assured a spot in Nora's line. Finally, he heard her sweet voice call "Next."

He was afraid she could see his heart beating through his T-shirt as he made the long walk toward her. He tried to smile but was so nervous he doubted it looked like a smile. She, however, wielded the same beaming, warm smile as before. He finally arrived at the counter.

"Hello again, Carl." This time, she definitely hadn't cheated by looking at the envelope. "Another contest?" she asked, holding her hand out for the envelope.

"Uh...no. I mean...not really," he stammered.

"OK. What are we mailing today?"

"Well, actually...actually, I'm not mailing anything."

"Oh, silly me. I thought you being at the post office with an envelope in your hand might mean you were mailing something." She laughed at his puzzled expression.

"Oh, yeah...that. Uh...no. I just wanted to talk to you for a minute." These two minutes lasted an eternity. He flashed back to high school and trying to ask Erica Chambers to the prom. The memory of her shooting him down remained quite vivid in his mind.

"OK. What would you like to talk about?" Nora asked, still smiling.

"Well, I rewrote 'Perfect Strangers,' with a surprise ending."

"Really? Cool! What did you change?"

"Uh, well, I was thinking that maybe you would like to read it." This wasn't getting any easier.

"Great! Is it in the envelope?" She seemed genuinely excited.

"Well, no. I don't have it with me. But I wondered if you might want to meet me at Coffee Hut after you get off work. We could have some coffee, you could read the story, and we could discuss it." There. He'd said it. It wasn't pretty, but it was out. All he needed now was "No," or laughter, and he'd be on his way.

70

"Hmmm…I don't guess I have plans tonight. We could do that. You're not a psycho killer, are you?"

"Um, no. A little strange maybe but not a killer."

"Would seven be OK?"

Carl couldn't believe she hadn't rejected him. "That would be great!" he said, louder than he'd intended.

Nora laughed. "See you there. Oh, and don't forget your story. I don't think the empty envelope will help us too much."

***

Not wanting to take a chance on being late, Carl arrived at the café at six-thirty. He still couldn't believe what was transpiring. He drank two cups of coffee as he waited, which didn't help his excitement problem. At 6:55, Nora came through the door. She wore a black T-shirt tucked into a pair of tight blue jeans and black boots. She had looked good in the postal uniform, but now she was just breathtaking. She smiled and headed over to his table. She was so out of his league!

"Hello, Carl. Do you have the story?"

"Of course! Would you like me to get you something while you read?"

"That would be very sweet of you. A large mocha cappuccino will be fine."

Carl handed her the story and scampered to the counter to order. He returned soon and sat quietly as she read. He couldn't help but stare at her beautiful face as he inhaled her sweet perfume and watched her read. Her facial expressions indicated she was really into the story. She'd smile in spots and raise her eyebrows in others. Occasionally, she would nod as if in approval. Twenty minutes later, she handed the story back to him. "Very good. I love it! That was a much better ending than what you had before…at least what you told me it was."

"Thank you very much. I'm glad you liked it."

"Just remember, you always need some surprise, twists, and a little mystery for a good romance."

When she said "mystery," he thought briefly about RL. Then his thoughts quickly returned to what was real, what was in front of him. They sipped coffee, talked, and laughed for three hours in the little café. She was everything he'd hoped she would be and more. Her looks didn't even compare to her intelligence, sense of humor, and energy. They couldn't talk fast enough to learn all he needed to learn, and the time passed by too quickly. It was like they had been friends forever. He was totally at ease with her now, not nervous like he was earlier. Unlike with friends, however, he definitely sensed a physical attraction between them. The way she stared at him, the way she smiled—there was definitely a playful flirtation. He tried to do the same but wasn't sure how it appeared on her end.

"Well, it's ten. I guess I'd better head home," Nora finally said.

Carl was sad that it was over. "So, can we get together again?" he asked, with just a little apprehension.

"Of course! I'd love to see you again." She produced a pen from her purse, grabbed his hand, and wrote a phone number on his palm. "Don't forget and accidentally wash it off."

"Oh, I'll never wash this hand again," he said, smiling.

"OK. That's a little gross." She laughed. "Good night, Carl." They both stood up from the table, and she extended her hand. In a way, he was disappointed with only a handshake, but on the other hand, it took away the ambiguity. They exchanged goodnights, and he headed back home.

***

As he entered his apartment, Carl couldn't remember ever being happier. Needing something to counteract the four cups of coffee he had just drunk, he danced over to the refrigerator and removed two beers. He sat down at the table and quickly wrote Nora's phone number on the pad. Then he turned on his computer as he took a large swig of beer. Suddenly, he remembered RL. He'd almost forgotten that he was supposed to instant message her.

He logged onto his webpage and saw an email from Romance Lover. He quickly opened it and read it out loud. "I'm sorry that I won't be able to chat tonight. Something came up. But if you get a chance, check out my profile. I lifted a little of the mystery." He quickly clicked on her name and waited a moment for the link to load. He stared at the picture in stunned silence. Somehow, RL had placed Nora's picture on her profile page. He was studying the screen, trying to figure out what it meant, when the phone rang.

He slowly stood from the table and walked over to the phone. "Hello?"

"Hello, Carl," a familiar female voice said.

"Nora?"

"Yes, and also RL. We're both here." She laughed.

"Huh?"

"Carl, I'm both."

"OK. One more time: huh?"

"I have a couple of confessions to make, and I hope you won't get mad."

Carl couldn't wrap his mind around anything at this point. "Please share."

"Well, first, I read both of the stories you mailed, which I'm pretty sure is a felony. Second, I wrote down your webpage address and phone number from the cover sheet. Then I checked out the website and created my 'Romance Lover' profile."

Several seconds passed before Carl could speak. "Why?" he managed to utter.

"I read your first story out of curiosity. I really liked it, so I read the second one. I liked it too, and I also liked you. I figured I could get to know you better anonymously and add a little mystery to your life—a twist and a turn. You know what RL and I say about romance. So, are you going to forgive me?"

"Wow! This has been some week. So the bottom line is, you like me, and RL likes me?"

"Yep. We both like you a lot."

"Well, I guess that's good enough for me. You're forgiven. You also might be dating me for a while."

"And just why is that?" she asked with a laugh.

"Due to your criminal behavior, you can either serve time with me or in the pokey."

Only Dead on the Inside

'Don't mourn for me too long, my love. Cry your tears, treasure the memories we made, and let me go. I promise I'm in a better place now. I'm free. Free of all the pain and burden we've carried for the past two years. You're free too, Glenn. You sacrificed so much to take care of me. You gave me more than any husband could provide. You always exceeded my wildest dreams.

'Glenn, I give you my permission to continue living. I'll be waiting for you when you're done. You're still young and have so much life to live. Let someone else experience what I was so blessed to enjoy. Give someone else the gift of your humor, your heart, and your love. Thank you for our life together. Although mine ended much too soon, I still enjoyed more than I deserved. I love you more than you'll ever know, enough to set you free.

'Until we meet again, Love Cathy.'

***

"So, G-Dog, what did you get into this weekend?"

Glenn didn't look up from his bag of Ruffles. "Pete, do you really need to call me 'G-Dog'? I mean, I'm a hundred years old."

"Nah, man. We're going to help you find your groove again. You'll be the hippest dude in the plant. Heck, maybe in the whole town," Pete grinned.

"Yeah, you'll be entertaining us with all your X-rated stories every Monday. Now, do you have any crazy ones from this weekend?" Billy asked.

"You guys are hilarious. I watched a Clint Eastwood marathon on Saturday, and I went grocery shopping and did laundry on Sunday. Does that get your motors' running?"

Pete shook his head. "That's the saddest weekend I've ever heard."

"Let me guess about your exciting weekend, Pete. You went fishing. And, Billy, let me take a stab at yours. You went antiquing with your wife," Glenn said.

"It's different with us. We're married. You're free and single, my man," Billy said. "We need to live vicariously through you."

"Vicariously? Wow, I'm impressed! Someone did some reading over the weekend. Well, I guess you vicariously did laundry yesterday. Was it as good for you as it was for me?" Glenn realized his friends' eyes had drifted up and over his left shoulder, and he turned to seek the source of their distraction.

"Hello, gentlemen. Care if I join you?" a tall blond woman asked from behind Glenn.

"If you have an ounce of sense, you will rethink that request," Glenn said.

The blond laughed and sat down beside him. "I'm Amy, Amy Vanderwahl. I just started in the Marketing department."

Pete and Billy quickly introduced themselves and shook hands with the newcomer. Before Glenn could speak, Pete introduced him. "And this is the man, the myth, the legend—G-Dog." Pete and Billy both guffawed.

"Wow! I'm surprised I haven't heard of you yet, G-Dog," Amy laughed.

"I warned you to walk away," Glenn said. He then abruptly stood. "Well, it was nice to meet you, Amy. Hopefully, you will make better lunch decisions in the future. See you later, Dumb and Dumber."

76

Glenn was a little late arriving at the lunchroom the next day. He immediately froze when he entered, carrying a brown paper bag and a can of soda. Pete and Billy were there, looking as goofy as ever. But a blonde female sat with her back to him, talking and laughing with them. He started to turn to escape, but he was too slow.

"Glenn!" Pete said. "You're late! Get over here."

Glenn walked over to the table; Pete and Billy grinned like mules eating briars. Amy turned and smiled warmly at him as he sat down beside her.

"What up, G-Dog?" Amy said. Billy and Pete laughed.

Glenn reached inside his paper bag and withdrew a peanut butter and jelly sandwich and popped the top on the can. "Amy, please don't encourage the goon squad. Glenn is fine."

"Dang, someone's panties are in a wad," Billy said.

Glenn chewed the first bite of his sandwich, trying hard not to grind his teeth. Although Billy and Pete were usually fairly entertaining, they could become super annoying quickly, especially if they knew they were getting under your skin. Glenn did look forward to eating lunch with them, though. It was a refreshing break from staring at spreadsheets all day. Now, this new person had intruded into this safe space. He had hoped yesterday was a one-off. They were fine with just being three stupid guys hanging out. They didn't need a fourth, much less a female. "They're thongs, thank you very much," he finally said.

Amy snorted and covered her mouth to keep milk from spraying out. It took several seconds of sputtering and coughing before she could speak. "You guys are a hoot!"

"Amy, I have to apologize for these two cretins," Pete said. "They should not be speaking of women's undergarments in the presence of a sophisticated lady such as yourself."

"Oh, don't sweat it. It's not like I wear them."

Glenn almost choked on his sandwich. He would have laughed at Pete and Billy's reddening faces if he were sure his face wasn't doing the same.

Amy laughed. "I grew up with four brothers. You're not going to offend me. If anything, I might offend you."

"So, Amy, what brought you to our awesome company? Are you from around here?" Glenn asked. He didn't want Billy and Pete to get too carried away with the new girl.

"I just moved here from a small town in Virginia. My divorce was final last month, and I needed a change—too much gossip in a small town. My sister and her husband have lived here for ten years and helped talk me into moving."

"Youngins?" Pete asked.

"No youngins. Thankfully, I didn't reproduce with my troglodyte ex," Amy said.

Glenn was afraid Amy would ask him if he were married, so he quickly changed the subject and asked about her job. The four proceeded to talk about work for the next ten minutes or so until their lunch break was over.

***

On Wednesday, Glenn had to run errands, so he missed the group lunch. He was relieved to enter the lunchroom on Thursday and see just Pete and Billy sitting there. He assumed his usual spot.

"Dude! You need to sit down for this," Pete said.

"Um, feels like I *am* sitting down."

Pete laughed. "You're never going to guess what happened yesterday!"

"You're right. So just tell me."

"Dog, Amy asked about you."

"You mean why I wasn't at lunch?" Glenn said. He took a large bite out of his bologna sandwich.

"No! I mean she wanted to know your situation," Pete said.

"Like she thinks your enormous, bulbous head is attractive," Billy added.

"Sure. Whatever."

"No. Seriously! I think she was like asking asking about you," Pete said.

"We told her that you were single and more than ready to mingle," Billy said.

"I will kill you both slowly!" Glenn felt nauseous for a moment. "Well, it doesn't matter what you told her. My situation is not interested." He finished his sandwich and downed his soft drink.

"Man, she is absolutely hot as crap!" Pete said.

"First of all, 'hot as crap' is possibly the worst description of a woman ever. Second, no thanks."

"Come on, man," Billy said. "You can't tell us you don't think she's attractive."

Glenn stood from the table. "I might have found her attractive when I was still alive." He turned and left the room.

***

Glenn had a dentist appointment during lunch on Friday and decided to take the rest of the afternoon off. He didn't have anything to do—he never had anything to do—but he just didn't feel like working. His world consisted of manipulating numbers in spreadsheets. It paid the bills, but most likely at the cost of healthy brain tissue.

It was a beautiful day, so he headed to the park after his appointment and walked several miles of trails. He had only resumed visiting the park earlier in the year. He and Cathy had walked there most pretty evenings. Now, he was finally getting to the point of being able to walk the trails without tears in his eyes.

He picked up Chinese food after his walk and headed home to watch a *Seinfeld* marathon—a pretty solid Friday afternoon and evening.

Saturday consisted of yard work followed by cleaning up to meet Pete and Billy for bowling. He didn't know why he had agreed to hang out with his work friends outside work. He guessed that just confirmed how pathetic his life had become. Hopefully, beer would make them easier to tolerate. And bowling wasn't something he had done with his wife, so at least there would be no sad memories entangled with the evening.

***

He paid for his shoes and turned to scan the alley for his friends. Dumb and Dumber were typically easy to spot, or more aptly, to hear. But he didn't see either. He did notice a tall blond smiling and waving in his direction. He looked over his shoulder to see whom she might be waving to, but no one was behind him. Suddenly, his blood ran cold. He slowly turned around to see her still smiling and waving at him. What the heck? It was Amy!

He ambled toward her with the same enthusiasm as a pirate walking to the gallows. He climbed down the stairs and was shocked when she greeted him with a hug. What the crap?

"Where's Pete and Billy?" Amy asked as she pulled away.

Glenn was too stunned to speak for several seconds. That was the first hug he had experienced since the well-wishers at his wife's funeral. It was most likely innocent, and Amy was probably just one of those annoying huggers, but Glenn felt strange. He tried to refocus his attention to the current predicament and not admit to himself how good her perfume smelled and how her warm body felt pressed against his. He sat on the bench and started changing into his bowling shoes. "I have a sinking suspicion they're not showing. When did they invite you?"

Amy sat beside him, changing from her high heels to her bowling shoes. "Yesterday at lunch. They said you had mentioned me joining you three on your bowling night."

"Son of a—"

Amy's smile fled from her face. "I take it that's not the case. I can leave." She started untying the bowling shoes.

"No," Glenn said, briefly placing his hand on her leg. "No. I mean I didn't say it, and we don't have a *bowling night*, but you don't have to leave."

"Why would they do this?"

"I warned you that first day to just walk away. They're idiots. And idiots do idiotic things."

"So, this is like a prank?" she asked.

"Probably not exactly. Billy and Pete are idiots, but they most likely had good intentions," Glenn said.

"Good intentions?"

"They're always busting my chops about being a hermit since my wife passed and trying to get me to date again. So, I imagine they've basically made this a blind date."

Amy shook her head. "This is embarrassing, but I might have unknowingly contributed to their idiocy."

"What do you mean?"

"I might have asked about you the other day. Like if you were married or dating anyone."

Glenn looked up at her. He could swear her cheeks were turning red. "Oh, those two clowns don't need any encouragement. They can screw things up perfectly well on their own."

Amy smiled again. "So, what do we do now?"

"Well, I suppose we can bowl. But you might be better off just leaving now."

"Why do you say that?" Amy said.

"First, I suck at bowling. Second, I'm about as much fun as a wet paper bag in a rainstorm," Glenn said.

Amy laughed. "Well, a sucky wet paper bag is probably still a little more fun than my typical Friday night. I say let's drink a couple of beers and throw some balls."

Amy went to buy them two beers while Glenn searched for a ball that fit his fingers. He quickly realized his heart was racing, and his hands were sweating. Although this wasn't a date, or a planned one at least, it did feel like a blind date. He didn't want to date! He knew what Cathy wrote in her letter, but he still wasn't ready to even think about moving on from her. Somehow the thought of even dating, much less a meaningful relationship, would feel like cheating on his wife. He was OK with his hermit existence. He didn't feel like he was missing anything, and he had plenty of good memories to replay in his head.

He should have just left then. But that would be rude. None of this was Amy's fault. She was new in town and was probably excited for a night out. She most likely wasn't thinking of this as a date either. It was just supposed to be a night out with new friends. He'd bowl one game with her, fake an injury or just say he was exhausted, and cut out. No harm would be done.

He returned to the lane with a ball just as Amy arrived back. She handed him a beer and sat down in the chair to program their names into the computer. Glenn couldn't help but laugh when he looked up at the scoreboard. 'A-Wow' and 'G-Dog' were Bowler 1 and Bowler 2.

"Maybe you're the third stooge the boys have been searching for, A-Wow," he said.

Amy scowled at him as she stood and walked over to the ball return. She grabbed the ball she must have selected before he had arrived. "Sit down and watch, grumpy old man."

Glenn did sit down, and he did watch. He hadn't paid much attention to her in the lunchroom, other than noticing her blond hair and pleasant smile. Now, it was hard not to notice the rest of her. Her faded jeans clung desperately to her long legs, and the tucked-in black T-shirt hid none of her curves. She was toned and either exercised regularly and ate healthily or was one of those rare freaks of nature that didn't have to eat grass and work out all the time to stay in shape.

He quickly tried to refocus on her bowling technique. She made a perfect approach to the lane, brought the ball way behind her back, and swung her arm with surprising speed. She kicked her right leg perfectly behind her left and released the sparkly, pink ball. It spun halfway down the lane, angling toward the right gutter, then gradually started to curve back toward the pins. The pins scattered with a crash and soon all toppled. Glenn couldn't stop his mouth from falling open.

"Oh yeah, I used to be in a league in college," Amy said as she walked back and sat down in the chair. She took a swig of her beer and turned to face him. "You're up, buttercup."

"But that was like what, thirty years ago?" Glenn leaped to the side to barely avoid a kick. He grinned and grabbed his plain, scarred black ball from the return. He hadn't bowled but a few times in the past ten years. He was decent in college, but he hadn't been enough since to become respectable again. And of course, now he was bowling against a ringer.

He lumbered toward the edge of the lane. Then his right foot slipped on the oily floor just as he tried to swing it behind his left. This caused his entire body to rotate to the left, and he almost fell to the floor. He couldn't stop his arm motion, and the ball flew from his hand after sticking momentarily on his thumb. It struck the lane with a loud thud and proceeded swiftly into the left gutter. Amy cackled loudly behind him.

Then came the walk of shame. Glenn slowly turned and reluctantly looked up. Amy was red-faced from laughter, stomping her feet and slapping the computer desk. "Gee, well, see you Monday at work," he said, walking as if he was going to retrieve his shoes.

Amy couldn't stop laughing until his ball finally returned. Glenn scowled at her and then retrieved the ball for his second roll. He took his approach a little slower this time. He didn't slip, and the ball managed to stay between the gutters and take out four pins. He didn't look up as he brushed past her to take his seat.

"Those are the four toughest pins to take out, you know," she said, bouncing up to grab her ball.

"How about we play another game? It's called shutty."

The subsequent frames didn't go much better. Amy kept throwing strikes and picking up spares, and Glenn was happy with six pins. She never got tired of gloating, though. They quipped and barbed back and forth. By the fifth frame, Amy had produced a second round of beers. The alcohol didn't help his bowling, but it made getting his butt kicked a little easier to accept.

In the sixth frame, he finally threw a decent ball. It felt good when it left his hand and stayed true to slam into the right pocket. The pins scattered quickly, and the big 'X' appeared on the scoreboard. He strutted back toward the bench, blowing on the tips of his fingers. Amy stood and gave him a high five. As she passed by him, her hand swung down and smacked him on the butt.

Glenn froze for a second in shock. He heard Amy laugh as she picked up her ball. He staggered over and dropped to the bench. The alcohol from the beers vanished from his system, and he was in total control of his faculties. He suddenly wanted to be back at his house…alone. He absently smiled as Amy threw yet another strike. He had to follow through with his initial exit strategy.

"Lucky yet again," he said. He walked past Amy to grab his ball.

"Lucky every frame, huh?" Amy replied.

It was time to execute fake-an-injury. Glenn made his usual wind up but purposely held onto the ball a little too long. It thudded into the lane and skidded quickly into the left gutter. He immediately shook his right hand and then grabbed his right thumb with his other hand. He turned to Amy, his face contorted in pain.

Her smile disappeared as she stood. "Are you OK?"

"My thumb got stuck in the hole and bent in the wrong direction. Hopefully, it's nothing serious." He sat on the bench and massaged his hand vigorously. "Go ahead. I'll be fine."

Amy frowned but took her turn. It took two throws to knock down eight pins. Glenn wondered if his injury had distracted her.

"Taking pity on me?"

"Yeah. I don't want you to start crying."

He took his position at the return and picked up his ball. He grimaced and hesitated. He then grabbed it with both hands and bent over to roll it like a young child. The ball meandered down the lane and eventually knocked down two pins. "Can't throw it with one hand. Although, the result is about the same with two."

He kept the act up for the final two frames. He felt a little guilty at being a major buzzkill for Amy, but he had to do what he had to do. "Well, I hate to be a party pooper, but I'd better get home and put a little ice on my hand."

Amy was visibly upset by the quick termination of the night. "Maybe another beer or two would help," she said.

Glenn shook his head. "I'm afraid not. Just ice and a good night's sleep. It was good to see you again. Have a good rest of your weekend." He held his shoes in one hand and the ball in the other, strategically keeping them between him and Amy.

She aborted her hug attempt and managed a half-smile. "OK. Hope your hand feels better."

***

"Dude."

"What?" Glenn grumbled. He was enjoying his Saturday morning coffee while reading the local paper. He was one of the few remaining dinosaurs that still received a physical newspaper.

"Uh, oh! You don't have, uh, company, do you?" Pete laughed.

"Well, good catching up, bye-bye."

"Wait! Just messing with you. But seriously, how'd it go?"

"I can't believe you two clowns did that. I was there to bowl with the guys, not for a date."

"Sometimes, the baby bird needs to be pushed from the nest. And as much as I know you crave my and Billy's company, I'm sure Amy brings a little more to the table." Pete said.

"A monkey would bring more to the table, but that's not the point. Not cool."

"Was it that bad? Bowling on a Friday night with a hot chick. And someone you could actually beat."

"Well, you'd be wrong on that. Amy kicked my butt. Turns out she used to be a league bowler. That was neat, too."

Pete couldn't respond for a few seconds until his laughter subsided. "Maybe you could arm wrestle her?"

"Is there a point to this call?" Glenn said.

"Well, how did it go?"

Glenn sighed. "It was fine. She was fine. But as I've told you a million times, I don't want to date, no matter how hot the girl is."

"Guy, you're not dead yet."

"Only on the inside," Glenn responded.

"Dang! I guess me and Billy-boy will give it up. If Amy can't break down your walls, nobody is going to. See you Monday."

Glenn was a little surprised that Pete ended the call that abruptly and seemed legitimately upset with him. Oh well. At least he and Billy could quit worrying about him. He was fine.

A little later, he grabbed his dirty clothes out of the hamper to do laundry, as he did every weekend. He noticed a faint odor from the shirt on top of the pile, tucked beneath his chin. For once, it wasn't a foul odor. He realized it was Amy's perfume from last night. Dang, but she did smell good!

His heart fluttered as he recalled the night before. He clenched his teeth as he threw the clothes into the washing machine, added detergent and fabric softener, and started it. He returned to the dining room table with his now cold coffee and paper. He stared absently out the window at the bright morning outside.

His mind raced beneath his stoic face, a flood of emotions battling inside. For the past two years, he hadn't truly felt alive. He trudged through the motions of life mainly because he was too cowardly to end it. It wasn't a choice to be devoid of emotions; it just happened. He was OK with it, though. He did reach the point where he could laugh a little with the guys or *Seinfeld* reruns, but he didn't even look at or notice women. He didn't want to replace Cathy. He didn't need a woman or love to be happy, or at least content. He had been privileged to have loved, and been loved by, the most incredible woman imaginable. He had thought his memories were enough to drag him through the next forty years or so.

But last night, he had felt something. Despite his defenses, Amy had stirred emotions deep inside him. It was shocking how quickly and easily it had happened. Maybe it was the first hug— the first human contact he had experienced since Cathy left him. Or perhaps he was just lonelier than he had realized. Now, just a faint whiff of Amy's perfume had his heart racing and his hands sweating again.

Dang it! He went to the liquor cabinet and added some Irish cream to his cold coffee. And a little rum. He sat back down at the table. He hoped the alcohol would slow the wheels of his brain. Stupid Pete and Billy! That one night of bowling had totally

85

upended his existence. He realized that it had been easy to stay dead since he hadn't allowed himself to live. Now, it was as if he had woken from a long, deep sleep. He was suddenly alive again. But he wasn't ready to be.

He recalled Cathy's letter yet again; he had it memorized. He knew she meant those words. That's who she was. However, it was still hard to imagine another woman in his life. He wiped a tear from the corner of his right eye. But Amy was a catch by anyone's definition. Would he be crazy to shut the door and walk away from that potential relationship? Now that he was alive again, with feelings, forty years might be a long time to go without love.

He tried not to think about Amy too much Saturday evening and night, immersing himself in a *John Wick* marathon. Violent, gruesome deaths had a way of taking the mind off other subjects.

Sunday started well, riding his exercise bike and then reading the newspaper once again. Then came his weekend pilgrimage to the grocery store.

***

"Hand better?"

Glenn spun around to face the voice. Holy crap! It was Amy! "Huh? Oh, yeah. Not too bad," he stammered. He looked down at the milk jug he held in his right hand. Dang it. "Probably not bowling condition yet." Amy wore black spandex tights with a blue tank top. It appeared she had just come from the gym or was getting ready to go. She didn't seem to be wearing much makeup and had her hair pulled back tight in a ponytail. But she was possibly even more attractive than Friday night.

"That's good. And you have a solid excuse for your beatdown."

"Nah. That was just flat-out letting you win. You know, with you being all new in town and at work." Glenn was still stunned at running into Amy here. What were the chances? He didn't even have a clue where she lived. Their town wasn't huge, but it wasn't Mayberry either. "So, do you live close to here?"

"Just over in Windhaven. I decided to rent for a while until I learned the town. You?"

"Just a couple of miles from you, over on Thompson Drive." What were the odds?

86

"Actually, I've probably jogged by your house and didn't know it. Which one is yours?" Amy said.

Was she being friendly or getting ready to stalk? "It's the gray and black house, straight back at the end of the cul-de-sac." But she was too hot to resort to stalking anybody.

"I'll have to wave at you if I see you out," Amy said.

"Sure. Stop by and say hey." Why had he said that? Stupid!

"Sounds good. Enjoy the rest of your Sunday."

Glenn finished shopping and headed back home to a beautiful day. He enjoyed a lazy day of watching TV, internet browsing, and reading. The afternoon was so pretty that he decided to fire up the gas grill.

***

"Hello?" The voice from the gate startled him from reading his phone on the back patio. He swung his head around to see what neighbor it might be. He spotted the blond hair before he even focused on the face. Guess she wasn't too hot to stalk.

"I decided to go for a run. I hadn't planned to stop, but I couldn't help but smell your burgers cooking. So, I thought I'd at least say hi."

Most of Glenn wanted just to exchange pleasantries and let her continue with her run. But part of him thought it wouldn't be the worst thing to share a burger with her. He stood from his chair. "Hungry? I could throw another burger on the grill. Or are you too healthy for a greasy, fattening burger?"

Amy opened the gate and entered the yard. She wore the same outfit she had on at the grocery store. "I exercise so I can eat fattening burgers and drink beer." She smiled big as she walked over to join him on the patio. "If it's not too much trouble, I could choke one down."

"No problem at all. I'll give you one of these two and then fix me another. Light beer work?"

"Sure! My Mom drinks light beer too," she laughed.

"You know, I could revoke your invitation."

They sat at the patio table eating burgers and drinking beer twenty minutes later.

"You've got an amazing place here. Hopefully, I can buy something in a year or two. Renting is OK but having your own private yard like this is awesome," Amy said.

"Yeah, it do not suck. A little more maintenance than renting, but it's worth it. I would light the fire pit, but it's a little warm for that."

"Darn! So, what's on your agenda for tonight?"

Boy, she was forward! Glenn swallowed hard. "Amy, I don't want to read anything into this weekend, and you are probably just being friendly. But if not, I want you to know that I don't think I'm ready for a relationship."

"Where did that come from?" Amy leaned back from the table, her face suddenly serious.

"I didn't mean to imply anything. But you know, with the bowling, and now this. It just feels like more than I'm ready for." Glenn wiped the sweat off his forehead with his napkin.

"Well, Friday was the fault of your idiot friends." Amy's face relaxed, and a grin returned. "And today—well, to be honest, I did jog this way hoping to see you out in your yard. I'm not sure if I would have knocked on your door or not. I mean, who knows what single men do alone on a Sunday afternoon?"

Glenn couldn't help but laugh, despite the awkwardness of the conversation. "Give you three guesses."

"Ew! But seriously, I do think you seem like a great guy. You're funny. You're easy to talk to. And you're not the ugliest guy I've ever seen."

"You do have a way with words."

Amy laughed. "Oh, and you suck at bowling. By the way, did you actually hurt your hand Friday night?"

Perceptive too. Glenn hung his head like a kid getting busted for wrongdoing by their parents. "No."

"So, you really hated our time together that much? Gee, and me the idiot thought we were having fun." This time Amy was completely serious.

Glenn shook his head. "No, it wasn't that. Actually, it was the opposite. I was enjoying it too much."

Amy leaned forward, resting her elbows on the table. "That makes no sense at all."

Glenn's face was hot, and he was sure it was glowing red. "I—I know—it's—it's just. I don't know."

"Cleared that up."

"OK." He breathed deep. "After my wife died, most of me died with her. I had no feelings at all, for anyone or anything, for the past two years. I was fine with that. I still loved my wife and resigned myself to living alone. I had Pete and Billy to do stuff with if I got bored occasionally."

"That last part is pathetic," Amy said. She smiled, easing the tension a little.

Glenn grinned and nodded. "I can't believe I'm telling you all this."

"You're doing good. I'll try to behave over here."

"Well, Friday night, I suddenly…I suddenly felt alive again, and it scared me. I had never anticipated experiencing feelings like that again and didn't know how to deal with them. So, I did fake an injury to end the night and return to my fortress of solitude."

Amy reached out and placed her hands on top of his. His first instinct was to jerk them away, but he didn't. Her hands were warm and soft and felt so good against his skin.

"I have no idea what it's like to lose a spouse you love. I hope I never have to. My ex and I wouldn't shed a tear if something happened to the other. But you are young! You still have more than half your life ahead of you. And you've mourned for two years. Heck, most of my Facebook friends are remarried three months after losing a spouse. Please don't say anything to them, but Pete and Billy told me about your wife's letter. You know what she'd want."

He bristled a little at the revelation that his friends had shared something that personal with a near stranger. But he let it slide. "I know. It's just—it's just complicated."

"You are trying to deprive yourself of feelings and possible happiness, of life, for what? It's obviously not for your wife. You're trying to be a martyr for no reason."

Glenn suppressed a quick flash of anger. He started to protest, but he couldn't muster much of a defense. "I know it's hard to understand."

"No, I don't think you understand it either. If you were truly dead on the inside, we wouldn't be having this conversation. Everything you're feeling just means you're very much alive again. Embrace it!"

Glenn's mind raced. It was too much. He wished he could just run into the house and lock the door. "I don't know."

"Look. I'm not talking about getting married. I'm still recovering from a nasty divorce from a Neanderthal. I'm just saying I like hanging out with you and hope we can do it more. If it leads somewhere, then great. If not, then oh well, maybe we'll be the bestest friends ever."

"So, you're saying I'm not marriage material?" Glenn smiled weakly.

"No. I'm just saying that you're a girly man that fakes injuries in efforts to avoid embarrassing beatdowns from girls." Amy laughed and pulled her hands away from his.

"That was extremely harsh and uncalled for, and I'm ready to settle the score this evening."

"Oh? And just how do you propose to do that?"

"A little game I like to call cornhole. Ever played it?"

Amy laughed. "My Neanderthal and I used to dominate in local tournaments."

Glenn shook his head. "Son of a—. Seriously? Gee, is hanging out with you always going to end in my humiliation?"

"That's the plan."

Glenn thought briefly about Cathy, but he was suddenly, finally at peace. He and Cathy had been dead for two years. But unfortunately, it wasn't his time yet. Cathy would always be the love of his life and irreplaceable. But moping around the rest of his life wouldn't bring her back. It was time to reenter the world of the living. He hopped out of his chair to retrieve the game. "We're arm wrestling if I lose."

First Love

You never forget your first love. It's a cliché we've all heard at one time or another and one that I would have to strongly agree with. I would even expand upon it. Not only do you never forget it, you never get over it. That first special person you give your heart to will always keep a piece of it, no matter how far you think you've left them behind.

I remember the first time I laid eyes on Julie. I was a senior in high school and the proverbial big man on campus. Quarterback and captain of our football team, I was about as important as you could be in our school. We were at the end of one of our late-summer practices when I saw her. The team was making its way off the field toward the locker room when we passed by the girls trying out for the cheerleading squad. Being the young studs we were, we had to show off, smile, and carry on for the ladies. The usual girls were there: Rebecca Mason, Cindy Green, Debbie Lang, Jenny Hart, and the rest of the squad. A few new freshmen faces were there too, but we didn't care. Seniors couldn't stoop to that level. I smiled at the group, and most smiled back. I knew them all well. Heck, I had dated most of them.

Then I spotted her—a new face in the back row and definitely not a rookie. I nearly stumbled to a complete halt. She had long, dark-brown hair; a tanned, flawless face; eyes bluer than the sky; and a smile that could stop time. She was perfect, from head to toe. Her eyes met mine, and she flashed a deadly smile. I stared dumbly for a second and then did my best to smile back. I stumbled into the locker room, my heart pounding.

My head was spinning in the shower. I wasn't one to fall head over heels over a girl. Sure, I had dated just about everyone I wanted to in the school and would not be caught dead on a weekend without a date. I'd never become seriously involved with anyone, though. The longest continuous relationship I'd experienced during high school was seven months, and most of that was just for convenience. I was tired of dating around and wanted someone to "settle down" with. Besides, I was the football team captain, and Jenny Hart was the captain of the cheerleading squad. We almost had an obligation to at least date, if not go steady. We ended our long-term relationship at the beginning of the summer. We still were friends and would probably continue to date occasionally, but not exclusively.

Now, suddenly, a new face had my head swimming and my stomach churning. It wasn't just that she was beautiful. It was something else about her, maybe because she was someone new—a mystery. In our town of three thousand people, it was seldom that anyone moved in or out. We hadn't had a new student in school for several years and definitely not one like this. I had to get to know this mystery person.

My chance came much sooner than I'd hoped. As I was leaving the locker room by the back door, she ran into me and stumbled backward, dropping a pompom in the process. I quickly reached out my hand, catching her shoulder and helping her regain her balance. My hand lingered for a moment as my eyes met hers. I was almost hypnotized by their depths as her perfume slowly enveloped me. I wished we could have stayed stuck in that moment forever.

The startled expression quickly left her face, replaced by the devastating smile. "I'm sorry," she said in the sweetest voice I'd ever heard. Definitely not a local accent. She bent down and retrieved her pompom.

"It was a good hit, though. You just have to remember to wrap your arms around my waist to complete the tackle. Maybe you should try out for the team," I said, trying to patch up the awkwardness of the moment.

"I'll be happy enough just to make the cheerleading squad," she said shyly.

"If beauty is a qualification, you should *be* the cheerleading squad." I knew it was a cheesy line, but I was willing to pull out all the stops for this girl. "I'm Max. Max Farmer," I said, saving her an embarrassing moment.

"I'm Julie Richardson and obviously new to Greeneville. I noticed you practicing. Are you the quarterback?"

"Yeah. At least I was last season. Of course, it's not that challenging of a position for a team that only passes about twice a game."

"I'm sure you're being modest. You're the team leader and have to lead all those other players and memorize all the plays. You must be a big shot around town."

I detected a touch of sarcasm in her voice. Everything she said was the usual shy, slightly flirtatious, high school "girl talk." Yet, something about her tone seemed to mock the usual boy-girl banter. I couldn't determine whether she was doing it playfully or a little condescendingly. "Yeah. I'm a real celebrity. Nearly as popular as Mr. Pete's talkin' pig."

She stared at me with a slightly puzzled smile and finally laughed. "Your town has a talking pig?"

"Some folks say so. Of course, they've usually been sipping Mr. Pete's moonshine when they hear it talking."

She laughed again. It was such a warm, sweet, sexy sound. "So, the town's really small?"

"Five restaurants, three gas stations, one grocery store, a post office, and a drive-in theater. Is there more to life than that?"

She laughed again, and I began to feel at ease with her. "Well, you could at least have a bowling alley," she replied with mock concern.

"Great! You've gone and ruined my surprise. I was saving the bowling alley for our date tonight." I was really going out on a limb now.

"Our date? I don't quite remember being asked out."

"I was coming to that. If you don't have plans yet, I'd like to give you a tour of our big town tonight."

"Boy, you don't waste any time, do you?"

"Well, you are new to town, and I am the only single male with a full set of chromosomes. I figure we would go out sooner or later, so it might as well be sooner."

"You're not going to take me to the drive-in too, are you?" she asked worriedly.

"Shoot. Now you're just being ridiculous. That's a fourth or fifth date, at least. How easy do you think we country boys are?"

She laughed again. "I'm not sure about you country boys."

"Will you go out with me tonight? Or do I have to make a fool out of myself and beg?"

"Now *you're* being ridiculous. That's not until the second or third date."

"Pick you up at seven?"

She shook her head and smiled. "I guess so. I live at 359 Lewis Circle. Do you know where that's at?"

"Wow. You're in the rich section of town! I'll be there at seven."

She laughed again and then walked to her car. I floated to mine.

***

I drove her around the town that night, showing her what few sights there were to see. Then we rode out to the old lake. I spread a blanket on the ground, and we sat in the moonlight listening to the bullfrogs croak. Stars twinkled in the cloudless sky, and the moonlight danced on the lake—a perfect summer night. In a pair of tight blue-jean shorts, a white T-shirt, and that intoxicating perfume, Julie was even more beautiful that night than she had been earlier. Her eyes twinkled in the dim light over her ever-present smile. It was going to be a difficult struggle to keep my hands, and lips, off her.

"So, Julie Richardson, tell me your life story."

"From birth to present or just the highlights?"

"The highlights will do." I laughed. Since breaking the ice earlier, we'd talked like long-time friends. We seemed to fit together like two pieces of a puzzle. Whatever direction the conversation took, we stayed on the same page. She told me she had lived most of her life in Philadelphia, where her father was a doctor. He had just become the administrator for our county hospital. He had been raised in Lewisville, a town just thirty miles away, and then left on a scholarship to Harvard Medical School. Now he had a chance to return home and run his own hospital.

"What do you think of the move?" I asked her.

She stared up at the moon and was silent for a moment. Then she turned to me. "I'm afraid that I am a city girl. I like to get out and do things. You know: museums, plays, libraries, shopping. I need some excitement. I have a feeling it's going to be a long year here," she said, staring at the ground.

"Year? Is your father leaving after that?" I asked, already upset at the news she wouldn't be staying forever.

"No. I don't guess so. But I am. I'm hoping that if I can keep my grades up and score well on the SATs, I can get into NYU."

"You actually want to go to New York City? I thought everyone was trying to get out."

"Oh, New York is great!" she said. "I've been there several times. There's so much to do, twenty-four hours a day. There is Broadway and

94

more museums and art galleries than you can count. Not to mention the opera and ballet, bookstores, nightclubs…."

"OK! I get the point. What about the muggings, murders, rapes, traffic jams, filth, homeless people, et cetera? Doesn't that kind of put a damper on things?"

"You listen to the news too much. Those things don't happen often and just if you're in the wrong parts of the city. Besides, you can learn to live with the crowds and traffic. New York is a city that's always on the go—alive. I can't wait to get there."

We sat in silence as I began to see that a long-term relationship was doubtful at best. We were two different people. Unless one of us underwent a major personality change, we had problems, and I was definitely not planning on going insane. "What are you going to study at NYU?" I asked, trying to rekindle some form of communication.

"Oh, I don't know yet. Most likely something in the arts, maybe acting or writing. I still have plenty of time to decide that." She paused for only a moment before changing gears. "Now, tell me about yourself, country boy."

I told her my story, which took all of five minutes. My father was a supervisor in a local pencil factory, and my mother was a clerk at the courthouse. A slightly above-average student and an all-sport athlete, I had not decided on my plans for after high school. A post-high school football career was doubtful; community college was possible; a job in the factory, likely.

"You're too smart to make a career of working in a factory!" she said. "Surely your parents could afford to send you to college." Her stern voice caught me off guard.

"So only dumb people work in factories?"

"Well, no! That's not what I meant. But many people end up working in them because they lack other options. Don't you have other options?"

"Probably. But I don't think that's what I want," I replied, trying to avoid becoming agitated.

"Isn't there anything you want to do for a living?" she asked. "Everyone has some sort of dream."

I stared blankly at the calm lake surface, wishing that the conversation would change directions.

"Come on. What would it be if you could do anything you wanted, with no limitations?"

I started to reply and then closed my mouth again. Julie was going too far, too fast.

"You have to give me an answer," she demanded forcefully.

With nowhere to run, I finally submitted. "I like to write a little."

"Really? That's great!" she exclaimed enthusiastically. "What have you written?"

"A couple of novels, a few short stories, and a poem or two."

"Wow! Color me impressed. You'll have to let me read some of them. I'm a good editor."

I had to change the subject this time. "Maybe sometime…Now, let's get back to you. You've made me uncomfortable enough. I'm going to turn you into a genuine country gal. You might forget all about New York in a few weeks."

Julie laughed. "Good luck."

We talked late into the night. Keeping our subjects light, we talked about our high school experiences, teachers, classes, loves, and all the trivial things that dominated our lives. She had dated some and gone steady a time or two but had never been serious about anyone. She told me about life in the city, and I told her about country life. Despite being from a very different world, I felt an attraction, a sense of rightness. Unlike with most first dates and new relationships, no awkwardness, long pauses, or moments of silence filled our time together. We were like long-lost friends, catching up on what we had missed over the past seventeen years.

At one point, she shivered slightly, remarking that the air was a little cool. I didn't miss the opportunity to pull her close and put my arm around her. She turned to smile, and we gazed into each other's eyes. I slowly leaned my head toward hers, giving her plenty of time to stop me. She didn't, and our lips met for the first time, sending pins and needles spreading throughout my body. I had kissed my share of girls but had experienced nothing like this. To this day, I still can't adequately explain the feeling and sensation of that first kiss. It was soft, sensual, and passionate, all at the same time. It seemed like time stopped, and we melted together into one person. There was no nervousness. Just like being together, it felt so right, so meant to be. When we finally pulled apart, she stared back up at the moon and didn't speak.

"What's wrong?" I asked. "Was that too fast?"

"It was kind of sudden…but, no, it was great. But…where are we going with this?"

I knew what she was getting at, and I didn't really want to think about it. "Let's just see where it takes us. You only live once."

She smiled and gave me another quick kiss. That ended our first date and led to many more. The next day, we went hiking in the nearby state park. For a city girl, she sure adapted well to the country. I had expected her to be scared of getting dirty, walking through spiderwebs, stepping on snakes, and all the other hazards of the outdoors, but she quickly proved me wrong. I think it was her energy that made her take to hiking so quickly. She ran and jumped and turned cartwheels. She seemed to be in constant motion. Before long, she left me behind.

Struggling to catch my breath, I sat down on a grassy bank beside a small, gurgling stream. Julie was rock-leaping across the creek, laughing and playing like a child. She looked up at me, frowned, and then quickly jumped over to stand before me.

"What's wrong, tough guy? Are you going to let this cheerleader run circles around you?" she asked impishly.

"Hey, I'm sore from two-a-day workouts for the past two weeks! I need to conserve my energy."

"Oh, poor baby! I didn't realize how tender you were." She leaned over and patted my head.

"I'll make you *think* tender in a minute," I said as I reached up and grabbed her arms. She fell off balance, and I pulled her down, spinning her, so she landed on my lap, our faces just inches apart. "What are you going to do now, pompom girl?"

"This." She leaned forward and kissed me. The kiss started innocently and then quickly transitioned to passionate. I lay her back onto the ground and laid down beside her, our lips still locked together. It was one of those incredible moments of unplanned passion that you experience only a few times in your entire life—the soft grass beneath us, the sweet fragrance of honeysuckle, the soothing gurgle and splashing of the water, a gentle breeze, and the warm sun caressing our bodies.

Yet, at the heart of our desire and lust, I felt something more. I was half-frightened and half-excited. I had known Julie only two days but was developing feelings I'd never felt for another girl. My palms were sweaty, my heart pounded, my head spun, and I had butterflies in my stomach. The hairs on my arm stood each time she touched me. I wasn't sure what it was, but I liked it. We lay together until well after the sun had set. We talked, we laughed, and we loved.

***

The following week flew by as we spent all our free time together. I showed Julie around the rest of the town and helped her register for school. Nearly every night, we ended up on our blanket at the lake, talking and holding each other for hours. I made team quarterback again, and Julie made the cheerleading squad.

We didn't talk any more about her possibly leaving the next summer. We both knew we had something special, and we didn't need to worry about something that far off in the future. We just enjoyed the time we had together. Somehow, it seemed that the fewer rules and less structure we made for ourselves, the better things were. We just knew that we wanted to be together as much as possible. What else did we need to know?

When school started back the next week, we were pleasantly surprised to learn that we had English class together. The rest of our classes were different, with her taking the honors classes and me taking "jock" classes. We still saw each other between classes and at lunch. After school, I had football practice, and she had cheerleading. After attempting to meet on the first few school nights, I quickly realized a major difference between us: she did homework, lots of homework. She was determined to make all A's to get into NYU. So we decided not to see each other on weeknights. But on the weekends....

Maybe it was actually good for our relationship, not seeing each other every night. By the time the weekend arrived, we were dying to be together. By not being around each other too much, we probably avoided many arguments. After Friday-night football games, we would stay out until two or three o'clock. Saturdays, we would hike, go to the mall, bowl, rent movies, or do whatever else we could think of. No matter what we did, we were never bored. We were just glad to be together. As time went on, I found it amazing how those feelings I experienced in the beginning never waned. Each kiss was still as exciting as the first; each touch still gave me chill bumps. It was such an incredible combination of friendship and passion.

***

The fall semester passed quickly, mainly because we lived for the weekends. What happened during the week seemed of little consequence. Julie made straight A's in all her classes. I maintained my A/B average, doing well enough to get into a local college if necessary. English was my best class, probably because Julie was in it with me. And I had always liked to write during high school. Every year, I would turn out a poem or short story that had my English teachers praising my work. With Julie interested in what I was writing, and usually editing it for me, I tried to make every piece I wrote praiseworthy. On many of those assignments, I

98

actually beat Julie, something I reminded her of frequently. She didn't get angry, though. She claimed it was because she was such a good editor.

Not long into our dating, we had to undergo the ritualistic meeting of the parents. Her mother had been killed in a car accident ten years prior. She didn't talk about her very much, and I didn't ask any questions. Julie's father, Peter, was in his early fifties. You could discern just by looking at him that he held some sort of respectable position. He was always neatly groomed and well dressed. I think he must have mowed his yard in a Polo shirt. He had penetrating blue eyes, which made me nervous every time they were focused on me.

One of his first questions was about my plans after graduation. I swallowed hard and glanced at Julie. She returned a smile that did little to comfort me. "I was thinking about going to the community college and taking some management classes and then getting a job at the local pencil plant. My father is a supervisor there."

Her father bored through me with those steely eyes. "And after that?"

I really wanted to leave. I could see that a factory supervisor was not Julie's dad's idea of success. Julie tried to bail me out.

"He's a great writer, Dad. You should read some of the papers he's written in English class."

Her father finally lifted his gaze from me and looked at his daughter. "It's tough to make it as a writer. He would be better off sticking to business. But a community college…." The phone rang, and Peter jumped up quickly to answer it—our cue to leave. We waved at him and quickly fled to freedom.

"Man, he's tough!"

"Oh, he doesn't mean anything by it. He's just making sure his little girl's main man has some sort of career plan. I don't think he wants me barefoot and pregnant, living in the trailer park."

"If it's good 'nuff fer ma, it'll be good 'nuff fer you, darlin'."

***

My parents loved Julie. They had always tried to push me to be more ambitious in my career goals. They wanted me to set my sights on something higher than my father's career path. Now, they saw Julie as someone who might be able to convert me to their point of view.

"Oh, that sounds exciting!" my mother exclaimed when Julie described wanting to go to NYU. She loved to travel and had always dreamed of life outside our country town.

"Why don't you take the boy with you?" my dad asked gruffly. He liked to joke and cut up with company, but I could sense a lecture coming on.

"I wish he would," Julie replied. "See? Even your parents want you to go."

I feigned a smile. "Why don't you take my parents with you?"

"Max…" my father began. I glanced toward the door, judging how quickly I could make an escape. "You need to listen to your girlfriend. You'll only be young once. You don't have to go to NYU but go to some good college. You need to find yourself. If you don't do something now, you'll regret it for the rest of your life. You don't need to be in that factory. Twenty years from now, you'll want out of there so bad you could scream. Then it'll be too late. Go to college for four years and get a degree in something. Then, if you want to come back here and work in a factory, you can. But at least then you'll have a way out."

Julie gave me a sly smile and was about to add her opinion when I interrupted. "Gee, look at the time! Our movie starts in half an hour." I quickly stood and walked toward the door, three frowns following after me. Julie stood, exchanged pleasantries with my parents, and followed me out.

"You have some really cool parents! Maybe you should listen to them."

"I can't keep from hearing them, but I don't have to listen. Why don't you take them home with you or to New York?"

"You can be hardheaded when you want to!"

"Can not!"

***

That fall was the best time of my life. Our football team went on a winning streak, and most of the school crowned me the hero. It was much more than that, though. Julie was the missing piece of my high school experience. It took a couple of months to finally realize what I felt. When the answer came to me, I was frightened. I was in love.

We were in my old Ford pickup bed watching *Fried Green Tomatoes* at the drive-in. We had a blanket spread over our legs, and I had my arm around Julie as I stared blankly at the big screen. I couldn't concentrate on the movie, and it wasn't just because it was boring me to tears. No. I had something else on my mind. Julie noticed too.

"What's wrong? You didn't even laugh at that."

"There was something funny in this movie?"

"Come on! You've been awfully quiet tonight. Are you mad at me?"

"Of course not. I've just been thinking."

"That's funny. I didn't smell anything burning."

"Your butt will be burning in a minute," I said, swatting her hip.

"We will come back every night and watch this movie until you tell me what's wrong." I knew by her tone that I wouldn't get out of telling her the truth.

I grabbed her hands and stared into her beautiful eyes. She smiled warmly. "Julie, these past two months have been the best of my life. You're everything I ever dreamed of in a girl. You're smart, funny, sweet, caring…and most of all, you're dating me." We both laughed nervously as I paused to take a deep breath. "I'll go ahead and spit it out before I make too big of a fool of myself. Julie, I love you."

Her smile quickly faded. She turned away and didn't speak. That definitely wasn't the reaction I'd dreamed of while working up the nerve to tell her. She was supposed to be hugging and kissing me and telling me how much she loved me back. "What is it? Am I the only one who feels this way?"

She slowly turned back around, revealing tears in her eyes. I wiped them away with my thumbs. She laid her head against my chest and said, "No, you're not the only one. It's…it's just…you just weren't supposed to say it out loud."

"You're not making any sense. If we love each other, why shouldn't we say it out loud? Heck, we should be shouting it to the whole town!"

She was sobbing softly now, her tears warm on my chest. I gently placed my hand on the side of her face and lifted her head to look at me. I again wiped away her tears and then kissed her on the lips. "You're thinking about leaving again, aren't you?"

She nodded.

"You can't think about that now! That's months away. Anything could happen between now and then. Let's just take it one day at a time. You make every day the best one of my life, and I want to cherish every one of them."

"I do love you, Max! I love you more than I thought I would ever love anyone. I just don't want to lose you. My heart couldn't take it."

"You don't have to lose me!"

"I can't stay here after school is out. I have to go to NY—"

"Let's promise each other not to worry about the future. Let's not ruin what we have now." She still wore a frown. "Come on, promise."

Her smile finally returned. "OK. I promise."

"Besides, you might flunk out of school between now and graduation."

She hit me hard on the arm.

***

Winter was quickly approaching. Football season had ended with our team falling two games short of reaching the state finals. Julie and I were nominated homecoming king and queen and were the hit of most parties and dances. Our love continued to build. I cannot remember a single argument during that period. We still spent most of our weeknights apart and fell in love again each weekend. We hadn't talked about the future since the night we'd admitted our love for each other.

Sharing the holidays together was great. We spent the cold days in my room, a cheerful fire crackling in the fireplace. We cuddled together, wrapped in a blanket in the old beanbag chair, talking and laughing the Christmas vacation away. Occasionally, we got out and drove into Nashville. Julie enjoyed shopping in the malls, especially in art and book stores. I patiently endured the throng of crazed shoppers to be with her. Julie seemed to adapt well to country life. Everything was relaxed, calm, and comfortable.

In mid-January, we received our SAT scores. Julie's weeks of studying paid off, with her scoring a 1510—well above what she had hoped for. She was more excited than I had ever seen her. With that score and her grades, she was pretty much assured admission to any college she wanted. I managed a 1240. She said that was really good, but I didn't really care. It meant little to me. The only good thing for me at that moment was that I was the beneficiary of all her joy and relief.

College brochures began pouring in to Julie over the next few weeks. Everyone in high school received some—I even got a fair share—but Julie must have received one from every college in the country. She mailed applications to several, all of them far away. She was ecstatic when NYU sent her their brochure. She must have read it to me a dozen times, pointing out all its strong points. She submitted her application the day after she received the packet.

I didn't receive one from them. I did humor Julie and mail applications to the three most respected universities that had sent something to me. I really didn't care what their responses were. My choices were community college or none at all, and I was pretty sure either would accept me.

***

102

"Julie, we need to talk." We sat in my truck at the lake on a clear, cold February night. Stars dotted the dark sky. Julie's head rested on my shoulder, and a blanket covered her.

"OK. About what?"

"I think we need to talk about our future together."

She was silent for a moment. It was a subject we had tried to avoid as much as possible, but we both knew this conversation was inevitable.

"OK," she whispered softly.

"Julie, I can't go to NYU or Penn State or any of those colleges."

"Yes, you can! You're smart!"

"I won't go to any of those schools. Julie, this is my home. Sure, it's a small, boring town, but this is where I want to be. I love it here. I love to hike and fish and hunt. I like going downtown and recognizing nearly everyone I meet. I like the laid-back pace and being able to stop and smell the roses if I want to. I like my friends. This is my home. I could never leave it for long."

"You can fish and hunt in New York or any other state! You can make more friends. And if you went away to college, you could come back home for the holidays and summer vacation. Then, after you graduate, you could move back here if you wanted to." Her voice was becoming a little desperate.

I shook my head. "I'm sorry, Julie. I just can't do it." We were silent for several minutes. I stared out the side window at the stars above. "Couldn't you stay here?" I finally asked.

"I think going to New York is as important to me as staying here is for you. It's all I think about, except you. Who knows? Once I've been there a while, I might not even like it. But I couldn't live with myself if I didn't at least give it a shot. Can you understand that?"

I wanted to give her an argument or at least tell her that she could meet new people at a local college. I decided not to. It would have been a waste of breath. We fell silent again for a while. "You know, it's kind of funny."

"What do you find funny?" she asked, surprised.

"In all the great love stories, love always wins in the end. The boy and girl are supposed to get together and live happily ever after. Where did we go wrong?"

Julie had been on the verge of crying; now, she could no longer hold back. I wrapped my arms around her and pulled her close, and she buried her face in my shoulder. Several tears ran down my cheek into her hair. I wanted to speak, but I knew my voice would betray my macho facade. We held each other for some time.

"What if you don't get accepted to NYU?" I finally asked, one last effort to find a ray of hope.

"I haven't really thought about it. I guess I would either go somewhere else or attend a community college until I could transfer there."

"So there's a chance that you could stick around here?"

She looked at me and smiled weakly. "Yes, I guess there's a chance."

"I love you. I will always love you."

"I love you too."

We made love that night in my truck. I think it was more to take our minds off our heartache than out of passion. We lay together until two in the morning. Then we went home in silence.

Our relationship began to change after that night. It was hard to point a finger at the differences. We still dated and were together every weekend, but there *was* a difference. We seemed to be becoming more like friends than we had been. We still shared moments of passion, but they were few and far between and not like before. I think we were both subconsciously distancing ourselves from each other. We were hardening our hearts for the pain that was rushing toward us. I didn't believe for a second that our love was waning. We were just building walls around it.

***

On the evening of March 14, a phone call from Julie dashed all hope. She was so excited; I could hardly understand her. Finally, I deciphered that she had gotten accepted to NYU. I never asked her to change her mind again. I had no doubt that she was going to New York, and no amount of tears would stop her. I listened to her talk about everything she had to do that spring and acted excited for her. I lay awake all night after we hung up. Despite the walls, my heart still felt the pain.

The rest of the school year was pretty miserable. My grades plummeted quickly. I just wanted to pass and get my diploma—A's and B's didn't matter. Nothing really mattered. It hurt to sit in class and stare at Julie. I remembered all those perfect nights we'd shared and the love we'd experienced together. Then I thought about her leaving forever. Sometimes I fought back tears.

She seemed as energetic as ever. She spent a lot of time in the library with some new friends who were also going away to fancy colleges, reading about their respective schools and cities. We were spinning in opposite directions. I spent most of my time with the worst crowd of friends I could find. We were all committed to a blue-collar future: forty-hour workweeks followed by weekends of drinking and partying. With them, I could briefly get my mind off Julie. Their true loves were whatever girls had just walked past. I really wasn't having any fun with them, but it was something. I needed something.

***

The final blow came two weeks after Julie's acceptance. We were in my room watching television on a Friday night. I talked and laughed, but Julie had been quiet most of the day. I was afraid to ask why. Finally, she said we needed to talk. I turned off the TV and braced myself.

"I'm not going to be staying here this summer."

I stared at the blank television screen, a dozen emotions flooding my mind simultaneously. "Why?" I finally asked, numb.

"I'm going to go to NYU for summer school. I really need to take calculus and some advanced science classes before the fall semester starts. Being down here for a year caused me to miss some honors classes. I'll be behind the other students if I don't go. Besides, that will give me time to learn the campus and city before all the other students get there. That way, it won't be such a culture shock."

"That's nice." I couldn't keep the sarcasm out of my voice.

"Don't you understand why?" she asked, hurt in her voice.

"Does it really matter? If you want to go, you'll go."

"That's not fair!"

"What is fair? Is it fair that the only person I've ever loved is leaving me for some college a thousand miles away? Is it fair that I'll never have someone like you to marry and raise a family with? Is it fair that I might never love, or love like this, again? Is being stuck in this town for eternity fair?" I vented months of pent-up sorrow and anger that night. The words came pouring out, and I was helpless to stop them.

Julie buried her head in her arms, which lay folded across her knees. She cried softly. I couldn't stand seeing her hurting like that. I finally wrapped my arm around her and rested my chin on her head. "I'm sorry. I didn't mean it."

She finally looked up, her eyes red and cheeks wet. "Yes, you meant it," she said softly.

"It's just so frustrating! We're alike in every way two people can be alike, except where we want to live. We love each other more than most people have ever loved in their entire lives, but we can't be together. There should be an answer somewhere. We should be smart enough to help love conquer all."

105

"I know," she whispered. "I just can't think of a way."

We lay back on the bed, my arm beneath her head, and stared at the ceiling. Half an hour passed before we spoke again. I finally broke the silence. "Julie, I still love you as much as I ever have. I will love you as long as I live. I know it in my heart. But I can't take this. I can't hold you in my arms...I can't kiss your lips and see your face and know that in a month, you'll be gone forever. It's tearing my heart in two. It's almost like one of us is dying. I just can't stand the pain."

"What can we do? We've both made up our minds."

I took a deep breath. "We need to end it tonight. Let's just make a clean break. We can cry all night long and then start putting the pieces back together again in the morning. I would rather die a quick death than agonize for another month."

Julie cried again. Tears rolled out of my eyes now too, and I didn't try to hide them. Julie finally spoke. "I love you so much!" We kissed for several minutes. "I guess you're right. We know we have to do it sooner or later. Maybe it would be better sooner."

"Now?" I asked.

"Yes. I don't want to think about it anymore."

We stood up, she gathered her things, and we walked to the door of my room. I held both of her hands and gazed deeply into her beautiful, sad eyes. "I hope New York lives up to your dreams. You be careful in the big city." I hesitated and sighed. "God, this is awkward!"

"I know. We could just wish each other a good life," she said, tears flowing again.

"Yeah. I guess that would say it all. You have a good life, Julie Richardson. May...may all your dreams come true. I...I hope you mar-marry somebody that'll t-treat you right." My voice quivered badly.

She wrapped her arms around me and hugged me tightly. "I wish it were you." We hugged for several minutes before either of us could speak again. "I hope you have a good life too," she said. "Keep writing. And don't settle for a life you don't really want. Follow your heart. You...you've got t-talent." She paused to regain her voice. "I hope you marry someone who will love you as much as I do."

We hugged each other for what seemed like hours before she finally pulled herself away. "Maybe we can write to each other after a couple of months, after we get over the hurt. And I'll be coming in for Christmas. We could at least remain close friends."

"Yeah," I said. "That would be nice."

We kissed for the last time. As I held Julie close and touched her lips, the previous eight months flashed through my mind. The best thing that ever happened to me was now leaving my life. It would be a long time, if ever, before I was over her. I watched her walk out of my room, and then I went to the window and watched her get into her car. Then I watched her drive out of my life. I cried all night.

***

That was twenty years ago. I had asked about her a time or two during those first couple of years when I saw Julie's father in town. He said she was doing well and really liked the college. After her first year, she got a job as an intern for a big publishing house. He said he didn't expect to see her but once a year. I thought about going over to her house each Christmas but could never bring myself to do it. I didn't see the point. After a few years, the urge to see her lost its strength as I slowly buried her memory.

I worked a very unfulfilling year in the factory and quickly tired of the blue-collar lifestyle I thought I wanted. It was the same routine every day and every night: the same friends, the same conversations, the same jokes, and the same tedious tasks. I felt like my mind was wasting away. The following fall, I decided to enroll in the community college and study English. I hated most of the classes, but they gave me a chance to write.

I wrote mainly short stories, most of them dealing with love going wrong, hearts getting broken, and people sacrificing everything to fulfill their dreams. I guess you end up writing what you know. I was never sure if my desire to write was for enjoyment or to share my pain with others. Whichever it was, I had plenty of motivation.

My professors bragged on my work. Their only complaints were concerning all the sad endings. I won a few college writing contests with my short stories, and those early victories further fueled my writing. After my first year at the community college, I transferred to the University of Tennessee. They offered a better variety of writing classes, and I could earn a degree in teaching. I didn't miss home as much as I thought I would. There was really nothing to miss.

I continued writing short stories and enjoyed some more successes. During my third year of college, I met my wife—a very beautiful, intelligent woman from California. Her name was Karen Stevenson, and she was getting a degree in accounting. I don't really know if I loved her or was just comfortable with her, but I know that what I felt had none of the passion I'd experienced with Julie. Our kisses were good, but they lacked that electricity. Her touch was just a touch, no chill bumps. I didn't

107

have the sweaty palms or butterflies or swimming head. We got along well and talked a lot but never quite shared a special bond. We married just before graduation. After we graduated, we moved to Lewisville, where I worked part-time as a substitute teacher and wrote the rest of the time. Karen found a job with a local accounting firm.

I continued entering and winning the occasional contest with my short stories, and I turned several of them into a novel during our second year together. After many rejections, I was finally published. I only made a couple of thousand dollars, but it catapulted me to the next level. With the contests I won and my novel, I found an agent. A year later, I published a second novel, and this one did much better than the first.

The honeymoon ended quickly for Karen and me. She complained about us not making enough money and that I spent too much time writing. She wanted me to teach full-time and write in my spare time. She also wasn't fond of where we lived. She talked a lot about us moving to California, where we could both make a lot of money. We argued back and forth for several years while I struggled to establish myself. Then I entered a dry spell. I had used up my book ideas; my motivation was dying out. I went two years without publishing a novel, which was too much for Karen. We divorced after five years of marriage. She moved back to California, and I never heard from her again.

I moved back to Greenville and got a job teaching English. I didn't marry again. I dated occasionally but never found someone I wanted to settle down with. I didn't see my old high school buddies much anymore, either. The ones still around were married and had children. I wrote from time to time but nothing of major worth. I liked teaching and didn't worry too much about writing.

That was until last year. Last year, I came up with an idea for a series of books. I think teaching high school students and observing their relationships brought back the memories of my own first love. I created a series of romance novels based on a group of high school friends. The series followed them through high school and then on to what paths they pursued afterward. It dealt with the entire young adult experience but focused mainly on first loves and what happened when the real world interfered. I targeted the teen-to-mid-twenties female market. Of course, the two main characters were based on personal experience.

My old agent loved the idea, and I was back in business. Each short novel I wrote increased in popularity. Their success nearly overwhelmed me, and I resigned from teaching to write full-time. Six months ago, after releasing my best-selling novel yet, *First Love*, my publisher wanted me to fly to New York to meet with them and work out the details of a book tour. I was scared to death but couldn't refuse the offer. I was off to New York City.

***

I had a three o'clock appointment with the senior editor of my novel, Ms. J. Edwards. When I opened the door to her office and walked in, my heart stopped beating. Behind the desk sat Ms. J. Edwards—or Ms. Julie Richardson. I had no doubt that it was her, twenty years older, probably a few pounds heavier, but just as beautiful. She wore glasses over her brilliant blue eyes, and her long brown hair hung to shoulder-length, but she was still the same woman I had loved. I stood stupefied.

She stood, her gray business suit hugging her still-shapely body. "Hello, Max. Surprised?" She obviously wasn't.

"A little," I stammered. "What…how?"

She walked around the desk and gave me a hug. I slowly responded and hugged her back, her perfume once again ensnaring me. She pulled away and flashed one of her deadly smiles. "Sit down, please," she said as she walked back and sat down in her chair. I fell into mine.

"I love your books, Max. I told you that you would make a good writer and that I'd make a good editor. I must say, I'm flattered that you would make me a character."

"You've been editing all my books?" I asked. It felt like I was in a dream.

"Just your new series. Of course, after editing them, I did read all your previous works. I cried through every one of them. I could have written every one of them." She paused for a moment and looked down at her desk. "Let's get out of here. We have a lot of catching up to do. Business can wait until later."

"What about my tour?"

"Oh, the big meeting on that isn't until tomorrow. I wanted you to myself today."

I smiled, dumbfounded.

We left her office, and she drove us back to her apartment. It was on the twelfth story of a beautiful new high-rise. Her apartment was a huge suite decorated in a contemporary black-and-white style with glass and metal furniture that appeared more like modern sculpture than functional pieces. A large glass door led out onto a narrow balcony. She was definitely doing well for herself.

We sat on her couch and talked until late in the evening. I told her a brief summary of my life since she'd left. She said it was sad that I had never found the right person. I told her that I had found the right person, years ago, but let her go. She then told me her story. She'd earned a master's degree in English at NYU while working as an intern at the publisher she worked for now. After graduation, she landed a full-time job as an assistant editor at the company. Over the years, she'd worked her way up to senior editor. She met and married her husband about five years after graduating college. A relatively well-known corporate lawyer, he was quite a bit older than she. He'd died five years earlier of a heart attack. She didn't speak much of their life together, although she didn't seem to show much emotion over him.

"Did you love him?" I don't know what possessed me to ask that question, but it was out before I could stop it.

She stared at me for a moment, slightly surprised. "He was a good man, very smart, good-looking, and wealthy. We didn't see each other very often, though. I worked twelve-hour days in quest of my next promotion, and he worked that much or more to ensure success in his career. We slept together and saw each other on weekends, and that was about it." She took another long pause. "We were good together. We were both successful, both levelheaded, and both comfortable." She paused again. Finally, she continued, "I guess we were content."

"No children?"

"No." She sighed. "We never had time for that."

"Did you want any?"

"Yes. And still do."

As we talked, I couldn't help but feel attracted to her again. It seemed like we were starting back where we'd finished so many years ago. We laughed and joked and smiled a lot. I didn't know where it was going, but I enjoyed it. Finally, I asked her a dangerous question. "Do you have any regrets?"

She thought for a moment and then smiled. "I love New York. The people are a little crazy, and the traffic is unbearable, but it's like nowhere else on earth. I love my job. I get paid big money to read books for a living."

"Sounds good," I said halfheartedly.

Her smile faded. "Not really. I sacrificed a lot to get here." She stared off out the window for a moment. "What about you? You must have it all now."

"Well, I'm getting paid a bunch of money to write books for you to read. I guess that's a pretty good living. I have a beautiful little cabin in the woods, and I get to fish and hunt year-round. It's a nice, quiet life. Sometimes it gets a little lonely."

We dropped that line of conversation, and Julie ordered supper. She ordered for both of us from some fancy Italian restaurant. We had antipasti, consisting of roasted artichokes filled with crabmeat in a garlic herb sauce; a salad; sautéed veal scaloppine with prosciutto, spinach, sage, and fresh mozzarella; and tiramisu for dessert. We shared a bottle of nice Chardonnay wine. She definitely knew what to eat in the big city. We filled in some of the missing details of our lives as we ate.

After we finished, she led me out onto the balcony. We held onto the railing and stared at the city. It was an incredible view. I never knew that many lights existed in the world. Cars still filled the streets, and many skyscraper windows still glowed. The sidewalks appeared to move and pulse with the throngs of people. It was loud and noisy but pretty in its own way. The air was a little cool. Julie moved back against me, her sweet-smelling hair touching my chin. I cautiously wrapped my arms around her, joining them over her stomach, and she placed her hands over mine. I pulled her close, feeling her warm body against mine and inhaling her perfume. It felt just like it had twenty years before. I felt the love again.

"You're going to get something started in a minute," she whispered back.

"Maybe I'm just picking up where we left off."

She twisted around, facing me, our arms around each other. "I can't go back to Tennessee," she said, her face serious. "Can you leave it?"

"Oh, I don't know. I've grown up into a big boy now. Does New York have any woods or streams in it?"

Julie laughed. "Ever heard of the Catskills or Adirondacks?"

"Nope. Do they have fish and deer and other varmints?"

"All kinds of varmints."

"That sounds good. I think I might be able to use a change of pace…."

She stepped closer and hugged me tightly. After a moment, I moved my head back, and she gazed up at me, her eyes watering. I cautiously leaned forward, and she pulled my head down the rest of the way and gave me a passionate kiss that sent my entire body tingling. Her lips were as soft and warm as they were so many years ago, and our kissing was just as great and natural as it had been back then.

We held each other for twenty minutes, hugging and kissing, before she finally broke away, her face serious again. "There are still a lot of questions. I don't want to have my heart broken again."

111

"You won't. And we can talk more tomorrow. I'm talked out tonight."

"You're not leaving, are you?"

"Nope. I'm going to pick you up in my arms, carry you to the bedroom, and make passionate love to you all night long."

She put her hands on her hips, her eyes wide with surprise. "Do you think we city girls are that easy?"

"You're not a virgin, are you?"

"Yes. A reborn one at least."

"Great. I'll be your first…twice."

I scooped her up in my arms and kissed her passionately on the lips.

"Do I have a say in this?" she asked, feigning anger.

"Nope. All I've had to stare at for fifteen years are sheep, cattle, and my golden retriever. I'm not going to let a beautiful woman like you get away from me."

"You beast!"

"You know what they say about us country boys."

"I still don't know what to think about you country boys!"

***

We married in Tennessee two months ago. Her dad gave her away, and my dad was my best man. Everyone finally got what they wanted—we were successful enough for her dad and my parents, and we were finally together. We didn't really regret the twenty years we'd lost. I believe we just met twenty years too early. Those eight months, so many years ago, were just a preview—a taste of the best yet to come. The twenty years in between were the ultimate test of our love. Our love never really died or even waned. It's as if we just pressed the pause button on the DVD player.

We split our time between her apartment and a house I bought in the Adirondacks. Both of us at last feel complete again. I just finished the final book in my series, *True Love*, which, of course, has a happy ending for the main characters. Now we're trying to think of a new direction for my writing, one that doesn't involve any more sad endings—we both like the sappy, happy ones. We're still working on the family thing and are optimistic that we'll be adding an entirely new element to our love soon.

You never forget your first love. The person who came up with that cliché was a wise one. You never do forget it, and if you're fortunate like me, you end up marrying that person—and living happily ever after.

Love Stories

Their first kiss—unplanned and wrong in every way—was the best kiss she'd ever had. Maybe it was the two drinks at lunch. Maybe it was the conversation. More than likely, it was just inevitable—too much attraction, too much closeness, too much time spent together, and too much pent-up desire. She quickly silenced the alarm bells as their kisses transitioned from tentative and gentle to hot and lustful. Soon, their mouths opened wide, allowing their tongues to touch as roaming hands joined their erotic kisses. She was quivering all over, the flood of animalistic desire quickly sweeping her away.

Finally, she mustered enough willpower to pull herself away from the brink of no return. They were both panting at this point. "We can't do this."

Ryan looked at her for a moment and then pulled his arms back from around her. He stared straight ahead out the window.

"I'm sorry," she whispered, rubbing his arm briefly as she removed her hands from him.

"No, I'm sorry. I know better. It won't happen again," Ryan said quietly, still not looking at her.

"Ryan, it can't happen again."

"I know."

They were both silent for several long minutes. "We can't do lunch anymore." It pained her to say that. Their lunches were the highlight of her days. They worked for a small mortgage company, and their boss was very lax on the rules, including lunch hours and breaks. Sometimes, they would go out and eat. Other times, they would get takeout and just park in a parking lot somewhere around town. They would talk and laugh and share everything with each other.

They were both aware of the underlying sexual tension, but they had managed it well—until now. Now, it would never be the same. They couldn't go back to just talking and laughing, at least not without thinking about the kiss and wanting more. It would eventually happen again and probably wouldn't stop with just a kiss. Kathy nervously awaited Ryan's response.

"I guess I knew that was coming."

"Do you agree?"

Ryan finally looked at her. "No. I don't agree. But I understand."

"We're still buds, right?"

"Forever."

"Deal!"

"Kathy, I'll just say this one time and never mention it again," he said, staring deep into her eyes. She nervously nodded in response. "I will always be here for you. If anything ever changes, I'll be here. Never forget that."

A tear ran down her cheek. She leaned over, and they exchanged a last hug, making sure their lips didn't meet this time.

***

The next few weeks were hell for Kathy. First, she couldn't see her best friend every day at lunch. They still spoke on the phone some and emailed, but it wasn't the same as being right beside him, talking and laughing. Second, she was dealing with guilt from the kiss. She even debated briefly about telling her husband, Andy, but decided against it. It would only bring him a lot of hurt and pain. She knew that it would never happen again, so it was better if she dealt with the hurt and pain of the guilt, plus the loss of a big part of her friendship with Ryan.

Andy was a good husband. Sure, she had never experienced the passion and desire with him that she'd felt in that one kiss from Ryan, but there was more to a relationship than that. He also wasn't one to share his feelings and emotions with her, as Ryan did. Nor would he sit and listen to her for hours on end. Andy was a man's man, strong and silent. Yet, he was safe and steady, a good provider and father to their two children. Until Ryan came along, she'd never really thought that there might be more to a marriage than what they had. Now, she just had to go back to

114

thinking that. She could never hurt or leave Andy unless he cheated on her or did something just as bad, which would never happen.

***

A few weeks later, Ryan emailed his first story to her. Kathy knew that he used to write in college and a little afterward, and he had talked about starting up again. She was ecstatic when he asked if she would read his story. She had no idea what to expect as she printed it and stuffed it into her purse to take home and read. She took it out and began to read as soon as Andy went to bed. It began with two friends who started developing feelings for each other.

> We both sat down wearily on one of the large rocks on the flat top of the peak. The air was cool, but the uphill, mile-long trail made for a challenging workout. We inhaled some deep breaths, shared a cold drink from the canteen, and took in the view. It was majestic as the deep blue, totally clear sky stretched down to merge with the surrounding purple mountain ranges. The large orange sun hung low over the mountains in front of us.

> As we watched the sun quickly descend and set, something came over me. I felt attracted to Paul in a way I hadn't felt before or at least hadn't acknowledged. He looked so rugged and strong, sitting beside me on the peak. His smell, a combination of cologne, deodorant, and healthy sweat, was overpowering. He turned and caught me staring. He smiled.

> Then, when he saw the look in my eyes, his expression changed. I'd never seen that look from him before. There were no words. He leaned toward me, slowly turning his head. I closed my eyes and leaned forward to meet him. It seemed to take forever for our lips finally to meet. But I had waited a lifetime for that kiss. It was so gentle, so sensuous, and so right. I felt his left arm reach around me and touch my back. His right hand extended and stroked the left side of my face. His every touch sent chills through my body. The kiss became firmer and more passionate as our hands began to explore each other's body.

115

> Slowly, I lay down on the flat rock, pulling him down on top of me. I couldn't believe this was my best friend, making me feel things I'd never felt before. Suddenly, I had never wanted anyone more.

That part sounded a little too familiar. Kathy began reading faster to see where Ryan was going with it. It ended happily with the two friends falling in love and living happily ever after.

She laid the manuscript down on the nightstand and turned off the light. She reviewed the story in her mind as she stared at the ceiling. Ryan was definitely a talented writer. She wasn't sure if he was trying to send her a message through the story, but it definitely hit home in a few places. She couldn't wait to talk to him.

***

"What did you think?" Ryan asked on the phone the next day. They talked on the phone frequently at lunch since they could no longer meet in person. It wasn't a terrible alternative.

"It was very good! I'm impressed."

"Really?"

"Yes. You're a very talented writer. Now you need to write me another," Kathy replied excitedly.

"Any story requests?" he asked.

"Hmmm…let's see. How about adding a little more spice to it, if you get my drift. You can decide the plot."

"Spice? You naughty girl!"

"But of course."

They both laughed.

***

A week later, she held the next story in her hands. Andy was once again asleep in bed when she started reading. Kathy couldn't believe how excited she had been all day since he gave it to her. She had fought hard to resist peeking throughout the day. She finally decided it might lose some of its effect if she read it in pieces, so she left it in her purse until that night.

> She was mostly joking when she asked Brian to rub her neck. She was shocked when he moved up behind her and placed his large, strong hands on her shoulders. He began rubbing and massaging from her neck to her upper arms.

116

Her apprehension and resistance quickly faded as her body trembled beneath his firm caress. The feeling soon became more than just relief to her aching shoulders and neck—her skin prickled, and the sensation quickly spread down her body. She was attracted to Brian but had never dreamed of pursuing it. They were both single, but he was her boss, which rarely turned out well. She didn't know if he found her attractive too, but they had occasionally teased and flirted with each other. She tried to control her feelings now. He was probably just giving an innocent massage.

Suddenly, she felt warm breath on her neck. Although her eyes were closed, she knew Brian's head was beside hers. She wanted to pull away or ask him to stop, but she was powerless now. When she felt his hot lips touch the top of her neck, she shuddered from head to toe. He slowly kissed and licked down her neck, from the hairline to her shoulders. He alternated from flicks with his tongue to gently sucking her skin.

She was now fully aroused, and all rational thought and restraint disappeared. She turned her head toward him, and his mouth quickly left her neck and found her parted lips. There was no hesitation or doubt with their kisses—they were hot and forceful. Their tongues quickly intertwined as his right hand moved from her shoulder to her chest.

Kathy laid the story down and took a deep breath. While reading this story, she had felt something different more than just admiration for Ryan's writing and storytelling ability. The guilt quickly hit her as she realized she had placed herself in the story, with Ryan as the leading man. Suddenly, she wasn't sure if reading his stories was a good idea. She found herself feeling some of the same tingling as the character in the story and decided she needed a break before finding out just how much spice he had added.

She hated that Ryan couldn't find a girlfriend. He was good-looking, funny, sensitive, caring, loving, and everything a man should be. He was just a little shy. If only a woman, besides her, could meet and get to know him, Ryan would sweep her off her feet. She knew him well and had no doubt that Ryan could be the leading man in his stories. He could be just as romantic, loving, and definitely passionate. She hoped someday he would find the right woman. She only hoped that woman wouldn't hurt her best-friend status.

***

"Do you know what I really want?" Ryan asked on the phone a few days later.

"Ryan, I'm married!" Kathy exclaimed in mock surprise. It had taken a while after their forbidden kiss, but they had finally gone back to joking and inserting some innuendo into their phone conversations.

"Yeah. You wish, honey. Anyway…my biggest fantasy, or one of them, is to write a collection of romance short stories and get them published. Can you imagine seeing a hardbound book of my stories with my name on it? I wouldn't even care about the money. Just seeing it and knowing that someone might be reading them and enjoying them would be great."

"Then do it! You're a talented writer. Just write a few more stories and start sending the collection to agents or publishers." Kathy fed on his excitement.

"Really? You think I could?"

"Heck, yeah, you can! And I'll be the founding member and president of your fan club."

"Sweet!"

"OK. Now that we've settled that fantasy, what are your other ones? You said getting published was one of them," Kathy said impishly.

"Oh, I guess I really just have one more," Ryan said with some hesitation.

"Really? Does it involve whips and chains?" Kathy laughed.

"Uh, well, I guess it could someday…."

"Hmmm…so are you going to share with me?" Kathy asked, a little perplexed.

"Nope. Not now anyway. For now, you just get the publishing one."

"Well, fine then!" Kathy said, feigning anger.

***

Ryan continued writing romance short stories over the next couple of months. His writing improved as he wrote more, and he was very creative in developing different plots and characters. Kathy's guilt remained, but she couldn't stop reading them and helping him to edit and rewrite. Her feelings for him grew even stronger, even though they rarely saw each

118

other. His writing opened a window into his soul, and she saw just how sweet, sensitive, and romantic he was.

He had just finished his twelfth and final story for his collection when tragedy struck. Early one Monday morning, the hospital called Kathy. Ryan had just been admitted to the ICU with what they thought was a stroke. She was frantic as she threw on her clothes and hurried to the hospital. Her mind raced. *He's so young and healthy!* He had been complaining of headaches a lot lately and some blurry vision, but they both blamed migraines and too much time spent behind a computer. This was unbelievable.

She had to wait for several hours before she could talk to a doctor. Since he had no relatives living close by, Ryan had listed her as his emergency contact, so the doctor was allowed to speak with her. He informed her that Ryan had indeed suffered a stroke. He was in stable condition but was mostly paralyzed on the right side and could barely speak. Then the news got worse. They had discovered a mass in his brain during the MRI—a tumor. They still had to do more tests to determine what kind it was, whether it was malignant, and how serious.

Ryan's eyes were closed as she entered his room. IVs ran into his arms, and tubes came out of his nose. Several machines attached to him monitored his pulse, blood pressure, and she wasn't sure what else. He appeared pale and frail, lying in the bed. She walked to his bedside and grabbed his left hand. His eyes opened, and he turned his head to look at her. It seemed to take a moment for his eyes to focus—or for him to recognize her.

Kathy smiled her best smile and squeezed his hand. "Are you just doing this to get me to hold your hand?" She laughed, trying to control the shakiness in her voice.

He smiled weakly and nodded. She sat by his bed and talked to him for half an hour. He didn't try to speak, but he smiled a half-smile and nodded where he could. Finally, the nurse came and told her visiting hours were over. She cried as she left the hospital.

She visited him every day for the next few days, and Andy seemed to be OK with it. Ryan gradually began to speak again. It was slow and hard to understand, but she managed. He also regained some of the sensation on his right side. They just made small talk and chatted about his writing and work as they tried to avoid the obvious subject.

They were together when the doctor came and gave the biopsy results on the mass in his brain. Ryan had the most serious type of brain tumor: glioblastoma. It was too large and had spread too deeply in his

119

brain to operate. The doctor recommended radiation and chemotherapy. He didn't want to give survival odds, but Ryan pleaded until he did. He had a ten percent chance of surviving the year.

They sat in silence for quite a while after the doctor left. Kathy finally leaned over and hugged him. He hugged her back with his left arm. She sat back down and held his hand again. "I guess you see the irony?" Ryan whispered.

She nodded, quickly wiping a tear away from the corner of her eye. His final story was about a woman falling in love with a man who had terminal cancer.

"I just wish I could have gotten my book published or at least have tried."

"You still can! You can beat this!" she exclaimed.

Ryan shook his head. "I don't think so, Kathy. I did a lot of research when writing my last story. This stuff is pretty bad."

"You still can't give up. It's not one hundred percent fatal."

"I won't give up."

"Good. And I won't let you even if you try!"

***

Ryan didn't get better. The chemo and radiation took their toll on an already weak man. He lost a lot of weight and strength. Many times when she would visit, he would barely acknowledge her or wouldn't have the energy to speak. She would stay with him anyway and talk or read to him. She even read him some of his own stories. One day, she read his last story to him.

> "I don't care what the percentage is, whether it's eighty or ninety or ninety-nine! As long as it's not one hundred percent, you're still in the game. If you're still in the game, I want to be in it with you. And if we're both in the game, we can still win it!" she pleaded.

> "I just can't do it. I've got no more fight left," he replied weakly.

> "I won't let you quit! I won't let you give up. You will beat this. We will beat this!"

> "You can't stay here all the time. You have a job and a life of your own."

120

"You are my life! My job can wait. I'll take a leave of absence. I want to spend every minute with you until you're better. I want to make every minute last a lifetime. We have too much left to do, too much left to say, too much to share, and too much love to give. Will you let me stay in the game with you?" she implored.

He briefly flashed his old smile. "Until the final buzzer."

They both had tears streaming from their eyes as she finished the story. It just wasn't fair. Ryan was too young to go through this. He had too much to offer the world. Kathy was positive and optimistic with him, but inside, she feared the worst.

On the drive home, an idea hit her. There *was* something she could do for him. She went to work on the details as soon as she arrived home.

***

A month later, she sat beside Ryan's bed, waiting for him to wake. Visiting hours were almost over when he finally stirred. He smiled weakly when his eyes focused on her and squeezed her hand.

"How are you feeling?" she asked.

"Guess."

"Great?" She laughed. She tried her best to keep the same banter they'd had when he was healthy.

"You got it," he whispered hoarsely.

"I have a little present that I'm pretty sure will brighten your day," she said, letting go of his hand and producing the wrapped gift from under her chair. She handed it to him.

He looked at her, puzzled, and then slowly unwrapped the package. He could use his right hand a little now, and he used both hands to remove the paper. He held up the hardback book so he could see the cover.

"Read the title and author to me," Kathy said, now standing beside him.

"*Tales from the Heart: A Collection of Love Stories by…*" Ryan stopped reading. He stared blankly at the book cover and turned to look at Kathy.

She nodded, smiling. "By Ryan Whitehall," she finished.

"What? How?" Ryan struggled to search for the words.

"You did it, Ryan! You're a writer!"

121

Ryan looked at the book again, marveling at it. Below the title was a picture of a man and woman's hands clasped together inside a heart. Flowers and hearts decorated the book's edges as a border. He turned the book over and saw a picture of himself and a short biography. Slowly, he opened it and flipped through the pages, seeing each of his short stories inside. He finally closed the book and laid it on his chest with both hands clasped over it. When he looked at Kathy again, he cried.

Kathy had paid to have the book published, only two copies for now, but she assured him she would get it published for real, and it would be in bookstores across the country. No matter how long it took, Ryan would be a writer.

The nurse came in to tell Kathy it was past visiting hours. Kathy leaned over, hugged Ryan, and kissed his forehead. "Now, at least one of your fantasies is fulfilled." Ryan still couldn't speak. "Oh, and don't forget to read the last page."

Kathy walked toward the door as Ryan opened the book and flipped to the last page. He read the words softly, "From my heart to yours, Love, Kathy. "

Kathy turned around to wave goodbye. Ryan stared at her, tears covering his face. "No. That's both."

Kathy leaned against the wall in the hallway after the door shut and cried. She now realized what his second fantasy was. She had given him both, but neither in the way they wanted.

The Affair

He sat in his old Chevy pickup truck in the far corner of the motel parking lot. It was cold with the engine not running, but he hardly noticed. He stared intently at the front of the building, at the long line of motel doors. He glanced at the clock and shook his head. Eleven o'clock on New Year's Eve. He had been there for an hour already. This was some way to bring in the New Year. The radio played country music softly. He hated country, but somehow, tonight, it felt right. He needed to hear some cheating and drinking songs. He briefly leaned his head back on the headrest and closed his eyes.

***

He remembered the first time he'd laid eyes upon her. It was his sophomore year of college and the first day of biology class. Time stopped as she entered the classroom. It was as if a ray of light shone upon her, bathing her in a surreal golden glow. She had long blond hair, big blue eyes, and a body that could have been carved out of stone. She wore simple but deadly clothes—a pair of tight, faded blue jeans with a black T-shirt. His heart skipped a beat or two, and his breath caught in his throat. Time finally moved again, only in slow motion. She briefly surveyed the quickly filling classroom until her eyes met his. She smiled and made her way toward him. By some miracle, or twist of fate, she chose the empty seat next to his.

He slowly turned to look at the goddess beside him, hoping his mouth wasn't hanging open and that no drool escaped his lips. The intoxicating smell of her perfume met him as he gazed upon the most beautiful smile he had ever seen, with full pouty lips and flawless white teeth. He nodded and smiled back; at least it felt like a smile. Then he turned back to stare straight ahead. He dared not risk speaking; he doubted he could.

***

He quickly opened his eyes and returned to the present. He couldn't risk missing anything. His eyes scanned the parking lot—no new vehicles or signs of movement. He hoped he was wrong. Maybe he was just being stupid. But deep down inside, he feared he was right. He tried his best not to think about what would happen, how he would react, how she would respond. No matter what, the outcome would be bad. His mind wandered again, back into the past.

***

She broke the ice. She was so warm and friendly, and he soon realized that she was not an actual goddess but just a human—a perfect one, though. His heart finally started beating, and his breathing resumed, and they began to talk. Her name was Beth, and she was from Pennsylvania. By the third class, they were laughing and cutting up like old friends, frequently getting reprimanded for their youthful exuberance.

They soon started seeing each other after class. Beth was so energetic and athletic. They played tennis and racquetball, threw Frisbee, played basketball, hiked, and did anything physical. They followed that by studying together at each other's apartments and then just spending every free minute together. They had it all: great conversation, similar interests, ambition, and an incredible physical attraction.

***

Eleven fifteen. *What is she doing?* The more he thought about the situation, the more upset he became. You were supposed to be with the one you loved on New Year's Eve. Or maybe she was. He only knew that he was alone, freezing in a motel parking lot. He reached for the bottle of Jack Daniel's in the passenger seat and quickly removed the lid. "Happy freaking New Year!" he said loudly and took a large swig.

***

They both landed jobs in Raleigh, North Carolina after graduation. She found one in an advertising department for a local television station; he became a manager at a large telecommunication company. They married a year later, and things slowly began to change. They both had

124

demanding jobs requiring late days and lots of hours, and they both wanted to do well and advance in their careers. The carefree college days were over. They were still in love, but the romance was not the same. Sex was a once-or twice-a-week appointment instead of daily bouts of passion. But they still spent their free time doing things together and traveled on vacations and weekends. They made the most of the time they had and were still happy.

Their first child was born two years later, and their second arrived eighteen months after. That was when the train derailed. Real-life caught up to them: colic, ear infections, sleepless nights, diapers, and bottles. What precious free time they shared before was gone. Work and children, that was all. They had no time for romance, no time for travel, and no time for each other. Beth gained some weight with each child, and afterward, she had no time for exercise. Her loss of self-esteem also contributed to their intimacy issues. As her body changed, so did his. He quit working out and exercising. He didn't have time anyway.

***

A car turned into the parking lot, quickly transporting him back to reality. He sat up and strained his eyes to see if he recognized it. After a tense few seconds, he realized it wasn't hers. The car pulled into a space in front of the building. A man and woman exited, laughing and swaying slightly as they met in front of the motel door. The man fumbled with the key before finally swinging the door open. She pushed him in and disappeared after. There was little mystery in what was about to happen in room 107. He took another swig of Jack and slid back down in his seat.

***

They took their stress and frustration with work and parenthood out on each other. Fights became daily occurrences: yelling, screaming, and crying. Early on, they made up by the time they went to bed and even occasionally enjoyed makeup sex. However, as time passed, there were no more apologies or making up, just reloading for the next fight. They turned into mere roommates rather than lovers as the years passed. Things became a little easier as the children left the diapers and bottles behind and began sleeping in their own beds, but their relationship just couldn't recover. They started keeping score. If one didn't do something, the other wouldn't. If one wasn't romantic, why should the other be? Neither was willing to make the extra effort.

They found themselves alone quite a bit when the children reached their teenage driving years. That should have been the perfect opportunity to rekindle the romance, to start over fresh. They didn't. They each found

125

hobbies to keep them apart. He golfed and fished. She traveled a lot for work and started taking classes: Spanish, painting, pottery—always something. They even quit sleeping in the same bed. The official excuse was that he liked staying up later and didn't want to disturb her. They both could have laughed at that.

***

Eleven thirty. He shook his head to try to stay alert. The time spent sitting, aided by the whiskey, had made him a little too comfortable. He picked up his cell phone and called his house. Maybe he was wrong. The phone rang until the machine picked up. Beth was still out. He thought briefly about going home, giving up, but only for a moment. There was no chance of that. One way or the other, he would have an answer that night—or morning, if necessary.

***

He'd thought about leaving over the past year or so. Their youngest was seventeen, and the oldest was in college. He was sure Beth had too. He wasn't really sure why they had stayed together. Maybe they had just been together too long to do anything else. Starting over would be tough. So they continued, maintaining the status quo, waiting for something to change but neither willing to be the catalyst.

That was until two weeks ago—when he noticed Beth spending a lot of time on the phone. Every night or two, she was on it. Sometimes, she called someone; sometimes, someone called her. She had different explanations. He overheard a man's voice on the phone on more than one occasion. She told him that it was her boss or a client. She also said she talked to her friend Heather and her relatives. He even answered the phone occasionally, only to hear silence followed by the other person hanging up.

He didn't ask many questions. He really didn't care. He just thought it was a little peculiar. Then last week, Beth had informed him that she was going out with friends on New Year's Eve, a group of friends from work and two old college buddies, Lisa and Linda. She asked if he cared, which he didn't, but she would have gone regardless.

His suspicions hadn't really been stoked until two nights ago when he had walked into the room as she finished making a motel reservation. He angrily asked her what that was about after she hung up. She just smiled and explained that it was for Linda and Lisa, but if she drank too much or it was too late, she might stay there too. He grudgingly accepted her answer. Her phone call volume picked up in intensity that night and the next.

126

But the last straw came the next day when he found the scrap of paper by the phone that read, "Midnight, Budget Inn, Rm. 105." Why did she have a room number and a time if she had just made reservations for friends? He didn't confront her about it, though. He wasn't going to give her a chance to lie or change her plans. He would find out for himself what she was doing.

***

A couple of more cars pulled into the motel lot. Neither was hers, and neither parked in front of 105. He stared at the window and door to the room. The light had been on since his arrival, but no cars were in front of it. He rubbed his fingers through his hair and shook his head. Then he suddenly noticed the song playing on the radio. He stared at the console for a moment and then turned up the volume to clearly hear *Your Cheating Heart*. "That's perfect. Just Perfect."

It was eleven forty-five when the red BMW turned into the lot. It pulled confidently into the spot right in front of room 105. His heart raced as he struggled to breathe. He really thought his feelings for his wife had been dead and buried for years. Over the past couple of days, he wasn't sure. He just couldn't bear to think about her with another man. They had been together for over twenty years. They weren't virgins when they met, but close to it. They knew everything about each other: the good, the bad, and the ugly. They had shared all their adult lives together.

The car door opened, and Beth climbed out. He held his breath as he waited for the other door to open, but it didn't. No Lisa, no Linda—and no man. Beth closed the car door and walked up to the motel room door. She quickly opened it with a key and disappeared inside. He was dumbfounded. *What is she doing? Is someone meeting her?* Five minutes later, the light inside the window went dark, replaced with a softer, flickering one. He realized it was a candle, or candles.

He grabbed the steering wheel and squeezed so hard he thought his hands might crush it. *Why isn't she with me tonight? We could be at home with candles lit.* They used to do that—candlelight, wine, massages—but he couldn't remember the last time. Now, she was doing that with someone else. He was nauseated. Why hadn't they done it for so many years?

Another thought occurred to him as the minutes ticked away. What if he was already in there? The light had been on all night. What if she had gone out with her girlfriends and was meeting him here afterward? The note said the room number and midnight. His head was pounding now, his palms sweating profusely. He would wait a few more minutes.

His anger dissipated somewhat as he waited. He realized that he really couldn't blame Beth for what she was doing. He had driven her to it. They hadn't had sex in months, and he never showed her any affection. She really didn't him either, but he could have been the one to cave and take the first step. If she hadn't sat beside him all those years ago and spoken to him first, they would have never gotten together. Why couldn't he have been the one to throw away the scorecard and make the effort to renew their love? She might have reciprocated if he had made the effort, and they could have fanned the spark again.

He thought about that as he stared at the flickering light in the window. They hardly knew each other anymore. With only one child at home, whom they hardly ever saw, they had plenty of time to spend getting to know each other again. They were settled in their jobs and were pretty much done climbing the corporate ladders. They could travel again. They could join a gym, start working out together, play tennis and racquetball, and hike and camp. They could have sex anytime and anyplace they wanted, maybe even meet at lunch for a romantic rendezvous. *We're only forty-four years old! Why have we been acting like we're eighty?*

His excitement was short-lived. Beth was either in there with another man or waiting on one. Either way, he knew in his heart that it was over. Though he couldn't blame her, he also couldn't accept it. Even if they wanted to try to work through a situation like that, he knew they couldn't. Their relationship was too fragile for such a conflict. He wiped at the tears that sneaked into the corners of his eyes and sniffed a few times to keep his nose from running. He reluctantly exited his truck.

It was a long walk to the door. It felt like his feet were encased in concrete or like a nightmare when you try to run and can only do so in slow motion. He finally made it and paused to gather himself in front of the door. He didn't want to see what he knew was happening. How do you get over something like that? He steeled his nerves. He wasn't sure what would happen, but he had to know. He had to confront his wife— and whoever was with her.

As he started to knock, he noticed the door stood partially open. *Beth must have really been in a hurry to get into the room.* Cautiously, he pushed it open wider, inch by agonizing inch. He saw the candle on the table in front of the window, the one he'd seen flickering from outside. He stepped inside and saw two more candles, one on each nightstand. He saw no one on the king-size bed or in the room, though. He surveyed the room in disbelief that his wife would be in such a trashy motel room with another man. Then he noticed the trail of clothes: her shoes near the door, her skirt in front of the bed, and her blouse near the television. Her bra and panties lay in front of the closed bathroom door. They were in there, either in the tub or the shower.

He strode quickly across the room and up to the door. He had to end it; enough was enough. He pushed the door open. The candles on the sink and sides of the tub flickered, almost extinguishing with the sudden breeze. Beth sat in the tub, her hair up and her face in full makeup. The bubble-filled water came halfway up her breasts, revealing her ample cleavage. Even at that moment, he realized how beautiful she was. Sure, she had aged and put on a pound or two, but right then and there, she was as beautiful as she was that first day of biology class. Her skin— smooth, supple, and flawless—glistened with the water and candlelight.

His eyes quickly searched the room, and he realized she was alone. He turned back to her and noticed the glass of champagne on the edge of the tub and the bottle in front of it. His eyes finally met hers, and she flashed her beautiful smile—the same beautiful smile that had taken his breath away so many years ago. It was a reflex that he smiled back. Then he quickly returned to the moment.

"What time is he arriving?" he demanded angrily.

"Who, dear?"

"Whoever you're meeting here! Whoever all this is for!"

Beth laughed. He seldom heard that laugh anymore and only at the TV if she did. Now, it only made him angrier. How could she toy with him like this? She was caught—busted. She saw his distress and stopped laughing, but her smile remained. "Oh. Him."

"Yes, him!"

She was silent for a moment, and her smile faded. "I'm afraid he's already here."

"*What?*" he exclaimed, looking back into the main room.

"Honey, he's right in front of me."

"Huh?" he mumbled dumbly.

"Tony, this is for you…and me…us. You're my affair."

"Me? Huh?"

Her smile reappeared. "I wanted to see if you still cared for me, if you still had feelings…."

"So you set all this up?"

"Surprised?" she asked coyly.

"Very." His mind was a jumble of emotions. He desperately tried to work through the moment and the past couple of weeks and understand what had just happened. "The calls?"

"The man was my boss, Mr. Sneed. The rest were my girlfriends."

"Lisa and Linda?"

"Oh, I did party with them tonight, but they wouldn't stay in a dump like this," she said, still smiling her deadly smile. "Besides, I had to be here by midnight."

He shook his head, still stunned. "What made you try something like this?"

She paused for a moment. "Over the past few years, I really questioned my love for you. Part of me thought it might be time to move on and start over, but another part still remembered the love we used to share. I knew I owed it to you, to us, to give it one more chance. I also knew I had to do something drastic, something that would really make each of us think about our relationship. Talking wouldn't have been enough. I figured if you paid attention to all the clues and actually came here, then maybe we would have a chance."

"And if I hadn't come?"

"I don't want to think about it. So, does your coming here mean that you still have feelings for me?"

He was silent for several seconds. Then he realized that it wasn't over. He hadn't lost his chance. "Beth, I realized tonight, for the first time in a long time, that I still love you, just as much as I ever have. I know I haven't shown it in a long time, but I never stopped."

Beth stared at him, tears running from her eyes and streaking through her mascara. "I love you too!"

Tony sat on the tub's edge and leaned forward to kiss her full, wet lips. The kiss was exciting and arousing, like the ones they'd shared so many years ago, not the pecks on the lips of recent years. It was as if he were kissing her for the first time, again. Finally, he broke it off and pulled back to stare into her beautiful blue eyes. He glanced down at his watch and realized it was midnight. "Happy New Year, baby," he whispered, hoping she didn't see the tears in his own eyes.

"Happy new life," she whispered back, trails of black now streaking down her cheeks.

"You know, I kept thinking all night that I wouldn't ever keep score again if I had a chance to do it over. But I think I've changed my mind."

"You're still going to keep score?" she asked with some concern.

"Yep. You're one up on me now. So I'm going to have to get even."

Her smile returned. "Just how are you going to do that, big boy?"

It was his turn to smile, as big as he had in years. "First, I'm going to help you from the tub, dry you off, and carry you to the bed."

"Hmmm…and then?"

"A full-body candlelit massage…."

"OK. Keep going."

"Followed by kissing every inch of your voluptuous body."

"Wow! And then?"

"You'll just have to wait and see, young lady. But I promise you: the best is yet to come. I'll be the only affair you ever need."

As Good as It Gets

I wasn't one to frequent bars, especially not to flirt with men in hopes of being 'picked up.' Sure, I had partied my fair share back in college and closed down a bar or two. But who hadn't? That night, I was only there to celebrate Cindy's 20th work anniversary. I had planned to cut out as soon as politically possible. I liked my coworkers OK, but eight hours per day with them was more than sufficient. Then, the 'Happy Hour' margaritas started migrating to the table—round after delicious round. Surprisingly, as the party was winding down, I wasn't quite ready to leave.

I bade goodbye to Cindy and the last of the partiers and wound my way through the semi-crowded floor to the bar. I was done with the sweet and sour of the margaritas. And since I was Ubering home anyway, I ordered a straight Crown Royal on the rocks. That was a good one for the road. Although, I knew I would pay dearly the next morning. It had been a long time since I had even been buzzed. Now, that train had long ago left the station. Hopefully, I wouldn't get sick.

"Nice!"

It took a moment to realize the voice addressed me. I slowly swiveled my head to the left. My heart did a quick double-tap. The man beside me could have stepped out of a GQ magazine. Or maybe at least off a Cabela's' catalog cover. He had a thick head of Italian hair, slightly tussled as if his hand had run through it a time or two. His eyes were blue—not smutty romance blue, but blue enough to remember. He either had a serious 5 O'clock shadow or hadn't shaven for a couple of days. Either way, it worked.

"My old boss drank straight Crown either after a terrible day or a great day. Never just after a mediocre day. So, which is it?"

Dang, his voice was even a perfect baritone. Not Trace Adkins deep, but definitely flutter-inducing. "Started out mediocre. Winding up with a strong 'not too shabby.'" What the heck was I saying?

He laughed. "Can't ask for much more than a 'not too shabby' on a Friday night in this town, huh?"

"No. That's about all this ole' gal can handle on a Friday night," I snatched my drink from the bartender's hand and greedily sucked down some of the precious liquid. I hadn't been hit on in, well, probably since one of those crazy college nights. I had only been divorced for three months and had yet to inject myself into any potential dating situations. Stupid anniversary party!

"Darn," he said. "I was wondering what might come after 'shabby.'"

Oh. There it was. He was here to pick up women. Heck, with his looks, he could have his pick of the litter. Or probably take the whole dang litter home. Well, it was flattering that he had at least noticed me. Maybe there was hope if and when I was ready to blossom into a woman again. "Just bedtime. Alone." There. Shot him down in flames.

He laughed again. "Don't guess you can get into any trouble there, huh?"

"Nope. Safe and sound and no drama."

He tipped his beer bottle toward me and took a long draught. He sat the empty bottle down and caught the bartender's eye, giving him a slight nod. "So, party girl, we haven't even introduced ourselves. I'm Colton. You can call me Cole, though." He extended his hand.

Colton? Cole? Of course, that was his manly name. I hesitated for a moment, staring down at his hand. I finally extended mine and allowed a grin to escape. "Susan." His large hand enveloped mine in a firm shake.

"Nice to meet you, Susan. What say we get a table? It's a little noisy here at the bar."

My inner voice screamed at me to say no and summon my Uber. It was late. I was buzzed. And this guy was obviously some kind of local bar Casanova. Yet another part of me, one that had lain dormant for many years, suddenly stirred from hibernation. Tomorrow was Saturday. I could sleep late. Besides, just talking to a guy, even if he were a womanizing jerk, wouldn't hurt anyone. That was as far as it would go. "Against my better judgment, lead on."

Cole took his fresh beer from the bartender, told him we were relocating to a table in the far corner, and guided us through the throng. We were soon sitting on the backside of a high-top table, facing the bar we'd just left. A waitress quickly found us, and she made sure to keep our drinks fresh.

"OK, Cole. Let's hear it. What's your story? Is this just your nightly hangout so you can take a different girl home every night?" I was quickly approaching that blurry line between buzzed and drunk, the one where your filters and inhibitions disappear to wherever it is that alcohol banishes them.

Cole laughed and shook his head. "No. But sounds like a mighty fine plan!"

"Jerk! Oh, come on. We're adults here. There's no chance you're taking me home tonight, so you might as well be honest."

"No chance, huh?"

I noticed just a slight slur to Cole's words for the first time. Good. He was tip-toeing the line too. "Not enough Crown in the town."

"What the heck, then. Let's give that crazy honesty thing a try."

He killed his latest brown-bottle victim. Dang, but he was cute!

"Actually, this is pretty much a monthly excursion. Usually, a few of us guys hang out and toss back some brews. And no, the purpose isn't to take women home. Tonight, Stu and Dave stood me up. But being the trooper I am, I gutted it out alone."

"Oh, you poor, lonely baby! So, then you started looking for a concubine for the night?"

"Concubine? Wow! Maybe 1,000 years ago…." He chuckled at his own joke. "No. Not really. I mean, if I met someone, that'd be fine. If not, I'd enjoy several beers, some group camaraderie, and have a decent night out instead of sitting at home watching HGTV."

I gazed at him as I finished off another glass of Crown. I shook my head at the burn, which still demanded respect, although it was lessoning. That had to be the last one, or there would be trouble before the night was over. I excused myself and made the long trek to the restroom. When I returned to the table, he had just returned from his own trip.

I resumed with the inquisition. "OK. Why's a guy like you still hanging out at bars? Why not married or in a serious relationship?"

"A guy like me? Uh oh. Do you think I'm cute?"

I swear his blue eyes smoldered at me. "I've drunk enough for a bar stool to look sexy. Now, answer the question."

This time it was a grin instead of a laugh. "I guess I'm not too good at long-term relationships."

"Oh, so it's all up to you? Not the girls coming to their senses and dumping you?" I wanted to dislike him. But I wasn't sure if he was cocky or if I just wanted him to be for being so darn sexy.

"Well, I'm sure there has been some of that too."

The waitress appeared, and Cole mercifully ordered us each a water. He sighed and continued. "I tend to end things when—when they are as good as it gets."

The cold water was good, although it would take a lot, and a while, to ease my swimming head. "As good as it gets? So, after you have sex with them?" I demanded.

He laughed, but it seemed a bit rueful. "No. Well, I guess it's happened. But I evaluate all relationships and the people I date. I think inevitably, relationships peak. And everything after that peak is downhill, or at best mundane and boring. So, I guess I'm just not ready for the downhill slide or mundane yet."

I shook my head. He sounded increasingly like a jerk. Honest. But a jerk. "Hmmm, I think that defines a relationship. So, you expect it to be great and awesome and exciting all the time?"

Cole rubbed his eyes and took a swig of water. "Something like that."

"Then, you, sir, are an idiot."

"Probably."

Most of me was ready to leave. I wasn't too enamored with my new friend, and the buzz was degrading into fatigue. But a small part of me, the moth-to-a-flame part, wasn't quite ready for the check. "What were your longest and shortest relationships?"

His eyes looked tired too, but still with some remnant smoldering. "I guess the longest was around a year. The shortest? Two days."

"When and why did the first one end?"

"Wow! This conversation quickly turned into an interrogation."

"Yes. And answer the question, or I will waterboard you." I couldn't stop my lips from curling into a grin.

"I'm thinking that might be more humane than the questions…. Let's see. I think that was after spending a perfect day at the beach, including a sunset picnic, and followed by some, uh, cuddling on a blanket in the moonlight."

I could swear his cheeks reddened in the dim light. "Cuddling, huh?"

"Uh, yeah. Maybe a kiss or two…."

"So, that was as good as it was going to get?"

He dropped his eyes to the water glass. Could he be ashamed?

"Probably as good as any relationship could get. But yeah. I knew we were at the point where we either needed to go further or part ways. As great as the girl was, and that day was, I didn't think she was the one."

I shook my head and finished my water. I picked my phone up off the table and scheduled my Uber pickup. "And the shortest?"

"First kiss."

"That's not so unusual. I've had several girlfriends that ended it with guys when they learned they couldn't kiss. You can teach men many things, but it's near impossible to turn a tooth banger or slobberer into a good kisser."

"Actually, it was the most sensual, passionate first kiss I've ever had. It's pretty much the bar for any first kiss now, and few can reach it."

"And you broke up because it was too good?"

"Yeah. She seemed like a nice girl, but I knew that one kiss was going to be the peak of anything I could reach with her."

I glanced at my phone and saw that my ride was one minute away. I stood and grabbed my purse. "Cole, my dear friend, you have broken my brain. But despite my Crown's, this has been a memorable night." He stood, and we shook hands.

"Wait, will I ever see you again?" he called out after me.

"This wasn't as good as it can get?" I asked over my shoulder.

"Not by a long shot."

"We'll see."

***

Saturday morning dawned painfully. What had I been thinking last night? I hadn't drunk that much in ten years. I hadn't been slammed drunk, but the after-effects apparently worsen drastically as you age. I shuffled numbly through the house with squinted eyes⎯a zombie in search of brains. Or, in this case, an idiot woman in search of coffee.

My Saturday to-do list was left undone. I drank coffee, and napped, and drank coffee. Surprisingly, my memory of the previous night was reasonably intact. I was recalling my conversation with Cole when Cindy called. Of course, I had to fill her in on my evening after she had left.

"So, I'm assuming you gave him your number?" she asked.

Dang! "So, one would think."

"What? Are you serious? No digits?" Cindy demanded.

137

"Hey, by that time, my head was spinning. Besides, I'm not sure if I want to see him again. I mean, really. As good as it gets? So, when would he dump me? First kiss? Second base? Our first sleepover?" The more I recalled my conversation with Cole, the more upset I became. "That's just stupid. He's just an immature guy that doesn't want to settle down or be in a committed relationship. I don't need that added pressure to my first time dating in a hundred years."

"But you said he was hot."

"Well, I didn't say I wouldn't do him." We both cackled.

***

Sunday dawned a little more productive. The ill-effects of Friday night were gone. I was well-rested, and my chore list beckoned. I finished my coffee and dove into cleaning and organizing with gusto. Around noon, while I was mopping and jamming to Lizzo, my phone ringing suddenly interrupted the song.

Without even taking my phone out of my back pocket, I squeezed the button on my headphone cord. "Hey, Cindy."

There was a pause before she-he answered.

"I know you drank a lot, but it's pronounced C-o-l-e, not Cindy."

I snatched the phone from my pocket and fell onto the couch, the mop handle clanging and bouncing off the floor. Cole? "Cole?"

"That would be me. Surprised?"

I could see his smug grin through the phone. Smug, sexy grin. "How in the heck did you get my number? I know I was feeling pretty good, but I'm fairly certain I didn't give it to you."

"Or did you, and you drowned those poor memory cells in whiskey?"

Dang it! Had I given my number to him at some point, maybe before switching over to water? Or did he get into my phone when I went to the Ladies' room? That was it; I was never drinking again! "I have my doubts about that. But be that as it may, what do I owe the pleasure?"

"It's a lovely Spring Day. We had a reasonably good conversation Friday night, and I'm bored. Let's go hiking."

"Reasonably good?"

"OK. Very intellectually stimulating. Better?"

"Well, I assume it wasn't the best conversation you ever had, or you wouldn't want to see me again." Ooh! That was a zinger.

"Ouch! A little mean and very much uncalled for. I might not have explained myself too well Friday night. Maybe the Bud's were doing some ventriloquism."

"Oh, I believe you were pretty clear."

"Give me another chance. Let's go on a short hike in the beautiful sunshine. If you still hate me, I won't call you again."

Crap! I had been looking forward to a full day of making up for slacking all day Saturday. But some fresh air and exercise would probably do me good. And I really didn't care whether Cole liked me or called me again because I knew this was a relationship that couldn't happen. Or at least not more than friendship. "Where and when?"

***

Thankfully, he stopped at the top of the first peak. I tried to hide the fact that I was sucking wind badly. To look at me, you would think I was in decent shape. To be inside my body, you'd be on the verge of death. Of course, Cole seemed unphased by the hike.

"Nice view, huh?"

I had been enjoying the lovely view of his tanned calves and khaki-covered backside for the past half hour. But the view he was pointing to was good too. We were on the top of one of many peaks in the mountain range the trail weaved its way over. There were no pine trees on this side of the path, with the steep drop, so we had an unobstructed view of the surrounding pine-covered mountains. But the sparkling blue lake in the foreground was what drew our attention. It looked almost too perfect—fake. Or maybe like a life-sized postcard. "Wow," is all I managed without revealing my shortness of breath.

"This is one of my favorite hikes and runs. It gets a little toasty in the summer months, but man, these views don't get old."

"So, you're a runner too?"

"And mountain biker. I like to stay in shape."

At least his mirrored sunglasses hid his blasted blue eyes. "So you can drink more at the bar every weekend?" I was finally regaining my wind.

He laughed. "Not every weekend, thank you very much. But it does ease some of the guilt of ingesting a few brews."

"And how many ladies have been on this trail with you? Or how many times was this trail as good as it got for them?" I regretted saying that halfway through.

"Wow, you don't cut any slack, do you?" He was still smiling, though. "No last dates on this trail."

He certainly had restraint and had obviously resisted the urge to slam me several times. Why in the heck had he invited me in the first place? It's not like I had given him any positive vibes on Friday night. At least I didn't think I had. Stupid Crown! "It is an awesome view. Like a postcard." There, I threw him a bone.

"Not too much further to the top. Then I've got a surprise for you."

"An oxygen tent?"

Despite a slight breeze and barely being Spring, the trail was hot and dusty. Soon, I was done checking out Cole from behind and just stared down at my feet as they plodded one step at a time. I didn't even care if stud-boy heard me gasping for air at this point. I'm not sure what his definition of 'not too much further' was, but it was a whole lot further than mine.

We finally stopped at the apparent top of the mountain, or at least as close as the trail wound. A small grassy clearing stretched between the trail and the precipice. The path continued around a bend and presumably wound its way down the other side of the mountain and up to the next peak. Cole strolled over to the middle of the clearing and then turned around to flash his Cole-grin. The mountain vista was even more stunning up here, as well as the unobstructed view of the lake far below.

I stumbled my way over to him on aching feet. My tennis shoes were OK for standard walks but not designed for mountain climbing. He had dropped his backpack to the ground and was rummaging through it. He quickly extended a canteen toward me, which I gladly snatched and drained a giant swig of the semi-cold water.

He continued rummaging, tossing various items from the bag. I watched in amazement as a picnic quickly materialized. Dang, he had used every square inch of that pack! He spread a small blanket on the ground and stacked miscellaneous food substances on it. Then he produced a bottle of wine and two plastic glasses.

"Sit down and take a load off," he piped cheerfully.

I shook my head and stepped forward, bearing a stupid grin I desperately wished I could hide. I sat down on one side of the blanket and he on the other. "I'm impressed, Mr. Cole."

"Wow! OK, that might be as good as it gets."

My grin quickly fled, replaced by a soul-piercing scowl.

"Just kidding! Now, let me tell you about the menu. This three-course meal features your choice of a Fuji apple or bag of seedless grapes, followed by a chicken or vegetable wrap. It concludes with a homemade brownie with walnuts. The feast, of course, is paired with a vintage bottle of white wine." He held each item up to show them to me as he rattled through the menu.

I shook my head again and smiled. "You're an idiot."

"Also known as a romantic?"

"Nope, just an idiot. I'll let you pick for me. Let's see how well you know me."

"Well, other than your thirst for Crown and tearing me down, not that well."

He laughed, and I couldn't stifle my own. I'm not sure if it was the relief at completing the uphill portion of the hike or if the scenery and picnic were working, but I was starting to feel very relaxed. And—and happy. Dang it!

"OK. No complaining, though. I will start you off with the grapes for your appetizer."

"Hmmm. Good choice. Why did you pick those over the apple?"

"Well, despite your obvious disdain for me, this is technically a first date. With you being a girl and all, I think you would see the apple as too potentially messy eating in front of a guy you barely know. Plus, your hands could end up being sticky, and you might not trust that I thought to bring napkins or wipes. Which I did, by the way."

I stared at him in disbelief. Although none of those thoughts had consciously entered my mind, I would have chosen the grapes for those exact reasons. "OK, smarty-pants, which one do you choose for my entrée?"

"I don't think you're a vegetarian. But, although you're not, I think you are health conscious. Chicken isn't unhealthy, but a vegetarian is healthier. Plus, there is no choice in having the brownie for dessert. So, you would pick the least calories and least filling since you'll have to eat the brownie regardless." He handed the veggie wrap to me.

Once again, he was spot on, even though I would have chosen the veggie wrap without any conscious thought of the reasons. "Have I told you lately I hate your smug self?"

"But with a little less gusto than at the bottom of the trail?" His grin displayed his perfect white teeth.

"Maybe just a little."

I didn't realize how much of an appetite I had worked up on our hike. Now, I was kind of regretting not choosing, or having chosen for me, the chicken wrap. We talked, laughed, and enjoyed the incredible view. And the wine. Maybe I was just a prisoner of the moment, but that had to be the best white wine I had ever drunk, just the perfect amount of sweetness.

He packed up our trash, other than our wine glasses, and slid over to sit beside me, so we were both facing the lake. I involuntarily shivered. The heat of the day was quickly dissipating, and the sun was hanging low in the sky. Cole took that as an invitation to place his arm around me. Suddenly, I felt like a sixteen-year-old girl at her first drive-in movie.

I cautiously turned my head toward him, only to meet his smoldering gaze. Stupid smoldering gaze! I couldn't stop my eyes from dropping to his lips. They were just the perfect thickness. I quickly looked back up at his eyes. Part of me screamed for him to kiss me. God, it had been so long! Then the rational part reeled me back in. He was the guy that had left a girl after their first kiss. This relationship couldn't have a future. What would be remarkable enough about me to be the one that was finally good enough for him?

Cole's grin faded. Either my facial expression had changed, or he could read my mind. He turned back to face straight ahead. He left his arm behind me, though. "Let me clarify something from the other night."

He paused, but I didn't speak. I, too, stared straight ahead.

"When I said I tend to end relationships when they were as good as they get, that's not exactly the way I meant to say it. I mean—I mean, I would never end a relationship if I were with the person I thought I was meant to be with, the girl I had fallen madly in love with. Deep down, I know when a person isn't the one. And that usually hits me in a moment when I realize that we have peaked. So, if it has to end, I'd rather end it on a good moment, a high, a memory that even the other person will someday relish. I don't want the relationship to inevitably degrade to the point where it's misery for both of us and ends with an angry, painful breakup. But I don't purposely seek out a great moment to end on, like with a kiss or sex. I just know when the time comes. Did that sound any better?"

I was silent for a moment. Part of me understood. Part of me thought he still sounded like an egotistical jerk. "Maybe slightly. Still pretty sketch, though."

"Think about it a little in your free time. I'm betting many people are doing the same thing. There might be better ways to describe it, or my timing might be different, but it's not as bad as it sounds."

I stood up and handed my empty glass to Cole. I wasn't going to kiss him or let him kiss me—at least not tonight. "I will think more on it. But we'd better head back down the mountain before we get lost in the dark."

***

It wasn't my choice whether I thought about Cole and his insane dating theory over the next couple of days. I could scarcely think of anything else. Cindy and I spent way too much time discussing and debating Cole at work. I swung from one side of the debate to the other,

142

ranging from him being an egotistical a-hole to him just being more honest and self-aware than most people. Cindy did well debating both sides too.

When Cole called Wednesday after work, my jury was still desperately deadlocked. "What?" I demanded, mostly playing.

"There's my cheerful girl," Cole's bubbly voice replied. "Bowling. 8:00. Be there."

"Wow! Demanding, aren't we? Bowling? Really? Did we just travel back to 1988?"

Cole laughed heartily. "I wish! Come on. It'll be fun."

I admit I didn't hate the idea. Bowling was always a solid, low-pressure date. So, two hours later, we were laughing and carrying on and throwing heavy balls at distant pins.

"Somehow, I thought you would be better at this. Like inviting me here to show off your mad skills."

After leaving five pins on his second roll, Cole walked back to his seat. "Yeah, I didn't think this one through too well. Or maybe I'm just tanking it to win some sympathy."

"Pity maybe, not sympathy." I grabbed my ball and made my approach to the lane. Then I suddenly turned around, catching him with his eyes staring straight ahead where my butt had been a second before. "Or did you bring me here just to check me out?" He definitely blushed this time.

"Guilty as charged."

I turned back around, smiling ear-to-ear, and threw the ball down the lane. The ball was just slightly off target but still took down eight pins. I walked back to the ball return, probably swinging my hips a little more than was necessary. "You should be focusing on my technique, which is kicking your butt."

We bowled three games, drank several beers, and shared a monstrous plate of cheese fries. I must admit that I didn't hate watching Cole's butt turn his Wranglers every which way but loose. We didn't talk about his dating theories or anything serious for that matter. It was just an honest to goodness second date.

We talked for another half hour at my car, me leaning back against it and he standing in front of me. There was no hiding our glances to the other's lips. We both knew we wanted to kiss, but neither was sure if this was the proper time and place. If it hadn't been for all the 'good as it gets' talk, I wouldn't have hesitated to initiate it. But that thought was permanently implanted deep in my brain, regardless of how much laughter and fun we had or how attractive he was.

He was absolutely the best-looking, sexiest man who had ever shown an interest in me. Once again, I was torn. Part of me wanted to kiss him now and just see where the relationship went. If he broke up with me at some point, I would be no worse for the wear. The other part wanted to remain friends and never put my heart out there to be inevitably chopped in two.

"Well, I appreciate you asking me to bowl with you and kick your butt. It didn't suck nearly as bad as I thought it would."

"You are a poet, my dear," Cole grinned.

I flashed him a smile to make sure he knew I was joking and climbed into my car. The kiss would have to wait.

***

Friday night, the battle within was finally won, or lost. We stood on my front porch after a night at the movies, followed by a few drinks at the bar where we had first met. I think it was the alcohol that finally tilted the scales of fate. Not Crown, but one too many Pina Coladas. When Cole finally leaned in for a kiss, I eagerly met him.

It didn't start as one of those heavy panting, moaning and groaning, tongue wrestling movie kisses. It started tentatively. Cole wasn't sure if I was ready, and part of me still had its doubts. Our lips furtively brushed together. His were as soft and warm as I'd imagined. His muscular arms wrapped around me as my hands moved behind his head to intertwine in his thick hair.

Then came the heavy panting, moaning and groaning, and tongue wrestling. My body tingled from head to toe, and I would have sworn every hair on my body was standing at attention. My knees were weak, but his strong arms held me tightly against him. His body was firm and warm against mine. His lips finally pulled away from my lips, and he moved his head so he could kiss and gently suck on my neck and ear lobes. His hands worked their way to my lower back, with promises of moving lower still.

I couldn't stifle a moan or two as my body experienced sensations it had never experienced before, even in the honeymoon phase of my marriage. Cole finally quit nibbling on an earlobe and pulled back to stare into my eyes. His eyes were glistening diamonds in the faint porch light. "Do you want to invite me in?"

Yes! Yes! Yes! Oh, man, did I want to invite him inside. But finally, that inner voice of caution sobered and spoke up. Although I knew we would end up taking it to the next level, and sooner than later, tonight was not the night. I needed to ensure that I was mentally and emotionally prepared for what came next. Plus, I had to make sure that he would call me again after that night. Maybe this was as good as it would get for him, and he just wanted to seal the deal before breaking it off with me. I could wait.

"Not tonight," I whispered hoarsely. "It's been a long time. I don't want to rush too fast."

Cole was slowly getting his breathing under control. He finally nodded and gave me a lingering good night kiss. Then he said he'd call me in the morning.

***

He did call the following day, bright and early. We spent the day hiking, this time on a trail that circled the beautiful lake we had picnicked above Sunday. We once again picnicked, this time right on the lake bank. Dessert was a hot and heavy make-out session. It was almost dark when we made our way back to his vehicle. He offered to take me back to his place, which I had yet to see, and I agreed after only the slightest hesitation.

He lived in a tidy one-bedroom apartment in town. It was very remarkable for a single guy. He even had some artwork hanging on the walls. "So, did you clean it up for me, or are you always this neat?"

"Heck, I didn't know these floors were hardwood until this morning's scrubbing."

We both laughed. Cole poured us a glass of wine, and we sat on his leather couch. He left the sixty-inch TV off as we sipped wine in the near-dark living room. After finishing the wine, we resumed kissing where we had left off at the lake. There was no tentativeness this time. It was rough, hungry kissing, accompanied by hands exploring bodies through our hiking clothes. Eventually, we had to separate long enough to gasp for air. I'm sure my cheeks were glowing in the gloom.

He abruptly stood and turned to face me, holding both hands out. I extended my arms and grabbed his hands, and he gently pulled me up to stand in front of him. Then suddenly, he scooped me up into his arms like a ragdoll. He was deceptively strong. He leaned over, kissed me briefly, and then walked out of the room and into his bedroom. I didn't protest as he gently lay me down on the bed.

We undressed each other. The lights were off, but the glow from the kitchen provided dim illumination. I was a little self-conscious. I wasn't in terrible shape, but I also didn't work out or exercise regularly. I was working on my mom-bod even before children were anywhere on the horizon. We had also spent the day hiking. Then I saw his upper body— good lord, he was chiseled out of stone! And his lips and hands quickly erased my insecurities.

The feel of his naked body against mine was indescribable. I would have been satisfied just lying beside him all night, our hearts beating together. But that wasn't an option. Soft touches and gentle caresses quickly led to passionate kissing and rough groping. A thin layer of sweat soon covered our bodies, which only aided them slipping and sliding together. He did things to me that I had never even imagined and touched and kissed me in ways I had never experienced.

I wondered at times if he was really eighteen, posing as a much more mature man. We made love countless times until the wee hours of the morning. I'm not sure if you can get too much of a good thing, but my body had to be very close. He was asleep in minutes, but he had earned some rest.

I lay in the dim light listening to Cole breathe deeply. I absently rubbed his back with my right hand, tracing the contours of the muscles. I fought sleep for a half-hour or so until I was sure he was deep asleep. I then gently removed my hand and inched my body toward the edge of the bed. He didn't stir, even when I sat up and then stood. I stared down at his sleeping form for a moment. I sighed softly.

Then I turned around and dressed. I opened the Uber app on my phone and arranged my pickup. It would be a long wait in the cool air at this time of the night, but that couldn't be helped. I then glided quietly through his dimly lit apartment. I gently opened and shut the door and headed out into the darkness, warm tears streaming down my cheeks. That night was definitely as good as it gets.

Ugly

Beauty is in the eye of the beholder. I'd heard that saying all my life, but I had never really thought about it or cared to understand it. After all, I was an expert on dating hot girls, and no one disputed their beauty. Then I met Emily when I was seventeen. That summer and through my senior year in high school, I learned plenty about true beauty and the eye of the beholder.

***

The rumbling grew steadily louder until I knew it was beside our house. Then it died down somewhat, and an annoying beeping joined it. After a moment, there was silence. I peered out my bedroom window to confirm that a moving truck had parked in the neighbor's drive and watched a car pull in behind it. We had heard that someone had finally bought the Robinson's house. Now it was time to check out the new neighbors.

"Josh!" my dad's voice rang out. I realized that meeting them was going to involve a lot of physical labor. I quickly headed downstairs and joined my parents as they walked out the front door. Our neighborhood was a very social, close-knit one. Neighbors always helped neighbors move in and out. Everyone was friends, whether they liked it or not. My parents relished the role of the welcoming committee and forced me to tag along each time. My only hope was that someday, a hot chick would move in next door. Today would be perfect timing since I'd just broken up with Angie two weeks prior.

I quickly evaluated my new neighbors as we made the short walk to their driveway. The parents appeared around the same age as mine, early fifties, and were probably middle-class professionals. Their son, tall and dark-haired with an athletic build, was about two years older than I. The daughter, whom I was, of course, most interested in evaluating, finally appeared from the car behind the moving van. I was instantly disappointed. She was ugly, or at least somewhere between nondescript and homely. She wore a pair of baggy navy-blue shorts and a powder-blue T-shirt. She had red hair, brown eyes, and very pale, almost pasty, white skin. She wasn't fat but carried a few extra pounds on her posterior and legs. Oh, well. Maybe the next girl to move in would have more promise.

My parents led the introductions as we all smiled and shook hands. They were the Clausons, and the girl was Emily, and her brother, Craig. After exchanging quick pleasantries, we started the strenuous process of unloading the moving van. Emily was surprisingly strong and carried her fair share. I did more than my fair share in an unspoken contest with Craig. There's an unwritten rule that teenage boys have to compete in everything, like young male lions in the pride. Although we both knew he was stronger, we still played the game.

"Oh boy, my stuff!" Emily happily exclaimed as I picked up a white dresser.

"I'm really glad Craig didn't say it was his," I joked, straining under its deceiving weight.

She laughed a surprisingly sweet laugh. "That's not to say we don't both wear panties."

"Shut up, brat!" Craig grunted as he walked past us.

She laughed again. "He loves me! Follow me," she ordered as she picked up a floor-length mirror and headed out of the truck. We walked through the front door, up the stairs, and into the first room on the left. By this time, I was really straining to keep from dropping the dresser as my legs quivered and my arms burned. I knew veins were bulging on my forehead, and my face was red. I shook my head to keep the sweat from running into my eyes.

"Where?" I managed to whisper.

"My, that looks heavy!" She smiled cruelly. "Um…let's see…maybe…."

"Hurry up, please!" I grunted between tightly clenched teeth.

"Geez! OK. I guess under the window."

I stumbled over to the window and let the dresser fall to the floor. I worked it side to side until it sat against the wall, perfectly centered. Then I collapsed onto my knees with my arms folded across the top of the dresser. I laid my head on my sweaty forearms.

"Hmmm…you know…I'm thinking it would look better over there."

I slowly raised my head and swiveled it to glare at her, my face clearly conveying my feelings.

She cackled. "Got ya!"

"You know, I don't know you very well, but I think I'd like to smack you right now."

"Big words for someone who just got his butt kicked by a little white girly dresser!" She grinned and quickly disappeared out of the room. I couldn't help but smile—the girl had personality.

The truck was empty two hours later. My parents were busy helping to set up the kitchen and living room downstairs, and Craig was taking care of his room. That kind of left me in an awkward situation. Emily noticed and quickly remedied it.

"Come on, muscles. You can help me."

"Oh, goodie. Can we play house too?" Although I was joking, I did kind of feel like a six-year-old boy playing with a girl for the first time.

"Sure! And then, doctor, as soon as it gets dark outside!" She brushed past me, hitting me intentionally with her shoulder while giving me a quick wink. I could definitely tell she had grown up with an older brother. She was very much a rough-and-tumble tomboy.

We set up her bed and arranged her furniture how she wanted it, and I finally sat down on her bed as she hung her clothes in the closet. An amazing transformation had taken place over the past few hours. Even though she was dirty and sweaty, she somehow looked a lot better than when I first saw her. She had a beautiful smile, and her laughter made her face light up. Her physical appearance certainly didn't hurt her confidence. She carried herself with the air of a beauty pageant contestant. Her personality was irresistible.

When she finished, she turned and walked over to stand in front of me. "OK. Me on top?"

"Huh?" I couldn't believe she'd just asked that.

She laughed and dove onto the bed beside me and then rolled over, supporting herself on her elbows. "Thanks for all your help today, meathead."

"No problem, peppermint."

She stared at me for a moment, her smile quickly disappearing. "Peppermint Patty?" she asked quietly.

"I…I was just joking." *Oh crap!*

Her bottom lip started quivering, and she turned away. "All my life, people have called me that. Do you know how much teasing I've endured? Do you know how much counseling I've been through?"

"I'm sorry!" I stammered. "I didn't mean anything by it. You know, you've been calling me names."

"That's why we moved here! I had to quit my last school." She rolled over, buried her head into the mattress, and sobbed.

I was mortified. What was I supposed to do? I finally put my hand on her back. "I'm so sorry. I didn't know. I think you're great."

"Really?" she asked as she spun around, tossed her hair to the side, and looked at me. Her eyes were dry, with no evidence of crying.

"Uh…yeah, sure," I stammered.

"God, you're easy!"

"You just made all that up?"

"Yeppers."

I shook my head. I had never met anyone like her. "That's good, because if you had been to therapy, you definitely didn't get your money's worth."

Her lip started to tremble again. Without thinking, I smacked her on the leg. "Don't even go there!"

She laughed. "Now you're catching on, aren't you?" she asked in baby talk. I finally laughed too.

"Josh!" my dad yelled from downstairs.

"Yeah?" I called back.

"Why don't you and Emily go get us some pizza?"

"Sure," I said, getting up from the bed. "Come on, spaz. Let's go."

"Oh boy, our first date! Are you going to kiss me? Huh? Huh?"

We walked to my house and climbed into my Ford Tempo. As I started the car, I sensed her staring at me. I slowly turned to face her. "Go ahead. Let's get it over with."

"No, this is a really sweet ride! But you aren't going to get all fast and furious with me in here, are you?"

"Feel better?"

"But of course." She laughed.

***

I spent all my free time with Emily over the next couple of weeks. She was addictive, and I couldn't really figure out why. We just hit it off so well. I would never have even spoken to her if I'd seen her at school. I only befriended good-looking girls, with the goal of being more than friends. Average or ugly girls weren't worth the time. Emily, however, was amazing. I never got along so well with any of the pretty girls I had dated. None could match her intelligence and wit. She was also more than just funny. We would lie on her bed or mine and talk for hours. We shared our life stories. I told her about my love life and current lack of it, and she told me about hers. She'd had many guy friends but never really dated anyone, other than going to a few dances and going out with groups of people. I knew why and realized what a shame it was.

One night, we lay on my bed talking about our dreams and ambitions. My parents were out at one of my dad's company dinners. They trusted us being alone, I guess because of our brother-sister-type relationship. She was a straight-A student and planned on becoming a doctor. Although I'd only known her for a couple of weeks, I had no doubt she would succeed. I told her I planned to take my A/B average and go into finance, probably as a stockbroker or investment banker.

"It's good for him to have dreams," she said with her baby-talk voice as she patted my head.

Suddenly, without thought, I rolled over on top of her, straddled her legs, and pinned both her arms down. "What are you going to do now?" I asked, my face mere inches from hers.

We had wrestled before. It was actually becoming fairly common. We did act a lot like brother and sister, but something felt very different about this moment. Time seemed to stop, or at least slow to a crawl, as I stared into her big brown eyes. They were pretty, in their own way. My eyes traveled down her face. Her skin was pale but very smooth and soft. Finally, my gaze fell upon her lips. I'd never really noticed how full they were, the top one slightly larger than the bottom. For some reason, she licked them just at that moment. They glistened with the moisture, shining in the dim light of my room. I felt stirrings within my body that I never thought I would experience with Emily. I wondered what thoughts were going through her mind.

"Come closer, and I'll tell you," she whispered.

There was no smile or bravado, but she had fooled me before. I didn't know what to expect as I leaned my face to within an inch of hers.

"A little closer," she whispered again.

My feelings were all over the place—fear, apprehension, and lust being the main three. I leaned closer, waiting for her to blow air into my mouth, bite me, or do some other trick. There were no tricks. My lips lightly brushed against hers as I hesitantly kissed her, and she kissed back. Kissing her was different from kissing all the other girls. There was something special about kissing Emily. It was more than how full and moist her lips were, more than how natural and right it felt. There was just so much feeling and emotion, way beyond lust. Everything faded away as our souls merged into one.

I shifted my legs so that one of hers was between mine, reached down, and rubbed the thigh of her other leg. Her leg didn't feel like it appeared when I first met her. Her skin was soft and smooth, and her leg felt shapely and feminine. I worked my hand underneath the leg of her shorts and slowly up toward her hip. We both started to pant as our kisses became more forceful and passionate.

Suddenly, we heard the slam of the downstairs door, and everything came to a crashing halt. I rolled off her, and we quickly tried to compose ourselves. I ran over to sit at my desk, and she sat up against the headboard and grabbed a magazine. A minute later, my parents came in to see how we were doing. I hoped they didn't notice our hearts trying to beat out of our chests and the flush on our cheeks.

"That was, uh...interesting," Emily said in a rare moment of nervousness after they left.

"Yeah. They saved you from a butt whoopin'," I joked.

She smiled. "Bring it, anytime."

I took that a couple of ways.

I worried about how things would be after that moment but was quickly reassured that our friendship hadn't changed. We spent almost every minute of the last week of our summer break together, having fun no matter what we did. We laughed and carried on and talked and talked. We kissed some more when the opportunity presented itself and even engaged in some heavy petting, but we never went further. I suppose we could have found a way, but neither of us was rushing anything. After that night in my room, though, I looked at her in a totally different way. She was beautiful and sexy. It had just taken me a while to realize it.

***

Things changed very quickly after school started. I gave Emily a ride the first day and helped her find her way around school. It seemed like a moment in one of those teenage movies, when the music stops, and everyone stares at the main characters. I hoped it was my imagination, but I doubted it was, at least not with the people who knew me well. Emily didn't say whether she thought the attention was strange or not. She was happy and excited to be in a new school. I tried to be happy too.

Our lockers were on different floors, and we didn't have any classes together, so we soon had to part ways. I was at my locker when Matt, Todd, and Bo came up behind me.

"What's up, dude?" Matt asked.

"Not much. You guys have a good summer?"

"Apparently, better than you," Todd replied to some snickers from the other two.

"What's that supposed to mean?" I asked, turning to face the three.

"Dude, what's up with the girl? I mean, I know you broke up with Angie and everything, but…."

"But what?" I quickly became agitated.

"Tell us she's just a friend, man, and one you can ditch now that school's back in," Bo chimed in.

I was upset but not sure how to respond. "Emily is a very good friend."

"Well, now you're back in the real world. You can't be seen with someone like that, man. You know that, don't you? We'll just write it off as being charitable to a new student. Oh, and guess what," Matt said.

"What?" I replied with some reservation.

"Tina broke up with Colt."

Tina Lockhart was the best-looking girl in high school, the one everyone wanted to date. I never had. We had talked about it off and on, but each time one of us was available, the other wasn't. She had been going steady with Colt for the past two years. "Really?"

"Two weeks ago. I hear it was pretty nasty too. Rebound time, bro!"

We all slapped hands and separated to go to our first classes. My mind was reeling. I felt terrible about what they'd implied with Emily, but how *could* I be seen with her and still be part of the "in-crowd"? Then there was Tina. I had pretty much dated every girl I wanted to date. She was the last one on my "list." She was so gorgeous, absolutely perfect. I had been with good-looking girls, but she was in a different league.

I stumbled into first period and sat in a desk by the windows. As I sifted through my thoughts, a voice snapped me back to reality. I looked up to see an angel, or Tina Lockhart, smiling down at me—five feet eleven inches tall, with long blond hair, glowing blue eyes, and curves in all the right places. She sat in the desk in front of me and turned around to face me.

"So, what have you been up to this summer?" She wore a white button-up shirt buttoned about one button too low, exposing her ample cleavage. Her perfume enchanted me as soon as she sat down.

153

"Oh, not a whole lot. How was your summer?"

"It was OK until two weeks ago. Colt and I broke up."

"I'm sorry," I said, mustering what fake sympathy I could.

"Don't be. He's a jerk. It's about time for a change anyway. Speaking of that, I heard you have a new friend."

My heart jumped into my throat. It's amazing how fast news travels around a high school. "Uh, yeah, I guess. It's my neighbor, Emily. She's new to school."

"Oh. Are you guys, like, together?" She stared intently into my eyes.

It was the moment of truth. The answer to that question could permanently change the course of my life. I knew what the correct answer was—but crumbled beneath the gaze of those beautiful eyes. "No. We're just friends. I was showing her around school."

"That's cool. Hey, I've heard rumors about a big back-to-school party at old Thompson Field. I was wondering if you'd like to go with me." She seemed genuinely excited about the prospect.

I had one last chance to change course. Once again, I failed. "Sure. Sounds great!"

***

It was a strange week. During the day, I hung out with my friends and talked to Tina as much as possible. Somehow, I looked past the fact that our conversations lacked depth. She talked about cheerleading, parties, fashion, girls, boys, the in-crowd, the out-crowd, and all the other high school drama. I went along with the conversation and chimed in as best I could. I tried to insert some humor, like with Emily, but it was lost on her. But she was gorgeous, and I couldn't stop thinking about Friday night.

I still hung out with Emily in the evenings. She talked about school too but not too much. She was adjusting well and had made some friends. I knew most of them, but they weren't in my social circle. She knew something was wrong with me, but I played it off as being tired. I also had to make excuses for why I didn't have time to talk to her at school. She accepted my answers and was her same bubbly self. She kept me smiling and laughing no matter how stressed I was. Even so, I started looking at her a little differently. I found myself comparing her to Tina, and she couldn't hold up to that comparison. I was forgetting everything I had learned and allowed myself to feel over the past few weeks. I knew it was wrong, but I felt powerless to stop it from happening.

I told Emily that Friday afternoon that I was going to hang out with some guy friends later. She simply smiled, told me to have a good time, and said that maybe we could hang out on Saturday. I felt bad for a moment, and then my thoughts turned to beautiful Tina and the anticipation of what the alcohol-filled night might bring.

The party was as wild and crazy as advertised: loud and crowded with plenty of alcohol for everyone. Tina and I both drank a lot and quickly became very touchy-feely. Sitting on a railroad tie next to the bonfire, we began making out in front of everyone. It didn't take long for us to slip away into the darkness of the small patch of woods near the field. Within moments, we were having sex. It wasn't great, but it was exciting, naughty, and satisfying for two seventeen-year-old kids.

***

The next day, I knew what I had to do. I had to end my relationship with Emily. I dreaded it so badly. I didn't want to hurt her. My hope was that we could still be friends. After all, that was mainly what we were. We sat on her bed that afternoon, engaged in our usual banter. I knew I had to say my piece before the darkness brought more than just talk.

"Emily, I need to talk to you," I said nervously.

"And that would be different from what we're doing how?"

"Shutty!" I joked. Then my smile quickly melted away. "I really like you. We get along great and are really good friends."

"Not liking the sound of this…" she replied, also not smiling.

"I'm kind of seeing Tina Lockhart." I breathed deeply and wished it were over.

"What do you mean 'seeing'?" she asked, her eyes turning glassy.

"I lied to you yesterday. I went to a party with Tina, and now we're kind of together…I guess."

She was silent for a moment as tears ran down her cheeks. This time, I knew they were real. "How could you do that to me? I thought we had something special!" She cried openly now and wiped angrily at her eyes.

"I'm really sorry! You're very special, and I want to still be friends and talk and hang out."

"Go to hell!" She whirled around to lie face down on her bed, her head buried in her pillow. "I don't *need* another friend! I've had plenty of friends. That's *all* I've had." She sobbed now, her back shaking with each one. "I thought you were different. I thought someone finally saw me for who I am on the inside…not what I am on the outside."

I didn't know what to do or say. I placed my hand on Emily's back, but she jerked away. "You *are* a really special person, and I *did* see it."

"You saw it, until your friends saw me. And I'm not pretty and popular and worthy of the in-crowd!"

"That's not true," I protested halfheartedly.

"So you throw me to the side to date Little Miss Perfect. Or Little Miss STD!" she continued.

"I'm sorry" was all I could mutter, tears filling my own eyes.

"Just leave! Get out of here and go do your thing! One day, you'll regret it. You're not like those other meatheads and airheads. You're selling out you and me to try to be like them. You're turning your back on someone who cares about you more than you'll ever know, for someone who will never love anyone but herself."

"Emily..."

"Get out!" she screamed.

I quickly obeyed her wishes. I was crushed by her words but relieved that it was over.

***

The following week was tough. Luckily, I didn't have to see Emily much at school, only catching an occasional glimpse between classes. I was still somewhat infatuated with Tina, but our conversations were becoming more and more excruciating. My conversations with my friends weren't much better. Suddenly, jock-talk and guy-talk weren't the same as in years past. I found myself thinking about the time I had spent with Emily. Our wits and senses of humor matched up perfectly. Our conversations were deep and meaningful, more than just high school chatter.

That weekend, while spending a lot of time with Tina, I finally realized what I had done. I tried to be playful and teasing like I was with Emily. At one point, I jokingly told her, "I'm going to have to slap you if you don't quit!"

"I'll call the police!" she said in all seriousness.

"I was just joking," I said with surprise.

"That's not something to joke about!"

A couple of hours later, she finally finished telling me about some scheme to get revenge on a new cheerleader who had somehow wronged her. After listening patiently, I said, "Good plan, Lucy. Now we just need to get Ethel on board."

"Lucy? Why did you call me that? Who is Ethel?"

Giving up on conversation, I just sat and listened to her nonstop babble. That weekend, I also found out that the passion was not what I'd hoped it would be. We kissed a lot, but there was nothing behind it, no emotion, and we lacked that special connection. I realized our first night together had only been decent because it was spontaneous, new, and enhanced with alcohol. Sure, she was beautiful and sexy, but as I touched her, my mind kept going back to the day I first kissed Emily and ran my hand beneath her shorts. I wanted that same feeling with Tina, but it wasn't there. It never would be.

***

The next couple of weeks were torture. I should have had everything a guy needed—cool friends and a hot girlfriend. Yet, I came to realize that I had let go of the only thing that truly made me happy. I found myself trying to find excuses to walk past Emily's locker. She wouldn't make eye contact, or she quickly turned away if she did. Still, I enjoyed those quick glimpses of her. I learned her class schedule and tried to walk past some of them conveniently as she arrived or departed. It hurt to watch her walk by like I was invisible. I missed the time we spent together: the long talks, the jokes, the horseplay, and, of course, the romance. Now, as I looked at her, she had transformed from the homely new girl to a radiant, red-haired beauty.

I also tried to catch glimpses of her after school and on the weekends. I felt like a voyeur, watching her work in their flowerbeds, wash the car, and walk through the neighborhood from my bedroom window. The thought of her doing all those activities alone nauseated me. I could have been out there with her. I picked up the phone to call several times, but I could never dial her number. I was afraid she would hang up, or I wouldn't know what to say.

The desire to talk to her only grew stronger as the weeks passed. I still went through the motions with Tina, but my heart was absent. Finally, I became obsessed with getting back what I had lost—or left behind. I knew she might curse me or hit me or just not speak, but I couldn't go on without at least trying.

***

My chance came the following Saturday. I knew she walked around the neighborhood every Saturday morning. Precisely at ten o'clock, she came out her front door and began stretching on the sidewalk. I hurried downstairs and peered out the window in the front door until she walked past. I let her get almost out of sight before leaving my house and trailed after her. My plan was to catch up to her when she was halfway across the neighborhood. Then she'd have to talk to me or at least listen—or try to outrun me back to her house.

I stealthily jogged after her, catching up after only a few minutes. She strolled leisurely, swinging her arms and checking out each yard and house she passed. She glanced over just as I reached her but quickly turned around and kept walking. I was terrified for a moment that she would bolt. "Emily, I have to talk to you!"

"No, you don't," she replied coldly, staring straight ahead.

"Well, then I really, really would *like* to talk to you."

She was silent for a moment and then finally sighed. "Whatever floats your boat."

I ignored her cold sarcasm. "Look, I was a complete and total idiot."

"Hey, we agree on something!"

"I caved into peer pressure and followed something other than my heart." I reached out, grabbed her right hand, and pulled it gently toward me. She stopped walking and turned to face me. I couldn't read her face or eyes. I grabbed her other hand too. "You were, and still are, very special to me. I love every minute we spend together. I love our deep conversations. I love our jokes and talking about stupid stuff. I love the punches in the arm and wrestling on the bed, and I love kissing your lips and touching your body."

Tears welled up in her eyes. "Then you shouldn't have walked away," she said softly.

"I know I shouldn't have! Like I said, I was an idiot, but I've suffered almost every minute since. Can you please find it in your heart to forgive me? I don't expect to be able to just pick up where we left off. I'd be happy to start over again from the beginning. Give me a walk through the neighborhood. Let me do some yard work with you. Heck, I'll rearrange your furniture for you!"

She pulled a hand away to wipe her eyes. A brief smile flashed across her face and then quickly vanished. "You hurt me bad! You just ripped my heart out and tossed it away. Do you realize that?"

I had to fight back my own tears now. "I know that, but I ripped out my own heart in the process. I just didn't know it right away. Just give me a shot at being your friend again; if it goes beyond that, then great. If not, then I'll be the best darn friend you could ask for."

"Josh, you have to know that if you want me in your life, you can't have everything else. I'll never be accepted in your social circle. You'll have to give up all your friends, your whole way of life, for me. Are you willing to sacrifice that?"

I was silent for a moment as I quickly processed that information. For the past couple of weeks, I'd known in my heart that it was a probability. "I'll sacrifice everything for you."

She wiped her eyes again and then stared deeply into mine. In that moment of vulnerability, she was as beautiful as I'd ever seen her. "I want to believe you. But I don't know if I can. What if another pretty girl catches your eye?"

"Emily, I promise that will never happen again. You're the only beautiful girl I want to be with."

"Take a week. Dump the bimbo, and tell your friends what you're doing. If you're still interested in me after all that, walk with me next Saturday."

"Thank you," I whispered. Emily continued walking, and I floated back to my house. I was upset at having to wait a week but exuberant about next Saturday.

***

Monday morning, I broke up with Tina. She took it well. She was still in love with herself, which was all that really mattered to her. Then I called my guys together and told them that I was really good friends with the redheaded new girl and would be hanging out with her a lot. Their reactions truly shocked me. They had a lot of questions at first as to why and comments that I had lost my mind. So I told them everything. They all pretty much shrugged and told me to do whatever made me happy. They would be my friends either way.

The following Saturday, I waited on Emily's sidewalk until she opened the front door. She appeared a little shocked. As she walked up to me, she let the smallest of grins appear. "Did you follow my instructions?"

"I did."

"And you're committed to this?"

"I am."

"Well, come on, lard butt; let's go walking."

We did start over at step one, but we quickly became close friends again. I proudly paraded her everywhere around school, and soon, the stares and whispers stopped. I was amazed that my friends actually gave her a chance, and her infectious personality quickly won everyone over. She also introduced me to her circle of friends, and they welcomed me with open arms. They were actually pretty cool. We opened up whole new worlds to each other. Tina and the cheerleading squad never really accepted her, but I think many other people's eyes and minds were opened that year.

***

Our friendship did develop into much more. Six years later, that red-haired, pasty-faced, homely girl married me. Today, we have two redheaded, freckle-faced hellions running around the house, with every bit of their mother's fiery personality. And they're just as beautiful.

One Year

"Then why don't I just leave?"

"I can't believe you!"

"Can't believe that I'll leave?" Charles thought maybe his threat had softened her stance some.

"No. That after fifteen years of marriage, you finally have a good idea!" Jessica said sarcastically.

"I'm serious. I'll go!"

"I'm serious too. I'll get the door for you!"

Charles had to fight his every instinct to stop himself from telling Jessica precisely what he thought about her at that moment. How could someone he had known for seventeen years, been married to for fifteen, and had two children with, become so hateful? He didn't even know who the person standing in front of him was. But to go on a cursing tirade would only let her know she'd gotten to him, and he wouldn't give her the satisfaction. "Wait a minute. That wouldn't count as housework, would it? We both know you don't do that!" Ah, he knew that one stung.

"Get out! Just leave, you useless, worthless excuse for a man!" Jessica's face was flaming red now, and her eyes were trying to kill as she strode over to the front door and opened it wide.

"My pleasure," Charles said and stomped past his wife and into the rainy, dark night.

Charles was sure steam must be trailing off his head as he walked quickly to his car. *Now, what am I going to do?* It was midnight on Sunday, and he was supposed to be at work at eight o'clock in the morning. He and Jessica had fought a lot over the past few months, and both had threatened to leave more than once. Neither had really meant it, though. He hadn't tonight, but anger and pride are a bad combination. *I can't go back in now, at least not tonight.*

He started the car and peeled out of the driveway, making sure Jessica heard his squealing tires. A block away, he smacked the steering wheel with the palms of his hands and emitted a guttural scream.

He drove into the nearly deserted town and into the Holiday Inn parking lot. He'd have to stay here for the night without his clothes or shaving kit. He'd go back to his house the next morning, after the Evil One left, and pack some things. He hoped work would accept his sick call-in.

His anger eventually faded during the long, sleepless night, leaving behind cold, stark reality. He had been close to leaving several times over the past few years, usually after similar fights. He had fantasized about it even more. In those exciting fantasies, he had imagined being totally free to come and go as he pleased—no more nagging or drama. He would just have to worry about himself. Then there would be the parties, hanging out with the guys, and dating hot women. But laying in that hotel room, at least that first night, he didn't feel like he had in his daydreams. He felt…sad.

***

The next day dawned rainy and cool. Charles ate the continental breakfast at the hotel, stretching it out until he knew his wife and children would be gone. Then he checked out and headed to his house. He received a text from Jessica as he packed his suitcase in their bedroom. His heart skipped a beat in a momentary rush of excitement. *Finally.* She had come to her senses and was going to ask him to change his mind and not move out. They could work things out. He picked up his phone and read the text.

"You better not take anything of mine or the kids!"

Wow! She was still unrepentant. The brief flash of excitement transitioned smoothly to anger. He quickly typed back, "It's all mine! I'm the one with the real job!"

Her response contained a few words he'd never heard her use before. At least he was holding his own in the jab department.

He finished packing his clothes and personal items and sped away. He'd have to get the big stuff once he figured out his living situation. He couldn't afford to stay in the hotel for long. He stopped and picked up some apartment guides and spent the rest of the day looking for a cheap one-bedroom or studio apartment.

***

"What did you tell Cody and Samantha?" After working up the nerve for an hour, Charles had finally called Jessica from his hotel room. He had lined up a relatively cheap apartment to move into the next day and had decided to take vacation for the remainder of the week to move in and set up as a bachelor.

"The truth: that their father is a selfish, useless SOB." Jessica's sarcastic voice cut like a knife.

"Spare me your clever barbs. What did you tell them?"

"I told them you had to go out of town on business. We need to figure out when and what we'll tell them," she replied with a little less edge to her voice.

"Well, we need to do it soon. I'm going to move and settle in tomorrow. I'd like to be able to see them by this weekend." Charles rubbed his head, the reality of the conversation sinking in.

"Well then, you should have thought about that before you left!"

Charles thought he heard Jessica's voice crack just before she hung up. *Nice…real nice. This is going to be a lovely process—just lovely.*

Charles borrowed a friend's pickup the next day and moved just enough stuff to give him the basics. The Spartan set up reminded him of college, minus the spool for a coffee table. That night, he again called Jessica. This time, the conversation went a little better. They talked to their children the following evening.

Cody was twelve and Samantha fourteen. They weren't totally shocked. Unfortunately, their parents hadn't done a good job keeping their frequent arguments quiet or hiding the constant tension. They were sad, and both shed a few tears. They had a lot of questions, most of which their parents didn't have answers for. Charles had to fight back his own tears several times. He hoped it would get easier for all of them.

***

Charles spent the rest of the week establishing his new existence: electricity, water, bank, post office, courthouse, etcetera. Jessica saw her lawyer on Friday, and he made an appointment with one the following week. He got to have his children that weekend, and they all three "camped out" on his apartment floor. It was a little strange for the kids,

163

and they were obviously nervous, but all in all, it went as well as could be expected.

He returned to work on Monday, and things actually started to feel a little more normal. He had to get used to grocery shopping, cooking, and laundry, but not fighting with Jessica was nice. It also dawned on him that he didn't have to answer to anyone. If he wanted to go have a few beers after work, he would. He could watch anything he wanted to on television, stay up as late as he wished, and eat what he wanted when he wanted. Once again, he felt like he was in college. Missing his children was the only thing that kept him awake at night and caused his tears.

The glamorous "college life" came crashing down around him during his lawyer visit. His lawyer estimated that he would pay $2,500 per month in child support and alimony—well over half what he brought home in a month. He returned to work and had to immediately start crunching the numbers. With his rent, car payment, and basic necessities, he might be able to break even. He would have nothing left for his fantasies of going out and partying, traveling, and dating, not to mention trying to save some money. Of course, then there were the lawyer fees. And the icing on the cake was losing half his retirement and 401(k).

***

"Wow. That sucks, dude!"

"Tell me about it. How can that be fair? She gets the house, the kids, and half my money, while I won't have enough money to pay for these beers!" Despite his newfound poverty, Charles had invited his best friend and coworker, Zach, to have a few beers at a local bar. It was the first chance he'd had to talk to anyone about his separation, and he really needed to talk.

"Doesn't seem fair at all. Can you fight it? Or try to get the house at least?" Zach asked. Zach was twenty-eight and had never been married. Charles had envied his bachelor lifestyle for some time—only their situations were much, much different now.

"I couldn't afford the house even if I had it. I could make her sell it, and us divide the money, but I don't want to put the kids through that. Apparently, there is nothing I can do about the money thing. I'm on the hook for alimony for eight years, or until she remarries, and child support until they turn eighteen."

"Hit man?"

"Are you offering?" They both laughed and then fell silent as they worked on their beers. "The good thing is, I'm free in a year."

"Here's to one year," Zach said with a toast.

They drank until late that night, the beer and conversation numbing the pain for a short while.

***

Charles had a lot of time to think and reflect at night. He dissected their marriage or at least tried to perform a postmortem. The easy path would be to crawl back home, tail tucked between his legs, and beg for forgiveness. That was at least appealing from a financial and parenting standpoint. But as soon as that option started sounding really good, the misery and pain of the last twelve years came back to him.

He had been so unhappy in his marriage, and so had Jessica. He'd dreaded going home in the evenings and dreaded the weekends as his coworkers talked about their big plans. He couldn't pinpoint exactly where the marriage had derailed. He guessed it was fairly typical, though. Once the children came, things changed.

It wasn't too bad with just Samantha. They could take turns watching her and taking care of the chores. But two children more than doubled the stress. He and his wife worked all day and then came home to crying children. They weren't bad children; they just took all their parents' free time. With the age difference and fighting, he would usually take one and Jessica the other.

The stress level steadily increased, and the only outlet seemed to be taking it out on each other. Jessica didn't trust babysitters with the children, except occasionally one of their parents when they visited, so they stopped having date nights. Work and children took all their attention—their positive attention anyway. By the time the kids were in bed, and they had alone time, they either had chores to do or were too tired for anything but sleep.

Stress and lack of attention festered in them, and their venting soon became personal. Charles began coming home later from work and occasionally went out golfing and drinking with friends. That, of course, only fanned the flames of Jessica's anger, which she took out on him, which, of course, led to his retaliation. They both began keeping score, too, of what the other did or didn't do. Once the scorecards were out, there was no turning back or reconciling.

As Charles replayed the last twelve years in his mind, he could easily see why so many marriages ended up the same way his had. Actually, it was a wonder any survived, at least with multiple children. But he could also easily see how they could have worked together and fixed it early on before it fell off the cliff. Unfortunately, gaining wisdom too late was about as bad as never having it at all—maybe worse.

"How's it going, bro?" Zach clapped Charles on the shoulder as he sat down at the table. Charles was already three beers ahead. Three months had passed since he'd left home.

"It's going, I guess."

"How are the kids?"

"Seem to be doing good. It really sucks not being with them every night. It's funny. When they were little and screaming and fighting all the time, I was coming up with excuses to be away. Now I'm away and trying to find excuses to be with them. Cody is playing Little League football. I try to catch his practices every day and all his games. Samantha is buried in homework and busy being a teenage social girl, but we talk every night on the phone."

"That's cool. And the Evil One?"

"She's not too bad…when I don't have to see or talk to her."

"What are you down to now? Nine months?" Zach asked, quickly chugging a beer in an effort to catch up.

"Yep! Nine more months and eagerly counting!"

They had resumed drinking and watching the college football game on the closest TV when Zach suddenly kicked Charles's leg. Charles looked at him in surprise and then followed his gaze to the door. Jessica had just walked in with several female friends.

"Oh, my God! She wouldn't ever get a babysitter or leave the kids alone for us to go out, but now she can go out with her gal pals?"

"I hate to say it, dude, but she ain't looking too bad," Zach said, receiving a death glare from Charles.

"Don't stare directly at it!"

"Will she turn me to stone?" Zach chuckled.

"No. Worse. She'll turn you into a poverty-stricken, bitter, woman-hating bachelor!" The bar was crowded now, and Charles and Zach managed to slip out unseen.

Charles's mind spun from more than just the beers after he was back safe at home in his tiny apartment. *Jessica going out on a Saturday night?* He had tried for years to convince her to get a babysitter, so they could go out. Just a few months ago, he had suggested leaving the children by themselves for a few hours while they went on a date. Samantha was fourteen, and Cody was a very mature twelve-year-old. Jessica wouldn't hear of it.

That was another part of their disconnect over the years. Back when they were dating, they always went out. They drank, sang karaoke, and went dancing and to movies and concerts. They had also enjoyed doing physical stuff together, like hiking, racquetball, and working out. They were best friends before they even started dating. They always enjoyed each other's company and loved to talk and laugh. Then, after the children were born, it was like they instantly became strangers—or, at best, roommates. Now, they were mortal enemies.

***

The following two months went OK. Charles adapted to living very cheap and tight. By wearing sweat clothes all the time in his apartment and keeping three blankets on his bed, he kept his heating bill to a minimum. He also learned how to eat cheap. Ramen noodles and macaroni and cheese transported him once again back to his college days. Canned and frozen foods were cheap. He downgraded as much as he could: car insurance, cell phone, cable, Internet—pretty much everything.

Relations between him and Jessica improved a little. Of course, barring murder, they couldn't have gotten worse. They occasionally spoke when they exchanged the children and texted some over her bills and household questions. They did manage to spend Christmas morning together at her house while the children opened presents. That helped them all. Some of the bitterness and anger faded in both of them as their new situation became the norm.

Single life for Charles wasn't as glamorous as he'd fantasized about. He occasionally went out with Zach and some guys from work, and he had friends over for Monday night football every couple of weeks. Zach even set him up on a few blind dates, but either the girls weren't right for him, or he just wasn't ready.

***

"Man, this place is filled with hot women!" Zach exclaimed as they entered the new bar. They had decided to go to a karaoke bar for a change. Chris and David, two friends of Zach's, had joined them. Zach was pushing Charles hard to find someone to date, or at least speak to, and Charles reluctantly went along with the plan.

They sat at a table near the back, ordered a round of drinks, and surveyed the scene. None of them planned on singing. Zach just promised that many good-looking women came out to karaoke night. So far, Charles had to admit that he was right. Zach and his young friends were chomping at the bit to talk to young, attractive women. After downing a quick couple of rounds of beer for courage, they started looking for prey to stalk. "OK. Here we go, guys," Zack said, nodding toward four women standing together near the bar.

167

"Have you even seen their faces yet?" Charles asked, heart pounding and palms sweating.

"Do you need to? I mean, look at the bods!" David interjected, clearly not struggling with nerves.

"What's the plan? Do we pick now, or just roll with it?" It was Chris's turn to speak. Charles thought he looked like a starving dog staring at a juicy bone.

"Nah. Let's just roll with it. We just walk up, chat for a minute, and each drag one to the dance floor."

"Sounds romantic enough," Charles commented weakly.

"Ah, come on, old man. You'll be a new man after tonight," Zach said, standing and heading toward the quarry.

"Or dead…" Charles followed the other three.

As the men reached the female group, two of the women turned to face them. Charles, arriving last, found himself in front of a blond in a tight blue dress. He did have to admit she had a good figure. She was the last to turn.

Charles froze like a deer in headlights. "*Jessica?*"

"Oh, my God!" Jessica exclaimed, not hiding her shock.

"Yeah. Nice to see you too," Charles muttered, his eyes darting around, looking for an escape route.

"Wait a second! Were you coming up to hit on me?" A smile replaced Jessica's stunned expression.

"Well, if you had been a human woman, I might have asked you to dance."

The other three pairs were so engrossed in their conversations that no one even realized Jessica and Charles were face-to-face.

"Now, Charles, that's a little rude. Or do you mean I'm like a goddess and not merely human?" Jessica laughed. It almost sounded like an honest laugh to Charles, not a mocking or sarcastic one.

"OK. You go with that. Would it look strange if I ran full speed out of here, screaming?" Charles felt more panicked as the other three couples headed to the dance floor.

"No stranger than you already look."

"OK. Great seeing you. Take care. Bye-bye," Charles said as he turned to go back to their table. He wasn't in the mood for exchanging barbs and quips. The bad thing was that Jessica looked really good. She had highlighted her hair and straightened it, like he had suggested in the past. She'd apparently lost a few pounds, too, because her body appeared

168

very shapely in that tight dress. She probably also looked better since she hadn't fixed herself up and gone out with him in years.

"OK. I'll be good. I'm going to sit at the bar. I'm way too sober. You're welcome to join me. We are married after all."

Charles hesitated as he processed the request. Every instinct told him to keep heading in the opposite direction. But with his wingmen on the dance floor, sitting alone at a table in a crowded bar was his only alternative. He was surprised to find himself walking up to the bar and sitting on the stool beside her. He immediately ordered a Long Island Iced Tea. Beer wasn't going to cut it.

"So, you come here often?" Charles asked, trying to ease the tension.

"Is that your best line?" Jessica asked, ordering the same drink.

"Well, the only one I haven't been slapped for."

"You know, this is pretty sad," Jessica said, sipping the strong drink.

"Us going out to find a date and ending up together at a bar?"

"Exactly! Is this town that small?"

"Apparently. Or the universe is in a cruel mood tonight," Charles responded dryly. They both laughed. "Let me ask you something."

"Oh, boy. OK," Jessica said, turning to look at her husband.

"I've tried for years to get you to go out with me, to have date nights. Now, since we've separated, I've seen you out at least twice. What's going on?"

Jessica took a big gulp of her drink and turned back to Charles. "I've had a lot of time to think over the past few months, as I'm sure you have. As bad as it pains me to admit it, you were actually right on some things. We should have been going out more and dating. I guess you just get caught up in real life sometimes. And once we started fighting all the time, I definitely wasn't in the mood to hang out with you. If I know I'm going to get back by eleven o'clock, I've been leaving them by themselves. If not, I've been having Jane's daughter, Kim, babysit. She's twenty."

They both turned back to their drinks and sipped in silence for a few minutes. "So, have you had any earth-shattering revelations?" Jessica asked, finally breaking the silence.

"I agree with you saying I was right." Charles laughed. The combination of the beer and the mixed drink was relaxing him, probably too much.

Jessica punched him in the arm. "Seriously!"

"Well, I can see exactly how we ended up going down this road. But I can also see how easy it would have been to fix it, at least early on. I think the thing we both lost sight of, as many people do, is that we met and fell in love with each other long before we had jobs and children. Marriage and children should just add to that love—expand it—not destroy it."

"Wow! Surprisingly deep. The Long Island?"

"Yup."

The bartender set another one down in front of Charles with perfect timing and then brought Jessica her second. Charles turned to her and held up his glass. "Happy five-month anniversary!"

Jessica laughed and toasted him. "So, how's the single life? As much fun as you dreamed?"

"Kind of like being in college...only no girls and no fun."

They both laughed.

"Dated much?" she asked.

"A few times. Not sure if I'd call it dating. More like helping to feed lonely women. Hey, maybe I could start a charity!"

Jessica laughed a little too loudly. She was definitely feeling the alcohol. "I don't remember you being this funny."

"I guess it was hard to crack jokes with the knife at my throat." Charles had to quit looking at Jessica. Her smile, something he hadn't seen much of in fifteen years, was making her too attractive.

"Good point! Although I'm sure you deserved it, at least half the time."

"I'll give you forty percent." He paused to take a swig of his drink. "How about your dating life? Hot and heavy?"

"Not! I've been out a few times too. But it's weird out here!"

"Tell me about it."

"Everyone wants to fall in love, get married, and have kids, all after one date. It's just so strange being our age and dating again. When we first started dating, we were just teenagers. We had no past. Now people have been married, some multiple times, have kids, maybe even grandkids, and have a whole lifetime of scars and stories. And I think since everyone's been married, they just think anything goes with dating." Jessica stopped to sip on her drink.

"Not like the movies, huh?" Charles asked.

"Not any I'd want to watch!"

They made small talk as they continued finishing their second drink. "Well, I think I'll quit while we're ahead," Charles said. "We've spent an hour together, and neither of us is screaming, bleeding, or crying. You're not driving, are you?" he asked after closing his tab, including paying for her drinks, and standing up to go.

170

"No. Stephanie did. She's only dancing, not drinking, tonight," Jessica said, a little surprised at Charles's leaving. "Thanks for picking up my drinks too!"

"No prob. You all be careful. I'll be over next Friday to get the kids."

"OK. Take care."

***

Their newfound civility was short-lived. The following Sunday, Charles was running late bringing the children back. He and Cody had been playing a heated game of Madden, and they couldn't just quit with a tie score in the fourth quarter. He arrived at Jessica's at eight-fifteen. Once he hugged the kids and they ran into the house, Jessica's eyes flashed the evil glare of old.

"We have a schedule, you know!"

Where was the smile and laugh he'd seen last Friday night? "I'm sorry. Our Madden game went into overtime."

"Then start it earlier next time! Or just turn it off. It's a game, Charles."

"What's wrong with you? I'm only fifteen minutes late!"

"You don't have to deal with homework and getting them into bed on time and up in the mornings. Just stick to the schedule, or I'll have the schedule changed!" Jessica turned and went into the house, slamming the door behind her.

So much for being buds…

***

The following month was fairly uneventful. Charles took a break from barhopping with Zach. He did go on one more blind date, but it ended about as well as the others. He and Jessica didn't have any more confrontations. They managed to avoid talking at all, other than for issues with the children.

Cody decided to play middle-school baseball that spring. Charles sat on the bleachers alone at the first game, watching the team's warm-up. He was shocked when Jessica walked up and sat down beside him.

"You're not expecting anyone, are you?" she asked.

"Uh, no. Unless a hot chick wanders up."

"She just did. So deal with it." Jessica flashed a slight smile.

"Oh, boy," Charles said sarcastically.

They sat together at each game for the entire season and even rode together to the away games. They never became quite as friendly as they had at the bar that night, but it was amicable. Jessica still wasn't dating anyone seriously. They talked about their dates, or lack thereof,

171

frequently. They also talked about the children and work. Samantha sat with them at the games she went to, but she also hung out with her friends a lot. She was a full-blooded teenage girl now.

***

Charles received a rare phone call from Jessica a couple of weeks after baseball season ended. Her shower was totally backed up, and she wanted to know if he could fix it. The children were spending the night with friends. *What the heck?* It might beat sitting at home alone—as long as the claws or fangs didn't come out.

As Charles worked with the drill and snake to bring up the clumps of hair, and who knows what else, Jessica came up behind him. "Hey, I was thinking about ordering a pizza as a reward for your hard work. Can you stay?"

"Sure," Charles answered without looking up from the gruesome task.

Thirty minutes later, they were sitting on Jessica's couch eating pizza, drinking light beer, and watching *The Hangover* on DVD. They laughed and talked like they had that night in the bar.

"Can I ask you something?" Charles finally asked.

"Uh…sure, I guess."

"We got along well that night at the karaoke bar."

"Yes. That was a surprisingly good night," Jessica agreed.

"But a week later, you were totally hateful to me. And I'm sure it wasn't just because I was a few minutes late. There've been many other times too when you have just been so hard to deal with. Then there are times like this when you're fun to be around." Charles nervously awaited her response.

"You really don't understand, do you?"

"I understand nothing when it comes to you or women."

"This has been really hard on me, Charles. You walked away from our marriage. You left me alone to raise two children. It's hard being a single mother! Sure, they are great kids and are very mature, but it's still tough. I have to grocery shop, cook, do the laundry, clean the house, help them with homework, run them to sports and school events, get them to bed on time, and get them up and take them to school in the mornings. Then I think of you, living alone, coming and going as you please, no chores that have to be done, no one you have to worry about. Sometimes, it all builds up and is more than I can just smile about and ignore."

172

Charles was silent for a moment, sipping his beer. "Don't forget: you held the door open for me to walk through and did nothing to try to get me to stay or come back."

"Don't even go there! You threatened to leave for years. You know you just wanted an opportunity to do it, and I wasn't going to keep begging you to stay after every fight."

Charles regretted asking the question. "You know, I understand what you're saying, and I'm sure it is hard, but don't think this has been a cakewalk for me. I live in a crappy apartment that could fit in the basement of this house because it's all I can afford. I eat frozen dinners and canned food and can't afford to run the heat or air-conditioning. I hate not seeing Cody and Samantha every night. Do you know I cried myself to sleep every night for the first month? That is when I slept. I hate not eating supper with them, helping them with their homework, hearing about their day at school, and kissing them good night on their foreheads. I haven't been able to practice football or baseball with Cody in the backyard. I missed seeing Samantha and her boyfriend going to her first homecoming dance, and I've hardly met any of their friends. I'm alone almost every night, with no one to talk to."

Jessica started to rebut his argument but instead thought about what he'd said.

Charles continued, "And you know, I could help you out with the children. I'd take them any night, drive them where they need to go, help with homework, babysit—anything. You might be a single mother, but the kids have a father."

"Maybe you could now, but you wouldn't have a few months ago."

They took a break from the conversation and stared back at the movie, working harder on their beers. Charles was the first to resume the conversation. "Well, do you think we can continue to try to be friends and be more like this than being mean to each other? We can't go back and undo what happened nine months ago. I can help you any way you want, to make things easier, but all we can do is deal with the present and solve current problems as they arise."

Jessica hated when Charles made sense. "Yeah. We can work on it. And maybe if you wanted to come over occasionally during the week and help out with repairs and maintenance like tonight, you can see Cody and Samantha more."

"That'd be great!"

***

They stuck to their pact over the next month. Jessica did call Charles some to help run Cody and Samantha here or there, and he found excuses to come over and fix things around the house and spend time with his children. He and Jessica continued to get along well. He was surprised to realize he'd started having some feelings for her again. When she was being nice, he saw what had attracted him to her many years ago. They talked and laughed like best friends. He also started feeling attracted to her, and she seemed a little playfully flirtatious with him too.

One night, he and Jessica found themselves alone on her couch after the children had gone to bed, laughing at a rerun of *Seinfeld*. During a commercial, Jessica turned to look at him. "You know…I was thinking."

"Oh, Lord! Nothing good ever comes from that."

Jessica punched his arm. "Shut up and listen!" She laughed. "I'm going to be childless a lot this summer. Cody has several camps he's attending, and Samantha has a cheerleading camp, plus lots of friends who like slumber parties. Maybe if neither of us is dating, and we're bored, we could just hang out and do stuff."

Charles pretended to think about it for a few seconds. "Yeah. I guess we could do that some."

***

Over the next two months, they spent almost every childless moment together. They hiked, played tennis, went to movies, went out to eat, and occasionally had a few drinks at a bar. It was nice, with none of the pressure of dating. They didn't have to try to impress each other or worry about kissing—or worse. Neither felt any obligation to call or text so many times a day or week. If they were free, they'd just do something. They did talk on the phone once in a while and texted a few times pretty much every day. There was also none of the tension of their married life.

Charles felt his attraction to her continue to grow. They did flirt with each other occasionally, and he was pretty sure she'd teased him from time to time while they were doing physical activities. The situation was so surreal. He had known her for over fifteen years and had raised children with her, but she was like a different person now—a familiar stranger. And it wasn't just due to being apart for almost a year. She had changed since they'd separated. She was much more confident and independent, much more relaxed and fun-loving.

***

"Got big plans for us tonight?" Charles asked as they walked past the Twister mat on the living room floor.

"Nah. You're too old; you'd hurt something." This time, Charles smacked her in the arm. "No, Cody and some friends got it out yesterday. They played for all of five minutes."

"Good thing it's not for us. I'd kick your aging butt!"

Jessica poured them both a glass of wine in the kitchen, and then they went and sat on the couch to watch some movies. They laughed, talked, and continued to drink. One bottle of wine led to two. It was Friday night, and Samantha and Cody were spending the night with friends.

"Let's do it!" Jessica suddenly exclaimed.

"Excuse me?" Charles asked, not sure where she was going with her exclamation.

"Twister! Drunken Twister!" She laughed as she leaped up.

"Oh, God!"

Jessica grabbed his hands and pulled him up, and they half-ran, half-stumbled, into the living room. Jessica spun the spinner, and the game began. Charles was very apprehensive and very nervous. Jessica wore a pair of short, thin blue shorts and a tight yellow shirt. As each turn brought them closer, he suddenly noticed her sweet perfume. He tried not to stare at her butt as she bent over to put her left hand on green. Her shorts rode up high, to the very tops of her toned legs.

Two more moves brought him directly behind her. He had to press against her body and wrap one arm around her to touch the circle at her feet. He couldn't hide his arousal now. Jessica spun again and had to try to reach her hand back between his legs to touch her circle. Suddenly, he lost his balance and tumbled onto his back. Jessica fell on top of him. She quickly rolled off, with her head resting on his outstretched left arm, so they were side by side. They both burst into laughter. After a moment, they rolled onto their sides to look at each other, their heads mere inches apart.

Neither mistook the look in the other's eyes. Their laughter stopped, and they gazed at each other, still smiling. Before he even realized it, Charles felt his head moving toward Jessica's. He was pleasantly surprised when she moved to meet him, and their lips met for the first time in a year. He felt as nervous as kissing someone for the first time. Her lips seemed even softer than he remembered. Their first kiss was gentle, their lips barely brushing. They were both hesitant, waiting for the other to break it off. When neither did, the kiss grew more passionate.

Their lips slid back and forth in unison and then slowly parted. His tongue thrust inside, quickly met by hers. She wrapped her left arm around him and pulled him even closer to her. Charles stretched his right arm down so his hand could caress her silky, smooth thigh. Very quickly, they were panting and kissing each other with more passion than either could remember. Charles rolled to his left, on top of her, as she rolled over onto her back. His kisses moved from her lips to her ears and then her neck. He alternated soft bites with gentle kissing and licking. Soon, their bodies were pressed together from head to toe, moving as one. Moments later, they ripped off each other's clothes and made passionate love on the Twister mat.

***

An hour later, they lay together, cuddling and kissing, naked in Jessica's bed. "Is it my imagination, or was that the best sex we've ever had?" Charles asked, stroking her blond hair.

"No. I have to agree with you. Where was that all those years?"

"Guess we just get better with age." Charles laughed.

"Hey!" Jessica exclaimed.

"Hey, what?"

"I just remembered something! I go to see my lawyer next week. Our year is up."

"Oh, wow! I forgot all about that!"

"What are we going to do?"

"This." Charles began kissing her again.

"So, cancel it?" she asked, pulling away.

"Of course! Oh, and by the way, happy one-year anniversary!"

Lovesick

I've been sent from the future to protect you."

I turned to look at the boy who'd sat down in the empty chair beside me. The two things that immediately stood out were his shaved head and pale skin. He appeared a little on the sickly side. He didn't smile as he awaited my response.

"You're too late," I whispered seriously. His puzzled expression was priceless. "Someone from the future came to me this morning. He told me to ignore the bald, pale idiot who would claim *he* was from the future in my US history class."

He stared at me for a moment and finally laughed. "A little harsh…yet clever. I'm Aaron, Aaron Spencer." He held his hand out for me to shake.

This was the strangest introduction I'd ever received, including drunken guys trying to pick me up at clubs. He was intriguing, though. I shook his hand. "Lori Anderson," I replied.

A moment later, Professor Schulz brought the class to order and introduced himself in a heavy German accent. For the next few minutes, he droned on in his deep, monotone voice, reviewing the syllabus and giving us a general overview of the class. I quickly realized this class would be torturous.

"Does anyone else see the irony in a German teaching US history?" Aaron whispered. I smiled and nodded, and he continued, "I mean, I can't wait to find out who won World War II!"

We laughed a little too loudly, causing the intense glare of the professor to fall upon us. Luckily, he didn't call us out. After an excruciating moment of silence, he continued his lecture. Aaron leaned close again once the professor regained his rhythm of monotony. "I ain't going in any shower. I don't care how much it counts toward our grade!"

I erupted into a fit of coughing to hide my laughter, once again drawing the evil gaze. The remainder of the hour was painful. The only thing that made it bearable was that Aaron and I started passing notes back and forth, or at least we wrote on our notebooks and showed them to each other. He was very quick and clever, and I think I managed to hold my own. Once we tired of making fun of our professor, we started on the other students. It wasn't mean-spirited, just good-natured fun.

I had never met anyone that I hit it off with that well so soon after meeting. We were on precisely the same wavelength, regardless of which direction our notes took. It seemed like I'd known Aaron for years, not just minutes. I felt guilty about not paying attention to the first lecture of the class but couldn't stop our sideshow.

Mercifully, nine-fifteen finally arrived. The other students gathered their books, shoved them into their backpacks, and dashed to the exits. I took my time, unsure how my goodbye with Aaron would go.

"Let's go ice-skating," he said casually, as if it were the most natural suggestion in the world.

"Ice-skating? It's nine-fifteen in the morning! Besides, I've never ice-skated before."

"Neither have I. Sounds fun, though, don't it?"

I shook my head and laughed. "You're an idiot."

"Didn't take you long to realize it, huh? Are you in or out?"

"I don't even know you! And besides, I have human anatomy at ten." I still couldn't believe how forward this almost total stranger was.

"When's your next class after that?"

"Two."

"OK. Meet me at the Combs Plaza Skate Land at noon, and we'll learn how to skate."

My every instinct screamed for me to just say "no," but my heart wasn't so sure. Aaron was so carefree and spontaneous, and those were two traits I lacked. Somehow, my heart overrode my mind. "OK. I guess, but you're still an idiot."

"But I'm growing on you."

***

I don't think I've ever laughed as hard as I did while we ice-skated. Aaron hadn't lied about not knowing how, but that didn't stop him from acting like he did. He attempted spins, jumps, and triple-toed something or others. Each attempt ended with a horrific fall, but he kept getting up and trying again. I wasn't much better, but I knew my limitations and tried to stay within them, although he did manage to pull me down a time or two in our efforts to couple skate. Aaron knew no restraint. He entertained me as well as everyone else on the ice. It was refreshing to be with someone who wasn't afraid to make a fool out of himself. That was rare, especially on a "first date." He did stop from time to time to catch his breath or recover from the falls. I wasn't really sure which.

Our friendship never slowed down or missed a beat after that first day. He was so exciting and fun. I couldn't imagine not saying yes to his next crazy scheme. Over the next few weeks, we went horseback riding, played tackle football in the rain, and went bowling, kayaking, spelunking, and rock climbing. Each activity was truly an adventure with him. He constantly entertained me and usually everyone else around. He never seemed to have a bad day or bad mood. He was like a little kid, fascinated and entertained by anything and everything. Aside from occasional breaks to catch his breath, he never stopped moving.

There was nothing other than friendship and fun between us during those first weeks. I did start feeling an attraction to Aaron, but I wasn't sure if it was physical or if I was just attracted to his magnetic personality. There were certainly a lot of differences between us, but we complemented each other perfectly. I provided reason and restraint to keep us both alive—and out of jail—and he constantly pushed me outside my comfort zones. He wouldn't let me have a bad day or get upset over a bad grade or family stress, and I gave him companionship and support in any endeavor he conjured up.

***

One Friday night, I really just wanted to stay in and relax, so I rented some romantic comedies and brought them over to his apartment. He acted reluctant to spend an evening indoors, but I finally convinced him. We sat on his couch with plenty of snacks and drinks and started watching the first movie. As we watched, I realized I really didn't know much about my new best friend. He never spoke much about his family or his past. We'd never really had any deep conversations. He kept

179

strangely silent during the first movie, only laughing or smiling if I did first.

Halfway into the second movie, I became really sleepy. I scooted a little closer to Aaron, watching his face for a reaction. He glanced at me, smiled briefly, and then turned back to watch the movie. I slowly inched closer and finally leaned my head against his shoulder. I waited nervously for him to move, or ask me to, but he said nothing. He finally moved after a few minutes, raising his arm up above me. I took advantage and leaned my head against his chest, and he placed his arm around me.

I was suddenly so warm and comfortable lying against him, and I felt my eyelids start to droop. After fighting sleep for a few minutes, I lost the battle. It took me a moment to realize where I was when I awoke. I was on the couch with Aaron, only somehow I had slid down, so my head was in his lap. I felt his hand lying on my side. My eyes focused on the television screen, and I saw that the credits were rolling. I quickly rolled over onto my back and looked up at Aaron to see if he was asleep. He wasn't. He was staring down at me, his eyes glassy, like they were full of tears. He appeared startled and then quickly smiled and turned to grab the remote control.

"Are you crying?" I asked.

He laughed nervously. "Stupid chick flicks! Now you've found out Superman's other weakness!" I hadn't seen him act nervous or unsure of himself, and tears were the last thing I'd expected.

I sat up, his right arm still around me, and stared at him until he turned back to face me. I suddenly viewed him in a different light. I don't know if it was the romantic movies, the closeness of sleeping on him, or his sudden vulnerability, but I felt urges I'd never thought I would feel toward him. He smiled at me and looked like he wanted to speak but didn't.

I leaned in toward him in a move that even surprised me. I closed my eyes and prayed he wouldn't try to stop me. Our lips finally met, joining together in a perfect kiss. Any remaining thoughts of friendship quickly evolved into so much more. His left hand gently caressed my cheek, and his right hand moved up and down my back, my skin rippling beneath his fingers. Our kisses quickly progressed from tentative and exploratory to rough and passionate. Our breathing became louder and soon transitioned to panting as our hands began wandering all over each other's body. I had kissed several guys before but never experienced anything like this. Just as we had special chemistry as friends, we had special physical chemistry.

Suddenly, it all came to a screeching halt as Aaron's hands moved to my shoulders, and he gently pushed me away. I opened my eyes and stared at him in surprise.

"I'm sorry," he whispered. "I can't do this."

"What? Why?"

"I just can't." He took his left hand off my shoulder and wiped his eyes.

"You can't tell me you didn't just feel what I did!" I exclaimed with a mixture of surprise and anger.

"No. Of course, I felt it."

"You don't have a girlfriend, do you?"

"No."

"Aaron, please tell me what's going on!" I pleaded.

He sighed and looked away for a moment before finally turning back and staring into my eyes. "There's something I haven't told you."

My heart sank into my stomach. I braced myself for the worst.

"I have lung cancer. Well, at the moment, I'm in remission, but there's a ninety-five percent chance it will return in the next year or two. If and when it does, it will be fatal."

I couldn't believe what he'd just said. I was too stunned to speak or even breathe. My mind didn't know where to start trying to process the information. Sensing my loss for words, he went on to tell me the entire story. He'd been diagnosed with lung cancer eighteen months earlier. His family discovered that his childhood home had high radon levels, and since his room was in the basement, he'd received the most exposure. He underwent several surgeries as well as chemo and radiation treatments over the next year. The cancer finally went into remission, but it left him a shell of his former self. He'd spent the past six months building back his strength. I realized that explained his bald head and frequent rest breaks while playing hard.

"I'm sorry," was all I could utter. Tears were flowing freely down my cheeks now.

"I really, really like you, Lori. I've been fighting falling for you ever since the first day we met. I never meant for things to get this far. I just wanted to be friends with you. Tonight caught me off guard."

I still couldn't formulate the words to speak. After a few more minutes of silence, I finally found my voice. "Why are you in college?"

"I completed my junior year before I was diagnosed. No one in my family has ever graduated college. That's the one dream my parents always had for me, so I'm going to graduate this year and give them that gift."

My tears flowed faster now. *Aaron would sacrifice that much of his life for his parents?* "And after you graduate?"

"I'm going to travel the world and live the heck out of life. I have a bucket list I'm gonna follow. My parents have given me the money—their gift to me."

I leaned back over to lay my head on his chest, and my warm tears soon soaked his shirt. He wrapped his arm back around me. I think I felt a tear or two strike the top of my head. We stayed like that for a while. The television was silent and changed to a blue screen at the end of the credits.

"What if I want to go with you?"

Aaron laughed for the first time in a while. "You can't do that. I couldn't let you. You don't want to waste a year or two on a man you know will die. You don't want to get attached to someone you're going to lose and have nothing to show for that time. I would love to have you with me, but that would be totally selfish. This is a trip I have to take alone."

Just when I thought I had cried out all my tears, they poured freely again. He hugged me tightly. "But we still have to be friends the rest of this semester and until you leave," I said. "You have to promise me that!"

"As long as we go back to just being friends, hanging out and doing stupid stuff."

"OK." Something was better than nothing.

"And no more chick flicks!"

***

We did just what we promised. The next day, we pretended nothing had happened the night before. The weeks and months flew by, and we spent every free minute together. He continued to keep us busy with every activity known to man. We even went skydiving. I never asked to see his bucket list, but I was sure he had crossed off several entries. We didn't kiss again, although there were moments along the way when we would stare into each other's eyes, and I had to fight the urge. Occasionally, we held hands while skating or climbing, and chills ran up my arm. I knew I was falling in love, despite trying to just be a friend. I had no way to be sure, but I thought he felt the same about me.

We talked more now about life and dreams. He told me about his pretty amazing travel plans. He listed about every spot on the globe that I knew anything about. Hearing him talk about the end of his life and hoping to make it home to die with his family made me sad. Life wasn't fair. He had such a great personality and love for life but would probably die by twenty-five. In my own selfish thoughts, I had met the greatest man I could ever imagine, one I could fall in love with and live happily ever after with, and yet I could never pursue it.

As the semester wound down and exams started, we spent more time apart. We both blamed studying, but we both knew the real reason. Doomsday was rushing toward us, and neither of us knew how to handle it. He planned to fly to Cairo on graduation night and begin his journey with the pyramids. Graduation day would be the last time I would ever see him.

We only saw each other a couple of times between study sessions during the last week. It was awkward and strange, without much laughter, fun, or talking. I wanted to hug and kiss him so badly but knew that I couldn't—it would only make things that much more complicated. So we did the best we could until our exams, and our short time together, were done.

***

Graduation day is supposed to be one of the best days of your life. Mine wasn't. I briefly met Aaron's family, and he mine. We all experienced the same unspoken emotions: joy and pride at college graduation and sorrow over Aaron's pending solo journey. My family knew about Aaron and his situation, so they understood my struggle. The speeches and handing out of diplomas were just a blur. I scarcely recall my walk and accepting my diploma. I do remember crying when Aaron received his, and his parents stood and cheered.

Aaron and his family managed to disappear afterward without me seeing them. I suddenly felt panic spread through my body as I fought against the tears and nausea. Suddenly, at that moment, I knew I had to see him. We had to talk one last time. I said goodbye to my parents and hurried back to my apartment. I had already packed my bags, so I just had to throw them into my car. Then I drove as fast as I could to Aaron's apartment. When I arrived, I saw that he had already left for the airport. I sped after him, praying I wasn't too late. During that maddening high-speed drive, I replayed our entire relationship in my mind: every act, every conversation, and every emotion. I knew what I had to do.

***

An hour later, I dashed through the airport, trying to locate gate forty-seven. I swerved back and forth, bumping and pushing my way past some of the slower people. I finally found the gate and was instantly relieved to see the area still full of people. I spotted Aaron's shiny bald head easily despite the crowd. He stood leaning against a column, reading

183

a magazine. As if sensing my approach, he glanced up as I neared. His eyes widened, and his mouth fell open in surprise.

"I'm sorry," he said before I could even speak. "I just thought it would be easier this way."

"Easier for who? Friends don't do friends like that!" I scolded, not hiding my anger.

He looked at me with a pained expression. "I'm really sorry. I don't know which one of us I was trying to make it easier for. I guess both."

"Aaron, you're the best friend I've ever had. It's been hard enough these past few months, knowing that you would walk out of my life forever. Now, you even try to take away the chance to say goodbye!"

I saw the tears appear in his eyes and suddenly felt terrible about scolding him. I stepped forward and hugged him, placing my head on his chest and wrapping my arms around him. He placed his arms around me and rested his cheek against the top of my head. My tears ran down my face and disappeared into his shirt. We just held each other for a minute or two, not daring to speak.

I finally moved away so we could look at each other. "I'm not going to let you say goodbye."

"Huh? What do you mean?"

I reached into my pocketbook and produced a plane ticket. "You didn't think they'd let me come this far without a ticket, did you?"

His facial expression was almost comical as his mind struggled to process the situation. "You bought a ticket just to come to the gate to say goodbye?"

"You're a college graduate; you should be able to figure this out." I laughed and received a slight grin from him in return. "I'm going to Egypt with you."

"What? You can't...."

"Can't I?"

"But..."

"Aaron, do you love me?" I boldly asked.

He didn't hide his shock at the question. We'd never discussed the subject or anything close to it. "Yes, I do. But..."

"I love you too!" I exclaimed with relief. "And it's been killing me ever since the first night we kissed, not being able to show my emotions for you or experience everything we could offer each other."

"But you know my situation! We can't do this."

"I thought I agreed with that, until today at graduation and during the drive here. It hit me that we've been idiots all these months and are on the verge of making the worst mistake of our lives."

"What's the point of pursuing things further if I'm dead in a year or two?" he asked, staring at the floor.

"What I realized is that there are no guarantees in life or in relationships. Anyone can die at any moment. When two people enter into a relationship and fall in love, they don't think about what might happen to the other person in the future. As in marriage, it's for better or for worse." I pleaded my case the best I could but saw he wasn't sold on it yet.

"Two people don't normally know ahead of time that they have to deal with something like this," he said softly.

"There are no guarantees in your situation either! Sure, the odds are against you, but it's just doctors giving their best guesses. The cancer might not come back. You could live to be one hundred. And if you do, you'll always wonder about what you missed along the way. It's great that you want to live life like you're dying, but you can't do that if you're afraid of living!" I grabbed both his hands and held them as we talked.

He struggled with what to say next. "So you're saying you want to come with me?"

"I want to be with you! I want to love you! If that means going to Egypt or China or the moon, then so be it. I can't turn my back on these feelings or on you. Love is too special to walk away from. If we only have one year or two years, it will be the best one or two years of either of our lives. A little love is better than no love at all."

His smile finally appeared. He released my hands, wrapped his arms around my waist, and hoisted me off the ground. I laughed as he spun us around in a circle, to the stares of many people. "I love Lori Anderson!" he shouted loudly. I leaned down and kissed him for only the second time in our lives. It was even better than the first. The rush of joy and relief, combined with the best kiss of my life, was surreal. I wasn't sure if I was floating or if he was still holding me. We kept kissing as he held me off the ground, neither of us caring what anyone thought.

Finally, he set me back down on the ground. "You know that we're both crazy, right?" he asked, still grinning from ear to ear.

"No. You are. I'm just your chaperone."

Schrödinger's Email

"What's the password for your Yahoo account?" I asked, not managing to hide my near exasperation.

"Yahoo?" Dad said from the couch.

"Yes. As if your other three emails weren't enough, you also have a Yahoo account."

He turned his head and stared at me for a moment, his brows furrowed. "Oh," he finally replied.

"Oh?" I rubbed my tired eyes, fried from cleaning up Dad's computer for four hours, including sifting through years of junk emails in three different email accounts. "Care to expound?"

His expression was unreadable until I spotted the mischievous twinkle in his eye, followed by a wry grin. "Nosy pest." He chuckled. "To be honest, my memory is a little foggy. Which, I'm sure, is not shocking news to you." He ran a hand through his thinning hair.

"I'm still shocked you had one email account, much less four."

Dad held up a fist and shook it a couple of times.

"Bring it, old man! Now, are you going to share your feeble memories or what?"

After a moment's pause, he began his tale. "Well, I suppose you remember the time your mother and I split up?"

"Uh, gee, no, I didn't notice anything like that in my most formative years.... And I believe divorce is a little more than a split up."

"Wiseass! Despite what your mother thought, I didn't start seeing anyone until after the divorce was final. It began as work friends, talking at lunch and on breaks. Then she created a Yahoo email account for me so that we could share emails after work. I wasn't looking for a relationship and wasn't much for talking on the phone. Keep in mind that this was before texting became the annoying thing it is now."

It was strange seeing my father serious and on the verge of sharing something intimate from his past. He was a great dad, but he was an old-school man, one that didn't express feelings—ever. "Just after the time of smoke signals?"

He scowled but continued. "We soon found ourselves emailing back and forth every night, as well as each day at work. We'd end each night with an email and start each morning with another."

"Wow, you were a player!"

He threw a pillow at me, which landed a little short.

"We gradually worked up to dating outside work. But we still shared good night and good morning emails every day. I guess it was kind of our thing."

He fell silent for a while. I wasn't sure whether he was willing to share more or not, but I was intrigued. It was strange hearing him talk about another woman. Mom had been dead for two years, and of course, he didn't end up with this mystery woman, but it was still a surreal moment. "So, what happened?"

Dad sighed. "She was a great woman, and we were both falling for each other pretty hard."

"But it didn't work out." I could have sworn Dad's eyes looked a little glassy.

"Because of me. In the end, I loved you and your mother more and wanted my family back. I broke it off with her."

"With an email?" I asked, not a barb this time.

Dad chuckled. "No. It was in-person late one evening. And it was the first night since we had become serious friends that I didn't send an email. I never checked that email account again."

"You never thought about it? Wondered if she had tried to contact you over the years?"

Dad nodded. "Every day for some time. Don't get me wrong. I loved your mother and was content with my decision, but I did wonder. But after a while, I realized that there was no good scenario. It wouldn't have mattered if she had or hadn't tried to contact me. I wasn't leaving you two again."

We were both silent for a couple of minutes. "What about now?"

"Huh?"

"What if she has contacted you over the years, wrote that if you were ever single again to send her an email?"

Dad smiled. "I guess that ship has sailed."

"Maybe not. Do you know if your woman ever married or where she's at now?" I found myself getting a little excited. I knew Dad was lonely, and he had grieved two years for my mother. It would be good if he at least had a friend.

"I know she married. I have no idea if she still is or where she lives. She left the company a year or two after we broke up."

"I say let's reset your password and take a look."

"No!" Dad's protest was surprisingly forceful.

"What would it hurt to look? She might not have ever emailed you. Or she might have emailed letting you know she's still interested and available."

"I'm still not sure if I'm interested in either result."

"Hmmm…."

"What?" Dad said.

"This reminds me of something I learned in physics last month. Have you ever heard of Schrödinger's Cat?"

"It sounds vaguely familiar. Refresh my memory, though."

"Quantum mechanics teaches that you can't know the state and position of a particle until you observe it. Well, this famous physicist, Schrödinger, proposed a thought experiment where someone locks a cat into a steel box with a flask of poison, a radioactive source, a hammer, and a Geiger counter. If the Geiger counter detects a single atom decaying, the hammer shatters the flask, which releases the poison and kills the cat. But since no one is there to observe whether an atom decays or not, quantum mechanics implies that the cat is both alive and dead at the same time. No one knows which state it's in until they open the box and observe the cat."

"What in the world is the point of that story?"

"Considering that I've forgotten most of the details of that lecture, probably that I should have paid more attention in class." I laughed. "It's a stretch, but your email account is kind of like Schrödinger's cat. There may or may not be an email in there. No one will ever know until someone looks in your inbox."

"Gee, so glad I dropped $80,000 on that education of yours," Dad said.

"That reminds me, I still need to find you that nursing home." I once again received a fist shake. My Dad's mind and wit were still as sharp as ever. "I say we look and end the mystery."

Dad leaned his head back on the couch again. I could sense he was wavering a little. "Even if I agreed to your hair-brained scheme, I have no idea what the password is. That was almost twenty years ago."

I stared at the login screen for a moment and then clicked 'Forgot Password.' "I don't suppose you still have the same cell phone number, do you?"

"I've probably had four since then."

"What has been your primary email account over the years?"

He rubbed his head again. "I guess Hotmail. What are you doing over there?"

I entered his Hotmail email address for the password reset. A minute later, I opened another Chrome tab and logged into his Hotmail account. "Ah-ha! I just sent a reset password to your Hotmail. All we have to do is click the link, choose a new password, and you're in."

Dad sat upright and turned to face me. "Don't reset the password! I need time to think about this. And if anyone is going to do it, it's me."

I held my hands up in surrender. "OK. OK. That's all I'm going to do. I won't mention it again. But now, if you ever want to check on Mr. S's cat, you know what to do." I stood up and walked to the couch. "Well, as fun as this has been, I've got to run."

"Alright, thanks for your help, Tommy. Love you."

I leaned down for our usual half-hug. "Love you too, old man." I leaped back to avoid the smack on my leg and headed out the front door.

***

"Dad?" I said as I re-entered the door ten minutes later to retrieve my wallet, which I had left on the desk. Dad sat at the computer, staring at the screen. His head slowly swiveled to look at me. For a moment, it appeared that he didn't recognize me. I was shocked to see tears streaming down his cheeks. Mom's funeral was the first time I had ever seen Dad cry, and I never expected to see it again. "What's wrong?"

A slow grin spread across his face, stretching toward the ears. "I guess the damn cat is alive."

The Long, Winding Road

'Virginia, you are my first and true love. No matter what happens between now and then, I'll be waiting for you at the end of the long, winding road. Love, Sam.'

"Awe! How sweet, Momma!" Rachel exclaimed. She handed the high school yearbook back to her mother. "And now you run into Sam here after all these years."

Virginia took the book and smiled down at Sam's words from sixty years prior. "It is hard to believe. We were all sharing stories from high school a few weeks ago, and I passed my yearbook around. A little bit later, a handsome gentleman rolled over to me and said he was Sam."

Rachel frowned. "Momma, are you sure it's him?" Her mother's mind was steadily deteriorating since she had placed her in Whispering Pines. She was easily confused.

"Well, I was a little skeptical too. But we've been talking for the past few weeks and sharing stories of the class of 1958. He knows many things that only Sam could know."

Rachel finally returned her mother's smile. She couldn't remember if she had ever seen her so happy, so glowing—at least not since before her father had passed away twenty years prior. "That's great, Momma. I'm so glad you've found a friend."

Virginia's smile suddenly disappeared. She grabbed her daughter's hand, squeezing it with her thin, wrinkled fingers. Her eyes glistened.

"What is it?"

"Do you think daddy would approve?"

"Of course! It's been twenty years. I'm sure he'd want you to be happy. Sam is an old friend from high school. Daddy was the love of your life, right?"

Virginia turned away and stared out the small window. The sun flickered and danced through the leaves of the willow tree. For a moment, her mind drifted back through time. She was gently pulled back by the squeeze of her daughter's hand. "Yes, your father was the love of my life. He should have been here with me, sharing our last days together." Virginia turned back to face Rachel. Her beautiful daughter had her father's eyes and smile. "But Sam was my first love. You never forget your first love."

"That was sixty years ago, Momma. You lived a happy and fulfilling life with daddy, didn't you?"

Virginia grinned. "Yes, I did, sweetie. He gave me the best years of my life. And you."

"So why did you and Sam break up back in high school?"

Virginia gazed back out at the willow—its branches swayed elegantly in the breeze. "To be honest, I had forgotten…until Sam and I started talking. He was hell-bent on leaving town and making something out of himself. He was going to head out to the west coast after graduation. I just wasn't ready to leave my family and risk everything for my first boyfriend and his crazy dream. Besides, I'm sure my family would have disowned me if I had."

"How did he end up back here?"

"His parents got sick about fifteen years ago. He left a good job out in Silicon Valley and came back to take care of them. With the money he made out there, and the money they left him when they passed, he just retired here."

"His wife?"

"Passed away from breast cancer ten years ago. Now, honey, let me ask you a question. Are *you* OK with Sam?"

Rachel laughed. "Momma, you're happier than I've seen you in a long time. I've been worried about you being depressed since you first came here. If he can make you this happy, then I promise that Daddy and I are both more than OK with it."

Virginia lit up again. "Thank you, dear. I am very happy. Now this place doesn't feel like a prison…or graveyard."

***

"I probably shouldn't ask you this," Virginia said, gazing at Sam. His eyes still looked as blue and young as they had so many years ago.

"Uh, oh. Probably not," Sam chuckled.

"Just for that, I will! Do you remember that time at old Smith's pond?"

"Hmmm…not sure. Which time?"

"Oh, I'm sure you do. I can remember it like it was last night. It was Saturday night after the homecoming dance. A big group of us went to a party in a nearby field. About midnight, me and you slipped off. Once we got away from the bonfire, the moon made it almost bright as day. It was a hot, humid night too. We walked to the pond, and you dared me to take off my clothes and jump in. I'm pretty sure you just wanted to see me naked, but I couldn't turn down a dare. So I slipped out of my dress and rushed headlong into the water. Then I had to dare you to join me— which of course, you did. Oh, we frolicked and carried on for hours in that old pond, never once worrying about snakes or snapping turtles."

Sam laughed. "Are you sure we only frolicked?"

"Well, Sam Miller! I'll have you know that I was the purest of ladies back then…and still am," Virginia said, placing both hands on her hips. Finally, she cracked a smile, and they both laughed.

"Those were some crazy times back then, huh?"

"Indeed they were. I'm sure we had worries, but the memories sure seem carefree."

Virginia was surprised when Sam reached over and laid his hand on top of hers, which now rested on the armrest of her wheelchair. Her eyes slowly traveled from his hand to his face. He grinned warmly. She nervously smiled back and turned her hand over beneath his, intertwining their fingers. Other than doctors and therapists, it was the first man's hand she had held since her husband had passed away so long ago. It felt strange but also comforting. It had been a long time since her heart had fluttered.

***

"Momma, I'm hearing some pretty juicy rumors around here," Rachel said, sitting by her mother's bed a few days later.

193

"Oh, you know how old people like to gossip," Virginia said, unable to suppress a smile. "Like a bunch of clucking hens around here."

"Well, I don't know if it's gossiping, but I'm hearing a lot about a certain young man and lady spending almost every day and evening together, talking and laughing like high school kids."

"Well, I suppose there wouldn't be any harm in that..."

"And it's also being said that they're always holding hands," Rachel continued, enjoying teasing her mother. Virginia's mind had been clear and sharp for the past few weeks, and she radiated happiness.

"Is holding hands some kind of crime now?" Virginia asked.

"I don't guess so. But what's next for those lovebirds? Making out?"

"Rachel Renee! I will have no such filth uttered in my room!" Virginia exclaimed, placing her hands on her hips.

Rachel burst out laughing first, quickly followed by Virginia. Virginia's laughter finally ended in a fit of coughing. She finally composed herself and took a few deep breaths. "I don't think those two will be doing any kissing. At their age, just sharing a talk and a little hand-holding is quite enough."

"I'm just glad you're so happy, Momma. Well, I'd better run. You try to behave yourself." Rachel stood, bent over, gave her mother a hug, and turned to leave. "Oh, Momma, what room is Sam in? If you don't mind, I'd like to meet him sometime."

"As long as you don't say anything to scare him off."

"Don't be silly! I just want to thank him for putting the smile back on your face."

"Room 110."

***

Rachel left her mother's room and made her way to the 100's wing on the other end of the facility. As she approached 110, she slowed her pace and took a couple of deep breaths. She didn't know why she was so nervous. She stopped just outside the door, before she could see in or anyone inside could see her. Then she read the name on the door, 'Frank Baker.' She checked the room number again and then the name on the door. She slowly stepped forward and peered inside.

A white-headed gentleman was sitting in a wheelchair watching the television. He turned and saw her before she could retreat. "Well, hello, young lady. Can I help you?" The man's smile was warm and inviting.

Other than the white hair and being confined to a wheelchair, the man appeared healthy. She could see that he was probably a handsome man in his prime. Even now, there was a charm in his twinkling eyes.

194

"Uh…um…I think I'm looking for a Sam, who I heard was in this room."

The man's smile quickly fled. He turned away from Rachel and stared down at his feet. "You must be Rachel, Virginia's daughter."

Rachel's mouth fell open. She had been prepared to quickly exit. Now this man that wasn't Sam knew who she was. "How do you know my name?" she finally uttered.

"Come in and have a seat. I suppose we need to talk."

Rachel walked numbly to a chair near the door and dropped into it. "So you *are* Sam?"

The man sighed. "No. I'm Frank...Frank Baker." He paused and turned to look at Rachel again. When she didn't respond, he continued, "I was Sam's best friend in school and a very good friend of Virginia."

"So why are you claiming to be Sam?"

"When Virginia started talking about high school and passing her yearbook around, it was obvious that she still had feelings for Sam even after all these years. I knew she was head-over-heels in love with him in school." Frank paused long enough to grab the glass of water on the nearby tray and take a long drink. He set it down and returned his gaze to Rachel. "I know Sam didn't love her back, though. Well, he might have thought he did, but he didn't. Sam was only concerned with one person— Sam. But I really cared about your mother. I had a crush on her all through school. I was the one that loved her."

"Did she know?" Rachel was still stunned but very intrigued.

"No. Sam was my best friend. And even though I know he didn't have your mother's best interests in mind, I bit my tongue. I always hoped that I would have a chance to tell and show Virginia how I felt one day. I was the one there for your mother every time Sam broke her heart—it was my shoulder she cried on. The funny part is, I was the one that talked her into going back to him each time."

"What about what Sam wrote in the annual?"

Frank chuckled. "Poor Sam didn't have a romantic bone in his body. I told him what to write. Then after high school, he just up and left town. He broke Virginia's heart one last time and headed to Hollywood to become famous." Frank turned away from Rachel and stared blankly at the television.

"So what happened to him?" Rachel was sitting on the edge of her chair now.

"He called me a time or two over the years. He never made it as an actor but did have some success behind the camera, directing and

195

producing some low-budget films and commercials. I heard from his brother about five years ago that he had passed away from a heart attack."

"What about the story you told my mother about Sam—about him coming back to care for his parents?

"That part was about me. I had also headed west but ended up in the computer industry. I did come back to take care of my parents and ended up retiring here."

They were both silent for a couple of minutes. "So why didn't you just tell Momma who you really are? You were a good friend of hers. This might have finally been your chance to be more than a friend," Rachel said.

Frank's eyes glistened when he faced her again. "I thought seriously about it. But I was scared of only being a friend once again. Sam is the one that she always wanted. He was her first love and the one that got away. Before I knew it, I was Sam. I remember enough of those years that I can play the part well enough."

"But that doesn't seem right to lie to my mother; to pretend to be someone you're not." Rachel was suddenly not feeling so happy about the story.

"She might think I'm Sam, but it's me that she's talking to every day. It's my hand she's holding. It's me putting that smile on her face. And is she not happier than she's been since your father passed away?"

Rachel wanted to argue, but she couldn't. "But what do you get out of it?"

"The love of a lifetime." Frank dabbed at the corner of his eyes with the sleeve of his shirt. "Your mother and I don't have a lot of time left. But we're both as happy as we can be. At this point, it doesn't matter whether I'm Sam or Frank. I'm the person with your mother now. She loves that person, and I love her. It might not be the same way we loved our spouses, but it's love. After sixty years of waiting, the long winding road led to here."

Rachel quickly wiped her own eyes. She stood and walked over and hugged Frank. "Thank you," she whispered and promptly left the room.

***

Virginia wasn't in her room when Rachel arrived the following week. Rachel figured she was somewhere with Frank and started to leave to find her when she noticed the yearbook lying on the nightstand. She quickly walked over, snatched it up, and sat on the bed. She flipped through the pages until she found Frank Baker. He was indeed a handsome young man. Then she found a picture of her mother, Sam, and Frank together,

196

leaning against an old car. Sam and Frank actually resembled each other. That's probably why her mother didn't question Frank being Sam now.

She flipped to the back of the book. Just below Sam's dedication was another one—from Frank. It was a long post highlighting their friendship and high school years together. It was the last two lines that caught her eye. She bet Sam had never seen it, and her mother probably never gave it a second thought.

> 'I will always be here for you, as a friend and a shoulder to cry on. And if that long, winding road doesn't end up where you want it to, I'll be waiting for you back at the start. Your friend forever, Frank.'

***

"Do you ever wonder what would have happened if we'd never been separated after high school—if we had spent our entire lives together?" Frank asked. They sat outside beneath the willow. The fall day was unusually warm.

Virginia squeezed his hand and smiled. "No. I had a good life with my husband, who I loved very much. And I wouldn't have my sweet Rachel. I know you loved your wife and children too. I think things worked out just like they were supposed to. You were waiting for me at the end of the long, winding road."

Frank laughed. "Well, since we've both ended up back in town, five miles from the old high school, it's like we ended up back at the beginning."

"Hmmm… I never thought of it like that, but I think you're right. Well, beginning or end, I'm just glad that we ended up together somewhere on the same long, winding road."

Dreams of Hope & Family

Open Field

"Come on, Tyler! Come on, Tyler! Get him!" James shouted from the stands. He stood, as did everyone else, as the play unfolded below. It was a tie game with a minute left in regulation. The winner went to the state championship game; the loser went home. The Falcons had just completed an out pattern to their star wide receiver, and he was running with open field in front of him. James's son Tyler, the free safety, was the only one who could prevent the game-winning touchdown.

The number of college scouts in attendance made the game even more critical. Several colleges had already contacted Tyler, but he hadn't received any official scholarship offers yet. However, this game was a huge showcase. So far, he had played great: six tackles, one sack, an interception, and no touchdown passes thrown against him. Now, it all came down to this one play. Tyler eluded the tight end's block with a juke and a stiff-arm and sped toward number one. The fans roared on each side of the field. Closer and closer, the two forces rushed toward each other. Number one realized he couldn't fake out Tyler, so he lowered his shoulder and head and prepared for contact. Tyler also lowered his upper body in anticipation of a crushing hit and a game-saving tackle.

"Go, Tyler!" Vanessa screamed from beside her husband.

"Hit him, boy! Hit him!" James yelled.

The two finally met, helmet to helmet, knocking the big receiver slightly backward and sending him tumbling out of bounds. Tyler's momentum was instantly halted, and his body dropped straight to the ground, facedown. He didn't move.

"Oh, my God! Tyler!" Vanessa shouted, staring down at her son in horror.

"He knows better than to lead with his head!" James shouted with his hands on the sides of his head.

"How can you even be thinking something like that?" Vanessa asked incredulously.

"I've only been drilling that into his head for twelve years now! Now he does it in front of all these college scouts in the biggest game of his life."

"I can't believe you!" Vanessa left his side and ran down the stairs to the field as the ambulance drove onto it.

***

"Mr. and Mrs. Davis?" the surgeon asked as he walked into the waiting room. They both quickly stood. Tyler had been in surgery for four hours. They knew little, other than that he had a severe, potentially life-threatening spinal cord injury.

"Please have a seat, and I'll tell you about your son's injury." They all three sat, with the Davises seated on the edges of their chairs. "Your son is stable but still in critical condition." Vanessa gasped and couldn't hold back her tears. James put his arm around her. "He sustained a fracture and dislocation between the C3 and C4 vertebrae. The good news is that his spinal cord wasn't entirely severed. We did a bone graft and inserted a plate between the two vertebrae."

"How is he?" James asked. "Is he awake? Can he move?"

"He's still in recovery now but should be awake and alert once the anesthesia wears off. He's breathing on his own, although we're giving him oxygen. However, he is paralyzed from his shoulders down."

"Oh, my God," James whispered, shaking his head and staring at the floor.

"Is it permanent?" Vanessa asked, tears flowing down her cheeks.

"There's about a ninety percent chance that it is."

"No...No..." James sobbed softly.

"There's still a chance he will get some sensation back and even regain some movement. We'll know more over the next few days. If he starts to regain any feeling and movement, then there is a chance that he may not remain quadriplegic."

"So he could make a full recovery and be normal again?" James asked, a spark of hope in his eyes.

"In a situation like this, we're not looking for normal. In a perfect scenario, Tyler could regain use of his upper body and possibly walk with assistance. But he won't be playing football again."

The three were silent for a moment. "When can we see him?" Vanessa finally asked.

"It will probably be another hour or two. We'll have to get him out of recovery and set him up in his room. The nurse will come to get you when he's ready."

"Are you happy now?" Vanessa asked James a few minutes after the doctor left.

"What are you talking about?" James demanded.

"You always had to push him, from the time he was six until now. Nothing was ever good enough for you. No matter how many tackles he made or touchdowns he scored, it was never good enough. He always felt like he had to give more to make you happy."

"I can't believe you're trying to blame me! It was an accident. He made a tackle, leading with his head, and now he's here. It could have happened to anyone on that field," James shot back.

"But it happened to our son! He wasn't just trying to make a tackle; he was trying to make one that would impress you. And because he was trying to live up to your unattainable expectations, he might never walk again. He might not even be able to take care of himself again!" Vanessa began sobbing too hard to continue speaking.

James stood and walked out of the waiting room toward the hospital's front door. He had to get out of that room and away from his wife. He needed some fresh air. He hurried through the front doors and out onto the sidewalk. He walked a short way and sat down on the concrete wall at the back of the emergency room parking lot. It was a cool, cloudy night, but it felt good on his hot, still-red face. As he sat there, his mind wandered back in time.

***

"Dad, did you see that? I made the tackle!" Tyler exclaimed as he ran over to the sideline.

"Son, you got lucky. You know better than to tackle that low. You'll never bring down a good running back like that. And you don't just hang onto him until he falls. Hit him! Put that shoulder into his belly and knock him down!" James shook his head as he watched his seven-year-old son walk over to the bench and sit down. He had to learn, though; he might as well teach him right from the start.

***

"Son, get over here!" James grabbed Tyler's face mask and jerked it up until their faces were inches apart. "What are you doing out there?"

"I thought he was going to run with it."

"You're the safety! You don't play the run unless he crosses the line of scrimmage!"

"I'm sorry, Dad. I messed up."

"Get your head in the game! This ain't Peanut League anymore."

***

"James!" a voice shouted, jerking him back into the present. "We can see him now." James turned to see his wife standing outside the doors. He jumped up and hurried inside with her. They walked quickly in silence to their son's room. After a momentary pause outside the entrance to steady their nerves, they entered.

Tyler appeared frail and small in the bed. Tubes and wires came from every part of his body, and the machines surrounding him emitted a steady stream of beeps, clicks, and whirs. The nurse smiled at them as she brushed past to exit the room. James and Vanessa walked over to the bed, one going to each side. Tyler's eyes were open, though not wide. He stared straight up at the ceiling.

Vanessa placed his left hand into hers and positioned her other hand on his head. "Hey, sweetie. How are you doing?"

"Great," he whispered in a soft, raspy voice. His face was expressionless.

"The worst part is over. Now we just have to get you better."

"Sounds easy enough…." Tyler whispered. "Dad?"

"I'm here, Son," James responded from the other side of the bed.

"Did we win?"

"I haven't heard yet. We didn't stick around for the end of it," James said with a halfhearted chuckle.

The three fell silent again, and his parents saw tears running down their son's cheeks. Vanessa grabbed a tissue from a nearby box and quickly wiped them away. "It's OK, Tyler. You'll beat this."

"Dad?" he asked again, his voice shaking.

"Yes?"

"I'm sorry. I'm really sorry!"

"Sorry?" James asked, wiping the tears from the corners of his own eyes.

"I messed up, Dad. I messed up really bad." Tears flowed faster than Vanessa could wipe. "I didn't mean to lead with my head. I tried to use my shoulder, but he leaned the other way at the last second. But…but I

204

should have gone lower, underneath his helmet. I should have been ready….”

“Tyler, you didn't do anything wrong!” Vanessa sobbed. “It was an accident. You were just making a tackle.”

The three were silent once again. Finally, Tyler spoke. “I'm getting pretty tired. I think I need to sleep now.”

“You get plenty of sleep, and we'll see you again in the morning. Love you, baby.” Vanessa kissed him on his forehead and squeezed his hand.

“Good night, Son,” James said.

“Night, Mom and Dad.”

***

“How does that make you feel?” Vanessa asked on the drive home.

“How does *what* make me feel?”

“Your son apologizing to you for getting paralyzed.”

“I don't want to talk about this.”

“Of course not. It's always about you.”

“I'm not going to listen to this now!” They didn't speak again for the remainder of the trip home. Vanessa went to bed as soon as they arrived at their house, and James sat down on the couch with only a lamp turned on. He didn't turn on the TV; he just stared at the blank screen.

***

“Dad, can I go camping this weekend?” Tyler asked anxiously.

“Son, what is next week?” James asked, looking over the top of the newspaper.

“Football training camp,” Tyler responded, staring down at the floor.

“And what do you think we need to be doing this weekend?”

“I guess practicing.”

“Very good. Tell your friends maybe sometime in the spring.” James went back to reading the paper. He knew his son was upset, but this was eighth-grade football, the last year before high school football—a critical year for his football future. Tyler would get over not going camping and someday thank him for pushing him.

***

James opened his eyes and wiped the tears away from their corners. Memory after memory flooded his mind as he replayed Tyler's entire life—a life dedicated to football. He shook his head.

***

“Dad, I've been doing a lot of thinking, and there is something I really want to do,” Tyler said, his voice shaking.

205

"What now, Son?" James asked, looking up from the Ford engine he was repairing.

"You know I won that writing contest in May."

"Go on," James urged, aggravated at taking time away from his project.

"Well, there's an awards banquet and writer's conference next week in Philadelphia. I'd get to meet a lot of professional writers, accept my award, and attend a lot of good workshops." Tyler became more excited as he talked.

"Son, you know this is summer training camp."

"But, Dad, I already talked to the coach. He said with my performance last year, I could miss a few days. And I'd only miss three practices. It's not like we do much for the first week, just conditioning and basic position tryouts. Coach said I'm the starting safety."

James shook his head. "This is your first year of varsity football. You have to start fast this year. Scouts might even be at some of your games. Just think if you can impress them as a junior."

"But I really want to do this! This is a great opportunity, and I really like writing. Mrs. Campbell thinks I could really be a writer someday."

"Are you going to get a writing scholarship to college?"

Tyler stared at the ground. "No, sir."

"But you *are* good enough to get a football scholarship. Once you get into college, you can study English and write and do whatever else you want to do. But right now, you really need to stay focused."

"Yes, sir."

***

James slammed a fist down on the arm of the couch. He stood and went into the kitchen—straight to the liquor cabinet. He removed the bottle of vodka and poured a glass half full. He usually mixed it with something but not tonight. He took his drink and sat back down on the couch.

***

"Dad, look at this!" Tyler exclaimed as he ran into the kitchen.

James glanced up from his breakfast and took the newspaper Tyler handed him. It was opened to the sports page. On the front was a picture of Tyler making a tackle. He had been named player of the week. "Not bad, huh?" Tyler asked, sitting down at the table as his father skimmed through the article.

"Looks like they left out some information," James said, setting the paper down and resuming eating his oatmeal.

"Huh? Left out what? I had an interception return for a touchdown, two tackles for losses, eight tackles total, and a sack."

"And two missed tackles."

"Hey, I was clipped on one, which wasn't called. The other one, I had help from the corner," Tyler responded defensively.

"Yet, they were still missed tackles. If they had resulted in touchdowns, your team would've lost, and you wouldn't have been player of the week. It was an OK game, but you have to step it up a notch. This is your final year of football, and you're being watched in every game—if not in person, then on tape."

Tyler stood up and walked out of the house, without a word, to go to school.

"Don't you think that was harsh?" Vanessa asked, turning from the stove to stare at her husband.

"I just don't want him to get a big head. He's close, dear, really close. It's no time to get cocky."

"I don't see how it would hurt anything if you gave him a pat on the back every now and then."

"Once he gets a scholarship to a football school, I'll give him all the pats he wants. Until then…"

***

That had been two weeks ago. James turned the glass of vodka up and drank it in two large swigs. He got up and filled the glass again. He couldn't take any more memories and was now struggling with the realization that everything his wife had said was true. It was his fault his son lay paralyzed in a hospital bed. A half-hour later, he was asleep on the couch.

***

"How's he doing?" Vanessa asked as soon as she saw the doctor at the nurses' station.

"Good morning, Mr. and Mrs. Davis. I actually have some good news for you. Tyler has regained some sensation in his arms and hands and even some limited movement. He also has some feeling in his legs and can wiggle his toes. That's exactly what we need to see."

"So he's not paralyzed?" James asked, some excitement in his voice.

"It's still too early to determine. It's definitely a good sign, but he does have a severe spinal cord injury. Let's be encouraged with his progress, but he still has a long way to go."

"May we see him now?" Vanessa asked.

"You may. He's awake."

207

James and Vanessa hurried to their son's room. "Good morning, baby!" Vanessa exclaimed as she ran over to kiss Tyler on the forehead. She grabbed his hand and squeezed it. "How are you feeling?"

"I'm OK, I guess. Better than yesterday."

"Good morning, Son," James said, grabbing Tyler's shoulder.

"Good morning, Dad," Tyler replied, glancing briefly at his father.

"The doctor said you're getting some feeling back," Vanessa said.

"Yeah. I can feel some sensation down my arms and in my fingers. Can you feel that?"

"Oh, that's great, honey!" she exclaimed as she felt his pinky finger move in her hand.

"And look down there."

They looked down at Tyler's feet and saw his left big toe move slightly.

"Wow, you're on your way back!" Vanessa exclaimed.

"There's still a long way to go from here to the football field, huh, Dad?"

James was silent for a moment, looking from his wife to his son. "Let's not worry about that. Just take it one day at a time."

Tyler stared at his father with some surprise on his face. "I'll get back out there. I'll make you proud."

James turned away, wiping a tear from his eye. He quickly composed himself and turned back around. "I *am* proud of you. I always have been."

"But I messed up! I'm the reason I'm here."

"*Don't* say that again," James said, raising his voice slightly. Vanessa and Tyler both stared at James, waiting for his next words. "Football is a game. You got hurt busting your butt making a game-saving tackle." James turned and walked over to the window. He stared outside for a few seconds before continuing. "Tyler," he began, a rare instance of using his son's name, "I've been an idiot all your life. You've always been a great football player, better than I ever was or ever dreamed of being. I pushed you way too hard, though. I expected way too much." He punched the wall beside the window. "*I'm* the reason you're here."

"It's not your fault!" Tyler exclaimed, not knowing how to react to this side of his father.

"It's no one's fault," Vanessa chimed in, looking at her husband as she spoke.

James turned back around from the window and walked over to the bed. He grabbed Tyler's other hand. "Tyler, I'm sorry. I'm so sorry."

Tears flowed freely out of James's eyes. He felt one of Tyler's fingers move slightly in his hand.

"You don't have to be sorry. I wanted to play football."

"But I made you sacrifice everything for it! I made you give up a big part of your childhood. And now…"

Tears ran out of Tyler's eyes and down his cheeks. "It's OK," he whispered.

James leaned over and placed his head on his son's shoulder. Vanessa let go of Tyler's hand and wiped tears from her own eyes. She couldn't believe the scene unfolding before her. She didn't speak. She didn't want to interrupt the moment.

"I'm going to beat this, Dad! I promise. I'll play again. Maybe I can walk on at Tech next year."

James raised his head to look his son in the eyes. "I know you'll beat it, and I'll be with you every step of the way, but you won't play football again. You need to leave that part of your life behind. It's time to move on."

"I don't understand. What are you saying?"

"You are a heck of a football player, one of the best to ever play high school ball in this state, but it's time to focus on the rest of your life. I know you'll walk again someday, but you won't be able to compete at the college level. It would be too dangerous anyway. You don't want to be here again or wind up in worse shape."

Tyler sobbed openly. Vanessa stepped forward and wiped the tears from his cheeks, trying her best to keep up with them. "What will I do? I don't know what else to do."

"You can do whatever you want to do. You can study whatever you want to study. It's your life now, not mine."

Tyler finally composed himself and smiled weakly. "That's a lot to think about."

"Well, you'll have plenty of time to think while you're healing, beating this. But can I make one suggestion…and only a suggestion?"

"Sure."

"Write. Once you get your arms and hands working, you need to write. It's time to use your talent. Take this as a blessing and an opportunity. There are no more rules or restrictions. This is your time. You're in the open field."

Tyler thought for a moment, and then a huge smile came across his face. "Thank you, Dad, for everything."

***

"Are you going to be able to forgive me for being a jerk all these years?" James asked his wife on the drive home.

Staring out the passenger window, she didn't respond right away. Then she turned to look at him. "In that room, I let go of the past. All three of us have a new beginning now. If you can stay the man you were in there and are right now, then I'll love you forever."

"Well, forever just started."

"Open field?"

"Wide open, baby. Wide open."

The Bum

Douglas lay on his back on the pure white sand, the golden rays of light caressing and warming his body as a soft breeze gently brushed his face. He listened to the hypnotic, steady crashing of the waves. A gull cried out from somewhere high overhead. Then he heard the sweet voices, laughing and talking, coming closer. He raised his head and saw his beautiful wife, her long brown hair shining in the sun, her tanned skin taut and glistening. A three-year-old white-haired boy held her right hand and a brown-haired seven-year-old girl her left. "Come on, Daddy; let's go jump waves!" the girl cried out. The boy ran over and dove in the air, his teeth showing behind a huge grin. The boy's knees struck Douglas's stomach hard, knocking the wind out of him. He jerked up into a sitting position.

***

He opened his eyes and then quickly squinted to avoid the sun's glare. A large figure loomed menacingly over him. Douglas raised his right hand over his eyes to further shield them. The figure shifted slightly, momentarily blocking the sun. It was a police officer, holding a nightstick in his left hand. He glared down with his coal-black eyes, his thin-lipped mouth curled into a sneer.

"Get off the bench, bum! Why don't you crawl back into the alleys with the rest of the trash? This park is for tax-paying citizens."

Douglas slowly stood, turned, and limped away from the bench. He didn't look at the officer or argue. He had learned the hard way what happened then. It was always the same routine. He walked toward the nearby trees. The sun felt good, and he wanted to stay in it, but he knew the cop was watching. His back was sore from sleeping on the bench, and his right knee hurt as usual. A car had given him the permanent limp the year before. His pains were always worse before his morning drink. He absently pressed his left elbow to his side and felt the comforting hardness of the bottle within his coat. *There's my medicine.*

Once in the sanctuary of the trees, he left the paved path and wandered down the trail to the small stream. He sat down on the soft grass of the bank. He liked the park. It was probably the only thing that kept him from losing all sanity. He took out the bottle of vodka and unscrewed the cap, stared at it briefly, and then turned it up. He lowered it again and wiped his mouth on his dirty sleeve. He would feel better, or at least experience less pain, in a few minutes. His dream had reopened wounds he had desperately tried to seal forever. It had been a while since he'd dreamed. As he leaned back against a tree, his eyes closed again.

***

"Down…set…hut…hut!" His seven-year-old son hiked the ball back to him and then took off running the route they'd drawn in the dirt moments before.

"One thousand one…one thousand two…" his wife counted, much too quickly. She jumped up and down, waving her arms to block his vision. She was so beautiful in her tight faded jeans and flannel shirt. No matter how tomboyish she dressed, she was still all woman.

His son pushed off his older sister and broke to the left. Douglas let the ball fly just as his wife reached "one thousand five." His wife continued charging even after the ball was long gone. She grabbed him around the waist and wrestled him to the ground. He didn't exactly fight it, and they hit the ground laughing. Then they both looked up to see what had happened to the pass.

His daughter, tall, thin, and changing into a woman all too quickly, leaped high into the air at the last moment. She grabbed the ball with a squeal of delight and charged toward them, away from her angry brother. He growled and raced after her. She tried to leap over her parents but was quickly plucked out of the air. She fell to the ground in her father's arms, followed soon by her younger brother diving onto the pile. All four wrestled around in the dry leaves, laughing and giggling in the fall sun.

***

He awoke to a stinging sensation on his face and chest. "Get a job like the rest of us!" the boys called out as they sped down the trail on their bikes. Douglas slowly leaned forward and looked around. He saw four quarters scattered on the ground. A couple of years ago, he would've been angry. Now, as he took another swig from his bottle, he needed all the money he could get. The day was early and his bottle, light. He slowly sat up, gathered the money, and stood and shuffled down the trail, further into the woods. He would rest again shortly. The soup kitchen and liquor store weren't far from the other side of the park. He hoped he could scrounge up enough money to buy his next bottle.

"Get a job," the young punks had yelled. Douglas would've laughed, if he remembered how. He used to make more money in a year than they would in the next ten. He shook his head and spit on the grass beside the trail. Heck, maybe it was just a dream. He barely remembered wearing the suits and ties, trading with tens of thousands of other people's dollars. He had possessed the Midas touch and found a winner, no matter how bad the market was doing. It was uncanny how he knew when to buy and sell. A tear crept into his left eye; a lot of good that Midas touch did him. A lot of good it was doing him now.

He was out of breath by the time he reached the bridge. He sat down beside it, his feet at the stream's edge. He hated what he had become. He was once on top of the world—perfect job, perfect family, perfect health. He used to turn away in disgust from the bums he passed each day on the way to work. He probably even told them to get a job too. It had been so easy living the good life, sitting high on his perch.

He fished the bottle out and took a deep drink. Only a few more remained, not nearly enough to stop the memories. He guessed it was the time of year. The trees had their full colors on display. He knew it was October, though he hadn't seen a calendar in more than a year. As the leaves changed, the memories stirred. He kept them in check most of the year, but now it was too close to the anniversary. He was powerless. All he could do was try to drown the thoughts as quickly as possible. But today, it was too early, the bottle too empty. He would have to endure.

He laid his head against the cold stone of the bridge wall, closed his eyes, and let the dreams flow.

***

The knock on the door caused Douglas to jump from his sleep. The clock on the wall said midnight. He stood up from the couch and quickly walked to the door. Apparently, his wife had forgotten her house key. He opened the door, but his wife and children were not standing there. He

213

blinked. A state police officer stood in the porch light, his face pale and expressionless. "Douglas Hodgins?"

Douglas nodded dumbly, unable to speak.

"Your family was involved in an accident…."

That was October 12. The funeral was three days later. A tractor-trailer driver had fallen asleep, crossed over into his family's lane, and struck them head-on. The officer said they died instantly. There was no viewing. Douglas attended the funeral, dressed in a black suit with a full-length black overcoat. He spoke briefly to his wife's family and then quickly left. He didn't call his own. All he really had was his alcoholic father in California. His mother had killed herself when he was eight years old. His father started drinking then and, to his knowledge, never stopped. His father never remarried, and Douglas remained an only child.

The brokerage firm was generous, letting him miss the first couple of weeks without saying anything. Then, when he didn't show up after a month, they mailed him a letter terminating his employment. He quickly sank into a zombie-like existence. It was as if his mind wouldn't let him think about his loss. Unfortunately, it wouldn't let him think about anything else either. He shuffled through life, surviving. He occasionally bought groceries but ate only enough to survive. The television stayed on twenty-four hours a day, though he never actually watched it. He sat and stared, but his eyes remained unfocused. He could have been staring out the window, even at a wall for that matter, but the noise was better than silence.

His money ran out a few months later. He sold his cars and other valuables to keep the house as possible, but soon, the bank repossessed that too. He found himself homeless, eating free meals at the soup kitchen, and sleeping in shelters on cold nights. He begged enough to get money for alcohol. That was really all he could obtain through charity.

He often thought about killing himself, but something deep inside wouldn't let him. He guessed it was the memory of his family. He wanted to be with them again someday, and the church had taught him that suicide resulted in going to hell, not heaven. He wasn't even sure there was a God and a heaven, especially after his family was taken without warning or reason, but it was worth a chance. He couldn't deal with the thought of never seeing them again.

So he existed, hoping and praying for death. Local gangs and hoodlums beat him often, but they never finished the job. Apparently, even they pitied him. He wished they would just put him out of his misery. He knew his lifestyle was taking its toll, though. He was sick frequently. Maybe pneumonia would take him that winter—if not that, perhaps cirrhosis.

***

Two approaching voices startled Douglas back into reality. He looked up to see two men dressed in fine suits walking toward the bridge from the other side. They were embroiled in a deep discussion on something dealing with money. He shook his head. He could almost see himself making that same walk, having that same discussion, just a few years earlier. He stared back down, avoiding eye contact. Their kind made him nervous.

Their shoes clacked loudly over the wooden boards of the bridge. Suddenly, their voices stopped, and Douglas sensed them staring at him from just a few feet away.

"Come on, Alex," one finally said to the other.

"No. This one might be the perfect test."

He cringed. Sometimes the upper class was meaner and more sadistic than the gangs.

"Oh, God," the first one responded. The two walked off the bridge and over to stand behind him.

"Excuse me, sir," the one called Alex said.

Douglas slowly turned to look over his shoulder. He knew ignoring them would only make things worse.

"Could we talk to you for a few minutes? I promise it will be worth your time."

Douglas squinted into the morning sun. Alex was probably forty, and his suit must have cost more than a thousand dollars. He was handsome and appeared intelligent. He didn't have that cocky, brash look he'd expected to see but rather a wisdom and compassion on his face. His younger companion lacked those qualities. He was obviously uncomfortable and wanted to be somewhere else. The corners of his mouth were drawn down in a look of disgust.

"Would you mind standing while we talk?" Alex asked.

Douglas shrugged. He was a little intrigued. This wasn't starting off like any of his street experiences up to this point. He slowly stood, favoring his right leg.

Alex looked into his eyes, making him immediately uncomfortable. The man's blue eyes seemed to bore into his soul. He felt naked. After a moment, Alex smiled, a genuine, warm smile. He glanced at his companion. "This is definitely the one." He turned back to Douglas. "Would you like to have a thousand dollars?"

215

Douglas stared hard at the man. *What kind of game is he playing?* He shrugged.

"Ah, come on! How many days of begging for change would it take to make a grand?"

"What's the catch?" Douglas croaked, his voice deep and hoarse. He hadn't spoken yet that day. He couldn't really remember when he last had.

"My friend here and I disagree on something. He believes that homeless people are homeless by choice; they end up on the street because they're weak or lazy. Even if you gave them money, they would only spend it on drugs and alcohol and wouldn't try to change their lives."

Douglas glanced at Alex's companion. His lips were still curled, his brow furled. The man quickly turned away as if embarrassed.

Alex continued, "I, however, disagree. While I agree that some meet that description, I believe that most of them, ones like you, are here through events out of their control. Some type of tragedy causes them to lose their identities and options, and they end up here on the street. I believe that if these individuals had a sum of money given to them, they could once again get back on their feet and rebuild their lives."

Douglas stared at the wealthy man but did not respond.

"With a thousand dollars, a man could rent a hotel room down the street, get cleaned up, eat some real meals, buy a decent suit, and go out and find a job."

"I don't want your money," Douglas said gruffly.

"You'd be crazy to turn it down! Why wouldn't you want it?"

"Your friend's right," Douglas said. "I would spend it on alcohol and wind up back on the street. I like it here."

"Told you," the first man said, turning back to the path.

"Wait a second. You would like it here, living in filth and begging for your next drink, better than having a job, an apartment, food, clean clothes, hot showers...."

"Yeah."

"Tell me your story," Alex said, not giving up.

"No! Why don't you two go back to your fancy offices and leave a bum alone?"

"Nope. We will stay with you until you tell us. You're not like most of the others out here on the street. I can see it in your eyes and face. You haven't lived out here long—your face isn't weathered enough. Your eyes give away your intelligence. I bet you used to be one of us. I have to know what brought you here."

Douglas wanted to protest again or try to escape. But then again, what did he care if they knew? He'd just relived it in his mind. He would share if it made them go away, just another persecution. He sat down and motioned for them to do the same. The first man began to protest, not wanting to wrinkle his pants, but Alex stopped him with a glare. They both sat down on the soft grass, and Douglas told them his story.

All three men sat in silence for a moment after he finished. "Wow, that's some story. I'm sorry to hear about your family. By the way, I'm Alex. My colleague here is Jason."

"Douglas," he croaked. He was tired. He just wanted the men to leave. "Now, can you two go and leave me alone?"

"Not yet," Alex said, obviously in deep thought.

"I don't want your money!"

"I understand what a terrible tragedy you went through, but you have grieved and done your time. Don't you think this is the opportunity to start over again?"

"Start over?"

"Think about it. Do you think your wife and children would want you to live like this? What if it had been you and your two kids in the car? Would you want your wife homeless, begging for change to buy alcohol? Or would you want her to go on with her life and be happy?"

"I…" Douglas couldn't finish. He'd never thought about it that way before. "But…" once again, he couldn't formulate a response.

"You don't have to answer. I'll make you a deal. I'm going to leave ten hundred-dollar bills here on the ground. You can take them or leave them. If you take them, you can spend them on booze and whatever other indulgences you wish. But if you want to start over, you can get a room in one of the cheap hotels two blocks from here, shower and clean up, and then catch a taxi to a decent clothing store. Buy yourself a suit and all the accessories. Be at the Charles Schwab building on Broadway at nine in the morning a week from today. Tell them you're there to interview for the broker job. Say Alex Streeter referred you."

Jason stared at his friend in disbelief. He looked at Douglas and then shook his head. Once again, he failed to hide his disgust.

Alex reached into his jacket and withdrew his leather wallet, counted out ten crisp bills, and laid them on the ground beside Douglas.

Douglas stared at the money for a moment and then back at Alex. "Why?"

"As I said, I believe many homeless people are here due to circumstances out of their control. If given a chance, they could become contributing members of society again. This is your second chance. Do it for your wife. Do it for your kids. Do it for yourself. You're a long way from dead. If you believe in a heaven and that your family is there, then one day, you'll be with them again. But today isn't that day."

Alex stood, and Jason quickly followed suit. "I hope to see you next Wednesday, Douglas."

The two men walked away, leaving Douglas to sit alone beside the money that could change his life. He watched them until they disappeared into the trees and shook his head. His life was fine like it was. He didn't want to go back to what he had. Then his wife's face appeared in his mind. She was so sweet, so caring, and so kind. It would break her heart to see him now. She would want better for him. He could almost see the heartbreak and disappointment on the faces of his two beautiful children. Their dad was a bum who begged for money to buy his next bottle. *God, what have I become?*

He grabbed the money and tucked it into his pocket. It was time to start living again.

***

Alex was the first to congratulate him upon his getting the job. "I knew you could do it!" Alex looked him up and down. "I can't believe this is the same bum we met last week."

"I have to apologize. I doubted Alex and you," Jason said, extending his hand. "I guess anyone could have ended up in your shoes."

"I will be forever indebted to both of you, not only for the money but also for making me realize what I had become. I'm looking forward to a new beginning."

***

Douglas moved into his new apartment. It was nothing fancy, but it was a start. It had furniture, food, and a hot shower. It took him a while to get back into the swing of life. He learned how to shop again, eat again, and dress again. He caught up on three years of world affairs. He visited the doctor for his leg and to get antibiotics for his bronchitis. He relearned the art of financial trading and started reading the *Wall Street Journal* from cover to cover each day. He went to church again. He'd always gone with his wife and children each Sunday. He met a few people there and found that he was at peace while in that building. He rediscovered hope and faith, and he found that this life made the pain of his loss a lot less than living on the streets. He replaced drinking with living.

***

A month later, Douglas had settled comfortably into his new existence. He wasn't exactly happy, but he also wasn't miserable. He existed. He went to work, came home, ate, and watched television. Occasionally, he would see a movie, by himself, of course. He read a lot and visited many of the bookstores in the city. He didn't date or put himself in situations where he would even meet women. For now, he was content with a life of solitude. Perhaps one day that would change.

***

One Monday morning, on his way to work, he stopped at the convenience store two blocks from the park he'd lived in just a couple of months earlier. He came here every Monday morning, just as he had while homeless. He used to take what change he'd collected from the weekend, not set aside for alcohol, and buy junk food. The little powdered donuts and Yoo-Hoos had remained two of his staples.

Jimmy, the store manager, was about as close to a friend as he had. He had waited on Douglas when he was homeless. Over those three years, Douglas had revealed his story. Now, Jimmy waited on the new Douglas. Jimmy was probably close to sixty years old, with a weathered face, a head of curly, graying hair, and a short, stocky build. He had shared his life story with Douglas too. He grew up on the streets close by. His life had been tough, but he persevered and succeeded. He started working as a stocker in the store when he turned sixteen. Over the years, he'd worked up to manager and now the owner. They wouldn't have exactly classified each other as good friends, but they were a substantial part of each other's lives.

"Have an exciting weekend, Doug?" Jimmy asked as Douglas approached the counter. A half-burnt cigar hung from the corner of his mouth.

"You know me."

"Find you a woman?" Jimmy asked, a sly grin on his face.

"Almost."

"Almost? What's that mean? You spotted one on the subway? You need to find you a good woman, somebody who will cook you some real food and put some meat on your bones!"

This was part of their regular banter since Douglas had left the streets. "Maybe…someday."

"Someday? Someday, it's going to be too late!"

A young black man dressed in baggy pants and a worn green coat with a black toboggan on his head came up behind Douglas. The man appeared nervous, his eyes landing only briefly on Douglas and Jimmy before looking toward the door. "You can go ahead. We're just shooting the breeze," Douglas said, moving off to the side.

The black man suddenly reached inside his coat and produced a nine-millimeter handgun. "Give me all your money!" he shouted at Jimmy. He then looked at Douglas to see his reaction. Douglas raised both hands over his head. Jimmy shook his head and began pressing the buttons to open the register.

"Hurry up, old man, before I cap you!" The gun shook in the man's nervous hand. He kept looking back and forth between Douglas, Jimmy, and the door.

"Calm down, sir. You don't need to hurt anyone," Douglas said calmly.

"Shut up, man, or I'll kill you first! Hey, you look like you got money! Give me your wallet!" The robber now pointed the gun at Douglas's face.

As Douglas reached into his suit jacket to get his wallet, Jimmy suddenly lunged over the counter and tried to grab the robber's arm. The young man saw the motion and spun toward Jimmy, striking his head with the side of the gun. As Jimmy staggered backward, the robber pointed the gun at his head.

This time, it was Douglas who rushed forward to grab the man's arm. The gun went off as the two fell to the floor. The shot missed Jimmy, striking the wall behind. Douglas tried to grab the gun but couldn't reach the man's hand.

Suddenly, the gun fired again. Douglas's ears rang with the proximity of the blast. A sharp burning pain exploded in his chest, and he smelled the acrid scent of gunpowder. He tried to rise but collapsed back onto the floor. The pain quickly faded into a dull burning sensation, and he felt the warm, wet stain spread across the front of his shirt. His vision began to dim, and the sounds around him became muffled, as if his head were underwater. He was vaguely aware of the black man scrambling up and running out of the store. Then he saw a face above him. He realized after a moment that it was Jimmy, a mixture of fear and shock lining his pale face. He felt Jimmy's hands slide beneath his head.

"Hold on, Douglas! Hold on! I called nine-one-one. They'll be here in a few minutes."

Douglas felt his body relax, and he experienced no worry or fear. A sense of peace spread over him, just as the warm blood spread from his chest down his sides. He grinned or at least thought he was grinning. "It's OK," he tried to say. His throat and mouth were so dry.

"Yeah, buddy. It's all OK. You've lived through worse than this!" Jimmy's face shone with sweat as he glanced over his shoulder, hoping to see flashing lights.

***

Douglas's dim vision suddenly flashed into a blinding white light. He blinked as he sat up. The brightness faded somewhat, and he realized he was staring at the golden sun. He looked down at his chest and saw no blood. He then looked around. He was back on the white-sand beach. The crashing waves and crying gulls were there, too, as were the sweet, magical sounds of the voices and laughter of his family. He stood as he saw his beautiful wife, hand in hand with his daughter and son, run toward him. They were laughing and crying at the same time, as was he. He spread his arms wide to embrace them.

***

Jimmy stared after the ambulance as it sped out of his parking lot. He shook his head and wiped the tears from his eyes as he walked back into the store to talk to the police. As Douglas had taken his last breath, his friend's face had been calmer and more at peace than Jimmy had ever seen it. It almost appeared like he died grinning. "Go home, Doug. Go home," he whispered.

The Field

Waves of heat rose off the tilled field, causing the blue hills beyond to ripple. No breeze stirred that day, nor had it yesterday, nor would it tomorrow. This was the reign of the Sun, and it ruled alone. Only one creature was brave enough, or desperate enough, to challenge the inferno. The man was stooped over, sweat running from his gray hair and falling to the earth, disappearing with a hiss. His bare back was deep red from frequent exposure to the July heat. Small clouds of dust rose from where his hands worked, making it appear that the dirt itself had caught fire.

The field stretched a hundred yards in all directions from the figure, rows of small plants running neatly in regular intervals along its length. Their leaves drooped, trying to escape the wicked Sun. They were smaller than they should be and wilting fast, but they lived. Their caretaker rose up and wiped his brow with the back of his hand. His face, a dried and wrinkled piece of leather, appeared much older than its years. It looked at home in its barren surroundings.

The man reached behind him for the bucket of water he'd carried from what was left of the creek. He poured the precious liquid around the shrunken broccoli plant. The ground hissed and crackled, seeming to reject the alien substance, but soon, the earth greedily sucked up the moisture. He moved to the next plant, even as the dirt around the first dried again. He sighed. There wasn't enough. There never was.

"George," a small voice cried, sounding shrill in the silence.

The man glanced behind him. At the far edge of the field sat his little white house, wavering like a mirage. A small figure stood on the porch waving at him. He waved back and set the bucket back down on the ground, looking around. Half-finished, half still waiting. He sighed again. *Man, it's hot.* He walked toward the house.

"Lunch is ready, dear," the woman said, holding the door open for her husband. "It's too hot to be working like that."

They walked into the dining room and sat at the table.

"Got to keep food on the table," George said with a tired voice and a wink.

"You old fool! You'll work yourself to death in that field one day," she said, smacking him on the hand.

"I hope so, Mary. I hope so. Is Chance up yet?"

Before Mary could respond, a tall black-haired boy entered the room. He wore an old gray sweat suit, and his face was several days unshaven. He yawned and dropped into one of the chairs.

"What's this? Gettin' up before noon?"

"Give me a break, Dad! I need to rest up this summer," Chance replied, grabbing one of the sandwiches.

"A little work wouldn't kill you," George said, smiling.

Chance stared at his father. "I've been working hard all semester."

His father stared back briefly and then looked back down at his plate.

"I passed all my classes," Chance said in defense.

George nodded and continued to eat. "All A's?"

"Well, I didn't like most of them. But next year, I'll graduate."

"If you don't like your classes, maybe you're studying the wrong subjects."

Chance shook his head. "It doesn't matter if I like them. Once I get my finance degree, I can be on my way to becoming a rich stockbroker."

George nodded again, not looking up.

***

Finally, the Sun began to drop in the sky, easing some of its relentless heat. George rubbed at his lower back and put his shirt back on. He looked back over his field. Not bad. Maybe he actually did some good. He walked toward the neighboring pasture to feed his cattle before nightfall.

He sighed. Despite the wretched heat of the days, the summer evenings were pleasant. Sometimes, a breeze would even blow. He liked listening to the night creatures. It was a peaceful time, a time to rest and forget about the day's troubles—a true gift from God.

"Did you finish?" a voice called out from behind him.

George turned and saw Chance approaching, dressed in blue jeans and a white button-up shirt. "Yeah. It was a tough one, though."

"I really don't see why you do it." Chance glanced back at the field. "I mean, look at the ground. Nothing's gonna grow in this drought."

"Why I do it?" George repeated, not understanding what Chance meant.

"Yeah. Why don't you just buy your vegetables? It's not like you don't have the money. Why spend all day in the heat when you could be inside relaxing? It's time to retire from this."

They reached the strip of trees separating the field from the pasture. "Sit down for a minute," George said, indicating a fallen tree.

"OK. But just for a minute. I have to meet some friends in town."

"Is food what you think this is about?" George asked, looking at the field. "I could buy all the food me and your mother need."

"Then why don't you?" Chance asked.

George ignored the interruption. "Son, farming isn't my way of making a living, at least not now. Farming is my life. Ever since I can remember, I've worked in the fields and with the animals. I don't know what else to do. I surely can't sit in the house with your mother and watch television all day. I'd go crazy. If I retire from farming, I might as well retire from life. Hopefully, I'm not ready for that yet."

"I can't understand that. What about all the money you've saved up? You could pay people to farm for you. You and Mom could be eating out every night, having people wait on you. Go take a vacation, a cruise, or something."

George chuckled softly, his eyes squinting, causing the wrinkles at their sides to bunch together. His eyes still sparkled with life despite the ancient face they were set in. "Money comes and goes, but raising something, creating life, can last forever. I can look at this field, the woods over there, the pasture, the cattle, our house, and especially you and say that I did that, or at least had a hand in it. That's the greatest joy I can imagine. Money can't buy that."

Chance was silent for a moment, lost in thought. Suddenly, he stood and looked down at his father. "Well, I'd better run. See you later."

"You know what I'm saying, don't you? You used to…."

Chance hurried back through the field, acting like he didn't hear his father. He would be glad when college started back. He was getting tired of living at home. He wasn't about to waste his life in that patch of dirt.

***

"What's wrong, dear?"

225

"Oh, I'm sorry. I didn't mean to wake you," George said, sitting back down on the bed.

"That's the second time you've gotten up. Is something the matter?"

"I guess I overdid it a bit today. I think I'm too tired to sleep."

"Do you want me to sing to you?"

"Lord, no. I don't need any nightmares," George said.

Mary kicked him softly in the leg. "Get to sleep, you old fool!"

A short time later, Mary heard her husband moan softly and slowly rolled over. A bright shaft of moonlight shone through the open blinds, striking George's pale face. He sat in the rocking chair, staring out the window. His right hand lightly massaged his left arm. His face was a mixture of worry and pain, a look she had seldom seen.

"George, come to bed! Please."

George once again climbed into bed. "Boy, I believe carrying water is work for a younger man," he said with what Mary knew was a halfhearted chuckle.

Mary sat up against her pillows and pulled George over to her. She placed her left arm behind him and laid his head on her chest. With her right hand, she stroked his head. "Just lie still, and I'll take care of you."

"You're a worry wart!" George said in objection. "But I love you for it," he added as he closed his eyes.

***

The following day dawned hot, with the insects already buzzing about when the first rays of the sun burned through the haze. The birds sang, but not for long. The early morning foragers scampered for the forest, running as much from fear of discovery as from the coming heat. This was the scene from the kitchen window as George sipped his cup of coffee.

"Nothing like the mornings, except maybe for the evenings. It's just the in-between-part that's so miserable," George said with a chuckle as he sat down at the table with his wife.

"Why don't you take the day off, dear? I hear tomorrow will be a little cooler."

"Believe it or not, the weeds still grow in this heat. I better get rid of them before they choke out my little plants."

Mary frowned. "I wish you would at least make Chance help you. Some honest work might do him some good."

"Now, Mary, he's a grown boy capable of making his own decisions. I'm not going to force him to do anything. Apparently, he doesn't like farming."

226

"Do you believe that?"

George stood, finished his coffee, and walked toward the door. "It doesn't matter what I believe."

***

A fierce struggle raged in the inferno. The distant figure doubled over in the middle of the field of dust. The struggle was not with the Sun but within himself. He dropped the hoe and clutched at the left side of his chest, trying to massage away the pain. It was a muscle spasm, nothing more.

George forced himself to stand back upright. He stared up to the sky, seeking some kind of relief. He put up a valiant fight, standing with pain few could have endured. He called upon God to help ease the pain, his brow knitted in a mixture of agony and worry. For the first time in his life, he was afraid. "Help me, God!"

The field slowly began to spin around him. It whirled faster and faster, the sky mixing with the earth, the blue with the brown. Waves of nausea wracked his body along with the pain. His left arm and chest were numb now. Finally, his strength wavered, and darkness swept in from the corners of his eyes. The warrior collapsed in the dirt, sending a cloud of dust slowly rising upward. Above, the Sun blazed on, uncaring, victorious. The field was silent.

"Oh, my God! Chance! Chance! Come quick!" Mary shouted from her position at the kitchen window. She had helplessly witnessed the struggle. She stood trembling in disbelief as Chance rushed into the room.

"What is it?"

"Your...your father!" She stammered, pointing out the window. "Call an ambulance!" she shouted as she ran out the door and into the field.

***

The funeral was simple. George was buried in the small family cemetery in his patch of forest at sunrise two mornings later, just as his will stated. Chance walked away from the small crowd of family and friends, deeper into the woods. He was still stunned, in a state of disbelief. His father had always seemed so healthy. "Seemed" was the problem Chance had. He had not really paid any attention to his father for the past several years. He was away at college most of the time, and when he was home, he was off with his friends. The doctors' presumed that his father had died of a heart attack from overexertion in the heat.

Chance walked further into the trees while his mother and the others returned to the house. The day was sunny but much cooler than the last few. It seemed the Sun regretted its killing. Chance followed a winding path that led all the way through the woods. The forest was still, mourning the loss of its protector and creator. The smell of rhododendrons wafted through the thick green foliage, intermingled with the damp, earthy scent of morning.

Chance's mind was a jumble of thoughts. Half were in mourning for the loss of his father, the other half confronting his own uncertain future. His mother was alone now. His father had always taken care of his family. His mother had never had to worry about money or work. George had been a good provider. Now she would have to learn how to take care of herself. The farm would quickly degenerate without someone's care.

Chance raised his head and surveyed his surroundings. It had been years since he'd walked through the woods. Now it was both comforting and sad.

***

"This land used to be open fields and briar thickets, Son. Then your great-grandfather bought the land. He tore it down and built it up again, molding it to fit his dreams. He planted all these trees, or at least planted the ones they came from. The animals slowly arrived once they realized there was food and shelter. He's gone now, but all this lives on. Money dies with its master. Grandpa will live forever in these trees and animals."

***

Chance marveled at the vision his great-grandfather, grandfather, and father had. They had a dream and made it happen. In a way, they'd created their own little land, where they were owner, president, and CEO—a living empire. However, they'd paid a great price in the building. Their lives had been hard. They had worked from daylight to dusk, breaking their backs to tend to the crops and the animals. They didn't enjoy any of the luxuries most people strive for. They had their family and their land, nothing more. They died relatively young. In the end, it had killed his father. *Was it worth it?* Could there have been some other way?

***

"Son, here on the farm, you can escape from the stress and hassles of the city. There are no lines or traffic jams, just nature and you. You make your own schedule, work when you want to work. Smell the air. It's fresh and pure. This life ain't for everybody, but it's the only one for me…."

***

Chance came to the ancient oak tree, the first one his great-grandfather had planted. It had changed little since being the center of his childhood world. Its huge limbs stretched out in a perfect circle, providing

228

shade no matter the time of day. Its leaves seemed to rustle in recognition. A warm, peaceful feeling surrounded Chance as he recalled the many hours he'd spent playing in and beneath the tree. He sat down against its thick trunk. It was a good place to relax and think.

A beam of warm sunlight caressed his cheek. He inhaled deeply and closed his eyes. He could stay here forever. If only it were that easy… He heard a shuffling in the limbs above. He glanced up and saw a squirrel chasing another one, chattering with joy.

***

"Should we really kill animals, Daddy?" the little boy asked, holding the shotgun unsteadily before him.

"Son, we have to take what the land offers. We have to have food, and we have to do our part to maintain the balance."

"What balance?"

"If we don't take some of the animals each year, there will be too many for this forest to support. They will run out of food. Then they'll starve and become sick. If we kill some, the remaining ones will be healthier and happier. There has to be a balance."

Chance squeezed the trigger. The large gray squirrel fell from the tree and lay still on the ground. "I got it! I got it, Daddy!"

***

Chance had only two weeks before he would return to college for his final year. It was something he had looked forward to. Now, it began to frighten him. Where had his life gone? He had always been so busy, too busy to enjoy the things that really mattered. He didn't even know what mattered anymore. The parties of years past didn't seem as important as they had at the time. He couldn't even remember most of them. But now, he did remember all the special moments he'd shared with his family on the farm. Those kinds of memories lasted a lifetime. They were the important things. The oak and the farm were still the same. His "friends" passed in and out of his life with no significant impact.

***

"I can't help you plant today, Dad. Me and some guys are riding up to the lake. Do you mind?"

"There's nothing wrong with having friends, but some things are more important. Your friends will not always be with you, Son. One day, it'll just be you and what you've made out of your life. What will you have left if you're not happy with what you've made? No. I don't care if you go with your friends. Just make sure it's what's most important to you."

Chance walked away to meet his friends.

229

Chance slung his suit jacket over his shoulder as he left the sanctuary of the tree. He needed to walk again and clear his head. He had too many thoughts and emotions battling inside. He wanted to forget the farm, put it behind him. It didn't fit in with his plans to make a fortune in some far-off city. He could probably land a job as a stockbroker in another year, making fifty thousand a year or more. He could live the fast life, with plenty of women and parties. One day, if he became successful enough, he could buy a farm twice the size of this one and hire people to take care of it for him.

As he walked along the trail, he heard a faint chirping coming from a patch of tall grass. He bent down on one knee and peered into the clump. In the middle sat a small bluebird, its short, downy feathers indicating its age. The bird opened its small beak and emitted a long, shrill chirp. Chance looked in the tree behind the bird and spotted a small nest wedged between the trunk and a limb. He smiled.

He rolled up his sleeves and began to rub his hands together vigorously in the dirt of the trail. His father had taught him that if you can disguise the human scent, a mother bird would sometimes accept her baby back into the nest. He bent over and gently scooped the bird into his hands. The bird struggled, but Chance held it firmly in his grip, careful not to hurt it. He walked slowly over to the nest and placed the bird back inside, beside two nest mates. He quickly walked away before the mother returned.

He walked lightly down the trail and soon came to the small, clear stream that dissected the forest in half. The small, pure creek had been one of his favorite haunts as a child. He couldn't begin to count the hours he'd spent fishing and playing in the merry brook. He'd dammed it up to make small ponds to float his wooden boats, turned over every rock looking for crawfish to catch, and pulled countless rainbow trout and red-eye from its small pools. His forefathers had even had a hand in routing the waters.

He knelt down beside it and washed the dirt from his hands. The cool water felt good, and he splashed a few handfuls onto his face. As he stood back up, he stared down the stream and noticed something amiss. A small tree lay in the water, leaves and smaller limbs and twigs gathering around it, effectively damming the stream and forcing it to detour around the blockage. The creek below the tree was almost dry. The ground around the jam had greedily drunk the precious fluid up, feeding an abundance of briars and weeds.

Chance strode up to the small end of the tree. With an intense effort, he bent down, pulled it up, and walked it back toward the upturned roots of its base. He waded through the middle of the creek, not caring about his shoes and pants. He carried the tree to the other side and lay it parallel to the water. The leaves and branches slowly broke free and made their way downstream. Quicker and quicker the water flowed, back to its old course. Soon, the debris washed away, and the stream was whole again. It seemed to laugh with joy as it splashed and gurgled along. He had restored the balance.

"What are you going to do now?" he softly asked the land around him.

The path finally reached the end of the forest, and Chance walked into the field his father had toiled in just three days before. The little plants his father had worked so hard to water were already in need of more, their stalks wilting over. In some spots, the grass and ragweed stood higher than the vegetables. Chance felt a lump growing in his throat. Seeing his father's pride and joy in such poor condition made it real that his father would never again stand in that field. It was a vision Chance had never thought could change. Every day of his life, he could look in the field or the pasture or the woods and see his father. Now, the land seemed void of life.

Chance slowly made his way through the rows of dying plants and found himself drawn to the spot where it happened. He slowly approached the sacred ground. The hoe lay beside the patch of crushed plants. He could almost see the outline of his father's body in the dirt. Chance knelt down on both knees and stared at the ground, tears flowing from his eyes. Without thought, he held one flattened plant up with one hand and scooped the dirt up around its stalk with the other until it once again stood upright. He did that with each plant until the rows were again in order.

He then took the hoe in his hands and stood, staring at it reverently. He moved his hands up and down its smooth, worn handle. It must have been fifty years old. It was probably the same hoe his grandfather had given his father. Chance dropped his jacket on the ground and removed his shirt. Then he took the hoe and began raking where his father had left off. He broke the dry dirt up around the delicate plants and expelled the weeds trying to choke them. He had no idea why he was doing it. Somehow, it felt right, at least for now.

He paused to wipe the sweat from his brow and glanced up at the Sun. It seemed to be rekindling its deadly fire. He looked around at the surrounding field; it needed water. He then glanced back at the nearby creek. As long as Chance had lived, the stream had always flowed. Some years, it was smaller than others, like now, but it was always there. With a little money and ingenuity, its precious liquid could be used to irrigate the field. A few pumps and a system of pipes could make the plants grow like never before. Mr. Jonas, a few miles away, had done the same thing with his farm. He would be willing to help. Chance's father had more than enough money in the bank to finance a project like that.

Chance then looked over at the distant pasture. Thirty head of cattle all had to be milked by hand. If he had a milking machine, he could milk twice as many head in less time. He had heard his father say that the local dairy was paying top dollar for milk. It seemed the drought had hurt production at some of the bigger farms. Their cows were still producing well with the creek and pond in the pasture.

He smiled as he turned back to the field and took up his hoeing again. He should be able to finish that row and maybe the next before feeding the cows. There was so much to do; he tried not to even think about it. After a few days, he might catch up. They were calling for rain by the end of the week. That would help.

After a few minutes, he paused again to wipe away the sweat before it could run into his eyes. *Man, it's hot.*

Strangers

The little blond-haired boy sat down beside a middle-aged man in a gray business suit. The man didn't look up from his newspaper. All the seats on the bus were occupied by a wide variety of passengers.

"My name's Billy," the boy said when the bus began moving.

The businessman grunted absently but didn't look up from the paper.

"Do you have a name?" Billy persisted.

"Harold," the man replied gruffly.

The boy fell silent for a moment, more likely from something else catching his attention than from the man's tone of voice. He looked at the people sitting across the bus from them. One man stared intently out the window. A black woman briefly met his eyes and then stared down at the floor. The whine of the bus's engine and the noise of the city outside were the only sounds.

Billy finally broke the silence. "Why's everyone so quiet, mister?"

"Huh? Because everyone is busy."

"Busy?" Billy gave the passengers another inspection. "They sure don't look busy."

"Well, I'm busy," the man said, not trying to conceal his annoyance.

"What ya' doin'?"

"Reading this newspaper!"

"Can't you do that at home?" Billy asked, chewing loudly on a stick of gum. By this time, some of the people nearby were observing the conversation.

"I *could* read it at home, but I can also read it while riding the bus," Harold replied, still not looking above his paper. After a moment, he placed the paper on his lap and turned to face his inquisitor. "Just what should I be doing, young man?"

"Talking to all us other people!" Billy exclaimed as if the answer was obvious.

"I don't know any of these people," Harold replied in a strained tone, realizing that they now had a large audience.

"'Cause you've been reading that paper."

Several chuckles arose among the spectators, and many exchanged smiles at the little boy's antics.

Harold was struggling on the defensive. "The bus ride isn't very long. I don't have time to meet everyone."

"Then just meet some of us. Maybe you can meet the rest of us later."

"There's not much use in making friends with people I will probably never see again."

The other passengers were now listening intently to the debate.

The boy stared down at the floor and stopped swinging his legs. He looked up after a moment. "My mommy said that Daddy was killed by strangers."

"I'm sorry," Harold said softly, stunned by the sudden turn in the conversation.

"Maybe if those men had been his friends, they wouldn't have killed him."

Harold squirmed uncomfortably and looked out the window. He wished he were at his stop. "We can't all know everyone."

"Dogs can! My dog meets every dog he passes," Billy responded, once again chewing loudly and swinging his legs.

"Yes, but dogs also fight a lot," Harold countered in a statement he hoped would get him off the defensive.

"I thought people were smarter than dogs."

The black woman leaned over to the man beside her. "It's too bad the rest of us aren't as wise as that little boy," she said and laughed.

"The city would be a lot friendlier a place; that's for sure," the man responded with a grin.

A college student turned to a man in a black suit beside him. "That kid ought to be on my debating team," he said, shaking his head.

"Or a lawyer with my firm," the man replied, chuckling.

Similar conversations erupted around the bus, which soon filled with the steady buzz of talk and laughter. Billy turned back to Harold. "Ain't that better?"

Harold laughed and rubbed the boy's head. "Yeah. It sure is, son. It sure is."

Dreams of Other Things

The Drive

Nick's eyes jerked open at the screaming car horn. He went from sound asleep to an instant state of heart-pounding, palm-sweating alertness. He reacted even before fully realizing the impending danger. He jerked the steering wheel to the right, pulling his car back into his lane just as the horn-blower sped past in the passing lane. He miraculously managed to straighten his fishtailing car, just narrowly avoiding the guardrail on the right.

"Damn it!" he cursed, furious with himself for falling asleep. He eventually relaxed his death grip on the steering wheel as his heartbeat slowed somewhat. It wasn't the first time it had happened on this trip. He was in the seventh hour of an eight-hour drive and had fought sleep most of the way—a combination of staying out a little too late drinking too much the night before, the dark, and the rain. The rain hadn't slacked up the entire trip. It was the kind that kept a constant spray on the windshield, faster than the wipers could remove, straining eyes and nerves.

He'd already stopped four times, buying peanuts, Skittles, and Red Bull. He'd feel fine for a few minutes, but the fatigue returned soon after getting back into the dark, raining night. "One more hour," he said out loud.

He couldn't wait to see his wife. She'd probably be asleep, but he knew she would wake when he climbed into the warm bed. Her hair would be messed up, her face tired and unmade, but still beautiful. He'd still be tired but could probably manage to participate in some missed-you sex—always had time for that. He grinned.

I-81 was awfully busy that night. He guessed the driving conditions, plus the few wrecks he'd passed, were jumbling everyone together. He couldn't wait to get home. It had been a stressful week, followed by an even more stressful drive. He was thankful it was Friday, and he was less than an hour away from a beautiful weekend with his beautiful wife. He could see her radiant smile, shining, thick black hair, and soft, sexy curves. *Maybe we'll go to the lake and enjoy some sun tomorrow. This weather's supposed to blow through and leave behind a beautiful weekend. Hmmm...wouldn't warm rays of sunlight feel great right now? One more hour...*

***

Squealing brakes and the sickening crunch of metal on metal woke him up this time. The scene around him was deadly chaos, with cars spinning and sliding on both sides of the road. He was off the left shoulder, sliding in the grass. Suddenly, a huge, blinding fireball exploded in front of him. He yelled, gripped the steering wheel, and waited for the impact. He closed his eyes as he entered the inferno, wondering whether the fire or crash would kill him.

He heard the roar of the flames all around him and felt the searing heat. But no impact. He finally opened his eyes and saw nothing but darkness and sheets of rain in front of him. Somehow, he'd missed all the cars and avoided contact. He quickly jerked his skidding vehicle back onto the asphalt, slowed, and looked in the rearview mirror.

The chaos had calmed somewhat, but the scene was grisly. Several vehicles were on fire, including a tanker truck. Other cars sat on both sides of the road in various states of disrepair, at least one on its roof. The sounds of sirens pulled his eyes from the mirror. Ambulances, fire trucks, and police cars were already approaching from the other side of the interstate. He was amazed at how quickly they'd responded. Deciding they didn't need his help, he cautiously proceeded toward home—pale, nauseated, and shaking.

He couldn't believe he had fallen asleep yet again. That time, he never even sensed it coming. One minute, he was awake; the next, he was waking up. That was the truly terrifying kind of fatigue. But he knew there would be no more sleeping that night. He was definitely wide awake now and curious about what had caused the massive crash, thankful it wasn't him. Maybe someone else fell asleep. He couldn't be the only one fighting sleep on this nasty night.

He wished his cell phone weren't dead and the charger wasn't in his wife's car. He wanted to tell her about what he'd just witnessed and help the last half hour go quicker. Instead, he found a good modern rock radio station and cranked the volume up nearly full blast. "I'm sexy, and I know it...." He laughed as he sang along. "Wiggle, wiggle, wiggle, wiggle, wiggle it...." Before he arrived home, a couple of ambulances rushed past him, sirens blaring and lights flashing.

***

Nick pulled his car into the garage beside his wife's red BMW and wearily stumbled out. He was so exhausted he didn't even get his briefcase or suitcase out of the car. They could wait until morning. He wasn't even sure about the missed-you sex now. Once inside, he crept down the hallway. The sounds of his wife crying and talking to someone in the bedroom quickened his pace.

"I don't know! Just let me stay on the phone with you the whole way!" his wife sobbed, talking into her cell phone as she quickly dressed, her long black hair tousled from recent sleep. She slipped into her old sweat clothes.

"Barbara, what's wrong?" Nick asked as he entered the room.

"No, Mom. I'll just meet you there." Barbara brushed past Nick and walked quickly down the hall. Her eyes were red from crying, and she didn't even wipe the still-falling tears.

Nick turned and followed close behind. It must be something with her father. *Oh, God!*

"Is it your dad?" he asked as he caught up to her in the kitchen.

Barbara quickly slipped on her shoes, grabbed her car keys off the counter, and headed to the garage, still talking on the phone. "Yes," she said as she walked.

"Do you want me to drive?"

"No. It's OK," Barbara said as she climbed into the driver's seat.

Nick wasn't sure why she couldn't just talk to him for a minute instead of the short answers. Growing increasingly agitated, he climbed into the passenger's seat. He was so tired.

She sped quickly into town, talking on the phone and sobbing the entire trip. From what Nick could gather, her father had been involved in a car accident. *Oh, God.* What if her father was in the one he'd just passed through? *I didn't even stop to see if I could help!* A cold chill shot down his spine. *Please, God, no.*

They arrived at the hospital ten minutes later. Barbara parked right in front of the ER, ignoring his protestations about blocking ambulances, and rushed inside. Perplexed and frustrated, he reluctantly got out and followed. Dreading what they'd face inside, he didn't rush this time.

Barbara already stood with her mother, talking to a doctor, by the time Nick found them. Whatever the doctor was saying caused her to burst into tears again and hug her mother tightly. Her mother was crying too, her eyes already red. Nick knew better than to try to interrupt. They'd let him in whenever they were ready. He was there for both of them. He was a rock. Barbara finally nodded to the doctor, and he turned to lead them through the double doors.

After several twists and turns, the doctor led them to an operating room. He opened one of the double doors and held it as the three passed through. The operating table stood in the center of the room. Unused machines and equipment surrounded it. He saw the raised shape of a body on the table, covered by a bloodied sheet. His wife and mother-in-law approached slowly, as though afraid something would suddenly jump up from beneath it. Nick followed but kept a respectful distance.

Barbara put her hand on the sheet and slowly peeled it back. After a brief, silent pause, she screamed a scream like Nick had never heard before. Her knees buckled, and she collapsed. Her mother half caught her, somewhat cushioning her fall to the floor. Nick stood frozen, unable to rush to her aid. Something was wrong. She loved her father, but this reaction wasn't right. And why wasn't his mother-in-law as upset? He quickly walked past the sobbing women to the other side of the bed. He gazed at the face on the covered body, a face badly charred and bloodied but still all too recognizable. It wasn't Barbara's father. Nick couldn't suppress his own scream—a scream not of the living.

How Do You Like Me Now?

"Let me wear your ring!" Kelly demanded with her impish grin. "Uh, why?" Eddie asked hesitantly.

"I don't know. Why not?" She reached her hands out and grabbed his. His heart instantly raced with her touch. Her hands were soft, smooth, warm, and feminine, but they were gone all too quickly, along with his class ring. "That's much better!" she exclaimed, happily inspecting her prize.

He was a little puzzled and a little confused but unbelievably giddy. He'd had a huge crush on Kelly for years. He had known her since the first grade. They had always been acquaintances but never good friends. She had always been so beautiful, perfectly evolving and blossoming into a full-blown eighteen-year-old woman. She had long brown hair, big green eyes, and perfectly tanned skin. Her body was more developed than most of her rival females, with a more-than-ample set of breasts and a backside that could stop traffic. And she always dressed in a way that maximized her gifts

She had also always been out of his league. She was a permanent board member of the popular kids, captain of the cheerleading squad, class president, homecoming queen, and on and on. If there had been a title for high school queen, that might have made her résumé a little shorter. As queen, she always had a plentiful supply of hunky boyfriends, including, of course, the high school quarterback, Brady Taylor.

Eddie, on the other hand, was nowhere near being a king—maybe vassal or serf at best. He didn't play any sports and wasn't part of the popular crowd. Tall and skinny, he sported a pair of glasses and more than his fair share of acne. His grades were pretty much straight A's, but he wasn't a real threat for valedictorian or salutatorian. A quick wit and good sense of humor were the only things that kept him officially above the geek/nerd level. He was a Tweener—stuck between cool and uncool.

There should have been no shot for him and Kelly to get together. That only happened in the movies. Although for the past few weeks, he wasn't one hundred percent sure he hadn't landed a movie role. They were in advanced chemistry class together and had been all year long, but things changed just three weeks ago—well, nineteen days, but who was counting? Kelly got into trouble for too much horseplay with her lab partner, Melissa, and Mrs. Stillwell swapped Kelly with Eddie's lab partner. That was the best day of his life.

"Here you go," she said, handing the ring back to him. "But tomorrow, I get to wear it again." She stood and quickly bounced out of the room and into the hall.

Eddie didn't even notice that the bell had rung and the classroom was already mostly empty. He slipped the ring back onto his finger, stood, and ambled into the hallway. The faces were blurs, voices just a conglomeration of noise. *She wore my ring!* But what did it mean? It couldn't mean they were going steady. She did give it back after all. But it had to mean something...

"What's up, Eddie?" Jeremy asked as he walked past.

Eddie quickly grabbed Jeremy's shoulder, nearly pulling him down. Jeremy started to protest, but Eddie forcefully dragged him into the boy's bathroom. Eddie promptly surveyed the room to make sure it was empty.

"What's going on, dude?" Jeremy asked, not hiding his irritation.

Since they'd started high school, Jeremy had been one of Eddie's best friends and was pretty much in the same social class he was. Although Jeremy was a track team member and wore a letterman jacket, he still didn't quite qualify as a jock or popular kid. His luck with women was a little better than Eddie's, but most were from the geeky realm. "Man, you'll never guess what just happened!"

"Uh, you lost your mind?" Jeremy looked into the mirror and adjusted his shirt, which had been violently rearranged.

"No! It's something with Kelly." Eddie's voice shook with excitement.

"Yep. You have definitely lost it," Jeremy responded absently, still primping.

"Dude, she asked to wear my ring! Then she actually took it from my finger and put it onto hers. Tell me *that* doesn't mean something."

Jeremy turned from the mirror, stared at his borderline deranged friend, and placed both hands on Eddie's shoulders. "Let me get this straight. She actually took your class ring off your finger and put it onto hers?"

"Yes!"

"Wow! That's definitely a little strange."

"I told you we were hitting it off really well lately. We laugh and talk, and she puts her hand on my arm like two or three times a day. Now, this!"

Jeremy looked down at Eddie's hand. "But I see she gave it back."

"Yeah. But then she said it was hers again tomorrow!"

Jeremy stroked his chin thoughtfully. "I don't know, man. I guess you never know. Maybe, just maybe, she might not be totally repulsed by you."

Eddie struck Jeremy in the arm with his balled-up fist. "Maybe she really likes me! Maybe she wants to have a bunch of little babies with me!"

Jeremy quickly ran to the sink and heaved as if vomiting. After a moment, he turned back around, barely dodging a punch aimed at his other arm. "Well, I hope so, buddy. Maybe it's your turn. I mean, stranger things have happened. We had Menudo and Boy George. Shouldn't have happened, yet they did."

***

The next day in class, true to her word, Kelly grabbed Eddie's ring from his finger and slid it onto hers. After that, their relationship only got better. Her wearing his ring emboldened Eddie. He began joking around with her more, even occasionally touching her hand or arm when they laughed and cut up. Mrs. Stillwell even called them down a time or two. He was a little more careful after that. If they got into too much trouble, one of them could be moved. That would ruin everything. At the end of each class, she gave his ring back. The next day, it was hers again.

This continued for the next two weeks. Eddie could hardly sleep at night between replaying the events of that day and the previous days, thinking about the next day, and fantasizing about all kinds of things for the future. Every other class was torture—time spent thinking about

245

Kelly. He knew he was in love with her. After eleven years of knowing he didn't have a chance, suddenly, he had a chance. It was unbelievable.

During those sleepless nights, he thought up a great idea to find out if she really liked him. She'd told him a few weeks back that she had broken up with Brady, close to the time of her first wearing his ring. The prom was a little less than a month away. *I'll ask her to the prom! What do I have to lose?* If she said no, they could still be really good friends and keep having fun together. If she said yes…if she said yes, his life would be forever changed.

***

Friday in advanced chemistry class, he knew he had to make his move. It would probably be too late if he didn't ask that day. He was so nervous he couldn't stand it. He wanted to throw up, use the bathroom, and pass out, all simultaneously. He hoped Kelly couldn't see how distracted he was as they worked on their lab project. Then he accidentally dropped the test tube. It hit the counter and fell to the floor, shattering loudly. Several barks from Mrs. Stillwell quickly silenced some laughter from the other tables.

When the other students had gone back to their projects, Eddie bent over to pick up the big pieces of the test tube. Suddenly, something squeezed his butt. He jumped forward, nearly hitting his head on the wall, and quickly whirled around to see a laughing Kelly. "What happened?" she asked with mock concern. Then she burst out laughing again.

Finally, Eddie laughed too. Behind the laughter, his mind was reeling. *She touched my butt!* Kelly Harper, the sexiest woman in the school's history, had touched his butt with her sexy little hands! That pushed him over the edge in confidence. He had to do it now.

"Hey, Kelly, can I ask you something?" His heart was pounding so hard he was afraid she'd see it through his sweater.

"Yes, dear?" she asked as she recovered from her fit of laughter.

"I was just thinking…I mean, wondering…I mean, would you like to go to the prom with me?" There. He had said it. For better or worse, it was out in the open.

Kelly stared at him for a moment and then burst out laughing again. Then she quickly realized that Eddie wasn't joking. "Uh…oh…" she stammered, trying to save some embarrassment. "You are so sweet to ask. But…but I think I'm just going to keep my options open right now."

Eddie felt like he had been kicked in the testicles and punched in the stomach at the same time. He was so sure she would say yes and that her yes would forever change his life. He never imagined her laughing and then totally blowing him off like she had. He had to say something to avoid even more awkwardness. "So you have a date already?"

Kelly shifted her feet nervously and turned toward the table to grab the Bunsen burner. "Well, I…not yet, I guess." She was silent as she struggled to compose a better response. "I mean, Brady might end up asking me again. We went last year. I'll probably just chill and wait and see. But thanks again for asking me. I'm sure we'd have a lot of fun."

"Yeah. OK. Well, if you change your mind, let me know."

The bell rang, mercifully. Kelly handed his ring back and quickly exited the scene of the crime.

As he plodded slowly and numbly into the hallway, a firm hand suddenly grabbed his arm. He snapped out of his thoughts and turned to see Jeremy's smiling face. "What happened, man? Are you prom-bound?"

Eddie shook his head. He couldn't even speak.

"What happened?" Jeremy asked with sincere concern.

"I…I don't know. She said she might go with Brady."

"Oh. That's not so bad. I mean, they *have* dated, like, forever."

"Yeah. I guess so."

"Well, I have to run. Maybe something will happen between now and then, like Brady getting hit by a train!"

Eddie smiled weakly as his friend darted down the hallway.

***

That night, Eddie once again didn't sleep. This time, it wasn't due to looking forward to tomorrow or further into the future. This time, anger and resentment filled him. *How could she do that to me? Why did she act like she was my friend? Why did she wear my ring, touch my arm, and even grab my butt?* Eddie knew he didn't know a lot about women, but he thought for sure he knew when he was being flirted with. Apparently not. Apparently, she was not flirting but teasing. She had just been teasing him, leading him along, toying with him. When it got serious, she'd kicked him to the curb. He wanted to cry. He wanted to scream. He couldn't even process all his emotions. He tossed and turned all night. Thankfully, the next day was Saturday.

***

He dreaded going into chemistry class all weekend and all day on Monday. How could he face her? What would he say? Finally, the moment arrived, and there was no escape. He slowly walked into the class and over to his chair. He looked up and was surprised to see Dale Umbarger in Kelly's seat. He quickly glanced around the room and spotted Kelly sitting on the other side. Somehow, she had switched partners. She must have met with Mrs. Stillwell before class. He was glad he didn't have to face her, yet it only infuriated him further. *Now she doesn't even want to be my lab partner?* He didn't look at her for the remainder of class.

***

The rest of his senior year was miserable. He couldn't quite recover from his incident with Kelly. She'd cut him deeply, taking his one chance at making something out of his high school experience, and life, and coldly crushing it. He occasionally saw her in and out of class, laughing and cutting up with other people like she had with him. Each time evoked intense anger that spilled over to all the popular kids. He lumped them all together: jocks, cheerleaders, and preppies. They were all high and mighty and thought they were better than everyone not like them.

The icing on the cake came when he saw Brady and Kelly together at a spring baseball game. He didn't notice them until it was too late to avoid them. He stared down and tried to scurry past, but Brady blocked his way. "Yo, Eddie, how's it going?" Brady asked with his usual cocky smirk.

"Absolutely great," Eddie responded with ill-concealed sarcasm.

"Cool. Hey, I just wanted to let you know I'm OK with what happened with you and Kelly, with you asking her to prom and all. I mean, we weren't really together, so no hard feelings on this end."

"Uh…oh. OK. Thanks." Eddie desperately hoped it was over.

"But hey, some advice, man to man: you might want to set your sights a little bit lower. I mean, I admire your nerve and everything, but you got to keep it real."

Eddie looked incredulously at Brady and then quickly at Kelly. She smiled faintly and turned away. Then she and Brady walked past, leaving Eddie standing alone. Something inside him snapped. He had been teased before. He had been rejected before. But the way Kelly had toyed with him and how her boyfriend Brady had added insult to injury? He vowed right then to get even with both of them. He didn't know how or when, but he would get even.

***

"Welcome Class of 1988," the hotel sign read as Eddie drove into the parking lot in his red Porsche. He couldn't believe it had been ten years since graduation. He had so looked forward to this day. Ten long years he'd patiently waited. They had been ten years well spent, though. He went to college and law school and was now part of a thriving law practice in Washington, DC. He lived in an expensive condo just outside the city

248

and enjoyed a lavish lifestyle. He wasn't officially rich, but he was very comfortable.

He had also undergone several physical changes, including growing another inch taller after high school and gaining nearly forty pounds. Some of it was natural filling out; the rest was muscle built from hard-core weight lifting. He'd started working out at the end of high school and really got into it in college. Even now, he found an hour or two a day to exercise. Contacts replaced his glasses, and he sported a well-trimmed goatee. His once pasty-white, acne-filled skin was now toned and tanned. He'd left a gangly boy and come back a wealthy, strapping man.

He parked his car and quickly hopped out to head into the hotel. He wore black slacks, a black sports coat, and a tight black T-shirt. He wore a gold chain around his neck, a Rolex on his wrist, and his high school class ring on his right hand. He strode confidently into the hotel lobby. A large sign indicated their reunion dance was in Ballroom C. He checked in, quickly carried his suitcase to his room, unpacked, and freshened up. Then he headed back down to find the ballroom.

His heart raced as he made his way through the twisting hallways. He wasn't sure what would happen or how it would play out. He just hoped and prayed that somehow his plan would work. A table stood in front of the doors to the ballroom. Eric Johnson and Michelle Morris, or Williams now as her nametag indicated, sat behind it, registering the guests and handing out nametags. No one was signing in at the moment, so Eddie strode up with a confidence he'd never displayed in school. "Well, hello, Eric and Michelle! How the heck are you?"

They both looked at him and then at each other. After exchanging confused glances, they turned back at him. "OK. I've guessed everybody right so far, but you've got me stumped," Eric said.

"Me too," Michelle echoed.

"OK. I'll give you a hint: it starts with Eddie."

Michelle and Eric glanced at each other again and then back at him. "Eddie Hawkins? No way, man!" Eric said. "Who are you really?"

"I'm sorry, but it's just Eddie," Eddie responded, enjoying their expressions.

"I'm afraid you're going to have to prove it. Let's see some ID." Eric was only half-joking.

Eddie shrugged and reached inside his jacket, pulled out his wallet, and flipped it open to his driver's license. He showed it to both of them. "Wow, man, you sure have changed. Good job!" Eric exclaimed, holding out his hand for Eddie to shake. Michelle stood and quickly walked around the table to give him a hug.

"Unbelievable! You're looking *fine*. And smell good too." She hugged him a little too long for comfort and then returned to her seat. It was funny that she hadn't even acknowledged his existence in high school. His confidence soared sky-high now.

"How's the turnout?" he asked as he placed his nametag on his jacket.

"Pretty good—pretty much everyone who was anyone," Eric responded.

"Cool!" He walked past the table and opened the doors to the ballroom.

Dozens of round tables were arranged around the sides of the room, leaving a large open area in the middle for dancing. A live band played in the front of the room on a small stage next to the bar. Streamers and balloons hung from the ceiling. He estimated there were probably two hundred people spread around the room, some sitting, some dancing, and small groups standing together. He took a deep breath and headed in.

Everyone in the room seemed to stare at him. He recognized most of the faces, despite the changes that ten years brought. He saw almost everyone glance at his nametag before greeting him. He received his fair share of "oohs" and "ahs" as he made his rounds and finally spotted Jeremy in one of the standing groups. He reached out and grabbed Jeremy's shoulder from behind. Jeremy turned with a polite smile and looked at Eddie's face blankly, down at his nametag, and back at his face. "Oh, my God! What happened to you?" he asked, giving his old friend a hug.

"I guess I grew up a little," Eddie said with some modesty.

"Yeah, and grew a new body and head! I can't believe it, man!" Suddenly, he remembered the woman standing at his side. "Oh, Eddie, this is my wife, Wanda. Wanda, Eddie."

They exchanged quick pleasantries, and Eddie did the same with the rest of the group. "Hey, Jeremy, why don't you come to the bar with me? You need a refill anyway." Jeremy nodded and walked with his old friend across the ballroom. They quickly compared notes on the past ten years as they walked.

"Is my girl here?" Eddie asked after they had ordered their drinks.

"Girl? Oh, Kelly?"

"That's the one," Eddie responded with a grin.

Jeremy smiled back. "Man, you'll blow her mind! Yeah. She and her hubby are over there, with the rest of the former jocks and cheerleaders," he said, nodding to the room's far corner.

"Brady?"

"That'd be him. Not quite so studly anymore, huh?"

Eddie couldn't help but laugh out loud. The former high school quarterback and stud of the school had changed as much as he had but in a different direction. He had gained about fifty pounds, but all in his belly. His once-thick black hair was gone, at least on top. And he appeared disheveled, with his white button-up shirt sloppily tucked into his khaki pants and his tie falling about two inches short of his belt.

"Hmmm…and she picked him over me?"

"Well, it was a little different in high school."

"So, what does Brady do for a living?"

"Two guesses. And the first one doesn't count."

Eddie laughed again. "Alex, what is a gym teacher?"

"We have a winner! Are you going to talk to her?"

Eddie turned his stare from Brady to Kelly. Her hair was shoulder length. She had put on a few pounds but was still beautiful—and certainly was not a good match for her husband. She wore a long black dress, low cut in the front and slit high on the side—it was also not a match for Brady's attire. She still carried herself with dignity and pride as she chatted with her old classmates.

"Yeah. I have to talk to her."

"This could get interesting!"

"I hope so." Eddie downed his freshly poured Long Island Iced Tea, for a little extra courage, and then proceeded across the room. "I'll catch up with you later, Jer."

"Good luck, man."

Kelly just happened to glance in his direction as he closed the final few steps. As she read his nametag, she couldn't hide her shock. He flashed the sexiest grin he could muster as he stared into her eyes. As he reached her, she finally produced a smile and extended her hand, which he bypassed to give her a hug. He pulled her tightly against him, smelling her perfume and hairspray as his head reached her shoulder. She smelled wonderful. He held the hug a little long before finally stepping back. "So, how's my old chemistry buddy doing?"

"Uh…good. And it looks like you're doing well," Kelly said, still looking stunned.

"Can't complain."

By this time, Brady realized someone new had joined the group and turned to greet the newcomer. "Man, someone's been hitting the 'roids!"

"And someone hasn't," Eddie responded quickly, extending his hand. Brady gave him a brief glare, followed by a halfhearted smile as he shook his hand. Eddie felt Brady trying to squeeze his hand hard, so he returned the favor. Brady's half-smile quickly disappeared.

"You sure have changed a lot. What type of nerd job did you end up with? Accountant? Insurance salesman?"

"Nothing that exciting—just a defense attorney up in DC." Eddie glanced at Kelly as he spoke. Her eyes widened, and her smile grew. "And I hear you're coaching now."

"Yeah. Teaching health and coaching football—can't get much better than that. Well, we're gonna hit the bar. Need anything, Kelly?"

"I'm fine, dear."

Brady shrugged, and he and three of his buddies headed across the room.

Kelly watched them walk off and then turned back to Eddie. They stood in silence, looking at each other. "I still can't believe you're the same guy from chemistry class."

"It's just little old me. Some of us are just late bloomers, I guess. Do you want to sit down and catch up?"

"Sure," she said, and they left the small group and made their way to an unoccupied table.

He learned that Kelly was also a schoolteacher—chemistry of all subjects. She and Brady had married while still in college, and they now had a six-year-old boy and a four-year-old girl. He wasn't sure if it was his imagination, but she didn't seem too thrilled with how the last ten years had gone.

"Let me ask you a personal question," Eddie said, steeling his nerves.

"Uh...sure; why not?" Kelly said, obviously a little nervous.

"Why did you turn down my prom invitation? And then have yourself moved across the room? Did you really dislike me that much?"

Kelly broke her gaze away from him and stared down at the table, absently toying with the silverware. "No. I really liked you. You were fun and funny and cute."

"Cute? Really?"

Kelly nodded and smiled.

"OK. Then why did you shoot me down?"

Kelly was silent again and fidgeted visibly in her chair. "I...I guess I just couldn't go to the dance with you. I mean, you weren't a jock or a cool kid, and I didn't know what my friends would say or if they would still be my friends. Not to mention Brady and the other guys. I just couldn't do it, even though I would have in a perfect world."

Eddie looked at her and shook his head, his smile disappearing. "So you were embarrassed to be seen with me?"

"No! Well, not exactly. I don't know. I was young and stupid. You know how high school was. Everyone was part of a clique, whether they wanted to be or not."

"Why did you move across the room?"

She sighed. "I just thought it would be less awkward for both of us."

"Hmmm. So, here it is, ten years later, and you got to marry the school stud, and you still have your popular friends. I guess everything worked out like you planned."

Again, silence.

"No. Not like I planned," Kelly said softly.

"Do you have any regrets?"

She stared deeply into his eyes. "Lots of them! I never wanted to end up back here. I wanted to get out and experience the world. Maybe live in a big city, like you. But Brady and I got married before we graduated college, and he was determined to come back here and be with all his buddies. So, here we are."

Eddie was silent this time. He'd learned all he needed to know for now. "Well, we still have a chance to dance, and we're already all dolled up. Would you dance with me?"

Kelly smiled, blushing a little. She quickly scanned the room until she spotted Brady with a large group of guys at a table near the bar. Beer bottles lay strewn about the table. The guys were loud and obviously feeling pretty good. "Why not?"

Eddie was glad to hear a slow song begin when they reached the center of the dance floor. He wrapped his arms around her, and she laid her head on his chest. They swayed back and forth to the music, only occasionally speaking. They shared several dances to a mixture of slow and fast music. They saw Brady and a few of his friends watching them once. They both smiled and waved, and Brady scowled and turned back around to his friends.

After they worked up a thirst, Eddie went to the bar and ordered them two Long Islands. They sat back down at their table and talked some more. Kelly asked Eddie about his love life. He explained that he'd had his share of girlfriends but nothing serious. He was waiting for his perfect woman. They drank their drinks fast, and Eddie was quick to retrieve them a couple of more.

Brady and his posse came to their table around ten, all either drunk or well on their way. "Honey, we're going down to The Tavern to shoot some pool and have some beers. Do you want to go or stay here?" he asked, looking from Kelly to Eddie.

"I really don't want to go there, but how will I get home if I stay here?" she responded, obviously agitated at the two options.

"I can give you a ride. I'm staying in town tonight," Eddie offered, not believing his luck.

"Yeah, nerd-boy can give you a ride," Brady slurred. His friends chuckled as he turned toward the door. Suddenly, he stopped and turned back around. "Oh, by the way, Eddie, she's still out of your league."

Eddie had to fight every instinct not to jump up and beat Brady into unconsciousness. He inhaled deeply and then allowed his smile to return. "Yeah. I guess I'm still not the stud you are."

"No, and never will be." Brady turned around, and he and his friends disappeared out of the ballroom.

Eddie turned to Kelly, who was shaking her head. "I'm sorry. He's like that sometimes."

"Like, every time he's awake and talking?"

"Yeah. Pretty much."

"Tell me again why you married him?"

"Young and dumb, I guess." She stared down at her drink for a minute and looked back up with a smile. "Let's go dance some more!"

They danced and drank for another hour, their dancing becoming less and less innocent and more and more provocative. Eddie knew the alcohol was affecting Kelly, and he made sure he kept a steady supply in her. He also was charming, witty, and romantic—three things Brady had never been. Their hands began to wander all over each other's body, and their lips came mere inches apart more than once. Instead of talking, he placed his lips close to her ear and whispered softly to her. She did the same with him. Soon, it felt like more than one-time friends catching up.

"What time do you need to be home to your family?" Eddie asked as they sat back down at the table with a fresh round of drinks.

"Never." She laughed. "Well, the kids are with my parents. Brady and his band of idiots will be out until The Tavern closes or they get kicked out—probably around three either way. But the reunion wraps up at twelve."

"That's way too early."

"Yeah. That sucks! We're just getting loosened up."

"Well, neither of us needs to be driving too far."

"Nope. And since I don't have a car, I'm definitely not."

"This is going to sound really bad…but what the heck? I have a room here tonight. What if we just go up there, put some coffee on, watch some TV, and talk for a couple of hours while we sober up?"

"What kind of woman do you think I am?" Kelly asked in a momentarily serious voice.

Eddie's heart skipped a beat. Everything had been going so perfectly. "One that's going to drink some coffee and watch some TV with me."

"Oh, OK. That works," she said, laughing. Eddie's heart resumed its normal beat. They finished their drinks and headed to the elevator, arm in arm, and up to his room.

They stumbled into the room and collapsed onto the bed, giggling like little kids. They quickly found themselves side by side, with Eddie's arm beneath Kelly's head. They gazed into each other's eyes with a look that neither misunderstood. "Do you still think I'm a little cute?" Eddie asked.

"No. You're gorgeous! Do you still think I'm cute?" she asked coyly, batting her eyelashes.

"You're still a hottie."

They lay there for a minute in silence, their hands lightly caressing each other. "This is really wrong," Kelly said softly.

"Yeah. But unless you stop me, it's going to get worse," Eddie said, slowly leaning his head closer to hers. She didn't resist and, in fact, moved forward to meet him. They kissed a long, passionate kiss. Eddie couldn't believe it was happening, after all these years. One kiss led to another. Then all the passion that had built up all night, through the dancing, teasing, and alcohol, boiled over. They nearly ripped each other's clothes off in a rush to get to each other's body. There was no more talk of right or wrong—just raw, uninhibited lust. In seconds, they were making wild, passionate love.

A couple of hours later, Kelly dressed, fixed her makeup and hair as best she could, and prepared to leave. After deciding it would be better if Eddie didn't drive her home, they called a cab. She was still feeling good, but the alcohol was wearing off. The reality of the situation was just starting to hit her. "What do we do now?"

"I have to head back to DC in the morning. Maybe we can call each other or email and figure out a long-term plan," Eddie said as he stood up from the bed, still naked.

Kelly couldn't help but admire his body once again. "That sounds good, but don't you forget about me!"

"Oh, I won't. I promise. You'll hear from me really soon." He winked.

They hugged and kissed, and Kelly headed back to her house, hoping desperately that Brady wasn't home yet.

***

"Hey, babe, there's a package for you," Brady said, handing Kelly a large envelope he had retrieved from the mailbox.

She took it, looking at it with a puzzled expression. Then she saw the sender's name: Eddie Hawkins. Her heart instantly skipped a couple of beats. *What could it be? Why would he send it here, where Brady could see it?* She also noticed that there was no postage or postmark on it. *Did he place it in the box himself?*

"Who's it from?"

She froze, her heart firmly in her throat. She knew she couldn't lie. Brady would grab it out of her hands if she did. "Uh, Eddie."

"Eddie. What would geek-boy be sending you?" He grabbed the package back from her and quickly ripped it open. Inside was a DVD and a note that simply read, "I hope you both enjoy. Your friend, Eddie."

Kelly had no idea what to think. *Why would he send a movie?* She prayed it was just a movie as Brady immediately went to the TV and inserted the disc into the DVD player. They both sat on the couch and watched.

Eddie appeared on the television, sitting close to the camera. "Hello, guys! How the heck are you—my two favorite people from high school? I'm sure you're not doing as well as I am right now. I only wish I could be there, sitting right there between you." Eddie smiled a smile that made Kelly's stomach turn. "I know we were all young and dumb in high school, but you still have to be responsible for your actions. Character is character. Brady, you haven't changed at all. You're still just an egotistical, brainless buffoon, only you've replaced being a star athlete with being a fat, lazy, balding waste of skin. Kelly, you're still all about status. You like me now because I have a good body and money, don't look nerdy, and am no longer beneath you. But I'm still the same person you crushed years ago because I wasn't cool enough or a jock. If only you had gone to the prom with me back then...

"So what you are about to see is a special gift for you both. I really hope you like it. But no matter what happens after watching the movie, I hope you enjoy the rest of your miserable lives, being washed-up high school celebrities turned insignificant nobodies, stuck in a dead-end town

256

and a dead-end life. Oh, and by the way, Brady, you were right. She isn't in my league. She's strictly minor league."

The DVD then skipped to a different scene, and Kelly gasped in horror. Brady couldn't even speak as he stared in disbelief. The movie was of Kelly and Eddie in the hotel room, having sex. Somehow, Eddie had hidden a video camera right in front of the bed. All two hours were on film, but Brady and Kelly didn't make it far into the movie before Brady stormed toward the front door, yelling and screaming as he went. Kelly followed, pleading and begging.

They missed the end of the movie, when Eddie came back onto the screen. "How do you like me now?" he asked with an evil laugh.

Till Death

Oh, God! It's happening again. I know better than this. I've done so well avoiding it all these years. But it has been so long. I'm still human, after all, with real feelings and emotions. The debate raged within as he stared down at the beautiful woman with her head on his lap and her body stretched out on the couch. He gently stroked her hair with his right hand.

He'd met Amanda a month prior, after drifting into the small town and finding the construction job. It seemed safe enough. Little did he know that a young, sexy blond woman worked in the office. It wasn't her looks or body that hooked him, though both were incredible. It was her smile and the way she arched one eyebrow, tilted her head to the side, and flashed her white teeth. He didn't know whether she did it on purpose or it was just how she smiled, but his knees went weak, and his heart skipped a few beats each time she did. He was drawn to her no matter how hard he resisted.

She had actually asked him out first. Since he was new in town, she said she could show him around. He had rejected so many women in the past, ones just as pretty, but somehow she broke through his defenses. He blamed her deadly smile and convinced himself that just one night out wouldn't hurt. He *was* new to town, didn't know his way around, and needed to eat after all. He hadn't even gone grocery shopping yet for his studio apartment. *Just one date couldn't hurt.*

They'd been together every night since. He told himself they would just be friends, that he could resist her charms, smile, and just hang out for a while. He had been lonely for a long time. Companionship was nice. He'd missed a lot of other things, too: the warmth of a woman's touch, the taste of a woman's lips, the intimacy and emotional bond formed through making love. But he couldn't afford to let any of those things happen. Just the companionship.

Their first kiss came a week later. Wall by wall, she continued to break down the barriers. The kiss came in a moment of alcohol-induced laughter at a local bar. They hit it off from the beginning, talking like old friends and never lacking for laughter. Their personalities meshed perfectly. This particular night, they were making fun of some locals singing karaoke. Somehow, amid a fit of laughter, they looked up simultaneously, and he gazed deeply into her green eyes. It happened so fast; he didn't have a prayer to defend against it. She leaned in, and he inexplicably met her. That first kiss was beyond words. Each step of their relationship built upon the last and drew him in further and further. Her sweet, succulent lips made his face flush and his body tremble. The kiss lasted for several minutes, as they forgot where they were and merged into one.

Once again, he drew an internal line in the sand. He would not take it to the next level and risk his feelings becoming even stronger. He would leave her before that. Yet, the next week, he allowed himself to lie on the bed with her, just to talk and cuddle. Very soon, another wall fell. It had been too long. No matter how much wisdom he had, how many scars from the past he bore, he couldn't resist that woman. They made love that night. Their lovemaking was incredible, as was everything else. They experienced no nervousness or anxiety as they explored each other's body and pleased each other in every way possible. It became a several-hour-long session that left them exhausted and panting in each other's arms, totally satisfied.

Damn! He was such a fool. She didn't deserve this. She had no clue what she was doing. He didn't want to go through it again. Yet, he was too far along, too hooked. He couldn't undo the damage. It was now just a question of when. The quicker he did it, the lesser the pain for both of them. It would definitely be easier for her, although it would still hurt them both. In the end, it wouldn't have been worth it. It never was.

Amanda opened her eyes, taking a moment to remember where she was. Then she felt the hand caressing her hair and gently stroking her head. She felt the firm muscle of the leg she'd used for her pillow. She grinned. She was exactly where she wanted to be. She rolled over onto her back and gazed up at Nathan, smiling as he stared down at her with his steely-blue eyes. For a moment, he appeared serious, as he often did, and then he finally grinned. She could always make him grin with her smile.

She never dreamed how her life would change when she first saw him walk into the office—tall, muscular, and dark-haired, with that pair of piercing blue eyes. Rarely clean-shaven, with several scars about his head and face, he was handsome in a rugged way. Although she hadn't asked yet, she figured he was in his mid-to-late thirties. She was instantly attracted to him. It was as if he'd stepped off the cover of a smutty romance novel and into her life.

He was a little on the shy side, and she found herself being a lot more aggressive than usual. It worked. He agreed to go out with her. They had an instant connection, despite his being a little reserved. He wasn't like any other man she had dated. He was so wise and mature. He loved to talk and listen to her talk. Although he was rough and tough, he was also very deep and sensitive. Every step of the way just got better. Their first kiss was the best of her life. He knew exactly what to do—how fast, how hard, which way to move, everything. Their lovemaking was even better than she had fantasized about, and she couldn't get enough. It, too, was the best of her life. He knew how to mix tenderness and caring with passion and lust. He was attentive to her every need and desire, pleased her in every way, and knew just how to hold and cuddle her afterward.

He was perfect, and it scared the hell out of her. He was too good to be true. There had to be something wrong with him or something in his past. Ted Bundy had probably *seemed* perfect to someone along the way. *Why is someone this great single? Why did he just drift into a town like this and take the first job he found?* He never spoke much about his past, and she didn't want to pry. They had only dated for a month. She'd asked a few questions, but he managed to change the subject or give vague answers. Someday soon, she would find out more about him, but she was very happy for now.

"Did you have a nice nap?" Nathan asked.

"Yep! It's always great when you're my pillow." Amanda grinned.

"Ah, you're so sweet."

"No, you are!" Amanda laughed. She reached up, grabbed his neck with both hands, and pulled him down to her. She kissed him as soon as he was close enough. She could never get enough of his lips.

Nathan's heart raced as she quickly aroused him. The power of her kisses was amazing. He had to tell her—if not tonight, very soon. Although he'd sacrifice a lot, now was better than the alternative.

"I have to tell you something," Amanda said as they finally ended their kiss. She hadn't intended to say what she was about to say but couldn't stop the words. "I think I'm falling in love with you."

Nathan's heart went from racing to not beating at all, his arousal forgotten. It had to be tonight. It had to be now. "I have to tell you something too but not what you want to hear."

Here it was. The shoe was about to drop. She sat up and turned to face him. What would it be: married, ex-con, escaped con, serial killer, gay, born a woman? How would he crush her heart and tear her world in two?

"I've debated about making something up to make it easier, but I owe you the truth." He grabbed both her hands.

"Go ahead," she whispered.

"How old do you think I am?"

Amanda suddenly perked up. *Age? Is that all?* She could deal with him being older or younger than she thought. "I'd say thirty-five."

Nathan laughed and nodded. "Not bad. That was my age when I stopped aging."

"Stopped aging?" Amanda's heart sank again. She had left just plain crazy off her list.

"I know you're not going to believe any of this, but let's talk it out anyway. Have you heard of the Fountain of Youth?"

"The mythical fountain Ponce de Leon tried to find?"

"Yes. Only it wasn't mythical."

"Why are we talking about this?" Amanda asked, perturbed.

"Ponce didn't find it, but I did. I found it in the First Seminole War in 1818."

Amanda's only response was the tears that ran down her cheeks. *Why couldn't he just be married?*

"I actually found it by accident. I was a soldier with Andrew Jackson, and we were marching to lay siege on Pensacola. While scouting alone, I fell through a sinkhole that opened up in the forest. I landed in a cave below, breaking my leg in the process. Through the dim light from the hole above, I saw a pool of water on the cave floor. I dragged myself over to it and drank the clear, cold water. I immediately experienced a warm tingling sensation in my throat and stomach that quickly spread to the rest of my body. I was frightened that I had drunk some kind of poison. I blacked out before I could even scream. When I came to, I felt different—alive and powerful and still tingly. It took me a minute to realize my leg had healed. I managed to find another way out of the cave, crawling out of a small hole on a riverbank."

"What are you *talking* about?" Amanda demanded, still sobbing.

Nathan continued, ignoring her question and anger. "It took a while to realize what I had found. Every injury I sustained quickly healed. I even regrew a hand. I really didn't understand why but never dared speak of it to anyone. A few years later, I realized I wasn't aging. When my friends and family noticed, I moved away. I finally realized that the pool in the cave was the Fountain of Youth. I was immortal. At first, I was excited at the prospect of living forever, of not being able to be killed. I served in the Second Seminole War and then the Civil War. I've served in almost every major war since. I was a Rough Rider with Teddy Roosevelt, fought alongside Eisenhower in World War II, and toured in Korea and Vietnam. I was just careful to avoid drawing too much attention to myself."

"You're insane!"

"Probably. It didn't take long to realize that immortality is a curse. I have to move every five or ten years, so people won't realize that I don't age. I've met and fallen in love with many women, only to watch them age and die, while I never change. I've watched all my family and friends be buried. I've seen everything there is to see in the world, done everything I've wanted to do, yet I'm still thirty-five. It's really a living hell. I destroyed the fountain with dynamite in 1900 to make sure no one else would stumble upon it."

"Why can't you just tell me the truth? Why are you making this crap up?" Amanda jerked her hands away from his and wiped her eyes.

"Don't you think I would tell you something different if I could? I never wanted to fall for you. I swore to myself that I would never allow myself to fall in love again and put someone else through this. I was weak, though, and you are incredible. I'm sorry."

"You're saying that you're in love with me yet will leave because you're really immortal?"

"Yes," Nathan said softly.

Amanda struggled to process his story. He seemed so sincere, yet she knew he was lying. *A fountain of youth?* She entertained the idea of playing along and trying to get him to stay with her for five or ten years, as he said he stayed in each place but quickly decided against it. For some reason, he didn't want to be with her. It hurt like hell, but she would let him go. Realizing he had mental issues did make it a little easier. She would be fine. "Leave then! Just go."

"I'm sorry," he whispered. Amanda turned, sobbing, and didn't look at him again. "I love you," he said as he walked out of her apartment and life.

***

Life went on for Amanda. She never forgot about Nathan, but the feelings did eventually fade somewhat. She met Roger a year later and began dating again. Eventually, they married and started a family. Roger was a good man, although she never experienced the same feelings and emotions or shared the same connection as she had with Nathan. They got along well, though, and loved in their own way.

It was strange that every now and then, every few years, she would think she saw Nathan somewhere around town. She'd just catch a fleeting glimpse or see a familiar face in the crowd. She didn't know whether that was why she never forgot him or her memories made her think she saw him. She couldn't help but occasionally think of what might have been, but she lived a long, full, contented life.

***

A figure cloaked in black knelt at the tombstone and laid the bouquet of flowers beside it. He touched the cold stone and partially traced the words with his fingers: "Amanda Wilkerson, b. 1979, d. 2060." A tear ran down his cheek, quickly washed away by the rain. *So young,* he thought.

"I love you, Amanda," he whispered as he stood and walked away. Immortality was hell.

End of a Dream

Learning to Fly

"It's pancreatic cancer."
That was how three words destroyed multiple worlds. My mother had been battling a mystery illness for a few months. She had first struggled with abdominal pain and lack of appetite, which had caused her to lose a lot of weight. The doctors treated her for ulcers and various digestive ailments. Then her skin began taking on a yellow tint. The doctors performed scopes and scans but couldn't see anything other than a possible blockage in the bile duct. They'd placed a stint in it a month prior, but the symptoms hadn't alleviated. She had been back to the doctor earlier that day. Apparently, the last scope had detected a growth in the head of her pancreas, and the biopsy confirmed it was malignant.

"Oh, no!" I didn't know what else to say. I knew enough about the disease to know that it was not a good diagnosis. "How advanced is it?"

"It has spread outside the pancreas—stage four," my dad answered.

"How did they not find it before now?" I asked, shock turning to anger.

"It's tough to detect and spreads fast. That's why it's so hard to treat," my dad responded. I'm sure I was only asking the same questions they had asked the doctors.

"What are the options? Can they do surgery?"

My father glanced at my mother and then back to me. "No. They can do chemotherapy and radiation to try to slow the growth and hopefully shrink it."

I felt like someone had kicked me in the stomach—or lower. I had to ask the next question. "What's the prognosis for treatment?"

"Let's not talk about that. Some people beat it," my dad said, weakly and unconvincingly.

I walked over and sat on the other side of my mother. I hugged her and kissed her on the cheek. "Well, there is no one else stronger than you. You'll kick its butt!"

She smiled weakly and patted my leg. "I'm sure I will."

***

I Googled articles on pancreatic cancer for several hours that night, reading them through tears most of that time. It was a nasty disease, with the highest cancer mortality rate. From my parents' description, she probably had six months to live with treatment, three without. That night, I prayed like never before.

***

"When do you start treatment?" I asked my mother the following night. My father was already in bed.

"I'm not sure if I am," she replied without emotion. She appeared weak and fragile, lying propped up by pillows on the couch.

"What? You have to!" I exclaimed in disbelief.

She turned to look at me. "I'm sure you did some research last night?"

"Yeah," I replied softly.

"Then you know that you're only talking a few months either way. I'm already so tired and weak. I'm not sure if I can handle the chemo and radiation."

"But some people live for years with it! And there are cases of remission!"

"Yes, I guess there are. A lot of those people are probably not seventy, though. Anyway, I'm still thinking about it. Try not to worry."

"Not worry? How? You're my mother!"

She reached over and squeezed my hand.

***

We were together again on her couch the next night. I'd decided to spend every night I could with her.

"Let me ask you something," I said.

She turned from the television and nodded.

268

"I've been tossing around an idea in my head. What dreams do you have that have never come true? What's on your bucket list?"

"Oh, you don't have enough paper for that." She chuckled weakly.

"Try me. At least the top ten."

"Well, I always wanted to own my own restaurant—or really a number of different types of businesses. I think I had a lot of good ideas."

"OK. That might not work. What else?"

"Let's see…travel, I guess. There are a lot of places I've never seen: the Great Wall, the pyramids, New Zealand, and Africa, to name a few."

I knew she loved to travel and was hoping she'd say that. "We can do that! I've been thinking, and if you and Dad can help fund it, I can take off from work with FMLA, and we can all travel wherever you want to go! I'll handle all the arrangements."

She reached over and patted my hand, smiling. "That would be great. But I'm afraid I'm too weak to travel, or at least to enjoy it. Thank you so much, though."

I was crushed. There had to be something we could do.

"I really hate that I never got to do those things. I think I could have run a really successful restaurant or flower shop or cooking school." She stared blankly straight ahead as she spoke.

"Why didn't you?"

"I wanted to. But your father was always very conservative about money and things like that."

"Did he actually stop you from doing it?"

She was thoughtful for a moment. "I don't guess so, but he wouldn't have approved."

"What about the travel? Why didn't you ever get to go to any of those places?" I asked, hoping not to upset her.

"Your father again. He never did enjoy traveling."

"Did you talk to him about how important it was to you?"

"No, I guess not really, but I'm sure he knew, and he wouldn't have enjoyed it even if he went." She dabbed at the corner of her eyes with the top of her housecoat.

I decided to drop that line of questioning. "Mom, it's your decision, but I really think you should consider the chemo and radiation. It affects people differently. It might not make you weaker, and it's worth a shot. People do beat this. And if you do start feeling better, then maybe we can do some traveling!"

"I'll think about it, dear."

***

She did start the treatments two weeks later. She did OK for the first few weeks, or at least felt no worse. Then her nausea began to increase, and her appetite decreased even more. She began to lose more weight and more strength. Her pain also steadily increased high in her abdomen. She didn't do much other than lie around and sleep in the afternoons after treatment. When the six weeks were complete, she was a shell of her former self.

***

Two weeks later, my mother had the follow-up exam. Another CT scan and scope confirmed that the treatments had not shrunk the tumor; in fact, it might have grown larger. I had to work late that day, so she was the only one still up when I made it over.

"What are the options now?" I asked, not wasting time with small talk.

My mother grinned weakly. "I'm afraid there are none. They could do radiation or chemo again in a few weeks, but even my doctor recommended against it. I guess we just wait."

"Wait for what?" As soon as I asked, I realized the answer.

"We just wait...."

We sat in silence and stared at the television, neither paying attention to what was on.

"I don't guess you feel up for a trip, do you?" I finally asked.

She didn't answer. She glanced briefly at me and shook her head. I saw her eyes glisten with moisture as she turned away to stare at the floor. "I hate that I never accomplished any of my dreams. I feel like I haven't done anything with my life."

"Mom! How can you say that?" I spoke a little more strongly than I meant to, but I was upset. "You have been married for fifty years to a husband who loves you more than you'll ever know and has always been there by your side, through the good and bad. Dad would do anything for you. You've raised a healthy, happy son who loves you very much too! You were a great mother and homemaker. You were also a great daughter to your parents and sister to your brother. You've lived a good life and have been blessed with a healthy, loving family!"

She dabbed at her eyes with a Kleenex. "I didn't mean to upset you."

"I'm not upset. But just think about all the good times and memories. Who gets to achieve all their dreams anyway? I'm sure when you were young, you dreamed you'd grow up, graduate high school, get married, and raise a family. You did that! You've fulfilled lots of dreams along the way. But dreams are just that. They are things to hope and strive for and to think about. Even if you checked off all the ones on your list, new ones would just take their place. You never stop dreaming—that's just part of living."

She slowly rose up and smiled. She leaned forward and gave me a hug and a kiss on my cheek. "You're definitely a dream that came true. I love you, honey."

It was all I could do to fight back my own tears. "And, Mom, I've been doing a lot of thinking since the last time we talked about your dreams. You know, if some of them had come true, like running your own business or traveling around the world, you might not have been available to help take care of Granddaddy after his heart attack or Uncle Bobby when he had his stroke or Granny when she was suffering from Alzheimer's. Maybe some dreams aren't meant to come true, just like some prayers aren't answered. But you were able to be the backbone for all of your family for all these years. You are your family's dream come true!"

She hugged me again, and we both cried.

***

As the days passed, it became apparent to everyone that the three-to-six-month prognosis was going to be accurate and probably on the long side. Mom did seem in better spirits after our talk that night, though. I hope she was more at peace. I'm sure she was in a lot of pain, but she didn't show it much. I just caught a glimpse of a scowl or frown from time to time. It was a Herculean effort when she resumed doing some cooking, cleaning, and trying to take care of my dad.

***

"There is a dream that only you can help make come true," my mother said as we sat on the couch eating freshly baked chocolate-chip cookies. I was trying to make sure she got as many calories as possible.

"Really? What?" I asked, excited at the prospect.

"I want to learn how to fly."

I stared at her blankly. "Huh?"

She smiled weakly. "I've always wanted to fly. When I was twelve, I climbed on top of my house, with wings I'd made out of pine tree branches, and jumped off. I flapped like crazy, but they didn't slow my fall. I nearly broke my ankle." She chuckled softly. "But I never gave up the dream of flying. I've flown on airplanes, and loved it, but I want more."

"Are you talking about skydiving?"

"Yes! I've always wanted to skydive."

I had skydived for years and was actually a certified instructor. As a local skydiving club member, I occasionally helped out a local company for some extra cash. "I thought you were scared of heights?"

"I am. But I think that would be different. And you're actually flying until you pull the cord."

"Are you sure about this? Deploying the shoot and landing can be tough on your body."

She smiled again. "At this point, do you think a rough landing will really hurt me?"

I couldn't argue with that. "What does Dad think?"

"That I'm crazy. But he understands. He just doesn't want to be there to watch."

***

We drove to the airport on a Wednesday morning. No dives were scheduled for that day; I had checked. I had called one of my club buddies, our pilot, and offered him some money to take off work and take Mom and me up. I gave her a crash course in tandem skydiving on the ground, explaining that we'd be jumping together.

"I need you to do one more thing for me," Mom said.

"Anything."

"I want to jump by myself."

"Anything but that. I can't let you jump by yourself; that takes a lot of training."

"Please, John. I want to fly by myself," she pleaded passionately.

"If anyone finds out, I'll be kicked out of the club and lose my certification and license." I was sick to my stomach.

"No one will know. It's just us. And the pilot is already on the plane; he won't see. Please let me do this!"

How could I deny a dying woman's request and take away her chance to fulfill her one last dream? So I gave her another course on solo jumping. I showed her how to read the altimeter on her wrist and explained how the one in her helmet would beep when it was time to pull the ripcord. I showed her how to pull the cord, deploy the emergency chute just in case, steer with the toggles, locate a landing zone, and land.

"Are you sure you want to do this?" I asked, still not feeling well.

"Oh, yes! I can't wait!" She was more energetic than I had seen her in months. She appeared ten years younger.

"I'll fall right with you, so nothing can go wrong."

"OK, dear. And thank you so much for our conversations over these past couple of months and being there for me. Thank you for making my

272

dream come true. I'm at peace now." She hugged me and kissed my forehead. I quickly turned before my tears started flowing.

We climbed onto the plane through the back door. Fifteen minutes later, we were at eleven thousand feet. I asked Mom if she would change her mind and jump with me one more time, but she wouldn't. So I nodded for her to get into position in the doorway. Another nod, and she fell out backward as instructed. I quickly jumped out behind her so I could catch up. I went headfirst, falling faster than she, and then pulled up and lay out flat when I was just a few feet in front.

She smiled and laughed like I'd never seen her smile and laugh before. It was amazing how alive she looked. She experimented with twisting around in different directions, including rolling over onto her back and checking out every position's view. She even figured out how to slow down and speed up. She was learning how to fly.

The altimeter in my helmet beeped, and I glanced at the one on my wrist to confirm we were at five thousand feet. I motioned for her to pull her cord. She just kept smiling and flying. Every hundred feet, the altimeter beeped again. I started to panic. Was her altimeter not working? I motioned again more frantically, making a pulling motion with my hand and arm. She was busy moving her arms from straight out to the side, to down by her sides, to out in front. We had a little time left, but we needed to deploy our chutes by four thousand feet.

At four thousand feet, she still hadn't attempted to pull the ripcord. I screamed as loud as I could for her to pull the cord and motioned wildly with both arms. She still gave no response. I changed my body position slightly and glided closer to her, reaching out to try to grab her cord. This time, it was she who gestured to me. She grabbed my hands and shook her head side to side. Then she smiled again. She mouthed the words, "I love you," squeezed my hands one last time—and let go. Then I think she said, "Thank you."

I shouted, "I love you, Mom," and reluctantly deployed my chute. My tears began splashing inside my goggles. I watched her flying farther away as my speed slowed. Then it hit me: at that moment, she felt no pain. She wasn't frail or sick or tired. There was no cancer. She wasn't seventy years old. There were no more dreams on her list. Unfettered from suffering and the failures of the past, she was fulfilling the one lifelong dream that not even cancer could steal from her. But this wasn't like jumping from the roof so many years ago. This time, she had learned how to fly. This time, she was free.

"Fly, Mom. Fly."

Eulogy

Janet Wilcox Sturgill
June 30, 1940 - January 12, 2012

There is no way to sufficiently describe my mother, Janet Sturgill, her life, and what she meant to me and her family. If you could look into our minds and memories, you would understand. If you could count all our tears and feel all our pain, you would understand. If you could measure the emptiness we'll carry in our hearts, you would understand. Since none of that can be shared, I'm left with only glaringly inadequate words.

I think the one best word to describe my mother is *selfless*. I've never known anyone who put everyone else above herself like Mom did. No matter what she was going through, she always took care of everyone else first—from her parents, to her husband, children, and grandchildren. No amount of pain or suffering could keep her from ensuring everyone else was happy. One of the last things I heard her say in the hospital and that she wrote when she could no longer talk was for Dad to go back home. She just didn't see any need for him to be staying there or for us to be driving down to check on her. I never once heard her complain or talk about her own situation. If she's looking down at this moment, she must be so upset that everyone is making this much fuss over her. Everyone has spent way too much time, money, and effort just for her.

275

At the heart of her selflessness was pure love. She was the most loving and caring person you could ever meet. If you met her even briefly, then you know. Family was so important to her. As her family grew, so did her love. She welcomed her daughters-in-law into the family and loved them as if they were her own daughters. The grandchildren were her greatest pride and joy. She was always supportive of all of us, through all of our failures and successes. All she wanted was for us to be happy.

There are so many things that come to mind as I reminisce on her life. She was an unbelievable cook. I know that everyone's mother is a great cook, but she was truly special. She loved to travel and experience new things. Her fear of heights didn't stop her from parasailing, and she sincerely wanted to skydive for her seventieth birthday. She loved animals almost to a fault, even putting some stray cats above her own needs. She loved going out with friends and playing almost any sort of game, from cards to Scrabble. She might not have won many Scrabble games, but she was always ready to play. Her true passion was probably plants, flowers, and gardening. She spent much of her free time tending to all the potted plants outside and inside the house. They might not have seemed worth the effort to most of us, but that's what she loved to do.

This has been a truly tragic and heartbreaking week for all Jan's family and friends. She was much too young, and we all still needed so much more from her. Although I'm sure even if she had been one hundred, we'd still feel the same way. But at least now, all the pain and suffering she's endured over the past few years is over. She can rest in peace now and be reunited with her parents, grandparents, and all those who passed before. Hopefully, she won't be allowed to worry too much about all of us until we can see her again.

Although she has moved on to a better place, I can't truly say goodbye. I can still see her in the people in this room. I can see her in my dad, my brothers, and all our children. We all have too many memories and too many vivid images in our minds. A part of her will live on within each of us until our day comes and we can be with her again. Thank you, Mom…for everything.

For More Information & Updates:

Follow on Facebook
https://www.facebook.com/crsturgillauthor/

https://www.facebook.com/dreamsfromtheheart/

Visit my Website
http://www.crsturgill.com/

Other Books by C. R. Sturgill:

Fantasy World

Blood Tides

Sea of Hearts